WITHDRAWN

THE DREAM

G·K Hall &C?

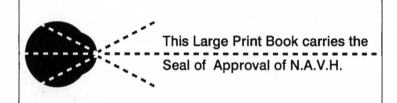

This Large Print Book carries the
Seal of Approval of N.A.V.H.

THE DREAM

Kat Martin

G.K. Hall & Co. • Waterville, Maine

Published in 2001 by arrangement with Zebra Books, an imprint of Kensington Publishing Corp.

G.K. Hall Large Print Romance Series.

The text of this Large Print edition is unabridged.
Other aspects of the book may vary from the original edition.

Set in 16 pt. Plantin.

Printed in the United States on permanent paper.

Library of Congress Cataloging-in-Publication

Martin, Kat.
    The dream / Kat Martin.
      p. cm.
    ISBN 0-7838-9535-6 (lg. print : hc : alk. paper)
    1. Nightmares — Fiction.   2. Businessmen — Fiction.
   3. Santa Barbara (Calif.) — Fiction.   4. Large type books.
   I. Title.
   PS3563.A7246 D7 2001
    813′.54—dc21   2001024844

To Maria Carvainis, for all her hard work and perseverance through some very tough years. To Wanda Handley, for her never-ending support and belief in my contemporary novels. Thank you, ladies!

A special thanks to my husband for all his help on this book.

One

Blood. Oceans of it, swirling pools of crimson that painted the walls of her mind and clouded her vision until it was all she could see.

Death and darkness.

Tides of it seemed to surround her, to pull at her, to drag and tug and fight to suck her in.

Then the voices rose up, chanting, but she couldn't see their faces, couldn't make out their muffled words. Great flames leapt up, blue-white and orange, red as the depths of hell, threatening to envelop her, threatening to char her pale flesh and leave her writhing in an agony that stretched through time and beyond.

Then the laughter rose up as it always did, high and shrill, surging toward the limits of sanity yet somehow strangely beautiful.

The flames burned brighter; the voices grew louder, louder. She could almost feel the heat, almost feel her soft skin melting away, feel the touch of the wicked fires of darkness. Pain. There was so much pain. She could not bear it. She could not stand the agonizing heat.

Dear God!

Genny Austin's eyes snapped open. A scream of terror lodged in her throat. Her heart was pounding, hammering, echoing in her ears, and a sheen of perspiration covered her slender shoulders. Her hands were shaking, her throat had closed up; it was all she could do to drag in great breaths of air.

"God in heaven," she whispered into the darkness of her bedroom, the black outline of once-familiar furniture now looking foreign and oddly out of place. She raked her trembling fingers through her shoulder-length light brown hair and sat up in bed, wondering how many more of the terrible dreams she could endure.

She sat there for moments that stretched like hours, propped against the antique oak headboard of her big four-poster bed. Allowing her heartbeat to slow, trying to calm her nerves, she worked to breathe a little more slowly and waited for the trembling in her body to ease. She knew exactly the things to do. The same sort of nightmares had plagued her for over two years.

Genny glanced at the glowing numbers on the digital alarm clock beside her bed. One-thirty. Last night she had slept until two.

Tilting her head back, feeling the sharp contours of the heavy carved wood, she stared up at the ceiling for long, turbulent moments, with images of the dream still slipping through her mind — swirling mists of crimson, spirals of flame, voices in the ink-black darkness — terror so thick and heavy she could feel it, even now that she was awake.

Her throat grew taut, constricted with unshed tears as she tossed back the covers and swung her long slender legs to the side of the bed. Wearily she came to her feet. It was Wednesday. Nothing special. The same as any other sleepless night among what had become an endless stream.

They had begun right after her husband died, about two weeks after Bill's funeral at the Crockett-McDermott Mortuary, followed by a graveside service in the Santa Barbara Cemetery on a beautiful green hill overlooking the sea. Until lately, she had believed the nightmares were a result of the shooting. The doctors had said so, the psychiatrists, and even the specialists at Cottage Hospital, where lately she had been going for treatment. They had an extensive program for the study of insomnia, which had developed as a defense against her dreams.

Everyone believed that once she had dealt with Bill's death, the dreams would end. But lately, she wasn't so sure.

With an unsteady hand, Genny turned on the Tiffany lamp on the small oak table beside the bed. Dressed in a simple white cotton nightgown embroidered with tiny pink roses, she stood up and went over to the closet. She wasn't in the mood for a walk along the beach, almost a nightly occurrence since the dreams had begun, the only thing she had discovered that would help her fall asleep.

Not tonight. Tonight she needed someone to talk to. Someone who knew what she had been suffering and might have a word or two of cheer.

It was September, still warm in Santa Barbara, but there was usually a cool night breeze sweeping in off the sea. She pulled on a pair of dark brown slacks and a beige cotton-knit sweater, then she slipped into her flat-heeled brown loafers.

A quick check of the mirror before she stepped out; she applied some soft pink lipstick and ran a brush through her nut brown hair. It curled thickly in the damp ocean air. She usually smoothed it with a curling iron and wore it slightly turned under.

Feeling a little more in control, Genny grabbed her beige cardigan off the chair by the door and headed downstairs. The condo she lived in was almost too big for her now that Bill was gone. Still, the place was home, and home and family had always meant a great deal to her.

The mortgage insurance had paid off the bank note on the property, so she owned it free and clear, and she had used some of Bill's life-insurance money to redecorate. She loved the feminine floral motif, the delicate cream and peach chintz of the sofa and curtains, and her California oak antiques. Mostly she loved her view of the sea and the boats bobbing down at the harbor.

Though the dream had long faded, her mind still churned with thoughts of the past two years. Bill had been murdered on the sidewalk, just outside the house. Genny had seen him lying there, though she barely recalled that night. She only knew for certain that her husband had been killed, her seven-year marriage had come to an end, and she was left alone.

She stopped in the kitchen and picked up her brown leather shoulder bag from on top of the ceramic tile counter. It sat beside her recipe books and several oak-framed blue ribbons she had won at the fair for her spicy dill pickles. The kitchen was done in cream and brown with pale peach accents, and it was always spotless.

She prided herself on her housework, though secretly she feared she was becoming a cleaning fanatic. It was probably some sort of sexual sublimation — at least she figured that's what the doctors would say.

It didn't seem all that likely, since sex with Bill had never really been all that great — a fact even Bill would not have disputed. He was usually too busy down at the office, too tired, or just plain not in the mood. And she had never been to bed with anyone else. They had met their first year in college, married when both of them were seniors at San Diego State. Bill was her first lover — and possibly her last if her life continued along the path it was presently taking.

Genny sighed to think of it, flipped on the

light in the two-car garage, opened the heavy door, which groaned and creaked, then she climbed into her brown Toyota. The engine hummed, reliable as always. That's why she and Bill had chosen it. Bill had driven a Volvo, but after he died, she had sold it. She backed her car out, turned on the headlights, and pulled into the alley behind the condo.

Since this part of Santa Barbara was near the beach, it was dense with foliage: big green-leafed shrubs, acacia trees, cymbidiums, hibiscus, palms. Anything that grew, grew bigger and taller in Santa Barbara. She passed the oversized plants, thinking how beautiful they were, yet wondering if the thick growth might have contributed in some way to Bill's murder. Perhaps his assailant had mistaken him for someone else, standing among the vines and flowering plants, or never even saw him until it was too late.

She would probably never know.

It didn't take long to reach the all-night Bob's Big Boy on the north end of Highway 101. She had discovered the place by accident two years ago when, desperate to escape her dreams and finding very few establishments open at three in the morning, she had seen the big brightly lit red and white sign and wearily gone in. Just as she did now.

Parking the car beneath a mist-dimmed streetlight, Genny crossed the parking lot and pushed open the heavy glass door, setting off a buzzer telling the hostess that someone had come in. The place was only half full, truckers mostly, a few teenagers in rumpled baggy clothes who should have already gone home.

"Hello, dearie," the gray-haired, wrinkled little hostess said. "Booth in the back, okay?"

"Fine, Peggy." She knew most of the waitresses by name since they wore little badges on their pink and white uniforms.

"I'll tell Dottie you're here. She's due for a coffee break, anyway. You want I should bring you a cup?"

"Hot chocolate, if you don't mind." She never drank coffee. She certainly didn't need anything that would keep her awake.

"Sorry, dear, I forgot." The frail little woman led the way toward a table in the rear, and Genny slid onto the tufted red plastic seat. When she looked around, she spotted Dottie and even from a distance Genny could see her welcoming smile.

Bright red hair pulled up in a wispy sort of ponytail, melon-round oversized breasts, rubber-soled shoes, and a little pink-and-white cap that always seemed to sit on her head askew. That was Dottie Marshall, the most unlikely friend Genny Austin had ever made.

And one of the dearest.

"Well, look what the cat's dragged in." Dottie reached the booth, leaned over and hugged her, then slid onto the plastic bench on the opposite side. She smelled a little like bacon and coffee.

13

"I guess your being here means you still aren't sleeping," Dottie said. "I hoped maybe things had changed."

"I suppose it has been a while since I've seen you. Mostly I've been walking on the beach."

"You know how I feel about that, girl. I hope you're being careful."

Genny smiled. "There's usually no one around, but even if there were, it wouldn't matter. I'd go if the entire U.S. Navy were bivouacked down there on the sand. As long as these dreams continue, it's just about my only salvation."

Dottie nodded, one of the few people who seemed to understand. "Bad one tonight?" she asked, as the waitress arrived with a mug of cocoa and one of steaming black coffee.

Genny sighed. "They're all bad, Dottie. Sometimes I don't think I can make it through another night."

"Hush, now — I don't want to hear you talk that way. The doctors say it's only a matter of time. As soon as you get used to your husband being gone —"

"I know that's what they say. Up until lately, I believed them. But the more I think about it . . . the more I analyze the dreams themselves. . . ." Genny rubbed the back of her neck beneath her light brown hair. "I just don't know."

Dottie didn't argue. She was a very good listener and wise beyond her years. She had been a soothing influence since the first night they

14

had met, the night Genny had stumbled into the place with eyes red-rimmed from lack of sleep, sat down in the same booth they were sitting in now, ordered a cup of chocolate, and proceeded to break into tears.

It was Dottie who had held her, taken her into the employees' lounge, and listened to her heartbreaking story. She had let Genny talk the whole thing out and by the time she had gone back home she felt better. It was the beginning of a tentative friendship that continued to grow over the weeks and months Genny came back to the coffee shop on Dottie's late-night shift.

"You might as well tell me the rest," the petite redhead said. "You won't be able to sleep until you do."

Genny sat up straighter in the booth, making her half a head taller than her five-foot tall friend. "All right. The truth is, I don't believe I'm still experiencing trauma. I miss Bill, yes. And I'm lonely. But I don't cry anymore. I don't feel lost and unable to cope. I know in my heart that I've put Bill's death behind me. If it weren't for these terrible dreams and the constant lack of sleep, I'd be ready to go on with my life."

"They've never found the men who killed him. Maybe that's the cause."

Genny shook her head. "I don't think so. I'd like to see the men who did it brought to justice, but I'm resigned to the way things are, and even if I weren't, I'm smart enough to know there's nothing I can do about it. I'm convinced I've finally let it go."

"I don't suppose you've discussed this with your parents."

"You know how they are." Her parents loved her, but they were overly protective. Her father thought psychiatrists were all a bunch of quacks and her mother worried too much, which was the reason she had let them think things were improving.

"What does Howard say?" Howard McCormick was Bill's partner in the computer business.

"Howard wasn't all that keen on my going to a psychiatrist in the first place."

"Then he thinks you ought to stop going?"

"I suppose. We haven't really discussed it all that much."

"But you have been seeing a lot of him lately."

"Howard is a very good friend."

"Are you sure that's the way you want to keep it? I think he might be interested in more than just your friendship."

Genny held up her cocoa and blew gently across the top to cool it down. "It's far too soon to think about something like that. Perhaps in time . . . I don't really know."

"You were telling me about the dreams," Dottie prodded, sensing there was something more. Dottie had been working in the coffee shop for the past ten years, ever since her husband had run off with a topless dancer, leaving a mountain of bills and a three-year-old daughter. Now, at thirty-nine, Dottie Marshall knew people. Her shrewd judgment and solid advice were part of the reason Dottie had won Genny's respect.

She took a sip of her chocolate, trying to choose the right words. "The truth is, I'm not really sure what it is that's bothering me. It's nothing I can put my finger on. Just a feeling, something that keeps nagging at me. Lately, I'm convinced more and more that my dreams have nothing to do with Bill's murder." Dottie looked up, ready to argue, but Genny cut her off. "I'm not saying his death wasn't the cause. It was obviously a catalyst of some sort, but I think there's a lot more to it. I don't believe this is about Bill *or* the shooting. I think it's something different, something not so simply explained."

"If that's the truth, then the dreams must be the key. Maybe in time, they'll tell you the answer."

Genny pondered that. "Maybe. In a way I'm afraid they will." She glanced away, her gaze drifting out the window to the shadows cast by the branches of a leafy eucalyptus waving against the steam-frosted panes. "Whatever it is," she said, "it's ugly. Brutal and cruel and ugly. I just pray it isn't something that's . . ."

"That's what?"

"Something that's deep down inside me.

Somehow a part of me."

"Now you stop that, Genny Austin. You're one of the nicest, sweetest people I've ever met. There is nothing ugly inside you. If the dreams hold a secret, sooner or later you'll find out what it is — and it won't be any reflection on you."

Genny tried to smile, but it felt tight and drawn. Reaching across the table, she clasped her friend's hand. "I hope you're right, Dottie . . . I really do."

It was nearly dawn when she left the café and drove back to her condo. The moment the first light of day tinged the sky, she was always able to sleep. She parked the car and went into the living room. From the sofa, she picked up the beige-peach-and-cream afghan her grandmother had knit for her, and curled up beneath it.

Thankful the library didn't open until nine, she closed her eyes and drifted at last into a dream-free sleep.

Jack Brennen hunched over the open ledgers on top of the chart table. His powerful shoulders were bowed as if weighed down by the entries he was reading. Sitting in the navigation room on board his eighty-foot salvage boat, *Marauder,* he braced himself on his elbows, his head hanging forward, long fingers thrust through his curly black hair.

"What's the matter, boy, can't sleep?"

Jack's head jerked up. He relaxed when he saw Charley Denton's familiar gray-haired figure outlined by the small brass lamp beside the compass on his teakwood desk. Charley, his partner and long-time friend, also lived on-board, along with a mangy yellow tabby cat named Felix.

"Haven't gone to bed yet," Jack said. Though his day on the boat started early, Jack was a night owl, always full of energy once the sun went down. He could honky-tonk with the best of 'em; he loved fast cars and even faster women.

"If you're looking to find a solution to our money problems," Charley said, "you ain't gonna find it in there." He was a leather-skinned, dry-humored man in his late fifties — barrel-chested and stoutly built, not tall, but not short either. He'd lived most of his life at sea and it showed in the swagger that was part of his walk, and in the hard-etched lines of his face.

In the early days, he'd been Jack's mentor in the salvage business. Back then, Charley had owned the *Marauder* and Jack had merely worked for him. But times had gotten tough. Charley needed money so he took Jack on as a partner and together they mortgaged the boat to pay off the debts.

Jack glanced down at the ledgers. "I wish you'd told me that two hours ago." He gave Charley a half-hearted grin, thinking he *had* hoped to find a solution in the books. "There's a helluva lot I'd rather be doing than going over these damn accounts."

In the years since they'd formed their partnership, they had paid off most of the debt they owed, but lately the recession had taken its toll. The final big payment was due on the boat and money was a problem again.

Jack's half-hearted smile slipped away. "I'm fast running out of ideas, Charley." He stared hard at the ledgers. The carefully inked-in entries held no clue to where the dollars might come from. "Nobody's willing to risk a new loan, the money from the work on the oil rigs won't be nearly enough, and the bastards aren't about to let us refinance."

Jack felt Charley's hand on his shoulder. "We got a couple of other jobs lined up, that ought to help."

"It'll help, all right, but not enough. We'll just have to hope like hell something major comes in." He could sell his car, but he hated to. Next to the boat, his '67 Shelby Mustang convertible was just about his most prized possession. Besides, he was making payments on that, too, so there wasn't all that much equity. Even if he sold it, they wouldn't have nearly enough. And his Harley was lying in pieces in Ollie Brown's garage.

"You've done the best you could," Charley said. "If it wasn't for you, I'd have lost the *Marauder* years ago."

"Yeah, well, somehow that doesn't make me

feel a whole lot better." Jack pushed back his chair and came to his feet, his head nearly bumping the ceiling. "But like you said, maybe something will turn up."

"Maybe." Charley glanced at the brass ship's clock hanging on the teakwood-paneled wall. "You'd best get some sleep," he gently chided, more like a father than a partner, and Jack felt just that close to him. "Five o'clock comes early."

He nodded. "Night, Charley." But he still didn't leave the room. Instead he stood staring at the books, wondering how in the hell he was gonna save their boat. He refused to consider that he might fail. Jack Brennen had failed at a lot of things in his turbulent thirty-three years. But he loved this boat and he loved his life at sea, and he was determined he would not fail in this.

Two

It had been just a typical day. Now it was proving to be a typical night. The minutes slid past, seconds ticking, ticking, hundreds of them, thousands. They grew into hours. Twelve o'clock. One. Two. It was fast approaching three.

Genny stared up at the ceiling. She had read for a while — an old book, James Michener's *Space*. It had been lying in a drawer for years. It was long and the print was so small she could barely see it. She hoped it would help her fall asleep. In her heart she knew it wouldn't.

Several hours later, she had laid the heavy volume on the small oak table beside the bed, turned off the Tiffany lamp, and settled into the quiet of the evening.

It was an odd sensation, insomnia. Not the tossing and turning most people believed, but a strange, nerve-tingling awareness that pervaded every part of the body. She could feel each beat of her heart, imagine the pulsing flow of her blood as it surged too fast through her veins. With her eyelids open or closed, her vision seemed to permeate the darkness, creating a keen sense of wakefulness as disturbing as it was exhausting. It drained her energy, yet the tension thrummed within her, as if an unseen cord of electricity sizzled at the ends of her nerves.

At dawn she might sleep for a time. The gray light on the horizon was oddly comforting. She would shower, dress, and drive herself to work. At noon, she'd grab a sandwich off the back of the lunchmobile, eat it in the coffee room at the library, then nap on the lumpy green plastic sofa in the ladies' room.

Genny blinked several times, bringing her eyes back into focus. Frustration lanced through her, making her feel even more wide awake. With a sigh of resignation, she swung her long slender legs to the floor and stood up. Her nightgown billowed slightly as she walked toward the closet.

Sliding open the mirrored glass doors, she pulled out a warm woolen robe the same nutmeg brown as her hair, drew it on over her nightgown, shoved her slender feet into a pair of open-toed slippers, and made her way downstairs.

She knew where she was going. There was plenty of light slanting in from the moon and its silvery path across the water beckoned her in that direction. Stopping for a moment to pick up the house key lying on the carved oak bureau beside the door, she stuffed it into the pocket of her robe then slipped silently out into the darkness.

It was quiet outside, except for the distant pounding of the waves, and the insects, and the far-away buzz of a low-flying plane. She had learned to take comfort in the sounds of the night, to enjoy them and not to fear them. They drew her now as they had for the past two years, offering solace from her dreams and the constant insomnia.

It was hardly a good idea, being out at this hour alone, but she refused to take sleeping pills, except on rare occasions, and with Bill no longer there, she had no one to really dissuade her. As she walked through the small wrought-iron gate leading onto the sidewalk, she glanced away, refusing to look at the spot where she had seen her husband's body, lying in a spreading pool of blood.

Instead, she concentrated on the waves in the distance, letting them catch her up, letting them soothe her, as she made her way along the deserted street that fronted the ocean. Crossing to the opposite side, she headed down the path through the ice plant that led to the beach. She left her slippers at the bottom of the trail and walked toward the water, enjoying the feel of her toes digging into the cool white sand.

Genny's gaze followed the path of silver moonlight to a ship drifting past on the horizon. She padded along the tightly packed ocean-drenched sand at the edge of the water. She wasn't sure how long she waded in the surf, absorbed as she was by the soothing roar of the sea, but her feet had grown used to the cold Pacific water, and the hem of her nightgown was wet where it skimmed her ankles.

Her wanderings had taken her close to the dock at the far end of the beach, where a number of fishing boats were tied. The night remained cool and clear, but a light mist hung in the air, along with the salty odor of fish and the musky tang of the sea.

Beginning to feel the chill and hoping enough time had passed that she might be able to sleep, Genny turned and started back toward her home in the distance. Her eyes were fixed on the dot of light that was the streetlamp near the path leading up through the ice plant. Only two short steps and she paused.

Not far down the beach, three men walked in her direction. She hadn't noticed them before but she should have; they were laughing loudly, jostling each other, and their footsteps looked decidedly unsteady. Two of them were Hispanic, she saw, black-haired and dark-featured. The oversized purple sportcoat on one seemed badly wrinkled, while the other one wore black leather pants. The third man was fair, blond and bearded, in a red-striped T-shirt, with an earring in his ear.

Genny's heart began to pump as fiercely as it did when she awakened from one of her dreams. Ever since Bill's murder, she had been fearful of the gangs that occasionally came into the area to cruise along the ocean or party on the beach. The police believed it was that sort of trouble between two warring factions that had gotten her husband killed.

An accidental shooting, they called it, a stray bullet from a gang member's gun, meant for one of their own, though no one was ever arrested. It had happened during Fiesta, early in August, when the town was full of tourists. An unseemly element had increasingly made its appearance at the festival, and that year had been one of the worst.

Were these three men the same sort of people responsible for killing Bill?

The beach was usually deserted this time of night and routinely patrolled. There wasn't much risk, she had told herself, since she needed these walks so desperately, but as the men drew near, a fissure of doubt crept up her spine. The men were staggering, swearing, and making lewd remarks. They were eyeing her drunkenly, and suddenly she wished more than anything that she had stayed home.

She moved away from the water, hoping to skirt them, hoping they would let her pass and leave her alone. Instead, one of them broke away from the others and started walking toward her. He was blocking her path, she realized; perhaps she should turn back toward the buildings in the distance, to the big fishing boats bobbing alongside the dock, to a place where there were lights and maybe a passing patrolman. Genny turned and started walking in that direction, each step a little quicker than the last.

The man increased his speed and so did Genny, until she was running flat out. Dear God, her heart was racing faster than her feet, her side was aching, her chest was burning as she sucked in great gulps of air. When she glanced over her shoulder and saw how close the man was, a strangled cry erupted from her throat.

Darting away from him, frantic now, she cut back toward the water. Terror drove her, making her pulse run wild. She could see the dock up ahead, but the other men had circled, placing themselves between her and the path of escape. Frantically she glanced around, searching for someone — anyone — who might help her, knowing with the loud crash of the waves it was probably futile to scream.

The sound of feet pounding against the hard-packed sand at the edge of the surf jerked her head in that direction and Genny cried out in terror. God, all three of them were running toward her!

"Help! Somebody help me!" She dodged one of them, tried to run, but the blond man's heavy weight plowed into her and knocked her into the sand.

"Gotcha!" he roared. The words were thick and slurred. His heavy torso was squeezing the air from her lungs. He reeked of whiskey and so did his friends as they formed a circle around her.

"Get away from me!" Desperately she tried

to dislodge him, fighting to bring her knee up and kick him in the groin as she had read in an article on women's self-defense. But the man was well over six feet tall and weighed at least two hundred and fifty pounds. Genny weighed less than a hundred and twenty, and her robe and nightgown had tangled in her thrashing legs until she could barely move.

"Let me go!" Sand filled her mouth and stuck to her eyelashes. "Let — me — go!"

"Hey, man, get off her. Let's get a look at what we got." A dark-skinned man with coarse black hair and round black eyes pulled his friend from on top of her, but he still gripped her wrists and the third man captured her flailing legs. She winced at her efforts to free them and realized she had twisted the left ankle in the heavy sand when she had fallen.

"Please," she pleaded, hating herself for the fear in her voice, but unable to control it. "Please let me go."

"What do you say, Ramon? Shall we let the lady go?" That one was standing above her, taunting her and grinning, his straight black hair hanging forward in his face.

The bearded man answered instead. "I don't think so." Reaching down he pulled the sash on her robe and jerked it open, then reached down, grabbed the neck of her nightgown, and ripped it open to the waist.

Genny screamed as the damp air hit her bare skin. And screamed and screamed and screamed.

Walking along the pier, his mind on the buxom blonde he'd been drinking with, Jack Brennen couldn't mistake the sound of a woman's cry for help. It rose plaintively above the waves, along with her fearful pleading and frightened weeping.

A quick glance down the beach and he spotted the three drunken men. Their vulgar words seared the air and he knew what they meant to do. Damn, he hated a bastard who would force himself on a defenseless woman.

He cursed his luck even as he started running along the dock in her direction. He had almost made it back to the boat, home from the Sea Breeze Bar, the locals' joint he frequented more often than he should. If he'd left just a few minutes earlier, if he hadn't been trying to nail the blonde, he wouldn't have seen the three men — or heard their helpless victim. But Vivian was an eyeful and he'd been randy as hell. If he hadn't had such a helluva long day tomorrow, he probably wouldn't have given up until he wound up in her bed, and he wouldn't have been here to hear the woman's cries for help.

Now he couldn't just turn away.

Swearing at his rotten luck, Jack increased his pace, jumping down from the dock onto the beach and running flat out across the sand. He was in good condition: diving, wind surfing, pulling line, and working out in the open kept him well-muscled, his body fit and darkly tanned.

It didn't take him long to reach the men. He grabbed the one unzipping the fly of his leather pants, whirled him around, and slammed a fist into his face, sending him sprawling into the sand. He jerked the second guy up by the back of his oversized purple sportcoat, spun him around, swung a punch to the bastard's stomach, doubling him over, then got him by the seat of the pants and the back of the neck and sent him flying out into the water.

As the third man, a strapping bearded giant he would have hated to have to fight sober, let go of the woman's wrists and staggered to his feet, Jack caught a glimpse of pale skin and pointed upthrusting breasts, but his attention quickly focused on the beefy blond giant who posed his greatest threat.

"You son of a bitch!" the man roared drunkenly, charging forward. "Before I'm through, you're gonna wish you'd minded your own business!"

He ducked Jack's first punch and landed an unexpectedly solid blow to the jaw — rocking Jack backward. He shook his head to clear the swirling circles in front of his eyes, sidestepped the second punch; and began a series of quick left jabs to the man's nose. The man began stumbling and finally a hard right cross slammed him to the ground to land in a red-striped heap.

A few yards away, the woman came unsteadily to her feet. She was pretty, he saw, her features fine and delicate. Her big brown eyes looked wide and frightened as she clutched her robe together, hiding her torn white nightgown and pale-skinned breasts.

He thought she might run, but she seemed unwilling to abandon him, a belated show of courage that, considering her slight frame and willowy build, almost brought a smile to his face. It probably would have, if his jaw hadn't been throbbing.

Then the guy in the leathers took off down the beach and the second sloshed out of the surf toward the shore, his baggy clothes streaming sea water, his black hair plastered to his face.

"I'll get you for this, man!" But he didn't seem to want any more of what Jack was dishing out, and he wasn't the least bit concerned for his big blond friend out cold on the beach.

Jack walked over to the woman. "You all right?" When she swayed a little, he caught a slender arm to steady her and felt her body trembling.

"Y-Yes. No. I-I don't know." Unconsciously Genny leaned toward him, her fingers holding tight to the front of her robe. "The truth is, I-I'm not all right at all." Fear still clogged her throat and tears began to trickle down her cheeks. She was shaking all over, frightened, and suddenly so cold she felt as if ice water ran through her veins.

"Those men . . . they . . . they tried to —"
She took a step forward, but her ankle crumpled beneath her and she started to fall. The stranger caught her up in his arms before she had time to hit the ground.

"I know what they tried to do," he said gruffly. "What I don't understand is what the hell you're doing out here alone. For Christ's sake, lady — it's three o'clock in the morning!"

"I-I know. I come down here quite often. I-It's kind of a long story." With a shaky hand she shoved her hair back out of her face, wiped the tears and the sand from her cheeks. "I'm feeling a little bit better. You can put me down now."

"I don't think you can walk." He stood at least six foot four. A huge pair of biceps bulged beneath the sleeve of his tight black T-shirt, where a pack of cigarettes had been rolled up. In the dark he looked almost as rough as those men.

"I-I can make it. You've done enough already. I don't know how to thank you."

But he didn't put her down. "I take it you live close-by."

"Yes. In one of those condos over there." She pointed in the direction with a trembling hand, and he started walking that way. When he glanced back over his shoulder, Genny did, too, and saw that the bearded man still lay unconscious, but that the other two were both long gone.

"I suppose you'll want to call the police," he said, but she could tell he really didn't want her to. And she didn't want to, either.

"No. No police. I don't want any more trouble."

He relaxed a little at that and began the long pull through the heavy sand toward the street-light in the distance. "Just a lot of red tape for nothing. The first two beat it to the parking lot and the big one will be gone before the cops could ever get here."

"I know." They certainly hadn't caught Bill's killer. She knew they were overworked and underpaid and that it really wasn't their fault. Still it was a loose end she would like to see resolved and perhaps was the reason for her dreams.

"You'd better put me down," she said. "You can't possibly carry me all the way to my door."

A corner of his mouth curved up. "I can't?"

"Well, I wouldn't think . . . what I mean is . . ."

"Just relax, lady. I'll get you home." He looked into her face. "What's your name?"

"Genny. Genny Austin. And you are . . . ?"

"Jack Brennen."

She said nothing more, but when they reached the path leading up from the beach, she unconsciously clutched his neck so that she wouldn't fall and she couldn't help noticing how muscular it was, with heavy cords running up from his thick-muscled shoulders. Beneath the streetlight, she saw that his hair was black and curly, and his eyes were a deep shade of blue.

"Which way now?" he asked. They crossed the street and approached the two-story building that housed several dozen expensive condominiums.

"The one on this end."

He moved forward, walking with an easy grace that seemed incongruous with his height and strength. When they reached the door he waited patiently while she fished out her house key. He took it from her still-shaky hand and opened the door.

He didn't ask permission to come in, just stepped into the entry, spotted the sofa in the living room, carried her over, and carefully deposited her on top of the peach chintz cushions.

"I-I'll be fine now, Mr. Brennen. I can't thank you enough."

"Are you sure? Something like that can be pretty traumatic." *Didn't she know?* "Maybe there's someone I should call."

She shook her head. "No, really, I'm fine."

"Where's your husband?"

The question seemed rather abrupt. She hesitated longer than she should have. If this man decided to attack her, he would not fail. It would be just her luck to jump out of the frying pan into the fire.

"I'm a widow." Inwardly she winced, but she was never very good at lying. Besides, the man had risked a great deal to help her. She owed him at least the benefit of the doubt.

"Listen, Ms. Austin, I know it's none of my business, but if I were you I'd do my beach-walking long before dark. Or at least take someone with you. Next time there might not be anyone around to save your pretty little . . . neck."

For the first time it occurred to her the man had seen her naked breasts. A flush rose into her cheeks, but she forced herself to ignore it. Jack Brennen certainly wasn't embarrassed. Or perhaps he just wasn't that impressed.

"That's very good advice, Mr. Brennen, as tonight proved only too well. Unfortunately, I'm often unable to sleep. Walking on the beach is the only thing I've discovered that seems to do any good. I won't let men like those drive me away."

He raked a hand through his curly black hair, combed back and glistening in the lamplight. "Then get yourself a weapon. A little twenty-two, or maybe a twenty-five, and get someone to teach you to shoot it."

"A gun? You're suggesting I carry a gun?" An image of Bill lying in all that blood came to mind and the bile rose up in her throat.

Jack Brennen merely shrugged. "It's better than being raped . . . or worse."

She swallowed hard and forced the image away. "Th-thank you, Mr. Brennen, I'll take it under consideration, but I don't think a gun is for me. Now if there isn't anything else —"

"Just this. My boat's docked down in the commercial section. The *Marauder*. If you see those bastards again, drop by and let me know. I've got some friends with the Harbor Patrol who might be able to help. That beach belongs to me, too. I don't want that kind of scum hanging around any more than you do."

Genny smiled a little uncertainly. "I'm sure that won't be necessary, but —"

"You don't need a key to get in. Just wedge a stick in the lock or use a credit card or whatever. Damn thing's been broken for years."

"As I said, I'm sure that won't be necessary, but I certainly appreciate the offer."

Jack merely nodded. Leaning forward, he gently probed her ankle. "Not a bad sprain. Stay off it for a couple of days and you'll be fine. An ice pack would help. You want me to make you one before I go?"

"No, thank you. I can take care of it myself. Again, I appreciate all you've done."

"No problem." He grinned. "A little exercise is always good before bed."

Genny flushed once more. "Yes . . . well . . . good night, Mr. Brennen."

"Good night, Ms. Austin." He moved to the door in that easy stride of his, opened it, and stepped out onto the porch. "Lock this behind me," he told her and then he was gone.

Genny stared at the place where he had been. Her mind was a jumble of emotions. The dreams weren't bad enough, tonight she had experienced a real-life nightmare. On top of that, there was Jack Brennen.

She had read about guys like him, muscle-jocks who bashed heads first and asked questions later. Of course, she had to admit she was glad he'd used that brawn of his tonight, and to give the man his due, she had to admit he was handsome.

In a reckless, devil-may-care sort of way.

He was close to her age, maybe four or five years older. She smiled to think what an odd combination they made, she a librarian, educated, a little straight-laced and old-fashioned. Jack Brennen was . . . some sort of boat person.

Still, now that he was gone and she felt safe, she was flooded with gratitude for what he had done. She had never met anyone like him, and she would probably never forget him. There was something about him. Something that tugged at the back of her mind. Something . . .

Whatever it was, it wasn't important. He was gone now and that was the end of it. Genny levered herself up off the couch, hopped across the room on her good leg, and bolted the door. Reaching into the coat closet, she pulled out a green umbrella with a crook-neck handle. Using the umbrella as a cane, she made her way into the kitchen.

The events of the night had left her more than a little unsettled. She was tired clear to her bones, but with her ankle throbbing she still wouldn't be able to sleep. As swollen as it was, she couldn't go to work in the morning, which in a way was a blessing. She would have to call the clinic and cancel her appointment, but perhaps she could finally get some rest.

If she slept during the day, she could recuperate over the weekend — catch up on her sleep debt, the doctors would say — and by Monday she would feel better. At night the nightmares would come — or the sleeplessness — but so far there was nothing she could do about that.

She wondered how long it would take to get her courage back up for another late-night walk on the beach.

Jack stepped off the long wooden dock and onto the *Marauder*, at ease the moment his foot hit the teakwood deck. Tonight he'd worn his boots, a pair of black lizards, instead of the navy blue deck shoes he practically lived in. Damned good thing, with all that blasted sand.

Crossing to the main cabin, he pulled the door open, ducked his head, and stepped in. His mind was still on the three men he had fought with and what had almost happened to Genny Austin.

In the light, she was even better-looking than he had first thought, in a hometown-girl, high-school sweetheart sort of way. Light brown hair, big brown eyes, slender but nicely curved. Sexy breasts, and the rest of her wasn't bad either.

He liked the condo she lived in, not all brass and glass but warm and homey, sort of old-fashioned. He wondered if that was the way she would be, then grimaced to think it might be true. Close to the beach, the way it was, the place was definitely expensive. He wondered what she did for a living, or if she went with some married guy, the way a lot of women did. Somehow he didn't think so.

He found himself wondering about a lot of things. Like why she couldn't sleep. Jack smiled as he crossed the deck and opened the door to the main salon. He'd lay odds ten to one, if she let him into her bed, he'd have her sleeping like a baby.

Not that it was going to happen. She was hardly his type, and he certainly wasn't hers.

At any rate, he had more important matters to worry about than Genny Austin, like how to get the money that was due next month on his boat.

Jack sat down on his wide berth in the captain's cabin, pulled off his boots, then jerked his T-shirt off over his head, a pack of Marlboros still rolled up in his sleeve. He'd quit three months ago. The smokes were just a security blanket now. So far, just knowing they were there had kept him from giving in to temptation.

He never should have started. He'd just been young and stupid and his father had forbidden it, which, if nothing else, insured he would take up the habit. At thirty-three he was smart enough to see the danger. He figured in another two months he'd be over the hump and able to quit for good.

He eyed the pack but ignored the temptation. Just like he'd ignore tempting little Genny Austin.

Three

Genny's weekend went better — and worse — than she had expected. The swelling in her ankle went down; the sprain was a mild one, just as Jack Brennen had said.

The sleep she had expected to catch up on came in fleeting naps during the day, but the nights . . . the nights were as bad as any Genny had experienced in the past two years. As she could have predicted, her insomnia had surfaced as protection against them. She slept little on Sunday evening and she arrived at the library Monday morning in a state of dull fatigue.

Situated on the corner of Anacapa and Anapamu streets, the building stood three stories high and was painted an adobe brown. High arching windows sat below a Spanish-style red tiled roof.

Seated at the sturdy oak desk in her small office behind the reference counter, Genny went over a list of recent book acquisitions. Once that was done, the stacks of newly purchased volumes would need to be filed and put away.

The list was long, and the monotonous job of

matching titles with invoices eventually had her eyes feeling leaden and slowly sliding closed, her head nodding downward toward her chest. She didn't realize she had actually drifted off until her associate, Millicent Winslow, lightly shook her shoulder. Genny jerked upward then sagged back down in her chair.

"Sorry," Millie said, "I didn't think you'd want the boss to catch you napping."

Genny shoved a tumbled lock of hair out of her face. "Thanks, Millie." She liked her job, needed it desperately with all of the problems she faced, but her boss was a stickler for propriety. A sleeping assistant branch librarian would be highly frowned upon, no matter what the circumstances.

"Rough weekend?" Millie asked. She was twenty-five and single, thin to the point of skinny, with a narrow nose, sharp chin, and deep-set blue eyes. Millie was a reference librarian, with old Santa Barbara money. She had gone to Smith College. Her job as a librarian was one of few her parents considered socially acceptable for the daughter of a Winslow.

"Worse than rough," Genny said. "It was terrible."

"I heard you sprained your ankle."

Genny nodded. She'd had to call in, of course. She removed the half-sized, tortoise-rimmed reading glasses perched on her nose, folded them, and set them on top of the long list of books.

"That wasn't the half of it." Briefly, she told Millie about the three men who had attacked her on the beach, about Jack Brennen, and the nightmares that had plagued her all weekend . . . when she slept at all. "Thanks for covering for me, Millie."

"No problem." They were friends of a sort, though they hadn't much in common besides their studious nature and lack of male companionship. Still, Genny liked Millie and Millie liked her. They shared what little happened in their usually uneventful lives and did their best to bolster each other's often flagging spirits.

"What about this guy, Brennen?" Millie asked. "He must have been something to risk himself the way he did."

Genny smiled. She'd had plenty of time to think about Jack Brennen. However unwillingly, all through the weekend he had crept into her mind. "He was 'something' all right. That's about the least you could say about him."

"What did he look like?"

"Well . . . he's tall — at least six foot four, and very darkly tanned — and the man has more muscles than one of those guys down at Venice Beach."

"Good-looking?" Millie asked.

She nodded. "He's got incredible blue eyes and sort of a lazy smile. He's extremely handsome — in a wild, rather reckless sort of way," she added, hoping Millie wouldn't notice the flush that crept into her cheeks.

"Sort of like James Dean," Millie said wistfully, rolling her deep-set blue eyes.

"More like Marlon Brando," Genny corrected, thinking of the rebellious youth Brando had played in *On the Waterfront.*

"Do you think you'll see him again?"

"I'm hardly his type, Millie. And he certainly isn't mine."

"Oh, I don't know. I think it would be exciting to go out with a man like that — just once — just to see what it's like."

"Well, he didn't ask me."

"That's too bad," Millie said, and oddly enough, Genny inwardly agreed.

It was ridiculous, she knew. They had absolutely nothing in common. Still, she had the strangest urge to see him again. Perhaps it was just curiosity, or a desire to repay him in some way for his kindness. Perhaps, if she was honest, it was simply because he was so incredibly good-looking. Whatever the reason, she kept thinking about him, remembering the name of his boat, the *Marauder,* and where it was docked, and that he had offered her his help.

"I guess a man like that wouldn't be interested in a simple librarian," Millie said a little morosely.

"I guess not." But the pull of attraction remained. When Millie changed topics, Genny was grateful.

"Today's Monday," Millie said, "that's your

day for Dr. Halpern, isn't it?"

"Usually, but this week she's on vacation. I'm supposed to see her again next week, after my visit to the sleep clinic. She wants to go over the results." Genny sighed. "I'm beginning to think I ought to save my money. Dr. Halpern was a big help in the beginning — I couldn't have made it without her — but lately . . . I don't know . . . I don't seem to be making much progress."

"That's probably normal. Two steps forward, one step back. I'm sure something as traumatic as you've experienced can't be all that easy to overcome."

"I suppose . . ." But Genny wasn't so sure.

Still, she trusted Francine Halpern, one of the city's most noted psychiatrists, the woman she had gone to see when her nightmares had first begun.

"In a way, dreaming is a psychosis," the attractive blond woman had told her. "It's a mental disorder characterized by symptoms, like hallucinations or delusions, that indicate an impaired contact with reality."

"You mean I'm mentally ill?"

Dr. Halpern smiled indulgently. "Of course not. But you have suffered a very severe type of trauma." She was thirty-five years old, tall, slender, and always wore fashionable clothes. "Your nightmares are a side effect of that trauma, the mind's way of helping you heal. In an odd way, it's actually therapeutic."

45

"I'm afraid I don't understand. How can such terrible dreams possibly be therapeutic?"

"It's simple, really. When you dream, you suspend reality. For a given period of time, you hallucinate. You believe, for that time, things that are obviously untrue. In your case, your dreams are a way of acting out what you imagine must have happened to your husband. Once you learn to cope with his death, your nightmares will end."

With Dr. Halpern's help during the next two years, Genny had been able to work through the shock she had suffered that terrible night in August.

They had gone over those moments again and again. Genny had described how she had come home late from a meeting with the Friends of the Library, a group dedicated to supporting the overburdened library system. How she had parked in the garage, noticed Bill's Volvo in its usual spot and assumed he was also at home. How she had gone into the living room and walked toward the window, calling his name, how she had felt when she glanced outside and saw Bill's body lying on the sidewalk in a thickening pool of blood — the top of his head blown completely away.

The agony she had experienced reappeared with each grisly detail, the torment and the tears, but each time the pain had lessened.

Dr. Halpern had been invaluable, and in most ways Genny felt healed. Unfortunately, even Dr. Halpern couldn't discover why the dreams did not end.

And the lack of sleep had long ago become intolerable.

Which was why, two months ago, the doctor had recommended she visit the Sleep Disorder Center at Cottage Hospital.

"You're going back to the Sleep Clinic?" Millie's thin-boned narrow face took on a look of incredulity. "Surely you don't have to go through all that again."

"Unfortunately, I do. They want to compare the results from the last time. Believe me I'm not looking forward to it."

"I guess not, all those wires and gadgets, and a room full of people watching you try to sleep."

"Don't remind me."

"Sorry." Millie left the room and Genny went back to her long list of invoices and books.

By five o'clock she was exhausted. As soon as she got home, she went upstairs and changed clothes, but she ignored the temptation of the bed and the rest she so desperately needed. A two-hour nap before bedtime would mean she wouldn't be able to sleep at all, and the doctors at the clinic had cautioned her against forming odd sleeping patterns. She napped only out of necessity.

Still, by nine P.M. she began nodding off. She climbed the stairs, crawled into bed, and immediately drifted to sleep. The first thirty

47

minutes were restful, NREM sleep, non-rapid eye movement it was called, she had learned at the clinic; and of course she'd read every book in the library on insomnia and sleep disorders.

Half an hour into REM, rapid eye movement sleep, she began to dream.

It was hazy at first, nondescript, yet the ominous overtones soon began to appear. She was standing among the lush green foliage, familiar from a dozen similar dreams. Broad-leafed plants surrounded her. Her fingers rested on the rough-ridged trunk of a palm tree; she could see heavy bunches of coconuts hanging high up in the wind-whipped limbs. Splinters of moonlight pierced the towering canopy, and spidery green-leafed ferns covered the jungle floor.

Chanting, chanting, she could hear it now, and she could feel the rhythm of the drumbeats all around her. The heavy rhythm drew her, called to her, beckoned her nearer. They were out there, she knew, as she moved in. Then she was watching them through the leafy branches, seeing their black, painted faces, their undulating bodies, writhing and moaning, throwing themselves on the ground in a frenzy of excitement. There were ten — no, twenty — some of them old, some young, all of them muttering, mumbling in foreign tongues. Their heads fell back, lolling about their shoulders as they repeated their senseless incantations.

She moved silently forward, closer to the

blazing fire in the center of the circle of men. There were women there, too, she saw, their breasts exposed above their long white cotton skirts, their huge dark nipples quivering, the lusty ripeness swaying in time with the rhythm of their bodies. Streaks of white paint had been slashed across their faces. They wore necklaces of colored wooden beads and bracelets carved from animal bones. Huge conch shell earrings hung from their ears, and rings made of wood and stone encircled their long slender fingers.

The headman was speaking, holding something in his outstretched hands. It was feathered and squawking, flapping its wings, beating them frantically toward the face of the tall, long-boned man who held the bird upside down as he gripped its ugly, rough-skinned red legs. He raised the bird above his head and repeated his incantation again and again.

The drumbeats strengthened, pounding like a heartbeat. The throbbing filled the jungle night. The throng of men and women drew closer, spiraling upward in heightened frenzy. Two of the women fell to the ground and began to speak in a tongue known only to the gods. Several more shouted curses or prayers invoking the deity they prayed to.

Dressed in nothing but a small white cotton loincloth covering his sex, the headman moved toward the fire. The man to his right handed him a long sharp machete. Its blue steel glinted in the moonlight. He took it in one hand and raised the flapping bird in the other. In an instant the head was severed and an eerie keening rose up from the crowd.

Blood gushed from the dead creature's neck, spraying those who stood too near and splattering in gleaming ruby droplets upon the ground.

The chanting increased, the drumbeats grew louder, more urgent. Crimson streaks appeared on faces and chests as men and women anointed themselves with the blood from the sacrifice. They were covered with sweat. Wailing and shrieking, they shouted their joy and their triumph.

A branch snapped and someone turned to stare in her direction. His face was streaked with blood. His torso was bathed in crimson. Their eyes met, locked. He cried out into the darkness, a sound so evil she must surely turn and run.

Instead she found herself laughing, a high, equally chilling sound that cut through the black night sky and suddenly silenced the chanting. The laughter continued, loud and shrill, echoing through the foliage, filling her ears and her dreams until Genny couldn't stand the terrifying sound any longer.

"Nooooo!" she screamed into the darkness, bolting upright in bed, her hands reaching out as if to protect herself from the rapidly fading vision. Her stomach clenched with wave after wave of nausea. Her trembling body glistened with a sheen of perspiration. She was shaking so hard she couldn't control the fingers she used to shove back her hair.

"Dear God," she whispered. The dream was still burning, the sights and sounds still echoing through her mind. And there was something else, something dark that always came when she awakened, a deep-rooted pain that felt close to grief.

Genny closed her eyes and lay back down, willing control back into her body, but her thoughts remained on the dream. For the first time in the past two years, she had seen something tangible. There had been images she could actually describe.

Before, they had always been vague: light and dark, feelings of blood and death, specters without form. Tonight she had seen real people. At least real shapes in bodily form. Tonight for the first time, something had actually happened.

Genny only wished she knew what it was.

And Genny was afraid she might find out.

Jack Brennen laid his cards facedown on the mahogany table in the main salon of the *Marauder*. "Three ladies, two deuces. A full house, boys. Read 'em and weep."

The other three men groaned as he raked in his winnings, the biggest pile of the evening, still not all that much since the table stakes were nickels, dimes, and quarters, all his friends cared to risk. It was the poker itself they enjoyed, and the camaraderie of long-time friends.

"I was hopin' my luck would be better tonight," grumbled Oliver Madison Brown, his thick black body sprawled back in the hard wooden chair. He was a former tailback who had been a friend since Jack's quarterback days at UCLA. His nickname was Owl, for the huge white circles around his dark eyes. Now he owned a garage.

"What the hell are you bitchin' about, Ollie? I'm the poor SOB who doesn't have two bits left to get his car out of the parking lot." Tall, lanky, and red-haired, Pete Williams was a friend from the Navy. Jack had enlisted when he'd dropped out of school.

He laughed and tossed Pete a quarter out of his pile of winnings. "Don't say I'm not a good sport." Pete worked for Oceanographics Limited, as a diver on the offshore oil rigs, a job Jack had helped Pete acquire.

"You ain't broke, Pete," Charley Denton, Jack's partner, put in. "Tighter than two turns on the capstan wheel, but never broke. Cough up another five and deal the cards."

It was getting late. Jack knew he should end the game and go to bed, but tomorrow's schedule didn't look so bad and he was enjoying his friends' company. He raised the ante and surveyed the two jacks in his hand of seven-card stud.

Standing on the dock at the harbor, Genny read the letters that spelled out *Marauder*, painted in black on the bow of the big gray salvage boat. It looked huge and forbidding, with its cables and towers, and antennae soaring thirty feet into the air. She pulled her blue nylon windbreaker more closely around her, and stared at the lights blazing inside the cabin, while wondering what Jack Brennen was doing awake at one in the morning.

She couldn't say why she had come. Curiosity, maybe. A determination to return to the beach, a resolve that her late-night walks would not be stopped by the likes of those three men. The old falling-off-a-horse philosophy. It was better just to get back on.

At any rate, she had worked the lock on the gate, just as Jack had said, and there she stood, feeling like a fool yet somehow unable to walk away. Worst of all, someone had just looked out the window. Or was it porthole, she thought, hoping whoever it was hadn't seen her.

If she meant to turn and leave, she hadn't the time, and deep down she wasn't sure she wanted to. The cabin door swung open; Jack Brennen ducked his head through the opening and stepped out onto the teakwood deck.

"Well, if it isn't the damsel in distress."

"H-Hello."

He glanced around, looking for trouble, she supposed, probably second nature to a man like him. "You all right?" He was as tall as she remembered, as dark and as startlingly good-looking.

"I'm fine. I was just walking. I remembered the name of your boat. I wondered what it looked like."

His eyes ran over her, noting her jacket and khaki slacks, a contrast to the robe and nightgown she had worn that night on the beach. She flushed to think he might be recalling the sight of her bare breasts, and vowed she would never be so foolish as to go out in her nightclothes again.

"Why don't you come aboard?"

She shook her head and unconsciously took a step backward. "Oh, no, I couldn't possibly . . ."

But already he was walking toward her in his long-legged, lazy gait, motioning to the makeshift wooden stairs that led up to the deck of the boat, leaning over and reaching for her hand.

"Come on up and I'll show you around." Dressed in faded blue jeans and a plain white T-shirt that stretched across his muscled chest like a second layer of skin, he grinned. A pair of dimples creased his cheeks. "You'll be a lot safer here than you'd be out on the beach."

She smiled. How could she argue with that? "All right." She climbed the stairs and Jack's dark, callused hand closed over her slimmer, paler one as he helped her aboard. She could feel the warmth and the strength of it, and an unfamiliar heat slid into the pit of her stomach.

"I thought sailors went to bed early."

"Lucky for you, I'm a night owl." Her insides clenched at the reminder and her smile slipped a little. "Sorry," Jack said. "I didn't mean to bring up an unpleasant subject."

"It's all right. For the most part, I'm over it."

"Good." His sexy male smile made her heart-beat quicken in a way she wouldn't have expected. A lock of his glossy black hair curled appealingly over his forehead, reminding her of the night he had carried her home.

"How's your ankle?" He paused in the midst of a long, lanky stride to stare down at her feet.

"Fine, thank you. You were right. It wasn't a serious sprain."

He nodded. "Come on, I'll introduce you to Charley and some of my friends."

She started to pull back. "Oh, no, I wouldn't want to interrupt. I only —"

Jack merely tugged her forward. He opened the cabin door and hauled her in. Three men sat at an oblong teakwood table playing cards. Short, dove gray pleated curtains hung from the windows. A built-in sofa and polished wooden tables rested beneath them, and an area at one end of the room served as a kitchen. It was nicely appointed and neatly kept, except for the empty beer bottles on the table, the peanut shells piled in an ashtray, and today's discarded newspaper, the *Santa Barbara News Press*, which rested in a tidy little stack on the gray tweed carpet.

At the creak of the cabin door, all three men stopped and turned in her direction. The gray-haired man on the far side of the table pushed back his chair and came to his feet.

"That's Charley Denton," Jack said, "my partner." A man in his late fifties, stoutly built and barrel-chested with short, graying hair. "And those two reprobates are Pete Williams and Oliver Madison Brown."

"Ollie will do, ma'am," the huge black man said, also coming to his feet, though it took considerably more effort. He looked to weigh at least two hundred and fifty pounds.

Pete Williams stood up, too, a red-haired man around thirty, tall and lean and attractive, though not nearly as handsome as Jack. "Pleased to meet you."

"Hello. I'm Genny Austin . . . the woman Jack rescued on the beach." All eyes turned to Jack, who said nothing to this, just shrugged his broad shoulders as if it were an everyday occurrence.

"You didn't tell anyone?" Genny said with some amazement. She'd thought surely a man like Jack Brennen would have bragged for hours on end.

"Nothing much to tell," he said. "It was over damned near before it got started."

"He's an arrogant fool most of the time," Ollie said. "When it counts, he don't say nothin'."

"Jack was incredible," Genny admitted, the

words coming out before she could stop them. "He fought three men all at once and saved me from . . . from . . ." The heat began to burn in her cheeks. She didn't even know these men. If she had any sense, she wouldn't even be there.

"They meant to rape her," Jack said gruffly. "They didn't get the chance."

Ollie grinned, his smile full of large white teeth. "That's my main man!"

"This calls for a drink," Pete said, heading toward the ice chest filled with beer. "You ready?" he asked Jack.

"I think I'll pass."

"How 'bout the lady?"

Genny shook her head.

"I promised Genny a tour of the boat," Jack said and all three men turned to stare at him. Their eyes went straying to Genny then back to Jack.

"Fact is, it's time the rest of us got to bed," Charley Denton said.

"Yeah right." Ollie scooped his change off the table with a meaty hand. "I got a long day tomorrow, got a half dozen cars down at the garage scheduled for service. And Bebe will be waitin'. I'd best be gettin' on home."

"I hope I haven't broken up your game," Genny said, feeling a little bit guilty.

"We've all got to work," Pete said. "We should have left before this."

The men headed for the door, shrugging into their jackets as they went. All but Charley

Denton, who seemed to be eyeing Jack with some speculation.

"I take it you live close by," he said to Genny.

"Yes. Just down a few blocks and across the street."

"What's a little gal like you doin' out this time of night?"

"Genny has trouble sleeping," Jack answered for her, bending to pick up a pack of Marlboros and stuff them into his T-shirt pocket. She'd forgotten that about him. God, she hated men who smoked.

"No man at home?" Charley asked bluntly.

"No, I . . . my husband was killed two years ago. He was . . . murdered . . . in front of our house." She nervously chewed her lip, unsure if she should go on. But Charley seemed to be waiting for her to finish. "Since that time, I've had a lot of trouble with nightmares . . . and insomnia. Walking helps me get to sleep."

"I suppose seein' something like that would give most folks trouble sleeping," Charley said. "Go on, Jack, show the little lady the boat, like you promised."

Jack just nodded. Already he was regretting his hastily spoken words. Genny wasn't his kind of woman, the no strings, no involvement kind. He didn't need any more problems.

"You don't have to do this," she told him, once the others had gone. "It's late and it's time I went home. I shouldn't have come in the first place."

"Why did you?"

"I-I don't know. The dream was worse to-night. It was different . . . a lot more vivid. It frightened me so much that I . . ." She shook her head. He noticed the mist was curling her light brown hair, making her look younger. "I had to get out of the house. You were so brave the other night, I thought surely I could be at least . . ." Her cheeks went pink and the words trailed off, as if she wished she'd said something else.

Jack looked into her pretty face, at the fine bones and softly arching brows, and thought how long it had been since he had seen a woman blush. He wondered if, in this day and age, a woman could possibly be as naive as this one appeared. She lowered her eyes to the floor, and thick dark lashes formed crescents on her cheeks. Her hair looked soft and silky, the brown seemed to sparkle with gold. He had always leaned toward blondes . . . until now.

He forced his gaze away. "Will you be able to get to sleep?"

"I think so. I usually can, once I get home."

"Wouldn't you like to see the boat?"

She glanced around, taking in the teakwood paneling, the brass ship's clock on the wall. Her face held a look of fascination, and yet she shook her head. "Perhaps some other time."

He should have been relieved, but he wasn't. The last thing he needed was a woman like Genny Austin. But one look in those soft brown eyes and desire tugged low in his belly.

"I've got an appointment with my banker tomorrow," he heard himself saying. "How about the day after? We'll be back at the dock about six. What time do you get home from work?"

"I-I get off at five. I work at the library."

Jack inwardly groaned. What the hell was he doing? Getting the hots for a damned librarian?

"I suppose I could stop by for a few minutes," Genny conceded. "I've never seen a boat like this. Actually this is the first time I've ever been aboard any kind of a ship."

He grinned at that. He was a sucker for anyone interested in his boat. "Great. I can walk over and get you if you like."

"That won't be necessary. I'm only across the street. I'll come down about six-thirty." Genny smiled, and he thought how different it was from Vivian's smile, how much softer and sweeter. He had never thought that kind of a smile could be so sexy.

"Come on," he said, "I'll walk you home."

"Oh, no, you don't have to do that. I got here on my own, I can certainly —"

"Listen, Ms. Austin, when you came onboard this boat, you became my responsibility. Once you're home, what you do is your business. The least I can do is get you there in one piece."

For a moment, she said nothing, as surprised as he was that he had suddenly become so protective. "Aye, aye, Captain." She gave him a smart little salute, and Jack grinned, glad to be back on familiar territory, and even more relieved that she had at least some sense of humor.

"I didn't mean to get so high-handed."

"It's all right. It's kind of nice to have someone worry about me. It's been a long time since that happened."

Jack merely grunted. The last thing he wanted was a woman he had to worry about. Then he looked at Genny Austin, saw the soft lush curve of her full bottom lip, felt the quickening of desire he'd felt since the moment he had seen her on the dock.

"Get your jacket and let's go," he said a little bit gruffly, but he was thinking, What the hell? It was obvious Genny Austin needed a good lay, even if she didn't know it, and he damned well wouldn't mind obliging. If it took a little effort, a little bit of time, so what? It just might be worth it.

The blonde at the Sea Breeze Bar would just have to wait.

Four

"Howard? What in the world are you doing out here?"

Howard McCormick, Genny's late husband's business partner, sat at the wheel of his shiny white Lincoln Continental, parked at the curb next to her condo. She had seen him as she had driven home from work.

"I tried to call you all weekend," Howard said through the rolled down window beside where she stood, "but your answering machine was on, so I figured you weren't home. I guess I should have left a message. This afternoon, I called you at the library, but Millie said you were helping someone with a research project. By the time I called back, you had already gone."

Howard was tall and well built with a mane of rusty brown hair. At forty he was attractive, intelligent, and a very good businessman. "I was trying to catch up on my sleep," Genny said. "I'm sorry I missed your calls. Would you like to come in?" They'd been seeing each other more often. Not really dating. Not exactly. Though Howard was beginning to think of it that way.

"Actually, I have a city council meeting beginning at six-thirty, but I wanted a chance to see you. Since I'm busy tonight, I thought we might have dinner together tomorrow evening."

She glanced off toward the water, then down toward the dock, feeling a little bit guilty as she thought of her meeting with Jack Brennen. "I don't think so, Howard. There's something I have to do. Perhaps another night this week."

"I'm tied up on Thursday. Why don't we make it Friday night?"

"All right. Millie's going out of town for the weekend. I have to feed her poodle and check on her parakeet. I told her I'd stop by and she could show me where things were. Beyond that, I'm free for the evening."

"Good. I'll pick you up at eight. We'll have dinner at the Plow and Angel."

"How about seven? If you bring me home early, maybe I'll be able to get some sleep." Howard frowned. She knew how much he hated it when she made him rearrange his schedule.

"All right then," he finally conceded, "seven o'clock it is." He reached out and squeezed her hand. He felt solid and strong, the way she always thought of Howard. He was also a little overbearing, and somewhat self-centered, but everyone had their faults.

"I'll see you Friday," Genny said.

Howard nodded and waved and started his engine. He glanced in the rearview mirror.

63

Genny stood on the sidewalk as he drove away. He'd been seeing her for the last two years, ever since Bill died. At first merely as a friend, but lately that friendship had blossomed — just as he'd intended.

Howard smiled with satisfaction. So far, he'd been going slowly, giving her time to get to know him, giving her a chance to grieve. When the time was right, he had long since decided, he would make Genny Austin his wife.

Howard braked and pulled up to the stop sign at the corner, thinking as he had a dozen times that Genny would make the perfect mate. Sweet and loving, loyal to a fault, she'd be a real asset to his burgeoning political career. She was quiet and well liked, with a spotless family background. As far as he knew, Genny Austin had never even had a speeding ticket.

Besides, he found her damned attractive, slender but well proportioned, with nicely shaped breasts, long tapered legs, and a tight little derrière. He was twelve years her senior, but he didn't look it. He still had plenty of hair, kept his six-foot, hundred-eighty-pound frame in shape, and he knew that women found him attractive.

He and Genny would make a handsome couple, he was sure, though he'd be glad when she got rid of all the doctors, got over the shock of Bill's death, and returned to normal. More and more he found himself imagining making love to her. He would take her slowly, gently, as a lady like Genny deserved. And he knew her smooth, sleek body would please him. He could hardly wait to get her into his bed.

Howard clicked on the radio as he waited for a car at the stop sign. It was amazing the way he'd always had a knack for making things work out. Even the times that seemed the blackest, times he'd done what he had to, no matter how hard it was. Still, it never occurred to him he would reap this kind of reward.

Howard thought of Genny, standing beside his car window, thought of how pretty she had looked in her simple navy blue suit. He would see her again on Friday. That night, he vowed, he would kiss her pretty mouth, instead of just her cheek.

Feeling an odd mix of emotion, Genny watched Howard's long white Lincoln round the corner. Since Bill's murder, he had been one of her closest friends. He was the first person she'd called after she found Bill's body, and from that moment on, he had simply taken charge. She couldn't imagine what she would have done without him.

He stepped on the gas, the Lincoln slipped from view, and Genny felt even more guilty. She owed Howard McCormick, and in the past few weeks she had begun to consider him more than just a friend. Their relationship was changing, just as Dottie had said. Genny had encouraged it. She had begun to think Howard might have a permanent place in her future.

Why then, had she refused his generous invitation in favor of a few short minutes with Jack Brennen? A man like Jack could never be part of her life. At best, he couldn't be more than just an acquaintance. What on earth could they ever have in common? She couldn't imagine Jack Brennen discussing the classics, or going to an opera, or attending a black tie benefit. She couldn't imagine him wearing a suit, let alone a tuxedo.

She sighed as she stepped up onto the sidewalk and walked back to her front door. Perhaps she was going through some kind of phase. Maybe she needed a change of some sort, needed some excitement in her life — just once — as Millie had said. Whatever the reason, she was going down to the dock tomorrow after work to see Jack's boat. He had invited her — old-fashioned, simple Genny Austin, Assistant Branch Librarian.

Maybe it was merely an act of kindness. Then again, perhaps it wasn't. At the very least, she was curious to discover what it was Jack Brennen thought of her. Beyond his physical appeal, she had yet to decide what she thought of him.

Genny dreamed again that night. But when she awoke at 2:00 A.M., she didn't walk the beach, nor drive down to the coffee shop to visit her friend. Tonight her nightmare was far too disturbing, too incredibly real. She didn't want to think about it; she certainly didn't want to discuss it.

Instead she bent the rule she had firmly set for herself after her first few months of insomnia. She broke out the bottle of Halcion the clinic doctors had prescribed, and took a dose strong enough to put her to sleep.

She rarely took sleeping pills. She had learned her lesson on that score right away. Her first prescription of barbiturates, a liberal dose of Seconal, left her feeling sluggish, and constantly depressed. When she tried to end her reliance on the drug, she suffered symptoms of withdrawal: headaches, nausea, and tremors.

She had tried other forms of medication, but the dependency she came to feel always scared her. Though the Halcion she took now was the most effective, it had initially been blamed for her nightmares, hallucinations being one of the side effects of the drug. Occasionally, she'd felt dizzy, and there was still the threat of becoming addicted. Better to discover the root of the problem and conquer it than to develop another, equally severe, different sort of problem by becoming hooked on drugs.

Still, occasionally, on nights like this one, Genny gave in to temptation and allowed herself to succumb to the lure of a restful, dream-free sleep. Already her eyes were drifting closed, beginning to feel heavy and limp. There would only be a moment more to remember the nightmare that had left her so shaken and disturbed.

Only a few more moments to remember that this dream had started just like the last. She had been standing in the same lush part of the jungle, hearing the call of the drum, drawn by it like the natives in the dream.

The woman in the dream had lifted her long full skirts up off the mulchy jungle floor and silently moved forward, closer to the dancers, closer to their half-naked bodies. The expensive Mechlin lace on one of her sleeves caught on a thorny acacia branch. She paused and jerked it loose, not caring that the beautifully woven lace tore free and dangled down the striped silk moiré sleeve toward her wrist.

Silently, the woman had moved toward the circle of dancers, edging closer. The dream was unfolding as it had before, ending with the sound of the natives' chilling screams and the woman's shrill, high-pitched laughter. Ending with Genny's eyes slamming open in the darkness, her heart hammering hard against her ribs.

She didn't want to think about it, wouldn't, she vowed, at least not till tomorrow.

Then she could examine the fact that the watcher in the jungle was a woman. And that the dreams were not set in the present — as she had always assumed — but at a time in the long distant past.

At 6:15 on Wednesday night, Charley

Denton shoved his bookmark between the pages of the book he'd been reading and left his berth in the first mate's quarters, the cabin he'd slept in since the night he'd signed his majority interest in the *Marauder* over to Jack Brennen on his thirtieth birthday, three years ago next month.

Jack had declined the captain's cabin at first, but Charley had insisted. It was Jack who needed the oversized bed, being as big as he was, to say nothing of the fact he got laid about three nights a week. Besides Jack deserved it. He worked his tail off on the *Marauder*, and he'd been more of a son than that worthless spawn, Robert, Charley's true flesh and blood, could ever hope to be.

Bobby was rotting in jail and had been, off and on, since he was fifteen years old and a high-school dropout. Charley had blamed himself, of course, though for the life of him, he couldn't imagine what he'd done wrong. He'd tried to help the kid mend his ways, made every effort at rehabilitation, but Bobby was just no good from the start. Thieving was easier than working. Drugs were a whole lot more fun.

Charley just felt grateful that God had sent Jack to help ease the pain and take the place of his son. Though right now, he'd like to aim a well-placed kick at the seat of Jack's pants.

Charley checked his watch as he climbed the ladder to the deck. It was almost six-thirty, the expected time of arrival of the woman named

Genny Austin, the girl Jack had invited aboard.

Unfortunately, Jack wasn't there.

Charley swore softly, calling his friend a fool and a few words far more choice. Jack'd had second thoughts about little Genny. She wasn't his type, he'd said. He only wanted one thing from a woman, and Genny wasn't the sort to give that up without attaching strings. To Charley's chagrin, Jack had strode off to the Sea Breeze Bar.

And Charley knew why.

Jack Brennen was scared.

Charley might have smiled if he hadn't been so damned disappointed. Good women always scared Jack off. He didn't want to get involved, he always said. He didn't want to be tied down to just one woman, and that was what Genny's kind always wanted.

But there was a helluva lot of difference between being tied down and being in love. When you loved someone, Charley knew, it was more like being anchored, having your own home port, a place of refuge in a storm. Charley had been married only once, to a woman named Sarah Mills — he called her Sassy. For twenty-three years she'd put up with his life at sea, his often nomadic existence. Even their problems with Bobby weren't enough to destroy what they shared between them — and not a day passed since her death that he didn't miss her.

But Jack was determined to live his life alone.

"Hello up there!" Genny Austin stood on the

dock in a pair of brand-new blue jeans and what appeared to be an equally new pair of sparkling white deck shoes. One look at the smile of anticipation on her fine-boned face and Charley could have booted Jack Brennen all the way to the Sea Breeze Bar.

"Come on up, missy. Here, let me help you." He went over and helped her aboard, noting the way her eyes searched the deck for some sign of Jack.

"I'm afraid our boy ain't here," Charley said. "At the last minute, somethin' came up. He asked me to show you around for him."

The eager smile slipped, but in seconds was firmly back in place. "I'd love to . . . Charley, wasn't it?"

"That's right."

"Are you sure you don't mind? I wouldn't want to be any bother."

"No bother a'tall. In fact it would be my pleasure." Charley found he meant it. There was something of warmth in Genny Austin's eyes that would reach out to the hardest man. He almost smiled. No wonder Jack had run.

"Why don't we start up top? That's the wheelhouse. That's where all the navigational work is done and it's where we operate the boat."

"How do we get up there?"

"There's two ways to get in. One outside, one up through the main cabin, where you were the other night." They went up through the inside passage, Charley explaining bits and pieces of information about the boat as he walked along.

"Those are the instrument panels." He pointed toward a chest-high wall of dials and gauges. "Oil, fuel, depth gauges —"

"And that's radar, isn't it?" She looked up at him for confirmation.

"That's right. And navigational gear. Most boats nowadays also use satellite navigation — GPS. This here's hundred-twenty-mile range Raytheon Radar equipment. The scanner's up on the radar bridge — that's that thing stickin' up way above us."

"I saw it when I came aboard." Her eyes took in the myriad dials, the charts on the navigation table, and the floating compass near the windows that looked out over the bow. She ran a hand over the smooth, well-worn surface of the teakwood wheel, then she glanced off to the right.

"You have a computer on board?"

"Jack insisted. We use it for navigation, and it's interfaced with the weather fax. Jack's gonna put our bookkeeping on there soon. Says it'll make things a whole lot easier in the long run."

"Yes, I imagine it will." They went back down the ladder, stopping for a moment in the main cabin. "Your kitchen looks very efficient."

"It's called a galley," Jack Brennen said from the open cabin door. Genny turned and so did Charley, who winked and smiled at him, surprised that Jack had returned but glad to see him just the same.

Jack glanced away, looking disgruntled and even a little bit angry. At himself, Charley surmised, for coming back to see Genny when he'd made up his mind not to court temptation.

"You got here just in time," Charley said. "I was about to show Genny the captain's cabin. Guess you'd probably like to do that yourself."

Jack said nothing.

"This is all very interesting," Genny said, feeling suddenly nervous. "I-I'm glad I came."

Jack's blue eyes swept over her snug-fitting blue jeans, bought just yesterday, washed and dried four times to fade them a little and get them to fit.

A hint of a smile curved his lips. "So am I."

Oddly warmed by his look, Genny followed him down to his cabin. He ducked his head and stepped inside. The cabin was roomier than she would have expected, everything built in, as neat as the rest of the ship, but even more Spartan. She flushed at the size of the bed, which would easily accommodate two. Jack's gaze followed hers and his blue eyes seemed to darken, as if he had guessed the train of her thoughts.

"The head's over there." He pointed toward a narrow wooden door, but his eyes remained fixed on her face.

"Head?" she repeated, and he grinned.

"The bathroom's called a head, the bed is a berth, and the windows are portholes. Come on, Miss Librarian. I'll show you the rest of the boat."

They took the ladder down to the engine room, where everything was painted gray and black, even the floors and the ceiling.

"The *Marauder* is eighty feet from bow to stern," Jack said, "with an eighteen-foot beam and a five-foot draft. She's powered by a pair of twelve-hundred-horsepower Caterpillar diesels. She carries 5,000 gallons of fuel and 1,000 gallons of water."

Genny nodded as if she really understood all that, and continued to survey the room. "What's this?" She pointed to a bulky piece of machinery along one wall.

"Generator. There's two on board, a 24 kw, which powers all our equipment, and an 8 kw for backup." He pointed out other various machinery, then led her back up on deck.

"The forecastle's up front. The main deck is where you came aboard, and we're standing on the aft deck. That's where we operate most of our heavy equipment."

Genny tilted her head back, angling it to look skyward. "That's a crane of some sort, isn't it?"

Jack nodded and she didn't miss the pride on his darkly tanned face. "We've got a twenty-ton knuckle crane and a ten-ton auxiliary winch. That little room with the three glass windows is the aft steering station. Sometimes we call it the doghouse."

"What do you use the crane for?"

"Lately, most of our business has been coming from the offshore oil rigs. Salvage is what we do whenever we get the chance. It's a lot more fun. Kind of like looking for sunken treasure."

Genny smiled. "I bet you'd like that, wouldn't you, Jack Brennen, hunting for buried treasure." All he needed was an earring in his ear.

He smiled that devastating, virile smile of his and her stomach flopped over, the way it did when she rode on a ferris wheel.

"I've done that a couple of times," Jack said matter-of-factly. "I worked with a salvage crew down in Florida. We were looking for gold bullion that went down with a sixteenth-century galleon that sank off the Bahamas. Never even found enough treasure to pay for the cost of the salvage operation. Eventually, the money man went away, and we all went back home."

"Still, I'll bet it was exciting."

"Some of the time. One day we brought up a solid gold cross inlaid with emeralds and rubies — *that* was exciting. A lot of the time, it was just plain hard work."

Jack finished the tour, pointing out the 7,000 feet of cable the *Marauder* carried, the aft capstan, which served as the anchor winch, the diving equipment storage locker, and a dozen sundry items she couldn't begin to remember. Then he led her back to the main salon.

"How about a drink?" Crossing the cabin in that easy stride of his, he opened a small wooden cupboard.

"I'm afraid I'm not much of a drinker."

"Might help you sleep." He took down two glass tumblers and set them on the counter.

"Actually, in the long run, liquor only makes matters worse . . . at least that's what the doctors say."

"Charley drinks white wine. Would you like a glass of that?"

"All right, wine would be nice."

Charley joined them, pouring himself a glass and handing one to Genny, while Jack poured himself a whiskey on the rocks.

"I heard you talkin' about gettin' some sleep," Charley said. "Those dreams of yours gettin' any better?"

She glanced up at Jack, wondering just how much she should say. She didn't want him to think she was some kind of crazy. She sighed. There was no use sidestepping the issue. If he didn't like her the way she was, there was nothing she could do about it.

"Actually, they seem to be getting worse. Or maybe it's just that they're changing."

"Changing?" Jack said. "How's that?"

"In the beginning the dreams were mostly disjointed and relatively meaningless. They were terrifying in one way or another, but mostly a jumble of fuzzy, ominous images — blood and darkness, swirling colors, glimpses of figures I couldn't quite see, that sort of thing. There were noises, of course — chanting and screaming, things like that. Often I felt as if the person in the dream was running for his life and that if he were caught, he'd be killed. Several times I dreamed about rooms full of spiders."

Jack shivered like a big wet dog. "Damn. That would keep anyone awake at night."

"And lately?" Charley prompted.

"The last few times, there've been people in my dreams. The setting seems to fit with the images that came before, the colors and sounds are right, but now the images are in focus. It's like watching a movie where the lens is finally set correctly. Lately, each time I've dreamed, the movie has more details."

"Then you've been dreaming about the night of your husband's murder," Jack said.

Genny shook her head. "That's what the doctors always believed, but oddly enough, the dreams don't seem to have anything to do with Bill's death. In fact, I don't think they're even in the same time frame."

"What do you mean?" Charley asked.

Genny chewed her bottom lip, uncertain if she should go on.

"You don't have to tell us if you don't want to," Jack said softly, surprising her.

She looked at the strong bones in his face,

noticing the tiny sun lines beside his bright blue eyes. "I just don't want you to think I'm crazy."

He smiled, making the same sort of creases in his forehead. "Don't worry about it. People have been calling me crazy for years."

"You can say that again," Charley grumbled.

Genny smiled. She liked Charley Denton, and as outrageous as it might seem, she felt more drawn to Jack Brennen than she had been before. Of course, most any woman would be, with those incredible blue eyes and that curly black hair. For God's sake, the man even had dimples!

With a face and body like that, it shouldn't have been surprising that she found him so attractive, and it wouldn't have been — if the woman had been anyone but her.

"Well?" Charley pressed.

"The lady isn't talking," Jack said stubbornly, and Genny felt a tug of appreciation for his concern.

"I don't mind, really. It's just that it's all so weird." Charley motioned her over to the sofa. She picked up her wineglass, walked over, and sat down across from his chair. Jack followed and sat down beside her, leaning back to stretch his long legs out in front of him.

Genny told them the details of her latest dream and about the old-fashioned dress the woman in the dream had been wearing. "It was kind of like something you'd see in *Gone with the Wind*, only without the hoop, and not quite so full. It was expensive, made of black and cream-striped silk and trimmed with black lace."

She went on to describe the clearing in the jungle, the natives, and the bloody pagan ritual they had performed.

"Sounds like someplace in Africa," Charley said.

"I can't imagine the place is real. It's probably some sort of symbol, don't you think? A way of dealing with my trauma?" She couldn't believe she was talking like that to men like these.

What could they possibly know about psychiatric trauma or psychosis? She hadn't known a thing about it herself until she had gone to Dr. Halpern. All that these men knew about were fistfights, buried treasure, and diesel engines.

"It might be real," Charley said. "It could be something you've seen in a movie, or watched on TV. Maybe it's something you saw as a child, something that scared you real bad. Maybe the murder brought it all to the surface."

"You read a lot, don't you?" Jack added. "Being a librarian and all. Maybe it's part of a book you've read."

Very astute on both of their parts, Genny thought with a slight raise of her brow. Perhaps she had pigeonholed the men a little too quickly.

"That's an interesting idea," she said. "Better than anything I've come up with. I'll have to give it some thought." She came to her feet and Jack stood up, too. "It's getting late. I want to thank you for inviting me here tonight. I really enjoyed the tour. You've both been terribly kind to me."

For some unknown reason Jack frowned. "Yeah, well I'm just glad you didn't get hurt too bad the other night."

"I would have been, if it hadn't been for you."

For a moment, he said nothing. "Come on, I'll walk you home."

"You don't have to, I can —" She caught his dark look and smiled. "What I meant to say was thank you. I'd appreciate that very much."

Jack smiled, too. "Smart lady, isn't she, Charley?"

"Real smart, Jack." He turned a warm look on Genny. "You come back and see us, little gal, you hear? And keep me posted on those dreams. I'd kinda like to hear what happens next."

She nodded. "Thanks, Charley."

Jack walked her home, as she knew he would have done with or without her permission. There was a streak of chivalry in Jack Brennen that even he hadn't seemed to guess.

"Charley knows a lot about psychology," he said, as they stepped off the boat and onto the deck. "He started reading up on it years ago. Had problems with his kid. Got interested in it then."

"I'll bet he knows a lot about a lot of things."

Jack smiled. "You can say that again."

It was dark by the time they reached the street, the sun having gone down some time ago, but a few determined stars twinkled through the mist and through the thin layer of clouds above their heads.

"Thank you again, Captain Brennen," Genny said to him, once they arrived at her door, "for a surprisingly pleasant evening."

Jack cleared his throat. "I was thinking . . . wondering . . . there's a big pool tournament over at the Sea Breeze Bar on Saturday night. I don't suppose you'd be interested in going?"

"A pool tournament? You mean like billiards?"

He answered as if she hadn't spoken. "I didn't think so." And started to walk away.

"I've never been to a pool tournament," Genny called after him. "I think I'd like to see one. Will you be competing in it?"

He nodded.

"What time does it start?"

"If you're serious about going, I'd have to pick you up around six-thirty."

"You have a car?"

He smiled with amusement.

"I'm sorry, of course you do. I just sort of thought —"

The smile turned into a grin, gouging the grooves in his cheeks. "You thought what? That when I'm not on the boat, I wind-surf my way

81

to wherever it is I'm going?"

Twin spots of heat rose in her cheeks. "Something like that, I suppose."

"Actually, I love to wind-surf. I like just about any kind of sport, and anything to do with engines and speed."

Genny mulled that over and clamped down on an urge to run. "Nothing in common" was putting it mildly. She couldn't even play a passable game of Ping-Pong. "What should I wear?"

"What you've got on now will do just fine." He gave her bustline a glance that made the heat rush back into her face. "A sexy tank top might distract the competition."

"I-I'm afraid I don't own a tank — I mean . . ." She smiled. "I guess I'll see you on Saturday."

Jack just nodded. He was staring at her lips. Nervously Genny licked them and she could have sworn she heard him groan.

He turned and started walking. "See you Saturday, Genny Austin."

Genny waved. "Good-bye, Jack Brennen."

"You like her, don't you?" Charley leaned back in his usual chair across from the sofa. There was a slightly worn indentation that exactly fit his back.

Jack took a slug of his drink, Wild Turkey on the rocks. "I'd like to get into her pants."

"Come on, Jack. Admit it. You like her."

He grunted. "She's got too damned many problems."

"I'll bet you asked her out."

"I told you, she looks like a good piece of ass."

Charley chuckled. "Genny Austin looks like anything but that — aside from having a damned fine figure. 'Course, in my experience, it was always the shy, soft-spoken ones who turned out to be the best in bed."

"Yeah, well, I guess we'll just have to wait and see."

Charley leaned forward in his chair. "Take it easy on her, Jack. She ain't like the rest, and you know it."

"Which is exactly why I must be out of my mind to be seeing her again."

"Come on, Jack. It might be fun to go out with a woman who can carry on an intelligent conversation for a change."

"Yeah, and while she's talking poetry and classical music, what am I supposed to be saying?"

"Don't give me that, boy. We both know you're a whole lot smarter than you let on."

Jack just grunted. He knocked back his drink and set the glass down on the counter beside the sink. "I'm going to bed."

"When are you seein' Bob Groller again?" Charley asked as he walked to the stairs leading down to his cabin.

"On Tuesday, but it doesn't look good." He

sighed. "The money market's too damned tight. We don't have any long-term contracts to back up our income, and that string of late payments we made last year is just about the crowning blow. Groller's taking our application back to the loan committee, but like I told you last night, he doesn't hold out much hope."

"Maybe something will turn up."

"Yeah, maybe." Charley had been saying that every day for the past three months. Jack figured there wasn't a chance in hell it was actually going to happen. Still, he wasn't about to sit there cooling his heels while his creditors took their boat. He was bound and determined that he would do *something*.

He just wished to God he knew what it was.

Five

Genny dressed with care that Saturday night. She had broken a cardinal rule and napped in the afternoon so she wouldn't be too tired to enjoy herself.

Now she tugged on the tight-fitting jeans she had washed and dried two more times. Then she slipped into the cotton-knit tank top she had bought at the Broadway on her way home from work Thursday evening. It was a navy blue stripe that clung to her bosom, defining the soft, upward-tilting curves.

Her breasts weren't huge, but they weren't small either. They were nicely shaped, and pointed, the way she had seen them on a model in an issue of *Playboy* she had once leafed through in the library. She couldn't believe she was actually wearing something that showed them off the way the top did, but for some crazy reason she felt good about doing it.

Besides, Jack Brennen had already seen them, she thought with a rush of heat — and apparently Jack approved. She attributed the sudden warmth to embarrassment but wondered deep down if it weren't something a whole lot different.

She still couldn't believe she was actually going out with him. Millie was the only person she had told, the only one she could think of who wouldn't laugh in her face. Howard certainly would have. Which was why last night at dinner she hadn't mentioned the three men on the beach, or the handsome man who had saved her.

The man who was taking her out to a beer bar, where he intended to compete in a game of pool!

God, she must be going through her second childhood, strange indeed, since at twenty-eight, she wasn't that many years beyond her first. Whatever the reason, she was determined to go through with it — she was going to have some fun for a change.

Other women did these sorts of things, why shouldn't she?

Still, she was pacing the carpet, her palms damp with nervous anticipation, and calling herself a fool when Jack knocked on the door, promptly at six-thirty.

"I can't believe you're ready," were the first words out of his mouth. The sight of him standing in her doorway, filled by his broad shoulders, with faded jeans riding low on his incredibly narrow hips, made her forget to breathe. Then she caught the look on his face and recalled the harshness she had heard in his voice.

"You don't seem too happy about it." In fact,

he seemed disgruntled and edgy, in some way as anxious as she.

He shrugged and stepped into the room. "Most women like to keep a man waiting. I guess they figure it makes him appreciate them more."

"Oh." She wondered if she should have done the same. She didn't have much experience at this sort of thing.

"Personally," he said, with a long, overly bold perusal, "I like a woman who's ready, willing, and eager."

A rush of embarrassment heightened the color in her cheeks. For the first time, she had major doubts about the evening. Jack Brennen seemed none too happy about it either.

"Come on, we're gonna be late." He started for the door, then stopped and turned. "You got a scarf?"

"A scarf?"

"Yeah, I've got the top down."

A convertible. She should have guessed. Heading back upstairs, she returned with a paisley silk scarf from Hermès, a gift from Millicent Winslow on Genny's twenty-eighth birthday, the only scarf she owned. She drew it over her hair and tied it beneath her chin.

"I'm ready when you are."

Jack said nothing, just assessed her in that too bold way he had done before. It was probably right in character, macho male that he was. But he had never looked at her quite that way, and it made her even more uneasy. Jack gripped her hand and hauled her toward the door. Genny grabbed a small leather handbag from the small oak table in the entry, locked the front door, and walked beside him to his car. She stopped short at the curb.

"Oh, Jack, it's . . . beautiful." In fact it was the sleekest, most gorgeous candy apple red convertible she had ever seen.

For a moment, Jack's dark look faded. "I have to admit, next to the *Marauder*, this little beauty's my pride and joy."

"What kind of car is it?"

" '67 Shelby 500 KR Mustang. And believe me she can run." Jack walked around the car, opened the passenger door, and helped her climb in. Returning to the driver's side, he slid in behind the wheel and reached for a pair of wraparound sunglasses. Hidden behind them, he glanced at her sideways and grinned.

"Hang on, baby, and I'll give you a little taste of what she can do."

In all her twenty-eight years, no one had ever called her baby. She should have been indignant — an insult to womanhood, women's liberation and all. Instead, something warm curled in her stomach. For heaven's sake, the guy was practically a caveman. How could she be pleased that he had talked to her that way?

Jack turned the ignition and the engine rumbled to life, along with the radio, which was blaring '50s music through four incredibly loud speakers. He reached over and turned it down a little, but didn't turn it off, which really made no difference, since the engine noise made it impossible to hear. Genny gasped when he reached across to fasten her seat belt. A jolt of electricity sparked from the spot where his arm brushed her breast. He snapped the catch, then fastened his own belt into place.

"I didn't think you'd be the seat belt type," Genny said to cover her embarrassment.

Jack just grunted. "I learned that lesson the hard way. Ten years ago, I went through the windshield on one of these little beauties. Damned near got myself killed."

Noticing the thin scar at the hairline near his temple, Genny swallowed weakly. Jack glanced down at her, gunned the motor once, twice, then popped the clutch, sending the car careening forward. He hit the gas and they were off to the screech of tires and the smell of burning rubber, while Genny's fingers were clawing into the black leather seat.

They raced up Shoreline Drive, Genny with her eyes closed more than half the time, Jack accelerating, then braking, cutting to the right or left to avoid a car, then accelerating again. He downshifted in front of the shopping center on the Mesa, slowed and pulled into the left-turn lane. Making a quick, wheel-tilting U-turn, he slammed the car into second gear, shifted again, and roared back down the hill the way they had come.

A few blocks past her condo, he finally slowed down and pulled into the parking lot of the Sea Breeze Bar. All the while, Elvis blared from the radio, singing "Blue Suede Shoes."

Genny didn't say one word. Finger by finger, she pried her grip loose from the seat she still clung to.

"Well, what do you think of her?" Jack asked as he popped open his door and slid out from behind the steering wheel.

Genny wet her bottom lip, still a little numb from where she had nervously chewed it. "Well . . . she certainly moves right along." With a shaky hand, she untied the scarf and shook out her hair, which now hung in light brown, softly curling ringlets.

Jack eyed her a little bit strangely but said nothing more, just rounded the car and opened her door. Her knees were trembling, she realized as she swung her legs onto the asphalt parking lot and tried to stand up. She swayed a little in his direction, and he steadied her against him, his big hand settling at her waist.

"That's all you have to say? She moves right along?"

"You . . . you seem to be a very proficient driver."

Jack's eyes ran over her face, which looked too pale, she was sure. Her legs were still unsteady and her heart thrummed a mad tattoo inside her chest.

Jack's hold tightened at the tremors he felt

running through her. He said a swearword beneath his breath. "I damned near frightened you to death. You should have said something."

She managed to muster a smile. "It's all right. I guess I'm just not used to going so fast."

Jack eyed her a moment more, swore again, then released a long slow breath of air. He shook his head, moving the black hair curling at the base of his neck. "I'm sorry, Genny. That was a rotten thing to do and the truth is, I did it on purpose."

Her back went rigid. She couldn't believe what he had said. "On purpose? You mean the wild ride up the hill? You were purposely trying to scare me?"

He nodded, a look of regret on his face.

"But why? Why would you do it on purpose?"

He sighed. "I was trying to prove something, I guess. I figured if I drove like that — the way I do when I'm alone — you'd scream like a scalded cat. I thought you'd pitch a fit and make me take you home."

Genny's heart twisted. "I see." She stared off across the parking lot, trying not to feel hurt. Jack's hand no longer touched her. She realized she missed the comforting warmth. "If you were sorry you asked me out . . . if you didn't really want to be with me —"

"It's not that . . . exactly."

"It's all right, Jack," she said softly. An odd pang rose in her chest. "I shouldn't have accepted in the first place. You were only trying to be nice and I —"

"I wasn't trying to be nice, dammit! I'm never nice to women." He raked a hand through his hair. "The truth is, there's only one thing I want from a woman and that's to take her to bed. You aren't that kind of girl, Genny. Any fool can see that. What the hell are you doing out with a guy like me?"

"You asked me out because you wanted to take me to bed?" Amazement laced her voice. She was just plain Genny, not some kind of *Playboy* bunny. She never imagined he had asked her out for sex.

"What the hell did you think?" This time it was Jack who looked embarrassed, the color creeping in beneath his tan. "Listen, baby, you're a damn good-looking woman — even if you are a librarian. You've got a great set of tits and a tight little ass — hell, I'm not some kind of eunuch."

She should have been offended, would have been if some other man had said the same thing. Instead she felt womanly. Sexy. "Hardly that, Jack." She did her best not to smile.

For a moment Jack said nothing, then his eyes swung back to her face. "I'm a real bastard, Genny. A girl like you'd be crazy to go out with a guy like me."

"Maybe that's the real reason you asked me

92

out in the first place."

"What do you mean?"

"You think I'm crazy already." Her mouth twitched. Jack saw it, and his own lips parted then curved upward. He started to smile, then he grinned.

"God, I wish I didn't like you so damned much."

Genny smiled. "I like you, too, Jack Brennen."

"You shouldn't. I'm nothing but trouble for a woman like you."

"Don't I know."

His features softened, making him even more handsome. "Still want to go to that pool tournament?"

"You still want to take me?"

"You know where I'd like to take you, but the tournament will have to do."

Her stomach did a free fall then curled with an odd rush of heat. She had never met a man so blatantly sexual. She couldn't begin to imagine what it might be like to go to bed with a man like Jack — couldn't imagine, yet thoughts of a night with Jack Brennen would haunt her as much as her dreams.

"If we're going, we had better get to it." Jack took her hand and heat licked up her arm. The calluses on his long brown fingers felt hard and male, the hair on his forearm was rough and sexy where it brushed against her skin.

You're playing with fire, Genny Austin. Beneath

her tank top, her nipples puckered and tightened, confirming the thought as the truth. Praying Jack wouldn't see them, Genny tried to will them back down. Leading her off toward the building in the distance, he stopped at the double glass doors.

"Next time you tell me if I'm starting to scare you. Okay?"

"A-All right." If he meant to put her at ease, to apologize in some way for what he had done, all she could think was that he had said "next time." Which meant he intended to see her again. Dear God, how could she even consider it? She'd barely survived the first twenty minutes of "this time."

And that was before he had mentioned taking her to bed.

Jack caught Genny's nervous glance and squeezed her hand. "Did I tell you, you look terrific?"

"No, but . . . thank you." She was blushing again. Jack liked the way she looked when she did, the way her cheeks turned a pretty shade of pink. He felt like an ass for trying to scare her, for trying to make *her* break their date because *he* didn't have the nerve.

He smiled with a trace of amusement. He wondered if she'd ever seen the inside of a beer bar. It couldn't be any more of a shock than the ride he had given her in his car. Whatever happened, the way things were going, it ought to be an interesting evening. He shoved open the heavy glass door.

The dimly lit room smelled of stale cigarette smoke. He inhaled a deep breath and unconsciously fondled the unopened smokes he'd shoved into his T-shirt pocket. In another couple of weeks, he'd leave them home.

"I don't suppose you've been in here before?" he asked Genny, who only shook her head. "I didn't think so." There wasn't much to it. It was nothing at all like the high-style places that graced most of Santa Barbara. There was nothing chic, nothing stylish about the Sea Breeze Bar.

There were no designer chairs, no expensive paintings on the walls, no soft music, no perfectly positioned spotlights. Instead, a jukebox blared oldies in one corner. The place sported small Formica-topped tables, low-backed captain's chairs, and a ten-stool bar. Two full-sized pool tables sat in the rear, one in a back room that had been added on. Narrow plastic Budweiser beer lamps hung above each one, emitting a harsh beam of light in the otherwise dimly lit room. A rack of well-used pool cues lined one wall, most of them too warped to use.

Neon beer signs — Bud, Coors, and Miller — formed most of the decoration, along with a few yellowing pictures of the owner, Pixie Murphy, a great big bald-pated Irishman, and some of his myriad friends. Boat people usually hung out there, guys who crewed on work or fishing boats, or some of the long-time residents who lived aboard their own small vessels down in the yacht harbor.

"Hey, Jack!" Pete Williams waved and began walking toward him. "About time you got here." He stopped when he saw Genny and his thick red eyebrows went up.

"Hi, Pete. You remember Genny?"

"Sure. Hi, Genny."

"Hi, Pete," she said a little shyly.

He smiled then looked over at Jack. "So how'd you talk a nice girl like Genny into going out with a guy like you?"

"It wasn't easy," Jack grumbled, not liking the way Pete was eyeing her. Taking her arm, he led her over to the bar. He saw the men begin to whisper, heard one of them chuckle aloud. He should have known the guys would give him a hard time about her. He usually showed up with some big-busted blonde.

"White wine okay?" he asked, ordering himself a beer.

"Perfect," Genny said.

He slid his hands around her waist and lifted her up onto the barstool. Just that small contact sent a twinge of desire straight into his groin. Damn — he'd never felt anything like it. He sure as hell meant what he'd said about taking her to bed.

Forewarned was forewarned, the way he saw it. His conscience be damned. From now on, Genny Austin was fair game. As far as he was concerned, she was on her own.

"Ever shoot pool?" he asked, trying not to notice the way the tank top clung to her breasts. Pete was staring at them, too, and Jack's jaw suddenly tightened. He must have been crazy to suggest she wear it.

"I watched a billiards tournament on *Wide World of Sports* one time when I was young," Genny said. "Fats somebody was the champion."

"Minnesota Fats. Come on." He lifted her back down from the bar stool and called to Buddy Dayton, the bartender, who dug out the black leather case holding his personal cue and handed it over. "They aren't quite ready to start. I'll teach you how it's done."

Another bad idea, Jack thought later, after he had assembled the two halves of his long, pearl-handled cue stick and given her a quick demonstration. That's when Genny bent over the green felt table.

Sweet Jesus, what a tight little ass. Those jeans were almost sinful. Talk about nightmares. He'd be having erotic dreams for the next three weeks, every time he thought of the way she looked bending over that table.

"Get over there, Jack," Pete prodded. "Give the lady a hand — show her how it's done."

Genny looked back at him over one shoulder. Her light brown hair hung in softly curling waves, as it had since their ride in his car. He liked it better that way, not so sleek and formal.

"Am I doing it right, Jack?" she asked.

97

He knew he shouldn't do it, but he couldn't resist. He came up behind her and bent over, matching her leaning stance with his. Her bottom fit into his groin and he went instantly hard. He closed his eyes, grateful to think that once he stepped out of the light, he'd be standing back in the shadows.

"Like this," he said, arranging her long slim fingers so they formed a resting place for the pool cue. He aimed the long wooden stick at just the right angle. "Whenever you're ready, ease the cue back and shoot. Just do it nice and slow."

"Now?" she asked, but the word came out like she couldn't get quite enough air.

"Now," he said, knowing exactly how she felt, his own voice rough and husky. Genny squirmed against him. Her hand had started to tremble so hard she wouldn't be able to hold the stick. "Take it easy, baby," he said softly, beginning to enjoy himself. Sweet Jesus, he wouldn't be happy until he'd made love to her exactly like this.

"J-Jack, I don't think —"

He pressed his hardness against her bottom just as she punched the cue. The stick scraped the table, nearly tearing the felt, the ball bounced once, twice, then flew off into the air. It landed with a crash against the jukebox, then bounced loudly onto the floor.

"Hey, you guys!" Pixie yelled. "Watch what the hell you're doing!"

By now both of them were standing back in the shadows, Jack still hard, Genny obviously embarrassed.

"I-I'm sorry. I guess I'll never be much of a pool player."

He ran a finger along her cheek. "Oh, I don't know. Maybe with a couple more lessons . . ."

She swallowed so hard he could see it. "I don't . . . I don't think so."

Jack just smiled. It slipped a little when he saw Vivian Sandburg walking toward them.

"What do you say, hotstuff?" Vivian eyed him as if he were a juicy piece of meat. Hell, if she'd done a little more of that the other night, he would have stayed around a while longer.

"Hello, Viv."

"I see you brought a friend. Kind of like taking sand to the beach, isn't it, Jack?"

The bar was always full of women, since it sat on the sidewalk across from the ocean. Most of the regulars, he had already been to bed with, or they didn't really interest him — except for Viv. She was really a looker, with long pale blond hair and a beautiful high round bosom. He'd been trying to take her to bed for over a month, ever since she'd roller-bladed into the bar and he had bought her a drink.

He still hadn't scored. Apparently what she'd been needing was a little competition.

"This is Genny Austin. Genny, meet Vivian Sandburg."

"Hello," Genny said.

Vivian eyed her up and down. Her usually seductive lips drew into a thin tight pout. "You and Jack been friends long?" she asked. She was wearing skin-tight yellow pants and a black stretch top that didn't quite reach her waist, showing a portion of her bellybutton. She looked like a sexy blond cat and any other time he would likely have been panting after her, just like the rest of the men in the bar.

Today, he felt strangely uninterested.

"Jack and I just met," Genny said.

"Better be careful," said Viv. "Jack's the big hot stud around here. He'll be into your jeans before you can say Jack Sprat."

Genny turned beet red.

"That's enough, Viv. Leave her alone."

A lightly penciled perfect blond eyebrow arched up. "What's the matter, Jack? You never get defensive when one of these bastards gives me a hard time."

"Maybe I figure you can take care of yourself."

"If that's what you think, you'd be right." She turned a cool look on Genny. "Nice to meet you, Genny. See you around, Jack." Vivian sauntered away.

Genny's gaze followed her progress toward the group of men sitting at the opposite end of the bar. "That isn't . . . that isn't your girl-friend, is it?"

"No."

"I mean if it is —"

"I said she isn't my girlfriend. I don't have a girlfriend. I've never had a girlfriend."

"Never?"

"Not since I was in high school."

"Why not?"

He turned a hard look in her direction. "Because I don't want one. Because I like my freedom. Because I'm a bastard, Genny, just like I said."

Genny made no comment. It was the flash of hurt in her pretty brown eyes that made him wish he could call back the words. What the hell was he doing out with a woman like Genny? He ought to take her home and come back for Viv. He and Viv were two of a kind, a pair to draw to. A night of fun was all Vivian wanted. She would have gone to bed with him long before this but she was enjoying the game.

Jack had known it. They were both world-class players, and he knew in the end he would win.

They both knew it.

Jack glanced over at the slender woman sitting beside him. She was staring at the bottles lining the back bar as if they held some great fascination.

"Genny?" He wanted to chase away that troubled expression, though he was damned if he knew why. She turned to look at him. The red neon Budweiser sign gave a pinkish glow to her skin.

"Yes?"

"I've never been to bed with Vivian."

She glanced down at the floor. "It's really none of my business."

"I just wanted you to know."

She looked back at him and nodded.

"One more thing."

"Yes, Jack?"

"I'm glad you came."

"You are?"

"Yes."

She smiled so sweetly, something pulled low in his belly. "Thanks, Jack," she said softly.

He finished the tournament in second position. Genny was enthralled with his less-than-perfect performance, but to his chagrin, the distraction she provided seemed to work best on him. He found it hard to concentrate. In fact, he just plain found it hard.

Hell's bells, he thought as he drove her back home. He wished he could blame it on Viv, but it wasn't Vivian he wanted. He wanted little Genny Austin, more every time he looked in her direction.

She wasn't as voluptuous as Viv, but in a sleeker, classier, more subtle way, she was far more attractive. And sexy as hell. The fact that she didn't seem to know it only made it more so.

"You gonna invite me in?" he asked when they stood on the front porch of her condo.

Genny wet her lips. "I don't . . . I don't think that's a very good idea."

"Why not? I think it's a great idea."

She only shook her head. "Not tonight. I can't . . . I'm not ready for you to come in."

His hand came up to her cheek. He drew a slow, lazy circle with his finger and a slight tremor rippled across her skin. "I bet I could help you sleep." Tilting her head back, he leaned forward and settled his mouth on her lips. They were as soft as he had imagined, as full and as sweet. He felt it the instant they softened, the moment she opened to allow his tongue inside. Jack groaned as he pulled her against him and Genny slid her arms around his neck.

He was hard and throbbing, aching to carry her upstairs and bury himself inside her. His hand came up to her breast, lifting it, feeling the delicious weight of it. When he cupped it and began to massage her nipple through her shirt, Genny went rigid and began to pull away.

"I-I can't, Jack. Not tonight." Maybe never, she was thinking. She had only been to bed with one man in her life. That man was dead and buried. This man was way out of her league, and if she did go to bed with him, he was sure to know it. It would be just like her trembling knees after the ride in his car, or the attempt she had made to play pool. She'd probably just make a fool of herself one more time.

"It's all right, baby," he said softly, surprising her. "I'm not in that big a hurry."

"You're not?"

He smiled that wicked, gleaming white smile

of his. "Well, I am. But I have a feeling you're worth the wait."

If he had said anything else, she might have been able to resist him. "I had an awfully good time tonight." Even now, it amazed her that she had.

"So did I."

He sounded like he meant it and that made her daring. "I-I've got tickets to a play at the Lobero Theatre on Tuesday night." Last night over dinner, she had meant to ask Howard, but somehow she had forgotten. "I don't suppose you'd consider going with me?"

"A play, huh? You mean like a stage play?"

"*The Lonely Heart.* It's supposed to be very good."

Jack smiled. "Why not?"

Genny beamed up at him. "It starts at eight. We ought to be there by seven-thirty."

"I'll pick you up at seven-fifteen."

She unlocked the door and turned to say good night, but Jack swept her into his arms. Hard muscle bulged beneath her fingers. Her breasts pressed into his rock-hard chest and his hardness thrust boldly against her. Her heart was pounding, thundering. The dampness began pooling in the place between her legs.

Genny made a small sound in her throat as Jack bent her over his arm, kissing her so thoroughly that her knees nearly buckled beneath her. Howard always kissed her on the cheek, she thought vaguely when he finally let her go.

"Good night, Genny Austin," he said in a voice gone rough. "I'll see you next Tuesday." He waited till she closed the door before he walked away.

Genny sagged against it, her heart still hammering against her ribs. Dear God, she thought, fighting the desire for him that still ran through her veins, I must really be going insane.

Six

Genny dreamed about Jack that night, an erotic dream, unlike any she had ever had before. He was making love to her, standing behind her gloriously naked. His body was tanned from head to foot and rippling with ridges of muscle.

They were standing in the Sea Breeze Bar next to the pool table, but no one else was there. She was wearing only her tank top and a pair of white lace panties. Jack was kissing the back of her neck, bending her over the green felt table. One hand cupped her breast as he massaged her nipple, the other moved over her bottom then slipped inside her panties. She could feel the calluses on his hand, his erection pressing against her, thick and hot and hard.

His palm stroked over her bottom, squeezing, caressing. A finger slid gently between her legs and he began to stroke her there.

"Jack . . ." she whispered, arching backward against his chest. Then his long fingers curled around her panties and in a single motion, he tore them away.

"Part your legs for me, Genny," he commanded in his rough, sexy voice; then he was readying himself, parting the folds of her sex and surging up inside her, filling her completely with his long heavy length. The feeling was so heady, so incredibly exciting, Genny moaned aloud.

Perspiration drenched her body. Her fingers trembled as they dug into the cool green-striped bedsheet. She licked her burning lips and shuddered at the heat pouring through her body. "More . . . Jack . . . please . . ." she whispered when his fullness began to recede, desperate to keep him inside her. "Please . . ." But Jack was already gone.

The beer bar had also disappeared. Suddenly, she was standing beside a huge four-poster bed hung with white silk draperies embroidered in huge Chinese red flowers. A red silk canopy arched above the soft feather mattress, and polished inlaid hardwood floors gleamed beneath high molded ceilings.

Soft weeping drew her attention back to the bed. A young black woman bent over it, much as Genny had been earlier in the dream. The girl was naked and trembling. There were welts across her back and buttocks, more welts along the backs of her stout black legs.

"I's sorry, miztress. Pleeze don' hit me no more." But the belt lashed downward just the same, smacking hard against the girl's bare bottom, then once more across her shoulders.

The woman wielding the belt felt a surge of excitement. It slithered through her limbs, shimmered deliciously, and mounted with every blow. There was a languorous tightening in her breasts and belly, a dampening in the folds of her sex.

Three more sharp smacks had the younger woman sobbing, begging her forgiveness and swearing she would never disobey her mistress again.

The woman ran a hand over the trembling girl's naked buttocks, caressing them, squeezing them, then she brought the leather strap down hard across them once more.

"Get out, Maizie," she commanded. "Get out and remember the lesson you learned here this eve."

"Yessa, miztress. Yessa, I-I shorely will." Moving stiffly, stooping like a withered old man, the black girl scooped up the slim, long white cotton skirt she'd been wearing, and her sleeveless blue flowered blouse, and made her way out the door, holding the clothes up in front of her to hide her nakedness.

The sound of her weeping carried down the hall, down the stairs, and across the parlor, fading until it finally disappeared. The woman sat down on the upholstered red silk bench at the foot of the massive canopied bed. Her hand moved upward toward the front of her low-cut gown. Fashioned of ice blue silk, it exposed her ripe breasts, the smooth white skin on her shoulders, and the tiny waist she was so proud of.

Her long pale fingers slid inside the bodice

and she began to fondle her lush full breasts, squeezing her nipples until they grew hard and distended. Through the heavy folds of her skirt, her other hand pressed against her sex.

She rubbed herself there, but she couldn't really feel it through the layers of silk. Disgruntled, she called to her maid for assistance in undressing, then grew petulant as the moments ticked by and the woman had not yet appeared. Then she thought of the hours that lay ahead, of the pleasure she would feel every time she remembered whipping the girl.

Tilting her head, she rested her cheek on the carved wooden bedpost, and then she began to laugh. The high shrill sound filled the silence, echoing across the bedchamber till it rang in Genny's ears.

Her eyes slammed open. She lay there a moment, with her heart beating frantically, her body bathed in sweat. She tried to block the dream, tried to deny it. She tried to will it away, then tried to pretend that it hadn't occurred.

When all of those efforts failed, she rolled onto her side, drew her legs up into her stomach, and began to weep.

Hot tears fell until they soaked her pillow. She didn't sleep for the rest of the night, nor did she leave her bed. She felt sick and guilty, embarrassed and ashamed. And she was frightened.

The woman in the dream was the one she had seen before. The woman with the awful bone-chilling laughter. What did the terrible images mean? Why was she the one to see them? What did they have to do with her?

Genny bit down on her trembling lip, but the tears continued to tunnel down her cheeks. What was wrong with her? Was she some kind of sick, sadistic monster? Perhaps she harbored secret yearnings. Perhaps her erotic fantasy about Jack had somehow unleashed a darker, more sinister side of her nature.

She tried to think back. Pain had never brought her pleasure. She wouldn't even watch something like that on TV. She forced herself to imagine the scene again, to see the young black girl weeping as she was being beaten. She forced herself back into the part of the woman, determined to see if the erotic sensations would reappear.

Nothing.

Not the slightest twinge of excitement. Still, the dream had been real enough. The woman in the dream had been part of it. Her mind had created it, but why?

She didn't fall asleep until sometime after dawn, then she tossed and turned fitfully in the brightly sunlit room. She slept on and off through most of that Sunday, finally getting dressed around three, but for the rest of the day, all she thought of was the dream.

By the time night had fallen, she was so upset she couldn't eat, and in tears over what she might dream if she managed somehow to actually fall asleep. Finally, she called Dr. Halpern at home, as she had never done before and certainly not on a weekend, not even in the days right after Bill's murder, though the doctor had given her the "for emergencies" number.

"Genny, is that you?" The doctor had answered on the third short ring, having just gotten back from her brief vacation in the Bahamas. "What is it, dear, what's happened?"

"I-I have to see you, Dr. Halpern. I can't wait until next Friday."

"Calm down, Genny. Take a couple of long deep breaths." Genny did as she was told. "Now I want you to go somewhere and sit down." She sat down in a high-backed oak chair in the kitchen, where the long phone cord could still reach.

"Are you sitting down, Genny?"

She nodded then remembered the woman couldn't see her. "Yes."

"Now I want you to tell me what's happened."

Genny started crying. "I-I can't. Not over the phone. Can I come in sometime tomorrow? I know I don't have an appointment . . ."

There was only a momentary pause. "Can you hang on until after work?"

"Yes." But tears clogged her throat as she worked to form the word.

"Are you sure? Perhaps I ought to come over."

"I'm all right, now that I know I can see you."

"Everything's going to be fine, Genny. Try to take it easy. Can you do that for me?"

"I can try."

"And get some rest if you can."

No chance of that, Genny knew. Sleeping through the day would mean being up all night. "I'll see you tomorrow," she said. "Thank you, Dr. Halpern."

By midnight, having been inside the house all day, she felt almost claustrophobic, more than ready for a walk on the beach. Even the thought of running into the men who had attacked her couldn't deter her. She thought of seeing Jack, but immediately dismissed the idea. Remembering her fantasy, she wasn't sure she could ever face him again.

She left the house and walked along the sand. A chilly night wind whipped her clothes, stimulating in one way, relaxing in another. The ocean felt icy cold, and a frothy surf slid up on the shore. The air smelled of fish and the seaweed that lay in clumps on the sand.

She returned to her condo sometime after one, turned on the television in front of the couch, and watched the late night talk shows. She read for a while, fell asleep for a couple of hours during an old John Wayne movie, then awoke to the morning news and the ringing of the phone. Noting the time on the antique oak clock on the wall in the kitchen, she realized that if she didn't hurry, she was going to be late for work.

Pushing back her sleep-tangled hair, Genny picked up the phone and sighed tiredly into the receiver. "Hello."

"Genny, it's Howard."

"Hi, Howard." She hadn't talked to him since their date last Friday night. She glanced back up at the clock, which ticked the minutes away. "I'm sorry, Howard, I'm running kind of late. Could I possibly call you back?"

"Why, yes, I suppose so."

"I'll phone you from work."

She hung up and hurried upstairs. Showering quickly, she dressed and set off for the library. Exhaustion was making her less efficient than usual. Her job had suffered, she knew, ever since Bill's death. She worked overtime and sometimes weekends to make up for her lack of concentration, occasional irritability, and the mood swings caused by her fatigue.

Her boss, Abigail Fowler — Crabby Abby to her staff behind her back — was watching Genny closely. After the murder, Genny had taken a short leave of absence, but she had decided she would rather be back at work. Her doctors' appointments bit into her schedule, and Mrs. Fowler had eventually discovered her insomnia and dreams.

The woman was unsympathetic. Abigail had warned Genny that any more infractions or tardiness would be dealt with severely. Genny knew her job was at risk and the thought of losing it made her feel slightly sick. She had worked hard to get through college. Under normal circumstances, she was good at her job and she enjoyed it. She hoped she'd be able to keep things under control.

She left the library precisely at five and drove straight to Dr. Halpern's office on De la Vina. As in most of Santa Barbara, the architecture was Spanish, with white plaster walls and a red tiled roof. Lush green elephant-ear plants angled up from the flower beds and hung out over the sidewalk, and tiny purple and white cymbidium orchids bloomed near the heavy carved front door.

Genny stepped into the waiting room: smoked glass tables, black leather and chrome, nothing at all like the building on the outside. The receptionist, Leslie Martinez, a pretty, dark-haired girl in her mid to late twenties, turned to her and smiled.

"She's just finishing up with a patient," Leslie said from behind the counter. "She'll be with you in a minute."

Genny sat down on an expensive black leather sofa, Italian in design and butter-soft to the touch. Her head had been pounding all afternoon, but she ignored it. Instead, she picked up a *Time* magazine from the stack on the table and nervously leafed through the pages.

"Genny?" Dr. Halpern stood in the doorway leading back to her office in the rear. Her perfectly coiffed short blond hair curved down smoothly to just below her ears, and her pink

Chanel suit reached precisely the proper line at her knees.

"Hello, Dr. Halpern."

"Hello, Genny." The doctor led her back to her office and Genny sat down in her usual place on the leather sofa, an exact match of the expensive black one out in the reception room except the color was cream. The blond woman sat down in a matching leather chair on the opposite side of the coffee table. Her huge black lacquer desk sat just a few feet away.

"So . . . where to begin." The doctor eyed her thoughtfully. "I presume this has something to do with your dreams."

Genny nodded.

"We've talked about them often. They've always been difficult for you to describe."

"Not anymore," Genny said darkly. "Things have changed, Dr. Halpern, since the last time I saw you." She went on to explain how, in the past two weeks, the dreams had begun a subtle shift, eventually becoming clearer. She said that there were people in her nightmares now, and that she had finally seen a woman, though she had yet to catch a glimpse of the woman's face.

"Go on," the doctor urged when Genny paused.

As objectively as she could, she told the doctor about the bloody pagan ritual with its half-naked natives, putting in as many details as she could remember.

"This is all very interesting," the doctor said

with her usual objectivity. "Is there anything else you want to tell me?"

"I'm afraid there is." Genny told Dr. Halpern that the dreams now seemed linked together, to begin again where they had left off before. "Or perhaps it's more like another separate part of the same story . . . and . . ." She swallowed nervously, working to compose herself.

"And?" the doctor prompted. When she still didn't answer, the tall blond woman leaned back in her chair. "I assure you, Genny, there is nothing you can say that will shock me."

Perhaps not, but Genny knew she had shaken her a little. That was clear by the pallor on the attractive woman's face when Genny finished her story of the young girl who had been beaten.

Dr. Halpern pulled a pencil from the golden hair looped behind an ear and scribbled a few more lines on the notepad she held on her lap. "You said earlier that this latest dream began with an erotic fantasy."

"Yes." Genny's face began to heat up, as it had when she had relayed the sexual excitement the woman in the dream had felt.

"What was this fantasy about?"

She glanced away, unable to meet the doctor's probing gaze. "Making love to Jack Brennen."

"Jack who?"

"He's the man who saved me from being raped down on the beach."

The doctor set her pad and pencil down on the smoked glass coffee table. "This is getting very complicated, Genny."

The throbbing in her head picked up its beat. "I know, Dr. Halpern." She filled the doctor in on the three men who had attacked her, and Jack's heroic efforts, then told her about the night they'd gone out to the Sea Breeze Bar.

"Did your dreams start to change before or after the attack on the beach?"

"After." Genny remembered that quite distinctly.

"Then it's likely there is some connection."

"I'm afraid I don't see what you mean."

"I'm talking about sexual fantasies. Most women harbor a number of them, including rape. That does *not* mean they really want to be raped — quite the contrary. But the fact remains, there is some primeval part of us, something instinctual, perhaps, that derives an erotic thrill from the imaginary thought of being held down by a man and forced to have sex. When it actually happens, it's extremely traumatic. No woman wants to suffer an actual rape, but the fantasy remains."

"I don't think I've ever secretly desired —"

"Perhaps not," the doctor interrupted. "The point I'm trying to make is that on some subconscious level you may have other, different fantasies, like the sado-masochistic one you experienced in your dream."

"I see . . . at least I think I do. But I have to

tell you, Doctor, I don't think that sort of thing excites me. When I remember what that woman did to that poor girl, it makes me angry, not excited."

"Consciously perhaps, but . . ." Dr. Halpern released a pent-up sigh. "I have to say, Genny, this has taken quite an unusual turn, considering what we've gone over in your last two years of therapy."

Genny said nothing.

"It could be explained by any number of things, but at this point I don't believe it's anything to worry about. Erotic fantasies — in any shape or form — are really quite harmless, and perfectly normal. The stress you've been under, combined with the attempted rape, has merely given rise to them in the form of these new dreams."

"I don't think so, Dr. Halpern. I think these dreams are the same ones I've been having all along, only now they're clearer. Now they're beginning to tell some kind of story."

"I'm afraid I disagree. I think we can be fairly certain the nightmares you've experienced up until now were indistinct images directly connected to your husband's murder."

Genny stubbornly shook her head. "A result of it, yes, but my nightmares aren't about the murder. I don't think they ever were."

The blond woman looked as though she wanted to argue. She caught herself, glanced at the clock, and smiled. "Whatever the case, we don't have time to discuss it tonight. If the same sort of dreams continue, we'll simply monitor their course and see where they lead. You're lucky you can remember them. Most people can't, you know."

"I wish I could forget them."

"I'm sure you do. In the meantime, I don't want you worrying overly about them. You have to go on with your life, keep things as normal as possible. We'll talk more about the attempted rape the next time you come in . . . and perhaps go a bit deeper into your childhood."

"My childhood?"

"Yes. As we've discussed before, clues to the present are often buried in one's past."

"But I told you, I had a perfectly normal childhood — better than normal, in fact."

The blond woman rose gracefully to her feet. "We're out of time, Genny, but I think we've made some very good progress, don't you?"

Genny sighed and stood up, too. She wished she could agree with the doctor, but in truth she felt nearly as confused as she had when she had come in. "Thank you for seeing me on such short notice, Dr. Halpern."

"That isn't a problem, Genny. You know you can call me any time you need."

She simply nodded. She did feel somewhat better. At least her latest round of nightmares were now out in the open. The dream had been hellish, but it was over. Perhaps the doctor was

119

right and the attack she had suffered on the beach had been the thing to set it off.

Besides, she wasn't the woman in the dream. That vicious creature had been far more amply endowed, and she'd had long thick, wavy black hair.

"I'd still like to see you on Friday," the doctor said, "after your night at the sleep clinic."

"All right." Genny checked with the receptionist on her way out for the time of her next appointment then walked out to the street. After climbing into her Toyota, she started the engine, pulled away from the curb, and headed toward home.

Half way down Chapala, she remembered she hadn't called Howard. Darn. She'd have to do it as soon as she got home.

Unfortunately, she forgot again and didn't remember until Tuesday morning. When she called his office, Howard wasn't in.

Oliver Madison Brown turned the last screw holding the oil pan in place and slid out from under the long white '58 Cadillac he had been working on all afternoon. The car was a classic, his specialty at Classy Classics Auto Repair, his small, almost-paid-for garage.

Across the yard, he saw his friend, Jack Brennen, step away from his shiny red mustang and begin to walk toward him. "Say, Jack," he called out, "what can I do you for, man?"

"Came to check on my Harley. I know it's been a real bugger, but I was kind of hoping you might have had a chance to get it fixed."

Ollie grinned. Wiping his huge pink-palmed hands on a grease rag, he pointed toward a tarpaulin draped over the motorcycle sitting in the corner.

"You're serious? You got it put back together?"

"Serious as a heart attack."

Jack walked toward it and jerked off the tarp. He admired it for a moment, then gripped the handlebars, booted the kickstand out of the way, and wheeled it into the sunshine.

"Lookin' good, ain't she?" Ollie said with pride.

"She looks terrific." Long, low and sleek, with a flaming, pearlized purple gas tank and fenders. The chrome spokes, pipes, gas cap, and trim shined like mirrors in the bright September sun. "Nobody but you could have done a job like this."

Ollie had rebuilt the blown 1360cc engine, then put the bike back together and cherried the whole thing out.

"When you gonna come get her?"

"Think I'll take her for a spin right now. I'll have Charley bring me back later to pick up my car." Jack swung a long leg over the padded black leather seat, but didn't crank the engine, as his gaze went drifting off for a moment.

"Say, Jack, if you don't mind my sayin' so,

you're lookin' a little down in the mouth."

Jack sighed. "I'm worried about the boat, Owl. That big payment's getting closer every day."

"You ain't gonna have to sell your bike?"

"I don't know. The trouble is, even if I do, we won't have nearly enough. If I don't think of something fast, Charley and I are gonna lose the *Marauder*."

Ollie grunted. "Damn, I hate to hear that. Let me know if there's anything I can do."

Jack just nodded.

"Say, how's that little gal who came over to the boat the other night? Pete says you're teaching her to shoot pool."

Jack's already dark look blackened. "There isn't much chance of that. Genny isn't exactly a natural athlete. To tell you the truth, I don't know why I'm taking her out."

"I do."

"Yeah, well, so far that isn't happening, either. She's a widow, you know. Probably still hung up on her dead husband. Or maybe she just feels guilty about sleeping with somebody else in her old man's bed."

"Or maybe she just ain't one of them gals who goes for one-night stands. Maybe she likes to get to know a guy a little before she hops into bed with him."

"Yeah, well that type isn't my type — remember?"

"So why you still seein' her?"

"I won't be if she doesn't start putting out. I figure she's got until tomorrow. I'm taking her to see a play."

"You're joshin' me."

"The hell I am." He grinned. "Now you see just how far a man'll go for a good piece of tail."

Ollie chuckled. He turned at the sound of his name and saw his wife, Bebe, walking toward him with a smile.

"I saw Jack out here. I figured the two of you might like a beer." She leaned over and kissed Ollie's cheek, pressed a cold Bud Light into his hand. She tossed a can to Jack.

"Thanks, Bebe." He popped the top, tilted his head back and sucked in a great long gulp of icy foam, working the muscles in his thick neck.

Ollie looked down at his pretty wife, thinking she still looked as good to him as the day they'd gotten married. "Jack's takin' his new girl to a play tomorrow night," he said.

"She isn't my new girl. She's a damned librarian."

"You gonna give her a ride on your Harley?" Bebe asked, pulling a fallen leaf from her short-cropped black hair. Big round earrings dangled from her ears.

"I doubt she'd be interested. I took her for a ride in my car and she nearly wet her pants."

"Must have been some ride," Bebe said.

"She must have done something right," Ollie

put in. "You're seeing her again, ain't you?"

"I think I'm losing my mind."

"Or maybe you're finally doin' somethin' sane," Ollie said.

"Maybe you're finally growing up, Jack." Bebe grinned, enjoying the repartee.

"If that means sitting home like a lump in front of the damned TV, I hope I never grow up," Jack said.

"Man's got a point there, honey."

Bebe took the beer from his hand and took a sip. "Settling down a little doesn't necessarily mean turning into a couch potato," she said. "It sure ain't boring 'round here."

"Yeah, well Ollie's the exception to the rule." Jack slugged down the rest of his brew and tossed the empty can into the trash barrel, which sat a good distance away. He grinned when he made the shot. "And you're one exceptional lady."

Gripping the handles on his bike, he stood up, brought his boot down hard on the starter, and the engine roared to life. Jack cranked the handles and revved it a couple of times. "Sounds great, Ollie. You did one helluva job. I'll pay you when I come back to pick up my car."

"You got it, Jack."

Pulling his wrap-around shades from the top of his head, Jack leaned back on the seat, turned the bike around, cranked the handles, and roared away.

"You meet his new girl?" Bebe asked.

"Sure did."

"What's she like?"

"A real lady. Jack might find himself in trouble with this one."

"Yeah, or maybe he'll finally luck out and find a woman who can handle him."

But Ollie couldn't imagine the sweet little librarian handling a man like Jack Brennen.

Seven

Just as promptly as before, Jack picked Genny up at exactly 7:15 on Tuesday evening. When she opened the front door, she was pleasantly surprised, and equally relieved, to see him dressed in a pair of gray worsted slacks and a navy blue blazer.

He wasn't wearing a tie, but his pale blue, button-down, Oxford-cloth shirt matched his blue eyes, and the coat fit perfectly over his thick-muscled shoulders. He was taller and more powerfully built than the men in magazines like *GQ*, but none of them were any more handsome.

He smiled at the look on her face. "What's the matter, you don't like it?"

She smiled. "You look terrific."

"You didn't think I owned a sport coat, did you?"

"To tell you the truth, I had my doubts."

Jack merely grinned, his dimples gouging grooves in his cheeks. He looked like a different man, spit-polished from head to foot, clean shaven, pants perfectly creased. Even his shoes were shined, a pair of glossy black wingtips. Dressed as he was, his manner somehow seemed different, more formal, almost sophisticated. She couldn't quite believe this was the same rugged man who had saved her on the beach.

"Ready?" he asked.

Genny nodded. Wearing a simple street-length plum silk dress with matching leather pumps, she picked up her small, matching silk clutch bag and started out the door. When she looked down and saw the top of a pack of Marlboros in the pocket of Jack's sportcoat, she paused.

"You always carry cigarettes, but I've never seen you smoke."

He shrugged. "I was up to three packs a day. I figured I could think of a lot more pleasant ways to die, so I quit. That's been over three months ago." He tapped the hard pack outlined in his pocket. "I carried these for so many years, it got to be a habit. Somehow it helps to control the urge. I figure in a few more weeks I'll be able to leave them at home."

Genny smiled. "I'm proud of you, Jack. I can only imagine how hard it must be to give up something like that."

Another of those broad-shouldered shrugs he was famous for, as if he took his accomplishments for granted. It was an interesting facet of his character. She wondered exactly what it meant.

They stepped off the porch and onto the sidewalk. The black canvas top was up on his car, which meant her hair would stay in place. Jack helped her in, waited while she tucked in her skirt, then closed the door. He drove sanely all the way to the theater, but refused to let the valet park his car.

"I used to park cars when I was in high school. I always took the hot ones out for a spin while the owners were inside."

"Why am I not surprised?" They went into the Lobero, Spanish in design with heavy beams and plush velvet seats. Theirs were in the orchestra section, third row center. Though the aisles weren't all that close together, Jack had to fold himself in.

"So how've you been?" he asked while the rest of the audience took their places. An obese woman sat in the chair on his left, crowding Jack even more. "Sleeping any lately?"

She sighed. "Not enough. Sometimes I don't ever think I'll catch up on all the hours I've missed."

He grinned. "I bet I could put you to sleep."

An eyebrow shot up. "I think I can guess what you have in mind." Her face heated up as she remembered the erotic fantasy she'd had about him the last time he had mentioned taking her to bed. "I'm afraid I'll have to pass."

"Whatever you say, pretty lady. Don't say I didn't offer to help." When he grinned again and winked, Genny glanced away.

The man was outrageous. Yet it wasn't really all that far-fetched. The clinic listed orgasm as a means of inducing sleep; it worked by releasing muscle-relaxing hormones. Unfortunately, since she had never personally experienced the phenomenon, she doubted that Jack's remedy would work.

Maybe she was sexually repressed, she thought, though Dr. Halpern didn't seem to think so. She said lots of women had trouble reaching a climax. Then again, perhaps the doctor was wrong and sex — or lack of it — was really the root of her problems.

"What's this play supposed to be about?" Jack asked, breaking into her thoughts.

"It's a drama about a man who leaves his wife and family for a younger woman. It's supposed to be a tragedy."

"I can think of times when it might be a blessing." His face had changed, his expression suddenly serious, and she wondered at his thoughts. Just then the house lights went down and the red velvet curtain began to go up. Genny settled back in her seat.

An hour into the play, she began to fidget. The actor who played the husband had little or no stage presence and the dialogue was stilted and dull. She was afraid to look over at Jack, wouldn't have, if she hadn't heard his loud, unrepentant snore.

Eighteen pairs of eyes swiveled toward the sound, then riveted on the man who sprawled beside her. His tall body was slumped in his chair, his long legs bent and cramped against the seat in front of him.

A second loud snore caught the attention of another thirty people. It seemed half the audience began to shift in their chairs and mumble among themselves.

"Jack," Genny whispered, shaking his shoulder. "Wake up."

A snorting sound came back in answer. Genny shook him harder. "Jack! You've got to wake up!"

He jerked upright, blinking owlishly and rubbing a hand over his face. "What is it? What's the matter?"

Fortunately, the house lights came up just then. The second act curtain had come down, signaling the intermission. People began to stand up and stretch, to slowly file out into the main aisle, heading toward the foyer for coffee and drinks.

"Come on," Genny said. "Let's go." She dragged him up on his feet and began to move along behind the others, hoping she wouldn't see anyone she knew.

"Where are we going?" he asked when they reached the entry.

"Anyplace but here."

He said nothing more, just continued on toward the door. They almost made it.

"Genny!" Inwardly she cringed. Howard McCormick's smooth baritone was unmistakable.

Genny turned and pasted a smile on her face.

"Hello, Howard."

"You were supposed to call me, remember? I had hoped to invite you to join me this evening."

"I had tickets of my own," she said lamely. "I called you at the office but you weren't in." Just then he noticed the tall man beside her. No more dodging the issue — she would have to introduce them.

"Howard, this is Jack Brennen."

"An introduction isn't necessary," Howard said coldly. "Mr. Brennen and I have met."

"How's the paper shuffling business, McCormick?" Jack said. "Levied any new taxes lately? Any unnecessary restrictions? That's about all you city fathers accomplish, the way I see it."

"Jack's upset over some of the regulations the city council has passed." Howard flashed him a look of disdain.

"Yeah, like the ones raising our dock fees, year after year. Howard keeps hoping we'll give up our spaces."

"Need I remind you, I also own a boat. I pay fees the same as you do."

"Yeah, well maybe that's true, but an eighty-foot yacht tied up in my slip would suit you a whole lot better than a greasy old salvage boat, wouldn't it? Since you own a major interest in that fancy restaurant across the way."

"Those are the breaks, Jack. If you can't stand the heat get out of the kitchen." Howard turned a hard assessing look on Genny. "I

131

wasn't aware that you and Brennen were friends."

Genny twisted the theater program she had rolled up in her hand. "We met on the beach a couple of weeks ago." Wishing at the moment she wasn't there with either of them, and especially not Jack, she forced a smile in his direction. "We discovered a mutual interest," she said with relish. "Mr. Brennen enjoys the theater almost as much as I do."

"Really?" Howard glared down the ridge of his nose. "I didn't realize he was such an intellectual."

Jack smiled wolfishly. "Yeah, I'm just full of surprises." He turned to Genny. "I'll get the car."

As he walked away, Howard's mouth flattened into a disapproving line. "I'm here with Mother. I must say I'm surprised to see you here with a man like Brennen."

"Yes, well, I'm somewhat surprised myself."

"I hope you don't intend to continue your association."

"After tonight, I doubt it very much." The point had definitely been made. They were just too totally different. She spied his bright red Mustang through an opening in the wide carved front door. "I have to go, Howard."

"I think we need to talk, Genny. I'll call you tomorrow at work."

Genny just nodded. She was feeling sick to her stomach. Between suffering Howard's displeasure, and Jack's obvious boredom, she felt about as popular as a case of the flu.

Jack leaned over the passenger seat to open her door. Genny climbed in and pulled it closed.

"It's a small world," Jack said. "I can't believe you know that jerk."

Genny bristled. "That 'jerk' happens to be my late husband's business partner. Which now makes him *my* partner. He's also a very good friend."

Jack snorted his disbelief. "McCormick's a pompous, arrogant asshole. He's a two-faced bastard who's out for no one but himself."

Genny gritted her teeth. "Is that so? Well, at least he doesn't talk like an uncouth dock hand — or snore in the middle of a crowded theater!"

Jack said nothing, just slammed his car into gear, spinning the tires and burning rubber, and forcing Genny to cling once more to her seat. It wasn't as bad a ride as the last one, but it was a far shorter trip home than it was to the theater. Fortunately, by the time they had reached her condo, Jack's temper seemed to have cooled and so had her own. He pulled the Mustang over to the curb and eased the car out of gear. It sat there quietly purring.

Jack turned to face her. His expression seemed a little bit grim. "I'm sorry about that scene with McCormick." Genny said nothing. "And I'm sorry I embarrassed you."

133

She hadn't expected an apology. Just like the clothes he wore tonight, it didn't seem to fit the image of him she had created. "It's all right. It could have happened to anyone." Not anyone she had ever known, but surely there must be someone.

"This thing between us . . . it isn't going to work out, you know."

"I know." Though she knew it was the truth, for some insane reason, hearing him say it made her stomach start to churn.

"Come on, I'll walk you to the door."

He turned off the ignition, got out, and came around to help her out. They said nothing as they walked toward the condo. Jack waited at the door till she found her house key buried in the bottom of her purse. He took it from her unsteady hand, slid it into the lock, and opened the door.

Another long moment passed. "Like I said, I'm sorry about the evening."

Genny just nodded. A tightness had climbed into her throat, making it difficult to speak. It was silly, ridiculous to be feeling this way, yet the tightness would not leave.

"Good-bye, Genny Austin."

She forced herself to smile. "Good-bye, Jack Brennen."

He started to walk away, but the sound of her voice caused him to turn.

"It really was a terrible play," she said softly.

"Yeah, it was, wasn't it?"

She smiled. "You look great in a sport coat."

Jack smiled, too. "You look great in just about anything."

"Good-bye, Jack."

He nodded, but made no move to leave. "I don't suppose it's much of an excuse, but we had engine trouble on our way in yesterday and I was up half the night trying to fix it. I suppose I should have called and canceled."

"I was getting pretty sleepy myself."

"Yeah, but you're used to it."

Genny said nothing. Her chest ached with every step Jack took farther away.

He walked a few more paces toward his car and Genny bit her lip to keep from calling him back. He hesitated a moment, then turned once more to face her.

"I was thinking . . . I don't suppose . . . you'd be interested in going for a ride on my Harley."

Her heart throbbed, skipped. "You mean as in motorcycle?"

"I've got an extra helmet."

The thought of it terrified her. Dear God, she'd been frightened to death in his car. "I-I've never ridden on a motorcycle. I'd love to."

"You would?"

Relief poured through her. "Yes."

Jack's whole body seemed to ease. "I've got one helluva week ahead of me. I have to go out of town on business for a couple of days, but I'll be back by Saturday. We could head up to Cold Springs Tavern."

"That sounds great." She bit down on her lip to keep from grinning like a fool.

"I'll pick you up at ten o'clock Saturday morning."

"I'll be ready." Her palms were still damp from the threat of his leaving. At the price of a cleaning, she didn't dare wipe them on the front of her good silk dress. She watched Jack walk away and climb into his car, then watched until the sleek red Mustang disappeared around the corner.

She was going for a ride on his Harley. His *Harley,* for godsakes. Whatever she had, it appeared she had it bad. To say nothing of the problems this created with Howard McCormick.

At that particular moment, while her heart was still oddly throbbing, Genny didn't care.

Jack stood on the deck of the *Marauder,* his hands braced on the rail as he stared out to sea. The day had turned cloudy. Whitecaps crested the tops of the waves, the swell was running at around six feet. The *Marauder* took them steadily. Her bow went nosing through the troughs as if they weren't there. Her diesel engines kept humming the even, reliable beat that Jack had grown to love.

In fact, he loved everything about the big work boat — and the sea that had become his home. It was hard to believe he'd ever been a landlubber, that he had grown up in the desert, in a small tract house in Apple Valley. Even then the sea had called to him. He had built model sailing ships of every kind, had read Hemingway's *The Old Man and the Sea* seven times. He'd read Richard Henry Dana's *Two Years before the Mast*, and of course, Melville's *Moby-Dick*.

In high school, like most of the students, he always spent Easter Week at one of the beach cities, usually Balboa down in Newport. They slept ten to a room, drinking and carousing until dawn, but in the daytime, instead of lying in the sand getting tanner than he already was, Jack hitchhiked down to the harbor to watch the boats come in.

That was almost as good as getting laid.

He turned, as Charley Denton crossed the deck and walked up beside him.

"Just got a call from the rig," Charley said. The wind whipped his thick graying hair and reddened his nose and cheeks. "They got a problem with their loading crane. They'll have to rig up a block and tackle of some sort and we'll have to use ours instead."

Jack nodded. Their equipment was in top-notch condition. It wouldn't be the problem for the *Marauder* that it might have been for another boat.

"You got in kinda late last night. You and Genny have a good time at the play?"

"Are you kidding? First I fell asleep, then we ran into that bastard Howard McCormick. The

137

evening was a total disaster."

"So what happened? You take her home?"

"If you mean did I take her to bed, the answer is no. By the time I brought her back, we were barely speaking."

"That's too bad. I thought you kinda liked her."

"For some unfathomable reason, I do."

Charley grinned. "She's a nice girl, Jack. Maybe you forgot what it's like to go out with a gal like that."

"Yeah, and maybe I don't want to remember." He could still recall Betsy Simmons, the girl he had taken to his senior prom. She had set her cap for him, and for a couple of lethal moments after they'd made love in the back seat of his Camaro, he'd been tempted to surrender, to give up his plans for the future, maybe even ask her to marry him. He'd dodged that bullet when he'd won that football scholarship to UCLA. The last time he'd seen Betsy, she had four rug rats and weighed nearly three hundred pounds.

"You gonna see her again?" Charley asked.

"Who?"

"Genny."

He nodded. "I'm takin' her up to Cold Springs on my Harley."

Charley scoffed. "She may be 'a damned librarian,' but she's hell for grit, that's for sure."

"What's that supposed to mean?"

"Means you're gonna break her in — or

you're just gonna break her. I may put my money on Genny."

Jack said nothing to that, just stared out toward the choppy waves and the black dot rising in the distance, the oil rig that was their destination. Alongside the boat, four big gray dolphins arched out of the water in unison, then dove beneath the surface. Their playful demeanor was in contrast to the darkening sky and heavily rolling sea.

"Heard anything from Bob Groller?" Charley asked, changing the subject.

He nodded. "The loan committee turned us down for the second time." Beside him, Charley's weathered hands grew tighter on the rail. "We might have had a chance if we could have produced some long-term contracts. I've got a meeting with the honchos down at Chevron in LA tomorrow morning. I'm hoping I can talk them into a servicing commitment. Then I'm going over to see Fred Withers at Lyon Gas and Oil. They've been using us for Oceanographic's diving operation for over a year. I don't see any reason to believe that's not going to continue. Maybe I can get them to put it in writing."

"What then?" Charley asked.

"There are other banks besides Santa Barbara National. Once I get the whole thing laid out, I'll find somebody who shows an interest and take the package there."

"You said Groller was our best shot."

"He was. But that doesn't mean I'm ready to give up."

Charley leaned over and rested a hand on his shoulder. "You're a good boy, Jack. The best. Whatever happens, don't ever forget I said that."

"Thanks, Charley." But just the thought of losing the boat made something twist in his gut. He had worked too damned hard — they both had. He couldn't stand the idea of letting the bank destroy everything they had struggled for. "You'll be all right without me for a couple of days, won't you?"

Charley grinned. "You ain't that indispensable. Besides, Pete'll be on board. He's always a good man to have around if something comes up."

Jack just nodded, his mind already back on the problem he faced with the boat. There had to be a way out, dammit. He just prayed to God he'd be able to find it before it was too late.

Genny tugged on her jeans, pulled on a sweatshirt and her nylon jacket over that, then put on a warm pair of socks. She shoved her feet into her brown penny loafers. Beside the bed, a reddish glow shone through the stained glass flowers on the shade of her tiffany lamp, and moonlight poured in through the sliding glass doors.

Unlike the last two nights when her insomnia

had kicked in and she had lain awake for hours, tonight she had slept . . . but she had also dreamed.

Genny went into the bathroom, brushed her teeth, and drew her hair back into a flat gold clasp at the nape of her neck. She would walk for a while, try to clear her head. If that didn't work, she'd drive over to Bob's Big Boy and talk to Dottie. It wasn't all that late, just a little past midnight. And the dream, although disturbing, had been a relatively mild one. Perhaps if she was lucky, she still might get a good night's sleep.

Genny left the condo and started down the path through the ice plant that led to the beach, but at the last minute, veered away from the path and continued along the sidewalk, making her way toward the dock at the end of the street.

Jack was out of town, she knew. Perhaps that was why she felt safe in heading toward his boat. Walking along the heavy planks of the dock, she spied the *Marauder* tied up exactly where it had been before, bobbing peacefully, amazingly graceful in its slumber. She was surprised to discover a light burning in the window of the main cabin, just as it had been before.

Perhaps Jack hadn't gone after all. Perhaps he and his friends were once more playing cards. Knowing she shouldn't, but somehow unable to resist, Genny climbed the stairs and stepped onto the teakwood deck. Almost at once, the door swung open and Charley stepped out of the cabin.

"Well, ain't this a nice surprise. I wondered who was out here. Come in, Genny girl, come in." She followed without hesitation, feeling as comfortable with Charley as she did with her own father. He had that warmth about him.

He opened the cabin door, but stopped and turned. "Jack's not here, you know. Had some business in the city. Los Angeles, I mean." He pronounced it Los Angles, making her smile.

"I know. I really didn't intend to come here, but I . . ."

"You what? Still having trouble sleeping?"

"Sometimes." She sighed as she followed Charley into the gray-carpeted salon. "I don't know which is worse — not being able to sleep, or sleeping and having to face my terrible dreams."

"Bad one tonight?" he asked.

"Not so bad, really. Just . . . I don't know, Charley. They mean something — I'm convinced of it, but I can't seem to figure out what it is."

"How 'bout a cup of hot chocolate? It's the packaged kind but it's pretty darned good."

"That'd be terrific."

"In the meantime, you can tell me about your dream."

"Are you sure? It's late and I know you have to work in the morning."

"I'm not sleepy yet, either. Besides, I'm interested in that kinda thing. Jack doesn't read much, but I do. A few years back I read a lot of self-help books, books on recovery, that sort of thing. Got a boy with some problems. Bad ones. He's in prison down in Arizona. His mother and I tried to figure out where we'd gone wrong. We took him to half dozen psychologists. Bobby didn't learn much, but I did. Made a couple of good friends, and got me to thinkin'. Got me lookin' into some other things, too."

He turned on the gas jet under the tea kettle he had filled with water. "All that reading Bobby's mama and I did never did Bobby any good. Maybe it'll be some help to you."

They sat down on the padded benches surrounding the built-in table in the galley. "All right, Genny-girl. You go on now and tell me about your dream."

She took a moment to collect herself. "Do you remember what I told you before?"

"About the natives and what you figured was some sort of ritual? I remember. I thought the dreams might be set in Africa."

"That's right. That was the first time I ever saw the woman. Since then, I've dreamed of her again, on more than one occasion. She's a vicious woman, Charley. Sadistic." She shuddered just to think of it. "But not tonight. Tonight she was charming. I caught flashes of a beautiful house, of fine antiques and crystal

143

chandeliers. There was a ballroom of some kind. I can't remember it clearly, but I think it had one of those black and white marble floors."

"Were there other people there?" he asked.

"I think so, but I can't remember very much about them."

The tea kettle hummed so he went and made their cocoa, and returned with two heavy porcelain mugs.

"There was a man, I think," Genny continued, "but I never saw him clearly. I think they may have danced — at one point I remember hearing music. At the time, I felt certain I knew the song but it slipped away when I woke up."

"That doesn't sound much like Africa. Maybe the first dreams weren't connected to these."

"I think they are. I *feel* like they are. I think the house might have sat at the edge of the jungle. And it was definitely sometime in the past — the woman was dressed in period clothing. What I can't figure out is why I'm dreaming about something like this. What could it possibly have to do with me?"

"Did you think about whether it could be a story you read, or maybe something out of a movie?"

"I've racked my brain, but I can't remember anything vaguely similar to this." She didn't mention the sado-masochistic dream she'd had. That might mean mentioning the fantasy she'd

144

had about Jack and she wasn't about to tell him that.

"You're a librarian," Charley reminded her. "Why don't you take a look at your records, see what books you've got that deal with the Africa of the past. See if there's something you might have read."

"Good idea. I should have thought of that myself." She straightened in her seat. "I get so tired, I don't think as clearly as I should, but I'll get on it as soon as I get the chance."

"Good girl."

"And through our computer link, I can access the film library, see what movies I might have seen."

"Now you're talkin'," Charley said. "Of course it could be a combination of what you've seen or read."

"Yes, but if that's the case, that brings us back to the why of it — why would I create a story like that and dream about it repeatedly?"

Charley took a sip of his hot chocolate. "What else happened in the dream you had tonight?"

"Nothing much. Compared to the nightmares I usually have, this one was relatively uneventful. I remember the woman walking outside. I remember the moist heat and the night sounds, and the smell of decaying vegetation." She set the mug down quickly and glanced over at Charley. "The man came out there, too — all of a sudden, I remember. He was older than she was. She kissed him, Charley. She kissed him and he wanted her — badly. But I don't think she really wanted him."

Charley watched her from above the rim of his mug. There were things he might say to her, avenues he might suggest, but he didn't have enough information, and he didn't think Genny would be willing to listen. His instincts told him to wait.

"Anything else?" he asked.

Genny sighed and leaned back in her chair. "Not that I recall. I woke up when the woman started laughing. They often end that way."

"What the devil was she laughing at?"

Genny's eyes seemed to glaze as she stared down at the cocoa in the bottom of her mug. "The man, I think, but I don't know for sure." When she glanced up, Charley caught the flicker of some turbulent emotion. "She seemed to want something from him," she said, looking suddenly pale. "I have a feeling that she's going to get it."

Eight

All week Genny had been dreading her Thursday night appointment at the Sleep Center in the Cottage Hospital on Pueblo Street.

That evening she hurried home from work, watched the news, called her mother — she had lately been lax in doing that — then went upstairs. She showered and put on slacks and a sweater, then packed her small tapestry overnight bag, taking a pair of shorty pajamas, a heavy quilted robe, her toothbrush, hairbrush, a little makeup, and of course something to read.

She left the condo at exactly 8:30 and arrived precisely on time for her 8:45 P.M. appointment. The sleep center sat on the fourth floor of the hospital, down a long narrow hall with an endless number of doors. She pushed one of them open and walked in.

Wally De Stephano, the technician on duty that night, was the same man who had been there before. He welcomed her but instead of leading her straight into the sleeping room as she had expected, he guided her down the hall to the doctor's office. She paused as she noticed the name on the door, *Benjamin I. Beckett.*

"What happened to Dr. Goldstein?" she asked.

"Took a job at the center in Rochester, Minnesota. It was a very big promotion."

"Good for him." Except that she now had to deal with someone new.

"Dr. Beckett is the head of the clinic now. He runs things somewhat differently, but he seems to be very good." Wally smiled. He looked to be nearing forty, stockily built with kind of a bulldog nose. "Why don't you have a seat? The doctor will be with you in just a few minutes."

She did as he asked, and sat down in one of two modest brown leather chairs across from the doctor's cluttered desk. There were the usual framed degrees on the wall, pictures on the desk of his wife and three children, stacks of medical journals were piled on the floor. They were dog-eared with signs of study. It was obvious the doctor was a very busy man.

"Hello, Genny," said a man's voice from the open doorway. "I'm Ben Beckett."

She stood up as he entered and he warmly clasped her hand. "Good evening, Dr. Beckett." Half glasses fastened to a silver chain around his neck rested on his long thin nose. His hair was gray and his eyes a very pale blue. He was reading notes on a clipboard.

"I've been studying your charts."

"My charts?"

He nodded, moving the silver chain up and down. "I've also spoken to Dr. Halpern. She

148

tells me your insomnia hasn't improved and that lately your nightmares have gotten somewhat worse."

"Unfortunately, that's correct."

"Before, when you were here, did you and Dr. Goldstein discuss your dreams?"

"We talked mostly about the insomnia, that it could be caused by a number of things."

He nodded. "Everything from stress to food allergies. It can be triggered by certain chemicals in the environment, changes in altitude, alcohol, drugs . . . or it may be related to trauma, as Dr. Halpern believes is happening in your case."

"Yes, I remember."

"Tonight we're going to test you again, see if anything has changed since the last time you came in." He turned and motioned her to follow. "I believe you know where we're going."

Down the hall to the sleeping room she had stayed in before. It was comfortably furnished, almost cozy, with a light blue comforter on the double bed and soft pale blue curtains over windows that weren't really there. A television sat beneath a hanging philodendron, and a stack of current bestsellers rested on the country maple bedside stand.

"We try to make it comfortable," the doctor said. "The idea is to make the patient feel at home."

That was a laugh, considering the video camera fixed over the bed, the infrared light, and the tangle of cables and wires by the nightstand. Still, they had obviously done their best.

"Why don't you get ready for bed?" the doctor suggested. "When you're finished, just ring the buzzer and Wally will come in and get you hooked up. We'll talk again in the morning."

She nodded and watched the tall gray-haired man walk out and close the door. In the bathroom adjacent to the room, Genny removed her slacks and sweater and put on a two-piece cotton nightie that gave them room to attach the wires needed to conduct their tests. When she returned to the room, she sat down on the bed and pressed the buzzer. A few seconds later, Wally De Stephano walked in.

He smiled. "If you remember, Ms. Austin, this takes a while." About thirty minutes as she recalled.

Working beside the bed, Wally rubbed her skin with an abrasive solution called Omniprep, which improved electrical conductivity. Then, one by one, he began to attach electrodes, twelve in all, each one smaller than a dime. They were fixed to her legs, face, and stomach.

Five of them ran to an electroencephalograph, an EEG, it was called, to record the electrical activity in the brain. The others recorded leg, chin, and eye movements, heartbeat, and rate of respiration. An electrode was placed on her forehead to reduce electrical interference.

Since she wasn't yet sleepy, the wires weren't hooked into the master plug, which left her free to move around the room. It wasn't until two hours later as she was reading, that her chin began to droop and the book in her hands felt heavy. Wally silently walked in and connected her into the system.

Wires from the electrodes were plugged into a polysomnograph, which amplified electrical messages and transferred them onto a graph. A microphone was attached to the top of her nightgown so that Wally could hear any unusual sounds, and a white noise machine was turned on to smother distractions.

As nervous as all of this made her, with the lights now out, eventually she fell asleep.

It was two-fifteen when she bolted upright in bed. She bit back most of the scream that nearly escaped her throat, but the microphone picked up the muffled sound and a few seconds later, Wally rushed in.

"Are you all right?"

Her heart was still hammering, her face and neck sweaty. "I suppose so."

"The graph showed a shift in brain waves, heartbeat, and respiration. It's obvious you were dreaming."

"Yes."

"Can you remember?"

Genny nodded. "Spiders," she recalled with a shiver, "big ones the size of my hand." God, it had been awful. She was running through the jungle, fleeing something she couldn't quite see when the massive web caught her in its sticky embrace. She was trying to cry out, clawing and fighting, trying to tear herself free when she had awakened.

"Spiders," Wally repeated, his mouth twisted up in a grimace. "Jesus, I hate spiders."

"So do I." Genny fell back against the pillow.

"Think you can go back to sleep?"

She shook her head. "Not for a while." She wished she could walk on the beach. She wished she could talk to Dottie or maybe to Charley Denton. She wished . . . for a lot of things, but none of them were going to happen tonight.

"I think I'll go to the bathroom, then read for a little while longer."

Wally nodded and unplugged her wires from the main connector, allowing her to walk around the room. Once she returned to bed, he came back and reconnected her.

"Sweet dreams," he teased with a smile that held a shadow of worry.

"Thanks, Wally." But her dreams were never sweet anymore. And sleep this night would elude her. For an instant she thought of Jack, but the rush of heat that came with his image embarrassed her, and she worried what the graph Wally charted might reveal. She picked up the new Meryl Sawyer novel she had just purchased and began to read.

Ben Beckett welcomed Genny Austin into his

office the following morning at 7:00 A.M. She sank down wearily in one of the chairs across from him.

She was a pretty woman, he saw, softer looking than most of the women he met these days, more fragile perhaps, more vulnerable. Her eyes were a warm shade of brown, though this morning there were smudges beneath them and her skin looked a little bit sallow.

"I hear you had a rough night," he said.

"I'm afraid so, Dr. Beckett."

He peered down his nose at the report Wally had laid on his desk, the graphs and charts and summaries. "I've gone over your test results. Just as before, the graphs show interruptions between the non-REM stages and the REM stages of sleep, but as near as we can tell there is nothing physiologically wrong."

He looked at her over his glasses. "You went to see Dr. Wharton, the allergy specialist?" he asked.

She nodded. "Right after I came here the first time. He found nothing out of the ordinary."

He studied the chart. "No hormone problems, no chronic pain, nothing we can assign your insomnia to except stress and trauma."

She sighed into the space between them. "I'm afraid that's old news, doctor. The question is, where do I go from here?"

Where indeed? He had seen severe cases of trauma affect sleeping patterns but none much

153

worse than this. He suppressed a surge of pity. It wouldn't do her one bit of good . . . but there might be something that would.

"My predecessor, Dr. Goldstein, entered this field from a background in neurology. In the cases he worked with, he focused most heavily on the physiological aspects. I presume you followed his suggestions."

"I've done my best, Dr. Beckett. I exercise regularly, never eat heavy foods before bedtime, and try to maintain a healthy diet. I live by a fairly normal schedule and always relax before I try to fall asleep."

"And if you should wake up and be unable to return to sleep within fifteen minutes —"

"I get up and do something else."

Ben noticed the tired way she slumped in her chair. She had tried all the usual suggestions, but apparently nothing had worked.

"Unlike Dr. Goldstein, my specialty was psychiatry. That means I view things from a slightly different perspective."

Genny's head came up. "A different perspective? Does that mean you've thought of something I can try?"

"It's obvious your insomnia is a result of the nightmares stemming from your trauma. Therefore it would follow that if you can stop your bad dreams, you can probably return to normal patterns of sleep."

"That's a very big if, but it certainly makes sense."

"Have you ever heard of lucid dreaming?"

Genny uncrossed her legs and sat up straighter in her chair. "As a matter of fact, I have. I ran across it during some of my research." She smiled. "As you might imagine, I've read quite a number of articles on sleep disorders in the past two years."

His mouth curved up. "Yes, I imagine you have."

"As I understand it, lucid dreaming isn't very well accepted. There are people who don't even believe it exists."

"There are always those who disagree, no matter the subject. The truth is lucid dreaming wasn't well accepted for a number of years because it came to the forefront through a doctor named Willems Van Eeden. Van Eeden was involved in parapsychology, a field that's been fighting for legitimacy for years. Recently the theory has been given more credence, with particular interest coming from those involved in the study of nightmares."

"Exactly how does it work?"

He laid his pen down on top of the folder bearing Genny Austin's name. "The object of lucid dreaming is to learn to control yourself in the REM dreamtime. Theoretically, once you can control what is happening during your dreams, you should be able to change them, to alter them in ways that suit you."

She looked at him intently. "No more spiders?" she said with a smile, and he thought how much he'd like to help her. Even in her dark brown slacks and simple cotton sweater she looked feminine and appealing. He wondered if she would ever remarry.

"No more spiders," he repeated. "At least that's what would happen if everything worked as it's supposed to. But like any idea in the developing stages, there are pros and cons to the notion itself. It might not be wise to control one's dreams. Science still isn't certain of their purpose. Our dreams may be trying to relay some sort of message through the subconscious. They might be pointing out a problem or offering some kind of solution. Or perhaps they're simply the mind's way of relieving undue stress."

He removed his glasses, which slid down their chain and settled against his white smock at the base of his neck. "Whatever the case, in your circumstance, I think it would well be worth the risk."

She pondered that a moment, with her eyebrows drawn together in thought. "How would I go about it?"

"Oddly enough, you've already accomplished the first step. Unlike most people, you can remember your dreams. The trick is to wake up *inside* the dream. You've got to know that you're dreaming, to become aware of it, yet remain asleep and in control."

He leaned forward. "For instance, had you been lucid dreaming last night, you might have been able to shrink the spider, then swat it away like a fly. You wouldn't have been afraid and you wouldn't have awakened."

"I see." A growing spark of interest reflected in her eyes. "How do I learn to do this?"

"There are a number of books on the subject. One by Celia Green simply called *Lucid Dreams* — that was written sometime back. There's one by Pamela Weintraub and Keith Harary called *Lucid Dreams in 30 Days*. Stephen LaBerge has written several texts on the subject. The library should have those and quite a few more."

"I'd certainly be willing to try it."

Ben rolled back his chair and came to his feet. "At the moment, that's the best suggestion I have. Why don't you read enough so that you feel comfortable with the subject, then call me with your questions?"

"Can you do it, Dr. Beckett? Can you control your dreams?"

"To some degree. There are others who are much more proficient."

Genny stood up, too. "I'll start just as soon as I can. I'll call and let you know how I progress."

"I hope you will, Ms. Austin." He offered her his hand and she shook it, then smiled as she turned and walked away. He watched her go out through the doorway and thought that perhaps there was a bit more lift in her step. He hoped so. He didn't know if she would really be able to master lucid dreaming, but he would help her in any way he could.

And he wouldn't be the one to tell her this might be just one more avenue leading to another dead end.

At nine-thirty Saturday morning, Genny stood at the window, staring out at the endless white-capped sea. Fleetingly she wondered how many times she had watched that same horizon, studying every detail, memorizing every line. Still, it never seemed the same. There was always something new to capture her interest, a subtle shift in the blue-green color of the water, the changing images of fleeting white clouds, the appearance of a ship on a distant wave.

She had always been drawn to the ocean, ever since she was a child. Though she had been raised inland, in the Southern California city of Riverside, her family had often traveled to the beach. Her sister Mary Ellen never much cared for it, but Genny did. She loved to look out at the water, to dig her toes in the sand, to hunt for sea shells or follow the flight of a sea gull as it soared out over the waves.

Being near the sea was the reason she had chosen to go to college at San Diego State. The reason she had been so happy when the job offer came in from the library in Santa Barbara.

She found the ocean comforting, and she needed that comfort now. It was Saturday morning. She'd had another rough night last night, in fact another rough week. Howard had called several times in the past few days, but surprisingly he had never mentioned Jack Brennen, and neither had she.

She'd agreed to see Howard on Sunday. He was taking her to church and then to a family picnic at Tucker's Grove. She wished she was looking forward to it instead of wishing she didn't have to go.

On Friday, Dr. Halpern had called her at work. She asked about her night at the clinic, though she had already spoken to Dr. Beckett, then asked that their appointment be postponed. The doctor's sister had started early labor and she wanted to be there for the delivery. The appointment was rescheduled for Tuesday after work.

Oddly enough, Genny felt relieved.

Unfortunately, that was yesterday and this was today.

Genny looked out at the sea and the clouds and tried not to think of the dream. Spiders again, this time a room full of them. There were small ones the size of an ant, some as big as a quarter, and the huge, hand-sized ones she had seen before, all of them with bent furry legs, beady little eyes, and thick black bodies. They were everywhere, it seemed, darkening the walls and the ceilings, their sticky webs clinging to the corners.

But that wasn't the worst part.

Genny's stomach twisted as the memory took

hold and crashed in. Tears stung her eyelids and began to blur her vision. Dear God, even now she couldn't stand to think of it.

And yet she could remember everything she had seen, every word that had been said.

"Bring the girl here, Maubry. The next time she thinks of sneaking off to visit Charles, she is certain to think twice about it."

"No, miztress, pleeze." The black girl twisted, trying to break the overseer's hold on her pudgy arms. He was a big man, powerfully built with ruddy skin and longish, dark auburn hair. He wore khaki pants, a plain white cotton shirt with the sleeves cut out, and well-oiled, heavy leather work boots. Thick muscles bulged in his arms, but only a portion of his strength was needed to contain the girl. "Miztress, pleeze — I swear, we didn't do nothin'."

"Do you also swear you've never slept with Maubry?"

The girl froze in her tracks and the big man's head swiveled toward her. His eyes were a little too close together, his lips chafed and slightly too thin. He wasn't attractive, except for his powerful body.

"That was a long time ago," he said gruffly. "You know it meant nothing."

"And Charles?" she said to the girl. "Does he also mean nothing?"

"But I didn't —"

"I saw you, Bereena." She smiled at her

160

coldly. "But after today, I'm certain you won't do it again."

The young girl started to tremble.

"Maubry!" The single command moved him forward, dragging the girl in his wake.

The black-haired woman opened the rotting wooden door to the shed, careful to keep her apricot skirts out of the way.

"Nooo!" the black girl shrieked, bracing her hands on the door frame, refusing to be dragged in. "I don't go in d'ere. Spiders in d'ere. I don't —"

Maubry shoved her in and the door slammed closed.

A moment of silence, then the echo of screams sliced the air. One after another, each more frantic, more hysterical than the last, they seeped through the rotting wood and permeated the hot moist air, the sounds eerily twisted as they drifted across the clearing.

The woman looked at the overseer and a smile touched her full ruby lips. "I'm feeling a little bit warm, Maubry. Perhaps we should go someplace cool and lie down for a while. You'd like that, wouldn't you?"

The overseer took an uncertain step in her direction. "You know I would," he said softly. The woman laid a hand on his arm and together they started walking away.

"What about the girl?" Maubry asked, glancing over his shoulder. Her screams still echoed from the shed.

"What about her?" the woman said, and then she started to laugh.

Genny jerked free of her painful thoughts as the pounding at the door finally reached her. Dear God, Jack was here and she was crying. She wiped her cheeks with the back of a hand, but the pounding continued, insisting she open the door. She unchained the latch but turned away as he walked in, hoping that he wouldn't see.

"Genny?"

She brushed away the last of the wetness and forced herself to smile, but her lashes remained spiked and glistening.

"I saw you through the window but you wouldn't answer the door." He took a long stride closer. "You look like you've been crying. What the hell is going on?"

"Nothing, Jack. Everything is fine." She tried to smile brighter but her bottom lip trembled.

"Everything sure doesn't look fine. Are you all right?" She hadn't expected concern. Not from a man like Jack. But his eyes had turned a stormy shade of blue and a muscle throbbed beneath the dark skin on his cheek.

She started to lie, to tell him it was nothing, that she really was all right, but when she opened her mouth, only a pain-filled sob came out.

Instinctively, he reached for her. Her name came slipping softly from his lips. Perhaps that was the reason she went into his arms, the

162

reason she let him draw her against his chest. Perhaps that was the reason she started to cry again, as if some great dam had broken.

Jack just held her. "It's all right, baby. Everything's going to be fine." They stood there like that, Genny crying against his shoulder, Jack's big callused hands sifting gently through her hair. She felt like a fool, but she couldn't seem to stop, and oddly enough Jack's presence only seemed to encourage her.

When her crying had finally eased, he handed her a white cotton handkerchief he pulled from the worn back pocket of his jeans. "Why don't you tell me what's wrong?"

Genny wiped her eyes and blew her nose. "God, I feel like an idiot."

"More bad dreams? Is that what this is about? Charley told me you came by to see him."

"I h-hope you don't mind."

"Of course not. If you've made a friend of Charley Denton, you've made a good one. And Charley's no dummy. He might even be able to help you."

"I already figured that out." She took a steadying breath, turned away from him to gaze out the window. "They're so awful, Jack. I'm trying to learn to control them. That's what Dr. Beckett told me to do, but I've only just started and so far I'm not having any luck. Last night was one of the worst."

She felt his hands on her shoulders, massaging them gently, helping to ease away the tension. "I-I went through all my resources at work, just as you and Charley suggested, but I didn't find anything that might be a connection. I don't *feel* like it's something I've seen or read; it feels like something real. And the worst part is the way I feel when it's over. Like I'm dying inside. Like my whole body aches with grief."

Jack slowly turned her to face him. "The dream you had last night — you want to tell me about it?"

Genny looked into the bluest eyes she had ever seen. The ache returned just to look at them. "Not really. I wish I could just forget."

Jack used the pad of his thumb to wipe the last of the tears from her cheeks. "If you'll trust me, give me a chance, I swear I'll help you forget. We'll ride up into the hills — stop at Cold Springs Tavern — then I know a place near the river where we can have lunch. You won't believe how beautiful it is." Jack smiled at her, and the tension eased inside her. "I promise I won't scare you."

Even the thought of riding on the back of his motorcycle wasn't enough to deter her. "I'd like that. I'd like it very much." She wanted to be with Jack Brennen, and she wanted to be someplace far away.

Jack leaned over and brushed her mouth with a kiss. His lips felt warm, soft. The pressure of his touch was feather-light. She wouldn't have believed that he could be tender. Not Jack Brennen. But the tenderness was there just the same.

His tongue touched the corners of her mouth, eased her lips apart, then tasted her more completely. A delicious warmth unfurled, buttery soft, yet her limbs began to tingle. Genny slid her arms around his neck and he pulled her against him, fitting them closely together. He deepened the kiss and the warmth began expanding, shafts of heat spreading slowly through her limbs.

She could feel his arousal pressing against her, the muscles across his thick chest, the pounding of his heart and her own heart pounding in return. She touched his tongue with hers, ran it over his bottom lip, then slid it into his mouth and heard him groan.

He kissed her so fiercely that she suddenly felt uncertain. Then Jack pulled away.

"I promised I wouldn't scare you," he said gruffly. "That's exactly what's going to happen if we stay here any longer."

A flush rose in her cheeks as she let go of his neck and backed away. She tried not to look at the heavy bulge pressing against his zipper. Jack shifted but the thick ridge remained.

Genny glanced away and he followed her gaze, which settled on the floor at her feet. When she looked up at him, deep grooves framed the grin on his suntanned face.

"I like your boots."

Boots. Temporary insanity. That's all she could think of to plead. The color in her cheeks deepened to a dull shade of rose. "I-I bought them last night on my way home from work. I thought if I was going for a ride on a Harley . . ."

"Yeah, right. If you were going out with a biker, you had to have a pair of black leather cowboy boots." He bent over and pulled up the pantleg of her jeans. "With eagles on the front."

Genny laughed softly. She would never know exactly what had possessed her to buy the boots except that she was tired of being depressed, tired of being tired, and tired of what she had now begun to see as her dull, monotonous existence. "It seemed like a good idea at the time."

Jack cupped her face in his hands, bent his head, and kissed her. "I think it was a great idea." He turned her toward the door. "Got your jacket?"

"Right here." She held up her blue nylon windbreaker. With her hair pulled back in a ponytail, she was as ready as she ever would be.

"Let's go." They left the condo, locked the door, and walked out to the street.

Whatever she had expected, it wasn't the outrageous low-slung, pearlized-purple motorcycle with the fancy chrome trim that Jack had parked at the curb. And yet it was exactly what she should have been prepared for.

She looked at the orange-red flames roaring

over the gas tank and part of her wanted to smile, but the other part suddenly wanted to run. What in heaven was she doing with a man like Jack Brennen? For God's sake, she was a librarian! She held a respected position in the community. She was an educated woman, the widow of a successful businessman. She couldn't go riding around with a guy in a black leather jacket on the back of a motorcycle painted with flames!

She might have turned around and marched right back inside the house if Jack had given her a few more moments to ponder. Instead he swung a long muscular leg over the seat, handed her a plain white helmet, and unsnapped the chin strap on his own, a black one with a panther etched in purple on the front.

"All you have to remember is to go *with* me, don't fight me. Whenever we turn, just lean the same way I do, not the opposite way. Think you can do that?"

"I'll try." She studied the bike and chewed her bottom lip. "What will happen if I forget?"

Jack smiled that incredibly masculine smile of his. "I'm not going to dump us, if that's what you're thinking. It just makes things work smoother."

That made her feel a little bit better. She pulled on the helmet and snapped the leather strap beneath her chin. Jack checked to make sure it was properly adjusted, then pulled on his own and told her to climb aboard.

Taking a deep breath for courage and pushing all her doubts away, Genny swung a leg over the padded black leather seat. She rested her shiny new boots on the footrests and slid her arms around Jack's waist. She was ready for the ride, but not for the jolt of electricity she felt when her breasts came in contact with the muscles across his back. Her mouth went dry and her heart started knocking against her ribs.

"All set?" he asked.

"Y-Yes." But all she could think of was how wide his shoulders were in contrast to his waist, how tight and round his bottom looked in his faded blue Levis, how hard he was all over. An unmistakable wave of desire washed over her. The feeling was so new, so exciting, that for a moment she didn't realize what it was.

With Bill, sex was a pleasant sort of bonding. What she felt for Jack was an all-encompassing, mind-numbing heat.

He raised a booted foot and slammed it down on the starter. The engine roared to life and a shot of nervous fear raised its head.

"Hold on," Jack said, but he really had no need. She was gripping him so hard she wondered if he'd be able to breathe.

Nine

They took the back streets, following Foothill Road out of the city, then they turned up San Marcos Pass. Jack listened to the perfect purr of the engine, appreciating Ollie's masterful hand with every smooth stroke of the pistons.

On the seat behind him, he felt Genny begin to relax. He found himself smiling, trying to imagine what she was thinking as she clung to him with a death grip that told him how frightened she was.

Still, he had to give her credit. She was hanging in better than he would have expected. He hoped by the time they reached Cold Spring Tavern she might actually be enjoying herself.

That brought a frown to his face. She sure as hell hadn't enjoyed herself last night. Or from what Charley said, not for a whole lot of sleepless nights before that. It bothered him the way she suffered, and it bothered him even more that it bothered him.

Just like this morning. Seeing her cry that way tore something loose inside him. He hadn't meant to kiss her, but once he did, he almost lost control. At the time, it was exactly what

169

both of them wanted, yet somehow it didn't seem right to take advantage when she was so upset.

Christ, what the hell was he thinking? He'd never worried about a woman's feelings before. He took what they offered and both of them were usually glad. Somehow he had known that Genny would regret it. Damn, the woman was getting under his skin. Involving himself in her troubles was the last thing he wanted, yet in some strange way he couldn't seem to stop himself.

They rounded a curve. The engine was droning the familiar roar that always set him free, and below them the Santa Barbara hills stretched all the way to the sea. The suburb of Goleta sprawled a ways to the north, where the houses looked like tiny Monopoly pieces. He pointed out the incredible view and Genny nodded. She was doing just as he told her, leaning with him on the curves and, he thought, starting to enjoy the ride.

She shifted a little and inwardly Jack groaned. He'd been trying not to think of the way her breasts pressed into his back as she sat behind him, the way her nipples kept rubbing against his denim shirt. The minute he did, he went hard, and that made him damned uncomfortable.

In a less physical way, he felt equally uncomfortable just being with her.

When Genny was near, he wasn't just good

old Jack Brennen, a little bit wild, a little bit reckless, always out for a good time. With Genny, he felt protective, concerned. Her feelings were as important as his own. What bothered him the most was the strange sense of rightness he felt when he was with her. Genny made him feel settled somehow, content in a way he hadn't even thought about.

Since emotions like "settled and content" were hardly on his list of priorities, he kept asking himself why he kept going back for more.

It was probably just a sexual thing, he told himself. He had come to her defense that night on the beach, and that had brought out some deep-rooted, primitive male instinct. It had also made him want to take her to bed. In the very worst way.

Which was probably more to the point.

Genny had turned him down. Not many women did that. Oh, she wanted him, all right, just the way he wanted her. But she was the type who needed more from a relationship than he was willing to give. So what the hell was he doing seeing her again? Christ, he wished she would just give in. He could take her to bed and get her out of his system. Couldn't she see it would be the best thing for both of them?

Jack leaned into a curve and felt Genny's head against his shoulder. She pointed to a red-tailed hawk that circled out over a canyon and he knew for sure she had finally put away her

fears. He pointed to the big bird's mate wing-
ing off toward its nest in the top of a tree and
she nodded.

A few minutes later, they crested the summit
at the top of the curvy mountain road and began the descent down the opposite side. The
steep ravines were thick with buck brush, yucca,
and sage. Outcroppings of huge granite boulders fell away at the edge of the pavement. He
grinned as he felt Genny clinging to him again.

He downshifted as they turned onto Stage-
coach Road. Cold Springs Tavern was the first
stop on his agenda. A Bud Light, some pretzels,
and a pit stop, then they'd head on down the
road to the place in the National Forest that he
had told Genny about. The Santa Ynez River
ran through it. He had a spot in mind where
they could spread out a blanket, eat the fried
chicken he had picked up at the Colonel's and
stashed in his saddlebags, along with some
apples and cheese. Then they could nap in the
shade of the trees.

Jack's smile reflected in his face mask. And
maybe, if he got lucky, Genny would finally
give in.

Motorcycles of every shape and color filled
the big dirt parking lot at Cold Springs Tavern
— a group of low-roofed hand-hewn log buildings which had once been a stage stop on the
route between Santa Ynez and Santa Barbara.

Genny had been by the place a dozen times,

even been there for dinner a time or two with Bill — in the evenings, the cuisine was surprisingly sophisticated. But she had never been inside in the daytime.

It was well known that the place was a hangout for bikers during the day and especially on weekends. From the number of motorcycles she saw, Genny expected the worst — an army of Nazi Hell's Angels — unbathed macho men in leather and chains, hair and beards uncombed, their posture belligerent and menacing. When she actually walked up on the patio, she saw mostly men and women who enjoyed the sport of biking, some of them pretty far out, but looking fairly harmless, and there were even a few professional men, doctors and lawyers she recognized from work.

"Surprised?" Jack asked, watching the expression on her face.

"To tell you the truth, I am."

"They aren't all social misfits, criminals, and delinquents. Lots of different people enjoy the sport."

"So I see."

"How did you like your first ride?" He pulled out a rough wooden bench at one of the outdoor tables. Genny sat down and Jack took a seat on the opposite side.

Genny smiled. "I have to admit it was fun."

"You weren't scared?"

"Not after the first ten minutes."

"Only ten?"

She laughed. "Well maybe fifteen."

A smile played on his lips. God, he was handsome with those thick black eyebrows and bright blue eyes. His lower lip had a sexy erotic curve that made her palms damp just to look at it. Yet beneath all that rough charm and good looks, there was a restlessness about him. Perhaps it was part of his appeal, part of the reason she felt so drawn to him.

She had never been restless herself. Her roots went deep when she put them down. Jack's roots went only as deep as the hull of his ship. Wherever his boat went, that was enough of a home for Jack. Somehow the thought made her sad.

It must have shown somehow, for she found him studying her face.

"Penny for your thoughts," he said, taking a sip of beer from the ice cold mug of Bud Light he had ordered for each of them. She could count on one hand the number of beers she had drunk in her life, but sitting here in the bright noon sun, sheltered by towering oak trees and listening to the ripple of a small babbling brook, the clean malty taste seemed just right.

"So what were you thinking?" he asked again, those incredible blue eyes drifting over her in lazy perusal.

"I was wondering about your family." It was close to the truth. "Your mother and father, brothers and sisters. I was wondering where they live and if you ever see them."

He took a sip of his beer, but the relaxed look was gone from his face. "My dad died a year and a half ago. My stepmother still lives in our house in Apple Valley."

"That's where you're from?"

He nodded. "I had an older brother named Phil, but he died when I was ten. He got run over on his bicycle."

"And your real mother?"

"Died just after I was born."

So much loss. It told her a lot about him. "Sounds like you had it pretty rough." Jack shrugged his broad shoulders. "Both my parents live in Riverside. Mostly I talk to them on the phone. I've got a sister in Seattle. She's married to a doctor. They've got two darling little four-year-old twin boys."

"How come you don't have kids of your own?"

She shifted on the bench, uncomfortable with the subject. "I-I never really wanted them, and neither did Bill."

"Why not?"

"I don't know." She evaded those inquisitive eyes. It wasn't a subject she liked to discuss. "What about you? You don't have children, either." She glanced up. "Do you?"

Jack grinned, displaying his dimples. "Not that I know of."

"My sister Mary Ellen always wanted them, even when we were little. She's a real homebody, just like my mother."

"Sounds like you must have had a pretty decent childhood."

She nodded. "Better than decent. My parents were terrific. Your childhood must have been very painful."

He shrugged again, but an uneasy look crept into his eyes. "My parents didn't get along. I don't know why they ever got married. After the first couple years, they never talked, never went anywhere together. They were totally wrong for each other. As different as night and day."

Sort of like us, she couldn't help thinking, and a pang of regret slid down her spine.

"My parents aren't like that," she said. "They have the kind of marriage people dream about. They've been together for thirty-three years and I honestly believe they're still in love."

The sound of laughter erupted at a nearby table, drawing their attention. A man and woman in matching brown leather pants and billowy long-sleeved white shirts held up mugs of beer in a toast to a friend.

Jack returned his gaze to her. "I never believed that kind of thing really happened. It sure didn't happen at my house. My dad was hardly ever home."

"If you met them, you'd see it's for real." She doubted he ever would. She couldn't imagine taking Jack Brennen home to meet her parents. She grimaced to think of them riding up to their house on his Harley.

"I suppose that's the kind of marriage you had with your husband." Jack reached into the bag of pretzels he had bought to go with their beer and drew out a salty figure eight, but his gaze remained locked with hers.

"It wasn't like that. Not really. Bill and I were more like friends. We were comfortable together. That was the reason we got married. I never understood that at the time, but now that he's gone I can see it's the truth."

"You're telling me you weren't in love with him?"

"I loved him," she said a bit sadly, "and sometimes I still miss him. But no, I don't think I was ever in love with him."

Jack said nothing. His gaze slid down from her eyes to her mouth, and her pulse picked up its rhythm.

"What about you?" she asked. "Have you ever been in love?"

Jack's bottom lip curled up. "Me?" He popped the pretzel into his mouth, flashing his white teeth, and the mood was broken. "Are you kidding? I told you, I don't believe in love."

Something squeezed inside her. "No, I don't suppose you would."

"This place is getting crowded." Upending his mug, he downed the last of his beer. "I think it's time to leave."

Genny took another brief sip and set her mug back down on the scarred wooden table. Hundreds of initials had been carved into the top, some of them surrounded by carefully constructed hearts. It seemed incredibly romantic, and suddenly she wished Jack had carved theirs into the wooden table, too. It was a silly notion. Jack didn't even believe in love.

They stopped by the bathroom before they headed back to his bike, then they climbed aboard and Jack fired up the engine. They set off down the narrow curving road, with Genny clinging once more to his narrow waist, her body pressed intimately against him.

They turned off San Marcos Pass at the bottom of the hill and headed east toward Paradise Campground. Some distance farther, Jack pulled off the paved road onto a narrow dirt trail that wound along the river among towering sycamore trees.

He stopped in a small clearing protected from view by a cluster of boulders beneath a broad-branched oak. A few feet away, the shallow Santa Ynez River flowed along the streambed, the ripple of water soothing as it caressed the rounded boulders in its path.

While Genny stretched her legs and worked the kinks from her neck and shoulders, Jack spread out an old olive-drab army blanket and unpacked the food from his heavy leather saddlebags.

"Come here," he commanded as he glanced up and saw her. When she reached him, he turned her around and urged her to sit on the blanket. Long brown fingers sank into her shoulders, massaging gently, deeply. Genny sighed at the feel of it, at the relaxing of her muscles and the boneless feeling that began to melt through her body.

He worked on her neck, back, and shoulders with a seductive skill she could too-easily imagine him acquiring. Though the pleasure was nearly overwhelming, she finally pulled away. The tiny bubbles of heat in her stomach and the clenching of her muscles a little lower down said it was time for him to quit.

"Hungry?" he asked, but a roughness had crept into his voice and his look said he was no longer thinking of food.

Genny wet her lips. "Yes." For a moment she thought he might kiss her; instead he drew away.

"There's apples, cheese, and fried chicken. There's a bottle of white wine, but by now it's not very cold."

"It sounds delicious."

They ate for a while in silence. Jack was watching her in a way he hadn't before. Every time he licked the chicken from his fingers, her stomach did an odd little roll. He took a bite off a big red apple and a trickle of juice ran down his chin. Genny fought an urge to lick the sweet taste away. He wiped his mouth on the tail of his faded denim shirt and handed her the apple. She could have sworn the taste of him lingered.

Fighting to keep her thoughts from straying any further in that dangerous direction, she finished eating the apple and started talking about the weather, always the safest topic.

Jack surprised her by chiming in, telling her about the importance of weather to the boating business, about the low pressure zone moving in, and the storm predicted for the end of the week.

"I've always loved storms," Genny said. "As long as I'm inside, sitting in front of a cozy fire."

Jack's eyes slid over her body. "Yeah, there's nothing better than making love on the floor in front of the hearth with a brisk wind howling and raindrops pounding on the roof."

Genny said nothing to that, but the erotic image of Jack lying naked before a roaring fire sent a trickle of perspiration down the V between her breasts.

He surprised her by changing the subject, pointing to a beautiful blue jay perched in the branches above them, then telling her about the coyote he had spotted near the river on his last visit.

"I suppose a person in your line of work would have to like the out of doors," Genny said.

"I'm pretty much a nature freak. Right down to the smallest creatures. See that web in the crotch of the tree? That's a wood spider. They help keep the insects away."

Genny's eyes fixed on the web and she shivered, thinking of her terrible dream.

"Sorry," Jack said, seeing the distressed look on her face. "Spiders aren't my favorite, either." He leaned over as if he meant to squash it, but Genny grabbed his hand.

"Don't. I didn't mean for you to kill it."

He grinned. "I wasn't going to. I just wanted to see how much of a web it had. I'm not much for insects, but like most of God's creatures, they've got their place in the scheme of things."

Genny glanced at the spider. "Normally it wouldn't have bothered me. It's just that my dream last night . . ."

Jack reached over and captured her hand. "I think you should tell me about it."

"I don't think . . ."

"I want to know, Genny." Sensing that his concern was real, this time she did, describing in detail the young girl, the awful shed full of spiders, and the vicious but beautiful woman who had locked the poor girl in.

"I don't understand, Jack. Other people have bad dreams, but I don't think they're anything like this."

"No, but most people haven't found their husbands murdered on the sidewalk. That had to be a terrible experience, Genny."

"It was, but this . . . it just doesn't make sense."

Jack squeezed her hand. "It isn't going to go on forever. Sooner or later you'll put what happened behind you. When you do, your night-mares are bound to end."

"That's what Dr. Halpern says, but I'm not sure I believe her." She sighed wearily. "If I could only piece them together, make the puzzle parts fit, maybe I could figure out what they're trying to tell me."

"They aren't real, Genny. You've got to remember that."

"Dr. Halpern thinks they may have something to do with the men who attacked me on the beach."

"What do you think?"

"I think she's wrong." She told him about the sleep clinic and about Dr. Beckett, surprised that Jack seemed so interested.

"Do you think this lucid dreaming might really work?" he asked.

"I thought so at first. But after the hours I've spent reading about it, and the times I've tried it, I'm not so sure."

"Why not?"

"Because most of the time, I'm not even in the dream. The woman with the long black hair is there, not me. I can't control her, so I can't control the dream."

He raked a hand through his curly dark hair. It was shining nearly blue-black in the sun sifting down through the leaves. "I wish I had an answer for you, baby."

She smiled at him softly. "You've helped already, Jack, just by getting me out of there."

He lifted her hand to his lips and kissed the palm, then stretched out on the blanket, apparently pleased by the thought. He didn't protest when she changed the subject.

"How did your business meeting go? You said you went down south."

Jack's soft release of air was long and weary. "Not too well, I'm afraid." He hesitated, his expression darker than it was before, then he told her about the final big payment that was due on the *Marauder*.

"I tried to get Chevron to agree to a long-term contract, hoping we could use it as collateral to refinance the note, but the terms they wanted were so damned unreasonable we would have lost money. I did get a promise out of Lyon Oil for an offshore diving boat contract, but by itself that isn't enough."

"What are you going to do?"

"What I'm not going to do is give up. I'll start looking for something else the first of the week, another contract of some sort. If I can find one, I'll start looking for a different bank."

"What will happen if you don't succeed?"

He sighed and leaned back, propping himself on his elbows, stretching the navy blue T-shirt he'd stripped down to across his massive chest.

"The truth is, if I can't raise the money in the next few weeks, we're probably going to lose the boat."

"Oh, Jack!"

"Yeah, life's a real bitch sometimes."

"I wish there was some way I could help you. I own stock in McCormick-Austin, of course, but Howard controls it till the end of next year. Bill made him trustee for three years in the event of his death. He figured that would give me a chance to learn the business before I decided what I wanted to do."

Jack was watching her with an odd look on his face. "I didn't ask you for money, Genny. It never even crossed my mind."

"I know that, Jack, but —"

"Don't be a fool, Genny. It was nice of you to think of it, but any woman who loans money to a man she's involved with is crazy."

Genny bristled. "We aren't exactly involved, Jack. We've only been out a few times."

"That's right" — a corner of his mouth curved up — "we aren't involved." He reached for her, pulled her down on the blanket beside him. "At least not yet." Jack kissed her hard. His tongue delved hotly inside her mouth.

Genny started to protest, but the warmth of his lips and the weight of his hard body angled over hers stilled the thought. He pressed her into the blanket, kissing her fiercely. His thick chest rubbed against her breasts. The kiss grew gentle, coaxing now, making the heat swirl low in her belly. Muscle rippled every time he moved, and inside the lacy cups of her bra her nipples grew hard and distended. They rasped against the lace in the most erotic manner, and the heat slid into her limbs. When his big hand began to massage her breasts, a swift ache rose in the place between her legs.

"Jack . . ." she whispered against his lips, which continued to nibble and taste while his tongue probed more deeply inside. Then he was unbuttoning her white cotton blouse, reaching inside her bra and cupping her breasts. His thumb flicked her nipple, rubbed it gently, plucked it until she moaned.

"God, I want you," he whispered.

"Jack . . ." It seemed all she could think of to say as her mind spun away and her fingers curved into his shoulders. She wanted to touch him as he was touching her, to feel those ridges of muscle, to taste that warm brown skin. But the voice was there, telling her she should stop him.

He was a womanizer of the very worst sort, interested only in her body. He was the kind of man she had always avoided, the kind who would take what she offered, but to him it would mean nothing.

He unsnapped the clasp on her bra with an ease that confirmed her fears, then pulled it apart to bare her breasts.

"Damn . . . you're even more beautiful than I remembered." Genny trembled as he drew her nipple into his mouth and began to suckle gently. A flood of heat slid through her, slick and warm and erotic. Her mouth was dry yet her body was damp and aching.

She had never felt like this. Dear Lord, she

didn't know a man could make a woman feel this way.

He kissed her other breast, caressed it, suckled it, then returned to kissing her lips. His hand moved down to the snap on her jeans, he popped it, and slid down the zipper. She was trembling all over, yet her mind screamed out a warning.

Don't do this, Genny Austin. Tomorrow you'll be sorry. Another of Jack's conquests, that's all she would be. Jack had so many women it was like taking sand to the beach.

Yet the voice of reason was fading with each of her too-rapid heartbeats. Her sanity was slipping away with every touch of Jack's practiced hands. She was losing the battle and she knew it. That's why she silently thanked God when she heard the unmistakable buzz of an engine and realized someone was coming up the narrow dirt road.

Jack heard it, too. He swore long and fluently even as he sat up, zipped up her jeans, and pulled her blouse back together over her naked breasts. Genny did the rest, hooking her bra with trembling fingers, then buttoning up her shirt. Jack was frowning at the gesture, obviously hoping, once the intruders were gone, to take up where he had left off.

Genny wasn't about to. Her silent prayers had been answered. Sanity had returned and Jack Brennen wasn't going to get a second chance.

"Christ," Jack swore as two high-powered dirt bikes dropped over the rise and the intruders rode straight toward them. They turned and sped past at the very last moment, throwing up a cloud of dust that drifted slowly back to earth.

What was left of their lunch was covered by a dusty film, so was the blanket. A layer of dust filtered over their clothes.

"Bastards." Brushing off his jeans, Jack came to his feet.

But Genny felt only relief. "They're just a couple of kids. You were probably just as full of mischief when you were their age."

Jack frowned and then he grinned. "Yeah, I guess I was." He watched as she began to repack their lunch, picking up the empty containers, dirty napkins, and empty plastic cups.

"Genny —"

"Don't say it, Jack."

"Just tell me you felt it, too."

Felt it? She'd nearly been bowled over by it. "The picnic was lovely, Jack, but the rest . . . it wasn't a good idea."

"You wanted me, Genny, admit it. Your nipples are hard even now."

Heat stung her cheeks. How could he say such a thing? "I-I don't deny I'm attracted to you, Jack."

"Attracted?" He took a step toward her, dragged her up from where she knelt on the blanket and straight into his arms. He kissed

187

her so thoroughly she dropped the plastic container holding the leftover cheese. Pressing her palms into his chest, she finally broke free, but her heart was pounding and her whole body shook with heat.

"Damn you, Jack Brennen," she said, and a heavy black eyebrow went up.

"So she does have a temper." His grin held no remorse. "I wondered about that."

"Well, you can just keep on wondering about the rest. It's time you took me home."

He stiffened and the smile slid from his face. "Whatever you want, Ms. Austin."

They rode down the hill in silence, but Genny sensed that Jack wasn't really mad. Disappointed maybe, but not angry. She liked that about him. He might be reckless, and volatile in a lot of ways, but he wasn't one to pout.

They reached the condo late in the afternoon, but Genny didn't ask him in. Jack seemed to know she wouldn't and perhaps he was even relieved. She didn't like to think about that.

"I had a great time today, Jack. I-I hope you know how much I appreciate your concern for me this morning."

For a moment his hard look softened. "My pleasure, Ms. Austin."

"I'd invite you in but . . ."

"I know — you're not ready for me to come in yet."

"Tired of waiting?"

"You can say that again." He ran a long dark

finger down her cheek and sweet fire rippled in her stomach. "But like I said, I've got a feeling you're worth it."

Jack leaned an arm on the doorframe. The angle was causing his muscles to bunch. God, he was so tall!

"I was thinking . . . as we rode home . . ." he said.

"Yes?"

"You told me once that you had never been out on a boat."

"No, I haven't." As much as she loved the ocean, in a way it seemed rather odd. Howard owned a boat, but he rarely used it, and they had only actually been dating for a couple of months. He and Bill had gone out, but Bill never enjoyed it, and until she met Jack, she had never really given it much thought.

"Tomorrow I've got a fishing charter, ten guys in town from the Newhall Elks Club. They're real nice fellas. I don't think they'd mind if you came along as part of the crew."

"Really?" Suddenly she wanted to go more than anything she could think of.

"Sure, if you want to."

"God, I'd love to."

"The boat leaves early. Around 5:00 A.M."

"I'll be there with bells on."

He gave her a lecherous grin. "If that's all you're wearing, that would suit me just fine."

Genny laughed. "No such luck, Casanova." But she went up on her toes to receive his good-bye kiss. Jack waved as he walked back toward his Harley.

"See you tomorrow," she called after him. Why did it always feel so good to know she'd be seeing him again? It was the last thing she should be feeling. In fact, she should be running for cover.

Then again she had never been much of an athlete.

And now that she'd decided to go, there was the matter of Howard McCormick. She would have to cancel her plans with him, her appearance at his family picnic at Tucker's Grove. She'd have to think of an excuse that wouldn't hurt his feelings and not be a bold-faced lie. Surely she could think of something.

She was going on Jack's boat, she vowed. Even the guilt she felt over breaking her date with Howard wasn't enough to keep her away. She was looking forward to it more than anything she had done in a very long time.

Genny didn't sleep well that night, but she didn't mind as much as she usually did. She spent the hours thinking of Jack, remembering their conversation about his family, his concern for her . . . remembering the way he had kissed her breasts.

She smiled into the darkness. Her body was flushed from head to foot, and damp heat throbbed between her legs. The way she felt, if she were still at the clinic, she would probably push those needles right off Wally's charts.

She did fall asleep for a while, and if she dreamed she didn't remember. She awoke when the alarm went off, and levered herself out of bed. She was tired, but excitement overrode her fatigue, and perhaps she could nap on the boat in the afternoon.

She dressed in her jeans, deck shoes, and a heavy cable-knit sweater, but took her tank top and a pair of shorts, in case it got warm later in the day. After a quick bowl of Raisin Bran, she headed out the door. Her body was energized with anticipation.

Ten

First light grayed the sky as Jack stepped out on the deck of the *Marauder.* Around him, gulls screeched and the smell of salt and sea hung heavy in the air.

He hadn't slept well last night, and his head pounded from the whiskey he had drunk at the Sea Breeze Bar. Vivian had been there and she'd been more than friendly. Too damned friendly.

He should have taken her home.

That he hadn't only made him feel worse. He knew the reason and it didn't set well with him. He should have screwed her and gotten little Genny Austin out of his system. What the hell was the matter with him?

Through the porthole, Charley held up a steaming mug of coffee. Jack waved at him and went back inside to join him. With only a muttered thanks, he took the mug and climbed the ladder leading to the wheelhouse. A few minutes later, he looked up from the charts on the navigation table and saw Genny approaching the dock. She was early. She still hadn't learned she was supposed to keep a man waiting. He smiled faintly and hoped that she never would.

" 'Mornin', Genny girl!" Charley called out, crossing the deck to help her aboard. The gray-haired man was grinning, obviously pleased that Jack had invited her along.

Jack had mixed emotions. Every time he was with her, his attachment seemed to grow. It was her sweetness, maybe, or just that she didn't play games. Hell, maybe it was just her ripe little body. He had no way of knowing for sure.

"It's good to see you, Charley," he heard her say with genuine warmth. Maybe that's what it was, that warmth that seemed so much a part of her.

Whatever it was, Charley must have felt it, too, for his smile broadened into a grin. "Jack's going over the nav charts. How 'bout a cup of coffee? You look like you could use one."

"Boy, could I."

"Get any sleep last night?" Charley asked.

"Not much. But to tell you the truth, I feel pretty good."

Another sleepless night, Jack thought, wondering how she stood it. He also wondered how she would sleep once he had taken her to bed.

That thought didn't last long. Not today. Workdays he was all business. The boat came first and the welfare of the men who had paid for its use. He went back to his final preparations, checking the gauges and mapping out their course. When he finished, half an hour later, he went down to the cabin and found Genny sitting in the galley, with Felix the cat purring softly in her lap.

"I should have known you'd like cats," he grumbled. The mangy yellow tabby rarely purred for him.

"I like most animals. I would have loved to have had a pet but Bill wasn't too keen on them."

Bill didn't seem keen on much of anything, Jack thought, but didn't say so.

"I'm really looking forward to this, Jack."

He only grunted. He wasn't much of a morning person and his head still hurt from his overindulgence last night. And he was chafing over his stupidity. Vivian Sandburg. And he had passed up taking her home.

"Thanks for asking me," Genny finished.

He glanced her way, saw those big brown eyes lit up with anticipation, saw the soft smile of gratitude that seemed to be reserved just for him. Why did she always make him feel like some damned hero? He was hardly that, and it galled him he should have to live up to that image.

"Just stay out from under foot once we make way," he growled, but his wet-blanket tone didn't dampen her spirits one bit.

A smile tugged at his lips. In a way he had to admire her. With the troubles she had, it was a wonder she ever found anything to be happy about.

"Where's Charley?" he asked, his voice a little less gruff.

"Your charter's arrived. Charley went to show them where to stow their gear."

A corner of his mouth curved up. Already catching onto the lingo. She had a damned quick mind . . . for a woman. "You want something to eat? There's a big box of doughnuts on the counter."

"I'm fine, thanks."

He left her there and went about his duties. He still had to rig the water to the portable bait tanks and make a last check of the engines. He wouldn't have much time for Genny, but right now she was too excited to care.

Somehow that didn't sit well with him either. He grumbled an oath but was soon swept up in his work. Only on occasion did his mind drift back to Genny Austin. When it did, he firmly shoved it away.

Genny watched Jack walk out of the galley and onto the deck. His long-legged stride looked confident and relaxed. He seemed different today, all business, every movement sure and purposeful.

It was a side of him she hadn't seen, a side she admired, and seeing it gave her a new respect for him. Then again, she was rapidly learning that first impressions of Jack Brennen were rarely what they seemed.

The cabin door opened and a group of men filed in, Charley Denton among them, and a younger man in a seaman's jacket who appeared to be one of the crew.

"This is Raymond," Charley said by way of

introduction. "He works for us whenever we need him."

"Nice to meet you," the young man said, dragging an upended sailor's hat off his head.

"It's nice to meet you, too." He looked to be in his early twenties, with big gray eyes, sandy brown hair, and a bit of an overbite.

Charley introduced her to the fishermen, repeating her first name and each of theirs, and they all smiled a greeting. They were dressed pretty much alike, in jeans and shirts and heavy woolen sweaters. Some wore short-brimmed canvas hats with fishing lures fastened around the crown. They ranged in age from thirty to fifty, from short and stout to tall and lean, from voguish rather-long hair to close-trimmed peppered with gray.

"Nice to meet you, ma'am," one of them said as he grabbed a doughnut and a Styrofoam cup filled with coffee and headed back out the door. The others quickly followed, and Charley motioned for her to come along, too.

A sunny, cloudless sky arched above their heads as she stepped out onto the deck, and a stiff breeze ruffled the light brown hair she'd pulled into a clip at the nape of her neck. She turned up the collar of her sweater and was suddenly glad she'd had the foresight to bring her blue nylon windbreaker along.

Jack and Raymond tossed off the heavy dock lines tying the boat to the wharf, then Jack climbed the ladder back up to the wheelhouse.

"Hang on, Genny," Charley said. "It'll take a few minutes for you to get your sea legs."

She gripped the rail and watched as Jack revved the two diesel engines, churning up oil-slick water, and the boat eased away from the dock. They chugged along slowly, passing several big fishing trawlers strung with heavy netting and row upon row of slips filled with power boats and small sailing vessels. Several people came out onto their decks as the *Marauder* cruised past. Some of them waved at Jack and he smiled and waved back.

"There's a five-mile-an-hour speed limit inside the buoys," Charley told her. "Once we're out in the open, we'll travel at ten to twelve knots — that's about twelve to fourteen miles an hour."

It wasn't long before they passed the last buoy. The bell inside clanged against the heavy metal. A big gray pelican perched on the top. Rounding the sandy point where the sea wall ended, they slid quietly through the channel between it and the pier.

The open sea lay ahead. She could just make out the hazy hump-back shadow of the Channel Islands in the distance. Beneath her, the deck of the boat began to gently tilt and sway. The big boat pressed forward, throwing a wide-spreading wake and bobbing from side to side in a manner she hadn't expected. Genny had to grip the rail to keep from losing her balance.

"Where are we headed?" she asked Charley, ignoring the dip her stomach had taken along with the rolling motion of the boat.

"Up north a ways. Supposed to be a place west of the kelp beds that'll bring us some decent fishin'."

Genny nodded, but suddenly found it hard to concentrate on what Charley was saying. With every dip and sway of the boat, her stomach rolled in a similar motion.

"I gotta go help the men get their fishing gear ready. You be all right?"

"Of course." But she was beginning to have her doubts. It had never occurred to her that she might get seasick. Not on a day like this. Not on a boat this big. She had never had any trouble flying, or in a car on a curvy road. Jack had never mentioned it and neither had Charley. God in heaven, she prayed her queasy stomach would settle down and she'd be okay.

But two hours later she wasn't okay. The boat had slowed near the kelp beds as Charley had said, but continued very slowly to pitch and roll. The bow dipped into a trough and the stern followed. The boat seemed to wallow from side to side. When Charley opened the below-deck tank and the first of the fish the men caught began to come in, Genny made her way to the rear of the boat and quietly threw up over the side.

She hoped that she would feel better. Instead she felt worse. She threw up the cereal she'd eaten that morning and everything else in her stomach. She threw up until her legs felt so weak she could hardly stand up, until she clung to the rail with her head hanging over the side, sure the next wave would wash her overboard. And almost wishing it would.

"There you are. Charley and I have been looking all over. For God's sake, Genny, where the hell have you been?" One look at her gray-green face and Jack had his answer. "Christ, I should have known."

She knew what that meant. She had failed the boat test, just as she'd failed at shooting pool. Only this test was far more important. "I'm sorry," she said between agonizing waves of nausea and painful stomach cramps. "It never occurred to me . . ."

"Jesus, it isn't even stormy."

Genny glanced away from him, fighting an urge to cry. She'd wanted to do this so badly. For the first few minutes, she had enjoyed herself as she never had before.

"I can't take you back," Jack said. "Not until the end of the day. Can you make it down to my cabin?"

"I didn't ask you to take me back," Genny snapped with a sudden show of spirit. It was quelled on the next wave, when she bent and dry-heaved over the side. Jack left her a moment, then returned with a small wet rag.

"Here. Wash your face and you'll feel better." She did and he helped her inside.

Unfortunately, she felt even worse in the close confining quarters of his cabin. Jack opened several portholes, letting in the freshening breeze as she lay down on his bunk. When he placed an empty wastebasket next to her, her cheeks went from ashen to rosy.

"I'm sorry, Jack, I really am."

"It's all right. I suppose I should have thought of it. It was just such a perfect day . . ." The rest went unspoken, but the accusing look in his eyes said more than enough.

She hardly remembered the rest of the day, just that it seemed endless. Charley came in several times to check on her, but Jack didn't come back again. Perhaps he didn't want to embarrass her. She hoped that was it, but she didn't really think so.

She slept for a while, out of weakness, she figured, and because she was so tired from the night before. She awoke and threw up some more. By the time they headed in, a little bit early, she was sure, she was barely able to lift her head. Her limbs felt shaky and her skin was so pale she could see the tiny blue veins beneath it.

She must have dozed off again. The opening of the door awoke her sometime later and Jack walked in.

"We're back in the harbor," he said. "We'll be docking in just a few minutes." Not a muscle moved in his face. His expression remained inscrutable, his eyes vague and distant as he ducked back out the door.

Genny got up from the bed. On unsteady legs, she made it into the bathroom — *head,* she corrected. She washed her face, rinsed out her mouth, sponged her neck and throat, then returned to the cabin to pick up the trash can she had been forced to use. There wasn't much in it, since her stomach was already empty, but she'd be damned if she'd let Jack Brennen clean up after her.

Nausea rolled through her as she dumped it in the toilet, flushing it as Charley had shown her. This time she was able to control it. She felt a little better by the time she finished rinsing it clean and putting it away. After smoothing the wrinkles from the top of Jack's bed, she made her way upstairs, stepping into the main salon just as he backed the big boat alongside the dock. She grabbed her jacket and the small canvas bag that held the extra clothes she'd brought along, and made her way out onto the deck.

"How you feelin'?" Charley asked.

She smiled wanly. "Better."

"Don't worry yourself about it. We've all been sick a time or two."

"Sure, Charley, especially Jack." She pushed her way through the men collecting their gear, receiving sympathetic words and glances, but none of the others had gotten the least bit seasick. "Tell Jack I'm sorry for the way things turned out," she said to Charley as she stepped off the boat onto the dock. "Tell him I know what he's thinking and he's right. Tell him it's okay."

Charley looked disgruntled. "He'll want to take you home. You know how he is."

"Not this time, Charley. The walk will do me good." If her shaky legs continued to hold her up. She didn't give him time to argue, just turned and walked away.

By the time Jack finished docking the boat and went in search of her, she was already halfway home. He caught up with her as she neared the condo. He followed wordlessly along at her side. When they reached her door, he took the key from her unsteady hand and opened the lock.

"Soda crackers are good. Maybe a little bit of broth."

Genny just nodded.

"I'll stop by after work tomorrow, see how you are."

"That isn't necessary, Jack."

"I know." He didn't say anything more, just handed her the key and turned to leave. Genny refused to watch him walk away. Instead she closed the door and wearily climbed the stairs. She wouldn't think of Jack and what had happened aboard his boat. She had never been so embarrassed.

She had never been so relieved to reach the peace and quiet of her home.

Unfortunately, that night Genny dreamed.

She was so exhausted and weak from her bout of seasickness, she sank into the nightmare deeper than she might have. Mired in the grisly scene, she couldn't escape it, couldn't fight it. Couldn't run.

Corpses. Three in a row, their bodies stretched out on the thick green grass. Palm fronds waved above the withered limbs, and leafy ferns whispered against the soles of their bare feet. Mostly she saw their faces — pale slumberous faces whose jaws had been tied shut. Small tufts of cotton protruded from their nostrils, a thick wad bulged from between their thin dry lips. Though their eyes were closed, they seemed to be watching her, accusing her. Their shrunken sockets were denouncing her even in death.

She stared at the wrinkled lips locked in a silent scream, at the hollows between the stringy cords straining at the bases of their throats, and her own throat closed up. She tried to swallow but couldn't. Her muscles had tightened and her mouth felt clogged with the same wad of cotton that protruded from the mouths of the dead bodies.

Then the corpses began to move. Brittle arms and limbs rose up. Each movement was rigid and jerky. They seemed like puppets on the end of strings. Stiffly they came to their feet and started walking toward her, a macabre sight that could only be envisioned by Satan. On the ground in front of them, she noticed signs that had been scratched into the dirt. An intricate five-pointed star and an odd assortment of symbols: crisscrossed circles, geometric figures, and a number of wiggly lines that seemed to mean nothing at all.

Candles smelling of whale fat scorched her nostrils and her swollen throat went tighter. As the corpses drew near, she tried to run, but her limbs were as rigid as those of the dead men. She fought to drag in air, but her nose and mouth felt blocked.

Her fingers frantically clutched her throat. She was suffocating, gasping for breath, yet none would come. She felt as if she were buried beneath a thousand tons of earth. As if she had taken the place of the corpses. A terrifying scream erupted from deep down inside her, then another and another, until her breath came out in one, long, shattering cry of terror.

Genny jerked up from the bed, drenched in sweat, gripping her throat. The last of her scream was still vibrating through the room. Trembling all over, she sat there gasping, dragging in great gulps of air. Through the partially open window, she heard someone calling, then pounding on the front door below.

"Genny — it's Pauline!" The urgent voice of her next door neighbor. "Genny! Are you all right?"

No! she wanted to shout. *I'm not all right!* Instead she forced her legs to the floor and grabbed her robe off the end of the bed with a hand that shook so badly she almost dropped the robe. Her throat still felt tight, her lungs still too empty. She gripped the handrail and made her way downstairs on legs barely holding her up, then unfastened the chain and opened the door.

Pauline Phillips, the middle-aged woman who lived in the condo next door stood on the porch in her robe and slippers. "For heaven's sakes, Genny — are you all right?"

The *no* still hovered on her lips. She wasn't sure she would ever be all right again. Instead she shoved back her sleep-tangled hair and leaned against the door frame.

"I'm all right, Pauline."

"Another bad dream?"

"Yes." The first time something like this had happened, she'd been forced to explain to her neighbor. Tonight she was glad. She knew she wouldn't have had the strength. "I'm sorry I disturbed you."

"It's all right, dear. Good heavens, it isn't your fault this keeps happening."

But maybe it was. Maybe in some way she didn't understand, she was the one who was ultimately responsible. "I'll be all right now. Thank you, Pauline."

"Is there anything I can do?"

She only shook her head. Pauline gave her a pitying glance and stepped down off the porch. "Good night, dear."

Genny nodded miserably and quietly closed the door. She felt exhausted and sad. Always so unbearably sad. She didn't understand it. None of it. It was slowly grinding her down.

Taking a deep calming breath, she crossed the room to the television set, flipped it on, turned the volume down low, and sank down heavily on the sofa. She didn't want to think about the dream; she could hardly bear to remember, and yet . . .

Shoving to her feet once more, she resolutely went into the kitchen. Taking a yellow legal pad from the drawer beside the phone and picking up a blue ball-point pen, she returned to her place on the sofa.

Recalling her nightmares was the last thing she wanted. She had done so in the beginning, as Doctor Halpern suggested, but the images were so indistinct it hadn't done her much good. Now something told her if she was ever going to escape them, remembering them was exactly what she must do.

Starting with the dreams after her attack on the beach, the first that actually seemed to have meaning, she began to write them down, using as much detail as she could dredge up. It was amazing how well she could recall them.

Then again it wasn't.

Every horrifying detail seemed burned into her brain.

Genny went to work that day exhausted. Still, by noon she had somewhat revived herself, and with the help of a tuna on wheat and a big Diet

Coke she felt able to make it through the day. She refused to dwell on her terrifying night-mare and the even more frightening choking and suffocating sensations that went along with it.

On Tuesday, she would see Dr. Halpern. She would discuss the dream then.

She also ignored thoughts of the day she'd spent with Jack, or at least the day she had spent throwing up on his boat. She did, how-ever, wonder if he would show up that night, as he had said. Somehow she didn't think so.

About that, she guessed wrong. At exactly six-thirty, Jack crossed the street in front of her condo. His long-legged gait carried him swiftly along the sidewalk, up the stairs, and onto her porch. He knocked on her door in that brusque, demanding way of his, and Genny hurried to open it.

"Hello, Jack." Her heart lurched at the sight of him.

"Hello, Genny." Though he stepped inside, he declined a seat on the sofa and remained standing, which gave her a pretty clear idea of why he had come. "You seem surprised to see me." A subtle tension burned beneath his calm surface.

"I am."

"I told you I'd come."

Genny didn't answer.

"How are you feeling?" His clothes still car-ried the salt tang of the sea. A button was undone on his shirt, giving her a glimpse of smooth dark skin.

She tried not to notice, to keep her manner as formal as his. "I'm not seasick anymore, if that's what you mean." She wasn't about to lie to him, tell him she felt great. After last night, she felt awful.

"Listen, Genny, I've done some hard thinking since yesterday . . . about what happened, I mean. It was my fault you got sick. I shouldn't have taken you out there in the first place. I should have known you weren't cut out for —"

"It wasn't your fault, Jack. I wanted to go. If I hadn't gotten seasick, I really would have enjoyed it."

Jack raked a hand through his shiny jet black hair. The damp air made it curl against his collar. "You're a good sport, Genny. And I like you — you know I do, but the truth is we're just too damned different." That was a fact. Yesterday had brought it home with a vengeance. "This thing between us — it's never going to work out. You know as well as I do that we haven't got a single thing in common. You're no good at what I do — I'm no good at what you do."

"I know that, Jack. I'm not a fool."

His hands came up to her shoulders. "No, you're not. You're a beautiful woman. You're sweet and loving — you've got a lot to offer a man."

"Any man but you," Genny said, hoping he

wouldn't read her disappointment.

"That's right, any man but me. You know it, and so do I."

She turned away from him, wishing she wasn't feeling the sharp pain stabbing into her chest. How could he make her feel so bad when she knew what he was saying was the truth?

"You've got a whole lot going for you, Genny." He gently turned her toward him. "You've got brains and class." Her eyes lifted up to his face. "You're a sexy, passionate lady — and I want you. I have since the first time I saw you. I think you want me, too."

Clamping down hard on her emotions, Genny glanced away. "Please don't, Jack."

"Why not? It's nothing to be ashamed of. What we feel for each other, it's real, even if it's only a physical attraction. It's there inside of us, on your part, just as much as mine."

He was right. Even if she wouldn't admit it. "It doesn't matter, Jack. There has to be more to it than sex."

"Why? Lots of people have purely sexual relationships."

Genny said nothing. She could still feel the heat of his hands on her shoulders, though he had already released her.

"I want to make love to you, Genny. If that's all there is between us, why shouldn't we take advantage of it? Let me make love to you, and maybe as time goes on, we can both let this thing go."

Genny just looked at him. A lock of his thick black hair hung over his forehead. She wanted to reach out and tuck it back into place. She wanted him to hold her, to kiss her, to touch her the way he had that day by the river. She wanted what he was offering, she realized. Wanted it so badly she hurt.

"I can't, Jack."

"Don't tell me it hasn't crossed your mind. If you say it, I won't believe you."

It had. She couldn't deny it. She looked at Jack, thought of his kiss, and a tremor of desire rippled through her. She had to admit there was a certain wild logic to what he was saying, the gritty sort only a man like Jack could unearth. Perhaps he was right. Maybe if she went to bed with him, the fascination he held would disappear. Maybe she would forget him and get her life back to normal.

Still, she had never done anything remotely like what Jack was proposing. She didn't really know the rules. "W-What about AIDS?"

A corner of his mouth curved up. "I'll be wearing a raincoat. There's nothing to be afraid of. Believe me, Genny, I know all about safe sex."

For several reckless moments, she actually considered saying yes. She could still remember the way she had felt down by the river, the warmth of his mouth, the thrill of his hands on her breasts. How would it be to lie with him naked, to feel his hard male length deep inside her? She wanted that. Now she knew for certain just how much.

"I won't deny it sounds appealing. I'd be lying if I did." And yet it could not be. In a clash of wills with her body, her mind had begun to function, to reason things out, logically and sensibly, to stir up all her fears. The urge to cry became almost unbearable. "But I just can't do it. As much as I might want to, making love under those conditions isn't something I can live with. I can't do it, Jack. I just can't."

Several different emotions flickered across his dark-tanned face. Disappointment, chagrin, perhaps a hint of admiration.

"I'm sorry, Jack. I wish it could be different."

His hand came up to her cheek. He toyed with a strand of her nut brown hair. "So do I, Genny. You'll never know how much." He bent his head and brushed her lips with a feather-soft kiss. "But I understand why you can't. In some crazy way, I'm glad you're that kind of person."

"Jack, I —" He pressed a finger gently against her lips.

"Take care of yourself, pretty lady."

She nodded, fighting hard to hold back the tears. "I'll do my best."

Jack frowned at her words, taking in the signs of her fatigue for the first time since his arrival. He studied her face a moment, noting the purple smudges beneath her eyes, the paleness of her skin, then he turned and crossed to the door. When he stepped out onto the porch, he paused.

"Charley will be wondering how you are. He's a good friend, Genny. He'll be there if you need him."

She nodded. But it wasn't Charley she needed, it was Jack. Why, she didn't know, only that it was the truth. The thought of never seeing him again turned her insides cold with dread, and a lump rose up in her throat.

"Good-bye . . . Jack."

"Good-bye, Genny." He stepped off the porch without a glance back and purposefully walked away. Genny closed the door, went into the living room, and sank down on the sofa. Exhaustion crashed in on her, dragging her down like a heavy iron weight, and with it another, deeper emotion she couldn't quite name. It made her heart hurt, it made her feel desolate and more lonely than she had ever been before. Not even Bill's death had left her feeling this way.

Jack Brennen was gone. It was the best thing for both of them. Jack knew it and so did she.

So why did it hurt so much?

Jack left the condo, feeling a lead weight in his stomach. After yesterday, he'd been convinced this was the right thing to do. He and Genny were oil and water; they were never going to mix.

And God knew, he didn't really want them to. He had no interest in a serious relationship. He was out for sex and a good time, that was all. So why did he feel so rotten? Why was it he could still see the pain in Genny's eyes when he had walked out the door?

And why did he want her so damned badly?

He had other women, at least half a dozen who would come at his beck and call. Even Vivian, if that was what he wanted.

The truth was, he wanted Genny. He had hoped she might agree to a strictly physical relationship. He could have handled that, accepted it for what it was. But in his heart he never believed she would agree.

There was a decency in Genny that gave her a certain strength, the kind of morality you could count on and respect, the kind that most men craved these days and rarely found anymore. A secret part of him was glad she hadn't agreed, just as he had said.

Another part thought he must be crazy. That he should have carried her upstairs and kissed her soft mouth and beautiful breasts until she begged him to take her to bed. He could have done it, he believed, he'd nearly had her that day by the river. But he couldn't imagine hurting her the way he now knew for certain that it would.

And she had more than enough trouble already. He could see the tiredness in her eyes, the toll her sleepless nights were taking. He prayed she'd find some way to stop her terrible dreams.

Striding along the dock, Jack stepped off the planking and onto the deck of the *Marauder*. Charley walked up to join him.

"How's she doin'?" he asked.

"She's feeling okay, but I don't think she's getting much rest. Maybe you could talk to her again sometime, see if there's anything you could do to help."

Charley nodded. "I guess that means you won't be seein' her again."

"She's better off, Charley. We both are. You know it and so do I."

"Whatever you say, son." But it was obvious Charley disagreed.

Jack ignored the knot balling hard in his stomach. For once Charley Denton was wrong. Genny Austin was gone from his life and things could return to normal. What he needed now was a woman, a sexy little number who could ease the ache in his jeans. After that he needed a solution to his money problems.

He knew exactly where to find a lady. He wished to hell he knew where to find the money to save the *Marauder*.

Eleven

Genny dressed for work on Tuesday morning, choosing a double-breasted gray worsted suit and a gray and burgundy striped silk blouse, but her mind raced ahead to her 5:15 appointment with Dr. Halpern. She usually felt a little better when she left there. She hoped today would be the same.

"Well . . . how was the ride?" A little after 9:00 A.M. Millicent Winslow stood in front of Genny's desk, holding a stack of books to her nearly flat chest, with a pale blond eyebrow arched in anticipation. Having taken an extra day off to attend her cousin's wedding, she hadn't seen Genny since last week.

"Which ride?" Genny asked. "The motorcycle or the boat?" She pulled her tortoise-shell half-glasses off her nose and rested them on top of the paperwork on her desk.

"He took you out on his salvage boat?"

Genny nodded. "Where I immediately proceeded to throw up."

Millie groaned. "You didn't."

"I did."

"Well . . . I guess if it only happened once —"

"No such luck. I managed to stay sick all day.

If you're going to do something, I always say, don't just do it halfway."

"I'm afraid to ask about the ride on his Harley."

If she hadn't been so tired, Genny might have smiled. "Surprisingly, that went fairly well. I have to admit, I actually enjoyed myself."

Millie broke into a grin. "So when are you seeing him again?"

Genny sighed. "I'm not. We're through, Millie. Jack and I decided to call the whole thing off."

"Are you crazy? You called the whole thing off — *before* you went to bed with him?"

"Millie, we are definitely not compatible. Now that I know that for certain, I can't just hop in the sack with him. There has to be more going on than just sex."

"Why?"

"Dammit, Millie, you make it sound like I'm some kind of prude. I don't think I am. And I don't think, under the same set of circumstances, you're the kind of girl who'd climb in bed with him, either."

Millie smiled somewhat forlornly. "Probably not. Actually, I was hoping to enjoy all this vicariously through you."

Instead of laughing, Genny frowned. "I see. You want me to wind up with a broken heart. Somehow that doesn't seem fair."

Millie leaned closer. Her deep-set eyes looked like big blue pools. "You like him that much?"

Genny sighed. "I've tried very hard not to, but . . . yes, I guess I do."

"Which is why you aren't seeing him anymore."

"Yes."

Millie threw up her hands and rolled her big blue eyes. "Maybe that makes perfect sense to you, but it sure sounds crazy to me."

"It wouldn't if you knew Jack. Look, Millie —" The phone rang just then, cutting off the last of Genny's reply. It was a call from the Lompoc Library wanting her to round up some historical information on early Santa Barbara for the city's upcoming Founder's Day celebration.

"I'll take care of it right away," Genny said into the receiver.

"I've got to go," Millie mouthed as she headed for the door, and Genny waved her away. She sighed as she hung up the phone. Maybe she should have gone to bed with Jack. No doubt, for the rest of her life, she would wonder what it would have been like. Well, it was too late now, and the truth was she had done the right thing.

She rubbed the back of her neck, tired though the day was still early. She hadn't slept well in over a week, and last night was no improvement. Still, she had a lot of work to do: correspondence to catch up on, books to catalog, and now working on this Lompoc Founder's Day project. Eventually, she would hand it over to Millie, since she was the reference librarian, but there were a few things she

217

wanted to see to first.

Shoving her fatigue aside, she struggled through the morning and afternoon, grateful for the brisk cup of tea Millie thoughtfully brought to her desk around three. A little after five, she picked up her gray wool coat, left the library, and headed for her appointment with Dr. Halpern.

By the time she reached the doctor's office, her nerves had reappeared. She wasn't looking forward to today's discussion, but she was determined to persevere. Taking her usual place on the doctor's cream sofa, Genny waited while the blond woman sat down on the opposite side of the chrome and glass coffee table. They exchanged pleasantries. Genny asked Dr. Halpern about her sister's new baby. The doctor was concerned about Genny's lack of sleep.

Then began the usual round of questions, and Genny launched into a discussion of her dreams.

Since it had been some time since they had spoken, she began with the dream about the spiders and the young native girl who had been locked in the shed. In the same objective voice, she relayed the awful dream about the corpses. She told the doctor about the symbols scratched in the dirt and how the dead bodies had threateningly approached her. She ended by describing the physical effects of the dream: the choking, suffocating sensations she had experienced.

When she was finished, she glanced over at the attractive blond woman sitting across from her, and found she had written only a few lines on her pad.

"Dr. Halpern? Is something the matter?"

The doctor's smile looked forced. "I'm concerned, Genny, that's all. This is extremely far afield from the ground we've been covering for the past two years. So much so, I can't help but wonder what we might have missed in our preliminary discussions."

"Which discussions are you referring to, Doctor?"

"I'm talking about your childhood, Genny. In cases like these . . . the answers to one's problem are very often found there."

"In my circumstance, I can't imagine there could be any connection. I told you, I had a very pleasant childhood."

"Yes . . . well, sometimes things that may seem trivial now are actually very important. Or there may be things we don't even recall. Some are so unpleasant we repress them."

"What sort of things?" Genny asked cautiously.

"Rape, for instance. Incest."

"Incest? You're not suggesting that someone in my family . . . that I was brutalized somehow and don't remember?"

"It's possible, Genny. I certainly think we should explore those avenues."

Genny straightened on the sofa, her fingers

biting into the butter-soft leather. "Well, I don't. I remember my childhood quite clearly. I have no memory lapses. I don't have secret fears I'm afraid to discuss. I recall my early years extremely well, and I can't remember a single incident that might account for what you're suggesting."

"All right, then, for the time being, let's put that possibility away and explore another avenue."

Genny remained tense. She didn't like the direction this was taking.

"Let's talk about the symbols you discussed." She glanced down at her notepad, to the few lines she had written. "The star you described — 'formed like an A with the cross bar extended. If you connected all the lines, you'd have that kind of star.' "

"That's right."

"There's a similar star used in the practice of witchcraft. Are you aware of that, Genny?"

She shifted nervously and brushed a piece of lint from the skirt of her gray wool suit. "I-I hadn't really thought about it."

"I don't mean to frighten you, but several of my colleagues have reported working with patients — extremely young children, mostly — who began to recall incidents in their early years involving witchcraft and ritual abuse. The ceremonies they described were violent and extremely bloody. Animals were often sacrificed, perhaps even other small children. These patients were sexually abused and even tortured. Your dreams, Genny, seem to have a great deal in common with what those children reported."

Genny wet her suddenly dry lips.

"And there are the sexual overtones we've discussed — the sado-masochistic episodes with the native girl. Combined with the rituals you described, you'll have to admit it's something to think about."

"If you're back to telling me something like that happened to me in my childhood, you can forget it, Dr. Halpern. I've also read accounts of the incidents you describe — they've been published in a dozen different articles across the country. The most recent accounts say those children may have been accidentally programmed by their psychologists, that their memories of those bloody rituals may actually be false — that they never really occurred."

"There has been that speculation, yes."

"And the rape you talked about . . . the incest people don't recall, then years later suddenly remember. Doctors are beginning to discount that — they're saying, the truth is, it never really happened."

"Genny —"

"I can tell you, Dr. Halpern, neither of those things happened to me, and convincing me they did isn't going to help me. The answer lies someplace else — I know it. I was hoping you could help me discover where it is."

"That's exactly what I'm going to do, Genny.

Perhaps if we tried hypnosis —"

"No!" she snapped a little too quickly. She had always been fearful of any sort of mind control. "You know how I feel about that. You said you didn't like to work with hypnosis, that you rarely ever suggested it."

"In this instance, it might be a viable alternative."

"No. I'm not willing to submit myself to something like that — especially not after the kind of things we've been discussing."

"That isn't a problem, Genny. We don't have to do anything you don't want to. Now, I want you to calm down."

Genny took a long deep breath, willing herself back under control. "I'm sorry. It's just that I find this extremely upsetting." She came to her feet in front of the sofa, then began to pace up and down. "The truth is, I think I need a break from our routine. You and I have worked together for a long time, but right now this just doesn't feel like it's working. I think what I need is some time to sort things through myself."

The doctor stood up, too. Not a wrinkle had formed in her immaculate dark green Chanel suit. "I don't think that's a good idea, Genny. Obviously something very serious is going on. You need my help now more than ever."

She forced herself to smile, but it took a tremendous effort. "If I do, I'll call you." She extended her hand and hoped the doctor wouldn't notice it was shaking. "I really appreciate all you've done for me, Dr. Halpern, but I think it's time I tried something else."

"What exactly do you have in mind?"

"I don't know, but I'm going to find out." She left the office totally depressed and at the same time totally determined. Francine Halpern had helped her to a point. Now it was time to look for answers in a different direction.

She didn't believe for a moment she had suffered some strange fate in her childhood. As Jack had said, the dreams weren't real, she had to remember that. Still, she had to discover why she kept having them.

Genny's hand tightened on her keys as she slid into the seat of her Toyota. She wished she had someone to talk to, but wasn't sure whom she should call. Her parents were supportive, but they would be frantic with worry and she didn't want that. Dottie would contribute in any way she could. Millicent was always helpful. Maybe Howard would have a suggestion. She thought of Charley Denton, but she couldn't go to Charley without seeing Jack and she wasn't about to do that.

That thought made her chest go tight. It was silly to miss a man she hardly knew, but the fact was she did.

As the days wore on and then the week, she wondered what he was doing, and how he was spending his time. She wondered who he was sleeping with, but that thought made her feel even worse. Instead of forgetting him, every day she seemed to miss him more. It was insane, but she couldn't stop thinking about him.

She wondered if Jack ever thought about her.

"What is it, Win?" Howard looked back toward the door of his office, irritated at being disturbed.

"Eduardo Fuentes is on the phone, Mr. McCormick. He's been trying to reach you all morning." Winifred Daniels had been Howard's personal secretary for over six years. She was attractive, with slender build and dark auburn hair. She was efficient and loyal, perhaps more faithful to him than even to her husband of fourteen years. It was what he liked best about her.

Howard walked behind his desk and laid down the stack of files he had just come in with. He'd been in meetings all morning; now his polished mahogany desk sat several inches deep in messages he had no time to return.

"Fuentes, you say? Go ahead and put him through." He sat down in his black leather executive chair and pressed the button on the speaker-phone while Win backed out and quietly closed the twelve-foot mahogany door. It matched the interior paneling and of course his expensive custom-built desk. He was proud of the changes he had made in the last two years.

He was also proud of the way things were

running. He didn't like problems.

"What is it, Eduardo? I thought everything was progressing right on schedule."

"On our end, it is, Señor McCormick. The chips are off the production line. They will be ready for shipment exactly as planned."

"Then why the devil are you calling?"

"It is Macklin Shipping, Señor McCormick. The bulk of the cargo they are scheduled to carry is a shipment of copper wire made of ore from the mines at Guanajuato, but Captain Macklin has been offered a bonus if he will wait a couple more days for a load of silver ingots to come in. If he does that, we will not make our scheduled departure."

"That bastard. I told him I needed those chips by the end of the month at the latest. That was part of the deal and he knows it."

"I think if you press him, he will do as he has promised, but I am afraid he will not listen to me."

"I'll press him, all right. That son of a bitch knows better than to screw with me. He had better not even think about it."

He could almost see Fuentes's dark-skinned face smiling into the phone. "*Muy bien,* Señor McCormick. I knew you would know best how to handle the problem."

Howard flipped the button on the speaker, ending the conversation, and dragged his stack of messages across the green leather-trimmed writing pad on the mirror-smooth surface of his desk. Then he reached for his Rolodex to look up the number of the marine operator who could reach Captain Macklin on board his ship.

Bob Macklin made plenty off the shipments coming into McCormick-Austin from Mexico — and he pocketed the money tax-free. Howard had known Mackiln since their days in the Merchant Marine. He was a greedy bastard, but he wasn't about to jeopardize the sweet setup the two of them had for an occasional piece of extra change.

One phone call and Macklin would do exactly as he had agreed. If he knew what was good for him.

Howard needed those parts and he needed them badly. And no later than the twenty-eighth, as had been agreed. There were a dozen waiting contracts to be filled, hundreds of thousands of dollars at stake.

Macklin had better perform, and the sooner he knew what would happen if he didn't, the better off both of them would be.

At the sound of the doorbell, Dottie Marshall ran her hands down the front of the ruffled pink apron she wore over her jeans, dusting off a coating of flour. She crossed the living room of her small second-floor apartment, and opened the door.

"Hi, girlfriend," she said with a smile as she motioned Genny in. "I hope you're hungry. I'm

fixing Southern fried chicken, mashed potatoes, and —" She broke off at the dismal look
on Genny's face. "I hate to say it, girl, but you
aren't lookin' so good."

It was only six-thirty. Genny had called yesterday afternoon and they had talked for a
while. Dottie had invited her over for an early
supper, since her daughter, Tammy, was re-
hearsing for a part in the high school play, and
Dottie didn't go to work at Bob's Big Boy until
ten.

"I thought I was getting better," Genny said.
"I felt pretty good yesterday. Today I feel like
shit."

One red eyebrow arched up. She had never
heard Genny swear. "How about a glass of
wine? That always makes me feel better."

"Why not?" Genny sank down on the sofa. It
was old but comfortable. With the autumn-
colored floral throw and matching pillows
Genny had helped her sew last spring, it actually looked kind of pretty. At least it didn't
clash anymore with the old brown shag carpet
on the floor or the olive green appliances in the
kitchen.

Dottie handed her a glass of E and J Chablis
and sat down in the beige recliner across from
where Genny sat on the sofa. "Another bad
night, I take it."

"I didn't get much sleep, if that's what you
mean, but this time my nightmares weren't the
problem."

Dottie studied her friend over the top of her wineglass, noting the circles beneath Genny's eyes that were clearly fatigue. But that didn't explain why she nervously chewed her lip, or why her eyes kept darting out the window.

"Lord, honey, I see man trouble written all over your forehead."

Genny's troubled eyes swung to her face. "I miss him, Dottie. I can't get him out of my mind."

Dottie sighed. "Some men are like that, honey — especially the tall, dark, handsome ones — believe me I know. When Jessie left me, I wanted to curl up and die."

That seemed to spark some life. "Well, you didn't. You got over him. And look what a good job you've done raising Tammy — and you did it all by yourself."

Dottie took a sip of her wine. "I'll let you in on a little secret, Genny. I never did get over him. I probably never will." She smiled, but it took more effort than it should have. "You just be glad you got out before the hurt got too bad."

Genny said nothing. She leaned back against the sofa, her soft brown hair fanning out around her cheeks. Dottie noticed it was growing longer, making her look even more feminine. She was a sweet girl, kind and compassionate to others, as good a person as they came. It didn't seem right she should have so damned many problems. She reached down and clasped her friend's hand. "I want you to promise me something."

"What's that?"

"I want your word you'll forget about Jack Brennen and get yourself a decent man."

Genny smiled forlornly. She was thinking that Jack *was* decent. A little too wild, perhaps, a little too reckless. He was nothing like her, but he was still a good man. He just didn't seem to know it.

"I'll try, Dottie." But she was also thinking Jack Brennen was a hard man to forget.

For the fourth time Sunday night, Jack lifted the receiver off the pay phone in the Sea Breeze Bar. This time he dropped in a quarter, then listened as the money clanged into the receptacle and he got a dial tone.

He looked down at his little blue address book, mashed and bent in the shape of the wallet he carried in his hip pocket, and thumbed through the pages. Finding the number he wanted, he dialed Genny Austin's condo, heard the phone begin to ring, then wondered if she would be home.

Half of him prayed she wouldn't be. Maybe in another couple of days this crazy fever would pass. Maybe he would be able to forget her. Maybe . . . but tonight his need for her seemed almost unbearable.

Three rings, four, then five. Jack's fingers tightened on the receiver till he heard her soft hello. He imagined her pretty face as she answered the phone, imagined her warm brown eyes and soft pink lips, and a tightness expanded in his chest.

"Genny? This is Jack."

There was a long, uncertain pause. "Jack?"

His mouth felt dry. He wet his lips. "I just called to see how you were."

"I'm fine, Jack . . . how about you?"

Not so fine. He wanted to see her. He'd been that way ever since the night they had parted. He couldn't seem to get her off his mind. "All right, I guess. Listen, I was just wondering . . . it's early yet. I thought maybe you hadn't eaten. I thought maybe . . . if I came over . . . we might grab a pizza and some beer."

Another long pause. It made his stomach clench.

"But I thought . . . I thought . . ."

"No strings, Genny, I promise. Just some pizza and a glass of beer. Maybe a little conversation. How about it?"

Her answer was so soft he missed it. He pressed his ear against the phone. "I'm sorry, Genny, it's kind of noisy in here. What did you say?" His knuckles looked pale where he gripped the receiver.

"I said, I'd like that, Jack."

Relief swept over. "Good. Great. I'll be there in about ten minutes."

He hung up the phone and leaned his forehead against it. Calling Genny was a crazy thing to do. Insane. He'd promised himself he'd call Vivian. Like he'd been meaning to do all week. Like he'd meant to do the night he had parted from Genny.

In the end, he had just gotten drunk.

He crossed the room to where Pixie Murphy — all six foot five of him — leaned against the bar. "You got any of those kittens of Cheesy's left?" The little gray cat in the alley behind the bar had delivered a litter several weeks ago. Pixie had been pawning them off on anyone he could think of who might be fool enough to take one.

Pixie grunted. "Yeah. The runt of the bunch is still out back. No one seems to want him."

"I'll take him."

"You? What about Felix? I thought you had enough of cats with him."

"This one's for a friend."

Pixie chuckled. "Couldn't happen to a nicer guy."

Lady, Jack silently corrected. He hoped Genny would want to keep the little pest and he wouldn't be stuck with a second cat. As Pixie said, Felix was more than enough.

"Here you go, Jack. I'll even throw in the litter box. Cheesy's bar trained — she always goes outside."

"Thanks, Pixie." Jack took the tiny gray kitten who rode in a shoe box on top of the litter box, complete with fresh litter, that Pixie handed over.

"You better put the lid on. I punched holes in the cardboard so the little guy could breathe."

Jack just nodded. He settled the lid on the shoe box and Pixie taped it shut, then he headed out to his car. Setting the litter box on the floor of the passenger side and the shoe box on the seat, he fired up the Mustang's big engine and rolled out of the parking lot. All he could think of was how much he wanted to see Genny. He prayed she'd be half as pleased to see him.

Twelve

Jack reached Genny's house at 7:20 and parked at his usual place on the street. When she heard his knock and opened the door, he strode in with his arms full, grateful for the distraction his odd load provided.

"Hello, Jack." He relaxed a little at the warmth in her expression. Genny glanced away a bit nervously, then back toward the boxes he carried. "What in the world . . . ?"

He couldn't help thinking how good she looked. He hadn't remembered her hair being such a golden shade of brown, or her eyes being quite so big.

"I brought you a present," he said, still a little uncertain. "Well, sort of a present . . . assuming you like it. If you don't you don't have to keep it."

"A present?" Genny stepped toward the boxes Jack set on the table. At the sound of a small muffled mew, she tore the tape off the shoe box and pulled off the lid to find the tiny gray kitten. "Oh, Jack, he's adorable." She lifted him up on her shoulder and the kitten sank its tiny claws into her thin beige sweater.

Genny laughed. "Oh, Jack, he's absolutely

darling. I've wanted a pet for years. Of course, I'll keep him . . . or is it a she?"

"It's a male."

"What's his name?"

"He doesn't have one yet, at least not that I know of."

"Well, we'll have to think of something before we get back."

She was dressed to go out, he saw, in beige wool slacks and a button-up-the-front turtleneck sweater. The clothes were simple, not the least revealing, yet looking at the way the knit clung to her breasts sent a jolt of heat straight into his loins.

"Jack, did you hear me?"

"I'm sorry, what were you saying?"

"How about Skeeter, since he's so small?"

He smiled. "Skeeter, it is." But all he could think of was how much he wanted to kiss her. It was crazy, the way he felt whenever she was near. "I hope you're hungry." He tried to keep his eyes on her face and not roaming hotly down her body.

"Starving. How about you?"

Yes, he wanted to say, but not for food. He nodded. "Pizza okay?"

"Sure."

"The top's down. You had better get your coat."

Genny went upstairs to collect her paisley scarf and a heavy wool coat. She paused at the top of the stairs to look down on Jack's dark head. She hoped he hadn't noticed how seeing him had affected her. Her insides felt fluttery, her hands were trembling, and her knees were shaking.

She was glad to escape upstairs for a moment to collect herself. She settled the scarf over her head and tied it beneath her chin. His top was down. Only Jack would drive around with the top down in rainy weather. Of course it wasn't really raining, just overcast and cold.

God, she was glad to see him. She shouldn't have let him come over, but she couldn't have said no if it had meant a month of dream-free sleep. She had thought of him endlessly, even last night when she had gone out with Howard. She still felt guilty about it, since he had spent a small fortune on an elegant dinner at the Four Seasons' Biltmore Hotel. But she couldn't get her mind off Jack, nor stop comparing the two.

Of course Howard had come out on top — at least when she looked at all the logical things a woman was supposed to. Like security, social position, reputation in the community, the fact that he would probably make a very good husband.

Jack won hands down in the illogical department. The crazy fun things she had done with him, his dark good looks and fabulous body, the overwhelming desire she felt for him. The extraordinary way she was drawn to him.

Carrying her coat draped over her arm, Genny descended the stairs to the entry.

"Ready?" Jack said.

"As soon as I fix Skeeter a place out in the kitchen." Taking the heating pad down from the cupboard, she turned it on low and covered it with a small soft blanket. She set out a bowl of canned milk and opened a small can of tuna. "Do you think he's old enough for regular food?"

"I think so. Pixie's been weaning the litter for the past two weeks."

Once the kitten was settled and she had put on her coat, Jack led her out to his car. The hand he settled at her waist felt oddly possessive. He let go to help her climb in, but once they had reached Rusty's Pizza up on the Mesa, the hand was firmly back in place as he guided her up to the door.

He stopped before he opened it. "I know I promised no strings and I intend to keep my word, but there's something I just have to do."

Leaning down, he kissed her, a soft gentle kiss that made the heat swirl low in her stomach. When he started to pull away, Genny cupped his face between her palms and drew him back for another soft kiss. She started to ease away, but Jack dragged her into his arms for a searing kiss that left both of them dizzy. They were shaking when he finally let her go.

"I missed you, Genny," he said gruffly.

"I missed you, too, Jack."

He gave her a brief warm hug, then pushed open the door, and they stepped into the noisy room. The walls were paneled with rough-cut planks and decorated with baseball pictures and driftwood. The tables were wood-look Formica. A group of Little Leaguers in miniature blue pin-striped uniforms fought over the video games.

Jack ordered a pizza and brought back an ice-cold pitcher of beer. As they sipped from frosty mugs and talked while they waited for their food to arrive, Jack seemed more nervous than she had ever seen him.

"So . . . how's work going?"

Genny smiled. "Until this afternoon, my boss has been gone out of town. That's always cause for celebration. Believe it or not, we actually get more done when she's not there."

Jack laughed. "I think I can relate to that. I never was too keen on authority figures."

"I can't imagine you were."

"My father was an accountant. He worked for a small firm in Apple Valley. That's what he wanted me to do."

"Your father wanted you to be an accountant?" It seemed incredible.

"Can you believe it? I don't think he ever had a clue what I was really like. I guess that's why we never got along."

Genny mulled that over. She took a sip of her beer. "What about your stepmother? What was she like?"

"She was a bona fide homebody. Cooking, cleaning, sewing . . . that kind of stuff. She worked around the house all day while my father played golf or went to Kiwanis meetings."

"Do you ever see her?"

"No." He reached over and squeezed her hand. "This isn't my favorite subject, Genny. Would you mind if we talked about something else?" His posture had subtly shifted, the muscles growing taut across his shoulders.

She remembered the losses he had suffered and squeezed his hand in return. "Any luck raising the money to pay off your boat?" she asked, and some of his tension seemed to ease.

Jack shook his head. "Not yet, but I did get a contract from the National Park Service to haul supplies once a week over to the islands."

Genny smiled. "That's great, Jack."

"Yeah, well, it's still not enough. I'm talking to Texaco now. They've been working with one of our competitors, a guy named Stan Louis. He owns Pacific Cargo, but it's a pretty small operation. I think Texaco's got more work than Stan can handle by himself. I'm just not sure they're willing to chance a long-term contract."

"At least it's a start in the right direction. Maybe something else will come up."

"Yeah, that's what Charley always says."

Their pizza came but Genny discovered she wasn't all that hungry. Jack must have felt the same, for more than half their pizza grew cold on the big tin plate.

"You can box it up and take it home," Genny

suggested. "Maybe Charley will eat it."

"Sure you don't want it?"

"I'm not supposed to eat a lot of junk food. It's just one more thing that might keep me awake. Of course I've done exactly what the doctors said for the past two years and it hasn't seemed to help one bit."

Jack started to speak, then glanced away.

"What is it, Jack?"

He wanted to tell her she hadn't tried *his* prescription, that making love was a sure fire way to get to sleep, but he'd made her a promise tonight and as tough as it was, he intended to keep it. "Nothing. I think we ought to be getting back."

Genny seemed almost reluctant to leave, and in a way so was he. They drove to the condo in silence. Being with her felt good — too damned good — but wanting her as badly as he did, he didn't trust himself to spend too long in her company. Not and keep his word.

Genny seemed pensive, too, staring out the window instead of talking, glancing at him from beneath her heavy sweep of lashes. He wondered what she was thinking.

"It's still pretty early," he said when he pulled up at the curb and turned off the engine, finding himself reluctant to leave. "How about a walk on the beach?"

Genny looked over at him and smiled. "I'd like that."

They locked the car and walked along the

239

sidewalk. There were no cars on the street. They crossed to the opposite side and headed down the narrow path through the ice plant. The beach was nearly deserted this time of night, except for a few distant couples he could barely make out in the moonlight, walking hand-in-hand just as they were.

They didn't talk much, just strolled on the hard-packed sand near the edge of the water and listened to the pounding surf, yet Jack felt oddly at ease.

"It won't be that late when you get home," he said. "Maybe you'll be able to get some sleep."

Genny didn't answer.

"Pretty rough week?" He could see he had hit on a nerve, but he was suddenly determined to know.

Genny glanced away, but not before he'd caught the flash of sadness. "Not one of my best. I've been napping as much as I can. I'm not really supposed to, since it disturbs my normal sleeping patterns, but it seems to be the only time I get to rest."

Jack squeezed the pale slim fingers laced with his own long tanned ones. "And the dreams?"

She swallowed and he noticed her bottom lip trembled. "Really bad, Jack. I don't know what I'm going to do."

"I wish there was some way I could help." He was certain he could, if only she would let him. He eyed her high soft breasts, remembering exactly how they'd felt in his hands, then forced his gaze back to her face.

"If you're that tired, can't you take a couple days off? You said you sleep best during the day." Since the time they'd left the restaurant, she had looked more and more fatigued.

"We're just too busy right now. Besides, the truth is, I need to work. Sometimes I think it's the only thing keeping me sane."

"Genny . . ." He turned her into his arms and kissed her. "I'm sorry, baby. I wish I knew what to tell you."

Genny leaned her head against his chest and a shudder rippled through her. Jack felt it and pulled her closer, his arms tightening protectively around her. Genny clung to him for a moment, her fingers curling into his shirt, her face pressed into his shoulder. Then she flashed him a look of embarrassment and hurriedly pulled away.

"I'm sorry, Jack. I didn't mean to bore you with my problems."

"You aren't boring me. Besides, nobody's got more reason to be upset than you do."

But already she was easing away from him, forcing a smile to her face. "I'll be all right now. I don't know what came over me."

"You're just tired. Maybe we ought to go in."

She nodded and they started back toward the condo. Neither of them spoke along the way, but he noticed Genny still leaned against him. He slid an arm around her waist as they walked through the heavy damp sand. They emptied their shoes when they left the path through the ice plant, then crossed the street and walked along the sidewalk. They stopped when they reached her front porch.

Genny unlocked the door, but made no effort to push it open.

"Genny . . . baby, are you all right?"

She only shook her head. "I c-can't, Jack . . . I don't think I can face it again tonight." She looked up at him and a mist of tears glazed her eyes. "I keep thinking about my nightmares, the terrible things I'll see. God, I don't want to go in there."

Jack's hand came up to her cheek. "We could go someplace else, if you want."

Genny looked up at him through the wetness spiking her lashes. "Why don't you come inside with me?"

Jack tensed, a jolt of heat sliding into his groin. "I don't think that's a good idea, Genny. Not if you expect me to keep my promise."

"I don't care about your promise. I want you to make love to me."

"Genny . . ." Jack took a long slow breath of air, finding it difficult to breathe. "You know the way I am . . . the way I'll always be. Are you sure that's what you want?"

Her lashes swept down and a tear slowly trickled down her cheek. "I need you, Jack. I want you to stay with me, make love to me. I want you to help me forget my dreams, to think only of you and the things you do to me. Make me forget, Jack — if only for tonight."

He pulled her into his arms and buried his face in her hair. It felt like silk beneath his fingers. "You won't be sorry, baby. I'll take you away from all of this darkness — I swear I'll take you to the moon."

A soft sob came from her throat as she clung to him, and Jack swept her up in his arms. He carried her into the entry, kicked the door closed behind them, turned the lock, and carried her up the stairs. He started to kiss her even before he reached the landing, his mouth taking hers in a way he hadn't allowed himself before. Genny kissed him back, her slick tongue so erotic it made him go rock hard.

Jack heard himself groan. It seemed like he had been waiting for this for a lifetime. He wanted to tear off her clothes, to throw her down on the bed and bury himself inside her. He wanted to suckle her breasts and knead her tight little ass, to plunge into her again and again.

Instead he forced himself to go slow. He was pulsing with desire for her, hot and hard and hurting. And determined that Genny would feel those same sensations.

Genny lay back on the wide soft bed. Even as Jack's mouth moved along her throat, she felt his hands unbuttoning her sweater. She trembled as he stripped it away, unfastened the hooks on her bra, and bared her breasts. His long brown fingers slid over her skin, gently lifting, firmly molding, and desire rippled hotly through her body. When his thumb grazed her nipple, Genny moaned.

Then his lips moved along her neck and across her shoulders, and she felt Jack's muscles tighten. Tension thrummed through his long hard body, matching the tautness in her own, yet his hands moved exquisitely slow.

"I want you," he whispered. His tongue began delving deeply, stroking the walls of her mouth. He touched, teased, and tasted — sampled her in such an erotic manner goosebumps pricked her skin. Her body trembled, shuddered. Damp heat slid into her core. When his mouth moved over her breast and his teeth tugged on her nipple, waves of pleasure washed over her, and Genny arched her back to give him more.

Jack accepted what she offered, opening his mouth to take a bigger portion. His tongue felt so hot she squirmed on the bed beneath him and tore at the buttons on his shirt.

"Jack . . ." she whispered, her hands moving frantically, gripping the muscles across his shoulders then threading through his springy black chest hair.

"Easy, baby, I've got you."

God, did he. But for all his efforts, she couldn't seem to get enough of him. Her fingers bit into his shoulders, strayed down his chest, curled around his flat copper nipple and made him groan. Jack's hands seemed less steady as they worked to unfasten the button on her pants and slide down the zipper. In seconds he had removed her shoes and socks and slid her slacks down her legs, leaving her in her tiny white cotton panties.

His warm mouth fastened on her stomach; his wet tongue ringed her navel. He kissed her through the panties, his hot breath heating the folds of her sex. She tensed as she realized what he intended.

"Jack . . . please. I don't . . . I've never . . ."

His dark head came up. "It's all right, baby. We'll take it nice and slow, if that's what you want."

She relaxed again, yet her blood heated up at the thought of Jack's warm tongue plunging inside her. She knew it happened when people made love, but it had never happened to her.

He slid her panties down her legs, and a long dark finger took the place of his tongue. She was wet and ready, so slick it moved in and out with just the right amount of friction.

"You like that, don't you, Genny." It wasn't a question, but the answer slipped from her tongue.

"Y-Yes, Jack." Unconsciously, her hips arched up as she said the words, and the finger delved deeper, probing, teasing, heightening her pleasure. Tendrils of heat licked up from her core and the ache there grew more fierce.

"How about this?" A second finger sank in and began to move, sending flames up through her body.

"Oh, God, Jack." He kissed her with fierce possession, stroking her all the while, making her tremble all over, wet and aching and on fire. She wanted to feel him inside her — she had to. "Jack, please . . ."

"Soon, baby, I promise." But her pleas went unanswered. He just kept on stroking. His practiced touch was relentless. He left her for a moment, then, naked, returned to the bed. When Jack wrapped her fingers around his shaft, Genny's eyes slid closed and fathomless heat rolled over her. Her grip tightened over the protective sheath he wore, felt his hardness pulsing, and began to move, wringing a gruff male hiss from his lips.

"Easy, baby." In seconds he was rising up over her, kissing her mouth and driving his tongue inside. "I've got to have you, Genny. Now. This instant. I can't wait a minute longer." He parted her thighs with his knee and his heavy shaft probed for entrance, then he was sliding his hard length inside, stretching her to fit his thickness, filling her to the hilt.

She whimpered at the feel of him, and a spiraling tightness gripped her. When Jack began to move, to slide his heavy length in and out, the tightness expanded, gripping her in a way she hadn't imagined, catching her in its thrall. She clutched Jack's shoulders and arched upward to receive each long deep stroke. He increased the rhythm, thrusting deeper, pounding harder, relentlessly driving toward his goal.

Waves of heat broke over her, scorching her from the inside out. Then her whole body clenched and an aching sweetness slid into her, a powerful jolt of pleasure that rippled through her body again and again.

Jack's deep thrusts continued, and a second wave broke over her, a white hot spasm of delight that brought tears to her eyes and wrung Jack's name from her lips. She felt him stiffen, knew he had reached his release, felt the last driving thrusts of his powerful body. She was crying when he began to spiral down, awareness slowly returning. Jack's big hand stroked gently through her hair.

"It's all right, baby. Everything is fine."

"Oh, Jack." She clung to him as she blinked away the wetness. "I can't believe it. I never knew . . . I never imagined . . . I never could have guessed how wonderful it would feel."

His hand stopped moving. "You never could have guessed how wonderful *what* would feel?"

"An orgasm. That had to be what it was."

Jack chuckled softly, a rumble inside his thick chest. "I guess you could say that." He rolled onto his side and curled her against him. "You're telling me you've never reached a climax?"

Genny glanced away, suddenly embarrassed. "No." She shouldn't have told him. Now he'd know how inept she was at sex, just like everything else.

Jack chuckled again. "If any other woman told me that, I wouldn't believe her."

Genny tried to roll away from him, but he caught her arm and pulled her back down on the bed. "Wait a minute. What's the matter?"

"I wish I hadn't told you." But hurt echoed in her voice. "I'm sorry, but I haven't had all that much practice."

"You little fool." Jack came up on an elbow to look down at her. "That was so damned good it was scary. And as far as your climax is concerned, can you imagine anything a woman could say that would make a man feel better than knowing he's the only one who's ever made her come?"

Genny's face heated up.

"It's one helluva compliment, lady." He leaned over and kissed her. "Now the trick is to see if I can do it again."

"Jack!" But already he was rolling her beneath him, spreading her legs and sliding his hard length inside.

Genny moaned at the feeling of fullness, at the shivers of heat spreading outward through her body. This time she recognized the tightness spiraling upward. As far as she was concerned Jack had already kept his promise to take her to the moon. She didn't doubt for a moment that he could do it again.

Arching against his deep rhythmic thrusts, Genny smiled, thinking this was one sport where she might actually excel.

When the numbers glowing on the digital

clock beside the bed read 2:00 A.M., Jack stirred and opened his eyes. He was hard again and wanting more of Genny, but when he looked at her and saw how deeply she was sleeping, the notion of waking her slipped away on quiet feet. He lifted a tendril of soft brown hair from her cheek, watched her deep even breathing, and found himself smiling.

Whatever course their rocky relationship might take, she couldn't fault him in this. He had given her what she had asked for — a decent night's sleep.

Jack sank back down against the pillow, closed his eyes, and tried to will away the hardness pressing against the sheets. He finally fell asleep but when he awakened with the first light of dawn, he found his body in the same condition, and Genny was already gone.

He tossed back the covers, got up and went to the bathroom, then used her toothbrush, and used her comb to slick back his hair. When he heard her coming up the stairs, he took pity on her, climbed back in bed, and pulled the sheet up to cover his sex.

"Good morning, Jack," she said softly, a hint of embarrassment in her voice, as he had guessed there would be. He couldn't remember when a woman he had taken to bed had been the least bit embarrassed in the morning.

"What are you doing up so early? You didn't have another nightmare, did you?"

Her pretty mouth curved up. "I slept better

than I have in the last two years."

Jack fought to keep from grinning. He didn't think it would be appropriate under the circumstances.

"I went down to check on Skeeter, but he was sleeping as soundly as I did last night." She stood at the foot of the bed, holding her warm wool robe together over her breasts. In the early morning light, her brown hair looked almost golden.

"Come back to bed, Genny," he said with gruff authority, figuring that's what it would take to get her there.

"What about work? Shouldn't you be getting back to the boat?"

"There's a problem with one of the engines. The guy won't be there to fix it till sometime after eight." He turned the bed back in silent invitation.

Genny hesitated only a moment, walked to her side of the bed, turned her back and untied the sash on her robe. She took it off and tossed it across a chair then hurriedly climbed into bed. He loved the thought of her inexperience. He never thought it would matter. Typical male. He wanted to have his cake and eat it, too.

"Come here." Reaching out, he pulled her toward him. He kissed her long and thoroughly. His shaft was already hard and throbbing.

"Jack?" Genny whispered as he nuzzled her neck.

"Uh, huh?" He nibbled an earlobe then trailed kisses along her throat.

"I-I want to thank you for my presents — both of them."

He paused, his head coming up. "Both of them?"

She smiled. "The kitten . . . and the trip to the moon."

Jack laughed softly and kissed her again. "Listen, baby, the ride has only begun." She was wet already, so he slid himself inside her, eager to have her again and confident he had told her the truth.

There was definitely a first-class ride coming up, and this one was just getting started. Jack inwardly smiled and slowly began to move.

Thirteen

Genny got more work done that day than she had in the past two weeks. Millicent marveled at her almost boundless energy.

"Good Lord, Genny, what in the world's gotten into you?"

Genny felt a rush of embarrassment. "I wish you hadn't put it quite that way."

Millicent pondered that, then she blushed, too. "You don't mean . . . not you and Howard? You finally did it — you actually took the plunge and slept with him? What did he do, ask you to marry him?"

Reaching up, Genny slid a volume of African history back into the rack above her head. "It wasn't Howard."

"It wasn't Howard?" Millie's eyes looked like big blue pin wheels. "You don't mean . . . are you kidding? You went to bed with Jack?"

Genny just nodded.

"I thought the two of you weren't seeing each other anymore. You told me you'd called it off. You said the two of you weren't suited."

"We aren't."

"My God — you did it just for sex! I can't believe it. I never thought you'd have the nerve."

"It wasn't exactly that way, but . . ."

"But what?"

"God, I don't know. Maybe it was."

Millie sat down on the rolling step stool parked in the aisle a few feet away. "I can't believe it." She leaned forward. "How was he?"

"Millie!"

The thin girl turned a guilty shade of red. "I'm sorry. It's just that . . . well, you know I'll never get a chance at a guy like that." She grinned. "The least you could do is tell me what he was like."

Genny laughed softly. "You want to know the truth — he was terrific."

"I knew it!"

"I'm seeing him again tonight, and every time I think about it, I get so worked up I can hardly keep my mind on what I'm doing . . . though I have to admit I'm a little bit sore."

Millie's eyes looked bigger than ever. "Oh, my God!"

Genny burst out laughing. "I'm only teasing, Millie." Well, mostly teasing, something she found easier to do, now that she'd met Jack. "He wants me to come over to his boat tonight. He thinks I should talk some more to his friend, Charley Denton, about my dreams."

"Why? Is he some kind of psychiatrist or something?"

"No. Actually, he's kind of a salty old bird but I like him. He's very well read, and apparently he's interested in psychology. Jack thinks he might have some ideas about what I should do to get over my nightmares."

"What about Dr. Halpern?"

"Dr. Halpern and I have agreed to disagree." She sighed. "To tell you the truth, I don't think lately she's doing me much good. I want to start trying something else."

"Like what?"

"I don't know. If you think of something, let me know, will you?"

"How about acupuncture? That's supposed to be good for just about everything. I even read where they used it in a zoo to anesthetize a giraffe while they worked on his teeth."

"You're kidding."

"I swear it's the truth. And there's always Chinese herbs. There's a place you can learn about that right here in Santa Barbara."

Genny pondered that. She had tried about everything else. "Maybe I just will."

Millie went back to her work and so did Genny, but several times during the day she caught Millie staring in her direction. She looked as if she couldn't quite believe Genny had actually gone to bed with a guy who rode a Harley, and her face held a definite trace of envy. Genny smiled. Thinking of the night she and Jack had shared, she had to admit she didn't blame her.

Charley Denton opened the cabin door for Genny and Jack at around 8:00 P.M. Rain pelted his face, and a stiff wind whipped the bottom of Jack's yellow slicker. Genny's beige trench coat dripped water all over the floor as she walked in.

"Nasty out there," Charley said. "Hope it's better by tomorrow." He helped Genny out of her raincoat. "It's good to see you, Genny girl."

She surprised him by leaning over for a quick warm hug. "You, too, Charley."

"You two kids eaten?"

"Yeah," Jack said, "we caught a bite on the way over here. What about you?"

"I'm fine. Had a sandwich with Pete before he left for home."

"He was good help today, but then he always is."

"Owl comin' over?" Charley asked. "I thought Pete mentioned something about playin' cards."

Jack looked almost embarrassed. "I canceled the game. I wanted Genny to have a chance to talk to you."

She looked up at him in surprise. "You shouldn't have done that, Jack. I know how much you like to play. I used to —"

"That's all right. There's always next week."

Genny started to say something else, but Charley cut her off. "Jack's right. Some things are more important. Now . . . why don't we sit down so we can hash all this over?"

Charley and Genny drank wine while Jack sipped a beer. They talked about Genny's latest dreams, about the sleep clinic, and her confrontation with Dr. Halpern.

"I just don't think she's on the right track," Genny said. "Dr. Halpern thinks something awful must have happened in my childhood. She acts as if the dreams are real, but they aren't. They're only hallucinations."

"Are you sure about that, Genny?" Charley said softly.

"Of course, I'm sure. I had a perfectly normal childhood."

"I'm sure you did."

"Then what else could it be?"

"I don't know," Charley said. "But I think you should try to find out."

She took a sip of her wine and set the glass back down on the built-in teakwood table in the galley. "Well, they aren't from something I've read or seen. I've gone through a dozen different indexes, including the video library."

"You said you'd started keeping a journal," Charley said. "That means you've got a fairly accurate account of what you've seen in your dreams so far."

"That's right."

"You remember what the clothes looked like, the kind of setting they were in, the way the religious ceremonies you described progressed?"

"Religious ceremonies — I never said that. These were half-naked savages having some kind of orgy."

"To some folks that is their religion."

Genny frowned. "Good point. I guess you can tell primitive cultures are not my area of expertise."

"Well, they're bound to be somebody's," Jack put in, then he grinned, gouging dimples in his cheeks. "How about that little reference librarian you were telling me about — Millie, what's her name — the one who's hot for my body?"

Genny laughed. "Jack Brennen, you are incorrigible."

Charley smiled and took a drink of his wine. "See if you can find a place that matches the setting in the dreams. You keep talking about Africa, but it might be somewhere else. There are jungles in South America. Or maybe it's the South Pacific. And search for a time in history that seems to jibe with what's going on."

"Even if there were such a place and time," Genny argued, "unless I've read about it somewhere, how could I know enough to dream about it?"

"Right now that isn't the question."

"Charley's right," Jack said. "If you discover the dreams are based on actual occurrences and aren't just hallucinations, you can find out where you might have come across it."

"I can't believe they're about anything real. Something that grotesque couldn't possibly be real."

"Maybe not," Charley said, "but you've got

to admit, accordin' to what you told me, parts of it did seem real. The clothing, for instance. You said it was from sometime in the past. And the fancy house you described. Can you remember the design? What kind of architecture it was?"

"Yes . . . it was Georgian, I think, but there again, I'm an administrative librarian, mostly. History isn't my strong suit."

"Finding out about it is," Jack reminded her. "And you've got everything you need right there in the library."

"Yes, I suppose that's true."

"Then you'll do it?" Charley pressed. "You'll try to track this stuff down?"

Genny drew in a deep breath. "I'll do it, Charley. I'll do whatever it takes."

"Good girl." He got up from the table and stretched, a twinkle glinting in his hazel eyes. "If the two of you'll excuse me, I'm gettin' kinda tired. Think I'll take myself off to bed."

Jack gazed at Genny with a look of undisguised heat. "I think that's a good idea," he said to her. "How about you?"

"The lure of a second good night's sleep? Are you kidding?"

Jack's wide chest rumbled with mirth. "I hope it's more than that."

Genny kissed him softly on the lips. "You know it is." Still, as she had hoped, after a vigorous round of lovemaking, she once more slept the whole night through and awoke feeling deliciously rested.

Genny spent the days buried to her eyebrows in work. Whenever she wasn't busy reading reviews, compiling lists of books for acquisition, or helping an employee shelve the volumes already received, she was digging into the reference books, looking up information that might be connected to her dreams.

Thinking of the five-pointed star and the symbols she had seen, she read up on witchcraft and had to admit that there were some definite similarities. The star looked pretty much the same, as well as some of the other symbols, but none of them matched exactly. Pagan rituals were often a part of coven ceremonies, and blood sacrifices were not uncommon. Women were often involved, and she had to admit that the woman in the dream was as vicious as any Satanist Stephen King could think up.

When she tired of reading the often gruesome texts, she studied books on Africa, since that seemed the mostly likely setting, particularly during the era of European Colonization. She also took note of the many different regions, each with distinctive customs and tribal beliefs.

Since the people in the dreams spoke English, she concentrated on British regions, but she discovered that Americans interested in black colonization had also established a colony — Liberia, at Cape Mesurado in 1822.

This discovery brought home the point that, assuming the dreams were based in fact — which she still very much doubted — narrowing down the time frame would have to be done before the place could be correctly established.

Since she recalled the clothes the woman wore, as well as those of the man on the terrace, she checked out volumes on clothing: *The Mode in Costume*, *Western World Costume*, *The Encyclopedia of World Costume*, along with a number of others. Since the men weren't wearing wigs, nor the women wide *panniers* — those rectangular metal hoops from the days of Martha Washington — it was easy to conclude that the time frame was after 1800. That was also the time that men began wearing ankle-length trousers, instead of knee breeches and hose.

The women wore high-waisted dresses with slender skirts until about 1815, which meant it had to be sometime later. In the dream, the woman's skirt didn't seem to be buoyed by a hoop, which began about 1850, and none of the styles after that seemed to fit.

Still, 1815 to 1850 was a pretty wide spread. Genny settled in to read descriptions of the clothes worn in between. As waistlines descended, she discovered, slim skirts grew fuller. By the mid-1820's the waistline was back to normal and the skirts fairly full, either gored or gathered. Sleeves in that period were large, with names like the Marie sleeve, the gigot sleeve, the famous leg-of-mutton sleeve.

Genny remembered the apricot dress the woman had worn that day outside the old wooden shed. The fabric was muslin, she now believed, and she recalled that the sleeves were large and puffy, yet fitted closely from the elbow to the wrist. By 1835, sleeves were round and full, which somehow didn't seem right.

Men's fashions were equally difficult to pinpoint, but she finally succeeded. It appeared men wore tailcoats that matched the one worn by the man on the terrace from 1815 to around 1835. Genny distinctly remembered his white waistcoat and loosely tied black cravat, which also fitted into that time slot.

In the end, she fixed on a date between 1820 and 1835 as the possible time frame of her nightmares. It disturbed her a little that the clothes she had seen in her dreams actually existed, but at least it was a start.

And it was a way to focus her studies, which she did whenever she could throughout the day and early in the evening, before Jack arrived at her door.

Crabby Fowler was in conference much of the time with her superior, Caroline Burkhardt, the library director, making plans for the new budget, which allowed Genny a little more freedom. She stayed late every night, checked out books, took them home, and read them with Skeeter purring softly in her lap. She even had Jack scanning the volumes, looking for something that might provide a clue.

Unfortunately, after a full week's research, she still hadn't discovered a location that seemed to match those in her dreams.

She did find out that many African societies were animistic, which meant they worshipped animals and often used animal sacrifices in their religious ceremonies.

Even if they did, she couldn't help thinking, what could it possibly have to do with her? She felt no real connection to what she was reading, no logical, rational reason to pursue the subject, since she was still sure the nightmares weren't real. But she had promised Charley — and who knew? — it might actually turn out to be important.

Her relationship with Jack was the only high point in the week, which started off in bed and ended in exactly the same place. Though the lives they led during the day were completely different, at night when they made love, she felt closer to him than she ever had with another human being.

And they did have fun. Jack promised that.

"Listen to me, baby," he had said as they stood beside his car, turning her to face him. "I can't tell you how this is going to turn out — but I can promise you one thing — we definitely will have some fun."

Genny had laughed as Jack lifted her into the driver's seat of his Mustang. She had made the mistake of telling him she'd never learned to drive a stick shift and Jack had immediately decided to teach her. They tooled around the empty parking lot of the Sea Breeze Bar, which hadn't opened yet. Jack grimaced as Genny ground the gears to his most prized possession.

Eventually, she had gotten the hang of it and he insisted she drive the road along the coast. She couldn't remember laughing so much, or enjoying so thoroughly the sun on her face and the wind in her hair.

Another time he took her to the movies — a big, action-adventure starring Arnold Schwartzenegger. She had never seen that sort of film, would never have thought she would enjoy that kind of picture. But when the movie ended, her palms were damp with excitement, her heart thumping madly, and her body racing with adrenaline. Outside the theater, Jack had grinned at the smile on her face and the rose in her cheeks. Playfully, he had tossed her over his shoulder and carried her all the way to the car.

She remembered thinking Jack was a lot like Arnold, only Schwartzenegger wasn't quite so good-looking.

Of course there were the not-so-good occasions, too. Like the night he took her bowling. Jack bowled an impressive 240 while she threw six straight gutter balls and wound up with a score of 46.

Or the fight they got into over Howard, who had called to ask her out to dinner. When she hung up the phone and Jack found out who it was, he made several wisecracks about Howard's two-faced business dealings, and called him a "horse's ass." Of course, she had staunchly defended him, telling Jack in no uncertain terms that Howard was the reason for McCormick-Austin's success. She called Jack small-minded, and angrily repeated what a good friend Howard was, saying it was Howard who would be there when Jack was long gone.

Jack had stormed off in a rage, gotten in his car and driven away, only to return a few minutes later. He'd apologized, kissed her soundly, then taken her straight up to bed.

Sitting behind her desk in the library, Genny thought about the week that had passed, their quarrels and their adventures, all they had shared. As volatile as their tenuous relationship was, she knew she was falling in love with him. Or perhaps she had started along that dangerous path the night he had saved her on the beach.

She didn't understand it, but that didn't alter the fact.

As the rain beat down on the panes of the high arched library windows, Genny wondered how Jack was feeling about her.

With the wind howling outside and a heavy spray of water beating against the portholes, Jack finished pouring himself a whiskey and Genny a glass of wine. Charley was over at a friend's, a doctor named Richard Bailey who spent the weekends aboard his sailboat over at the yacht harbor.

Jack took a hefty slug of his drink, hoping to dull the tension he was feeling. Then he carried the wine across the room to Genny. She was wearing jeans and a bright yellow sweater. Her nut-brown hair was pulled back at the nape of her neck and tied with a matching yellow ribbon. In that soft way of hers, she looked sexy as hell, and he felt himself start to go hard.

Christ! Jack's hold grew tighter on the bowl of the wineglass. His jaw went taut at the thought that she could affect him so easily. He caught Genny's glance and saw the way her eyes clung to his. She noticed how edgy he was, wondering where his thoughts were leading.

Lately, he had been wondering the same thing himself.

He crossed the room and handed her the glass. Her fingers brushed his as she accepted it. She took a small sip then set the glass on the coffee table. For the first time, he noticed she had picked up the dog-eared paperback lying over the back of the sofa. The back of his neck went warm.

"Charley said this was yours."

He nodded and took a long sip of his drink.

"The *Odyssey* and the *Iliad?* Where on earth did you get it?" The pages were rumpled, the cover nearly torn off, but it wasn't from overuse.

"I found it in my locker I was supposed to read it in high school but I used Cliff Notes instead. I thought I might give it another try."

Surprise moved over her face. "Charley said you didn't like to read."

"I don't."

"So why are you —"

"Because I figured you had probably read it. I thought it might be something we could talk about, something we had in common, but it isn't going to work." He hated the roughness in his voice, but he'd been thinking about Genny, about their growing closeness, and he'd been brooding and ill-tempered all day.

"Why isn't it going to work?"

"Because the damn thing bores me to death, that's why." He turned away from her then, angry at himself for being so brusque, but mostly for being so honest. Genny had a way of doing that to him and he didn't like it one bit.

"It wouldn't be my favorite reading matter, either," she said gently.

"Why not? It's not much duller than that godawful play you took me to."

Genny ignored his biting words. "Because reading it wouldn't be all that much fun."

"So when did fun have anything to do with it?"

"Jack, if you read things you enjoyed, you'd discover it's a great deal of fun. Why don't you let me bring home a few things from the library . . . choose some books I think you might like.

That's part of my job, you know, and you might be surprised to discover —"

"Thanks, but no thanks. I think I'll skip the literary efforts for a while." It was a stupid idea to begin with. All he had done was prove once more how ill-suited they were.

Genny frowned at his tone, but he didn't care. He felt claustrophobic tonight, like he needed to be someplace else.

"What's the matter, Jack?" she said softly, coming up from the sofa and walking toward him. "I can tell something's wrong."

"Nothing's wrong . . . exactly."

"So what *exactly* isn't wrong?"

Jack turned a hard look in her direction. "Look, Genny, you and I have been together every night since the first of last week. I'm not used to that kind of confinement. Tonight . . . well . . . I just feel like I need a little air."

Something flashed in her eyes, uncertainty or hurt, he couldn't be sure. Then she gently touched his arm and a ripple of desire slid into his groin. She looked so damned pretty. Not hard, like the women he usually had, not so brassy, not so . . . used. Her lips were pink and full and he knew exactly how soft they would feel when he kissed her. He knew how perfectly shaped her breasts were, the smooth sleek outline of her tight little round derrière.

They'd made love a dozen times, but it hadn't been enough for him. He could think of fifty different ways he'd like to have her, a hundred different things he'd like to do. And yet there was this feeling . . . this prickle at the back of his neck that told him that was the worst thing that could happen.

"It's all right, Jack," Genny said. "You should have said something sooner. I know the kind of life you lead. I know you like your freedom. I didn't mean to get in your way."

"You're not in my way . . . exactly. It's just that . . . well . . . Pete Williams and some of the guys are getting together tonight and I kind of . . ."

"You kind of wanted to go with them. There's nothing wrong with that. Look, why don't I go on home? You can go out with your friends and later, if you feel like stopping by, you know you'll be welcome."

Jack smiled, feeling like a weight had been lifted off his shoulders. Pete had been on him all day, ragging him about being pussy-whipped, saying he was getting in too deep with Genny. And dammit, it was the truth.

"Thanks, baby." He leaned over and kissed her, ignored another quick swell of desire for her. "Finish your wine and I'll drive you home on my way out."

She only drank part of it, sensing he was eager to be away. She was being a damned good sport about it. Most women would have pissed and moaned and tried to make him feel guilty. Not Genny. Not that it didn't bother her — he could see very clearly that it did.

But she had gone to bed with him with her eyes wide open. He hadn't pulled any punches and apparently she was willing to accept whatever came.

"I'm ready whenever you are," Genny said a little too brightly.

"Let's go." Jack grabbed her windbreaker and his Levi jacket, and headed for the door. He was anxious to be on the loose, out on the prowl again, off on his own. He was looking forward to it. At least part of him was. If he was honest with himself, another part didn't want to go. If he wasn't so uptight, a cozy night in front of the fire with Genny would be a helluva lot better than a night out getting drunk.

Which made him more determined than ever to go.

Jack Brennen pussy-whipped? Not on your life!

A few minutes later, he dropped Genny at her condo then headed down Shoreline Drive to the Sea Breeze Bar. Pete Williams and a couple of blondes were standing beside Pete's navy blue Camaro in the parking lot. Jack pulled his Mustang over to the curb, turned off the ignition, and unfolded his long body out from behind the steering wheel.

"Say, Jack! You actually made it. I'd just about given you up." Pete leaned back against the Camaro on his elbows, his lanky frame warmed by a set of round hips and big tits on each side.

"No chance of that," Jack said.

"I hope you're ready for a hot night on the town." Pete grinned. One of the blondes smiled at him and ran her long-nailed fingers through his close-cropped red hair.

"Has a cat got an ass?" Jack said.

"This is Kelly and this is Sue." Pete patted one of the girls on the ass. "Ladies, say hello to Jack Brennen."

"Hi, Jack," they both said in unison.

"We gonna stand out here all night slinging the bull," Jack said, feeling suddenly restless, "or go get something to drink?" Some remote part of him kept asking what the hell he was doing here.

Pete just grinned. "Ladies . . . after you."

The Sea Breeze Bar was packed, every seat full, standing room only at the long mahogany bar. Jack elbowed his way through, ordered a straight shot of Wild Turkey, tossed it back, and ordered another. By the third straight shot, he started to relax — and stopped feeling guilty.

Dammit, Genny Austin was nothing but bad news. She was great in the sack, but that was all there was between them, and the odd stranglehold she held on him just wasn't worth all the effort. Tonight was as good as any to get her the hell out of his blood.

"Say, Jack, look who just walked in."

At first he couldn't see her, surrounded as she was by a half-dozen gawking, leering men.

But when she started toward the bar, the men made way, parting in front of her like the Red Sea before Moses. For a moment all he saw was a great set of tits and a cloud of long blond hair. Vivian Sandburg paused just a few feet in front of him.

"Well . . . if it isn't Jump 'em Jack Flash. What happened, honey? Mama let you out of your cage?"

A corner of his mouth curved up. Jack challenged her with a glance, then gave her a long hard perusal that started at her bulging cleavage, moved over her shapely behind, down her long legs then returned to settle on her breasts. He noticed that her nipples had peaked beneath her tight black T-shirt.

"I'm out of my cage, all right, and I'm definitely on the prowl." Leaning forward, he slid a hand beneath her hair at the nape of her neck and dragged her mouth up to his for a kiss. He shoved his tongue down her throat then around the walls of her mouth, ignoring the fact she was trying to break his hold, slamming her fists against his chest.

Instead he hauled her roughly against him and deepened the kiss, cupping her buttocks and pressing her into his hardened sex. Vivian went stock still. A shiver ran through her, then her arms slid up from his shoulders and slowly encircled his neck.

She kissed him back just as hotly as he had kissed her. When he finally let her go, both of them were breathing too hard.

"You got any plans for tonight?" he asked, his eyes holding hers, daring her to walk away.

"I do now, cowboy." She straddled his leg and pressed her breasts against his chest. Jack leaned backwards, propping his elbows on the bar and bringing his knee up between her thighs raising her a little bit off the floor. Viv hissed in a deep sexy breath.

"How 'bout a drink?" he asked, his eyes still fixed on the two stiff peeks beneath her blouse. He could see the outline of her large aureoles and an image of Genny's small tight nipples flashed at the front of his mind.

Vivian wet her lips. Her fiery red lipstick was a little too bright for her pale blond hair. "I thought you'd never ask." She gave him a sexy come-on smile.

With looks of disappointment from her bevy of admirers, a few of grudging respect, the men around her faded away. Even Pete Williams looked impressed.

"Well, tiger," he said to Jack, "looks like you've got your hands full tonight."

He would, all right. He'd be squeezing her big lush tits, but he'd be thinking of slightly smaller, uptilting, perfectly shaped ones. "What are you drinking?" he asked a little more tonelessly than he intended.

"Tequila. Straight up," Viv said.

Jack's smile should have come easy. She'd be drunk by the third or fourth round, but that wouldn't stop her. Vivian always drank a little too much.

"You're looking good, Viv," Pete said, voicing Jack's thoughts as he continued to assess her luscious curves. She *was* looking good, in her low-cut sleeveless T-shirt with the push-'em-up bra underneath, and her skin-tight black pants. As usual, she wore a pair of high-heeled shoes to make her legs look longer.

"She feels good, too," Jack said, giving her a pat on the bottom. Viv just laughed. He ordered another round of drinks, downed his, and ordered another. For some crazy reason, he was reluctant to leave with her and that made him even more determined that he would.

"You ready, Jack?" Pete nuzzled one of the blondes.

"I'm always ready." He cupped Vivian's rump, squeezed, and for the first time noticed it felt a little fleshy. She was rounder than Genny, he thought vaguely, not nearly so lean and sleek.

When he realized Genny had once more crept into his thoughts, he swore fluently and dragged Vivian out of the bar and off toward the parking lot.

"Let's go to your place," Pete suggested. "It's a helluva lot closer than mine."

"Sounds good to me." Charley was gone. The couch folded out and his own bed was empty. The bar in the galley had plenty of liquor and he was randy as hell.

He loaded Vivian into the car and climbed into the driver's seat, grateful that as much as he'd drunk he was only a few blocks from the harbor. Oddly, he still felt far too sober. Pete followed in his Camaro with the blondes, and a few minutes later, they walked the long wooden dock toward the boat. Jack stepped aboard the *Marauder* and helped the girls aboard, then the five of them went inside the cabin.

While one of the girls went to the head, Pete loaded a Bruce Springsteen disc into the stereo, set out some Rod Stewart, some Rolling Stones, and some Michael Bolton for a little later on.

They were ready to party. And to get laid. For him it was long past the time it should have been done. Jack walked to the cupboard, pulled out a bottle of whiskey and one of tequila and began to pour the liquor into glasses. He didn't usually drink this much, but somehow tonight he needed the booze to see this thing through.

The thought was a grim one. It did nothing to lift what was starting to become a less than festive mood.

Fourteen

Genny pulled on the bright yellow sweater she had worn earlier and the pair of jeans which were the only ones she owned. It was almost 1:00 A.M., dark outside, with only a sliver of moon. The rain had stopped long ago, but storm clouds hovered over the ocean.

Though she'd been sleeping better lately — she had to give Jack that — she had gone to bed early, knowing that without him, she would probably have trouble tonight. She tossed and turned for a while, worrying about the depth of her feelings for him, remembering what Dottie had said, and knowing she should try to lessen her involvement.

She tried not to think what he might be doing, tried to tell herself that on some level he cared, then wound up wishing he would come home to her, no matter what time he got in.

She had finally fallen asleep, but then she had dreamed.

It was hazy at first, just lights and colors and odd birdlike sounds that might have come from the nearby jungle. Then the images began to take shape and eventually came into focus: clear blue skies, towering green trees, and wide swatches of manicured lawn. Across the clearing, she saw the big Georgian mansion atop a sloping hill.

It was three stories high, and built of stone. The huge main structure and two distinctive wings were opulent and impressive. Rows of paned windows traveled across the upper and middle floors, where the entrance appeared to be. Great stone arches thrust the house up from the ground and sheltered the floor beneath. It looked out on a magnificent expanse of lawn and a large rock-lined pond, floating with white-flowered lily pads.

The scene shifted, grew blurry, then came sharply into focus. She stood inside the mansion, in a majestic entry hall beneath a crystal chandelier. A sweeping mahogany staircase climbed to the bedrooms above. The mahogany rungs and banisters were polished to a sheen only matched by the inlaid hardwood floors beneath her feet.

An elegant salon furnished with exquisite marble-topped tables and expensive Oriental carpets sat off to one side; a magnificent chandeliered dining room with a long polished mahogany table, each of its twelve chairs upholstered in brocaded silk, stretched out on the other.

Someone called down from the bedroom. She seemed to float up the staircase, her feet barely touching the thick runner of carpet. Then she stood in the hall outside a locked bedroom door.

She didn't want to go in, but something compelled her, forcing her to turn the beautiful silver knob. From some vague corner of her mind she fought it, thought of Dr. Beckett, and tried to manipulate the dream. She tried to awaken inside it, to somehow extricate herself from its terrible pull. Or simply to awaken.

Instead she turned the knob. The silver felt cold against her palm, and the locked door swung wide. In a rose silk gown, a black-haired woman stood inside the lavish bedroom, her small frame poised at the foot of a high four-poster bed that was draped in ice-blue silk. As the scene unfolded, she saw that something lay atop it.

A man she discovered, older than the beautiful woman with the ebony hair. His jaw was slack, his gray hair slightly receding. The flesh on his neck looked thick. He was dressed in formal evening clothes. His long black tail coat reached nearly to his knees, and his white neck-cloth and pleated white shirt were spotless. A long white pique waistcoat was buttoned across his torso beneath his black coat. The man's gray trousers touched his ankles and a strap wound its way beneath shiny black evening shoes with small gold buckles on the front. A tall narrow-brimmed hat rested in the crook of one bent arm.

The force drew her forward though she didn't want to go. She tried to pull back. Part of her was disturbed by the silence and the pallor of the man's fleshy face, yet another part felt oddly unmoved by it. The petite woman in the rose silk gown just stared at the figure lying so still on the thick feather mattress, his hands as pale as his cheeks, his eyes closed, his thin lips tinged with blue.

In that moment, she knew that the man was dead.

She knew that he was the black-haired woman's husband.

And that the woman had killed him.

The shock sent Genny up from the darkness of sleep, plunging toward the safety of wakefulness. Her hands were shaking, her lips dry and trembling, her heart thudding wildly inside her chest. She lay there a moment, taking long, calming breaths, then she forced her shaky hands to reach for the light. She picked up the notebook resting on the table beside the bed, fumbled for a moment with the pen that lay on top, then began to scrawl out the words describing her dream.

When she finished, she sank back against her pillow feeling exhausted and unnerved, and that strange overwhelming sense of grief she had felt so many times before. Setting the pen and notebook aside, she shoved tangled brown hair back from her face and swung her legs to the floor, then crossed the room in search of her clothes.

She dressed in the jeans and bright yellow

sweater she had worn before, and now as she wandered along the beach, she replayed the scene in her dream, as well as the implications of what it might mean.

There were no answers, of course, just more disturbing pieces of a puzzle she could not solve. Perhaps Dr. Halpern was right after all, and these were nothing more than the mind's way of dealing with her husband's murder.

Somehow she just didn't believe it.

She thought of the dream and the magnificent plantation house — for she was certain now that's what it was. She shivered to think of the death that lurked inside it. But seeing it again tonight had given her more food for thought. Always she had felt as if the people were English and living somewhere in Africa.

Now she wasn't so sure.

As she walked along the beach, Genny stuffed her hands into the pockets of her jeans and kicked through a little hill of sand. Tomorrow she would continue her research. Only this time she would focus right here in the U.S.A., somewhere in the deep South. There were houses in Georgia like the one she had seen, built by English planters in the eighteenth and nineteenth centuries. Perhaps she should start there.

She wrapped her arms around her, ignoring the chill, barely hearing the crash and glide of the waves. She kept thinking of the woman in the rose silk gown, wondering what could have driven her to such brutal lengths. Wondering why she had been chosen to discover the woman's story.

For she was beginning to believe that was exactly what was happening. And she was becoming more and more certain that the only way to end the dreams was to fill in all of the missing pieces, to make the story come to an end.

An especially large wave broke on the shore and the water rushed toward her shiny brown loafers. She hurriedly stepped away and for the first time, she noticed how far she had come. The lights of the harbor were not that far off; she could hear the clatter and clank of ship's rigging in the silence between each set of waves.

Knowing she should turn around and walk the opposite way, she kept going till she came to the wharf. She passed the ship's chandlery, passed the yacht broker's office, and the Sailors' Emporium. When she reached Dock H, where Jack's boat was tied up, she searched the ground for something to use as a tool, picked up a broken seashell, and opened the lock on the gate.

She knew she shouldn't be there, that she should give him the space he had asked for. She told herself it didn't matter, that Jack was out with his friends, not aboard the *Marauder*, and that even if he was, she wouldn't disturb him.

Then she reached the spot where the big work boat rocked gently beside the dock, saw that the lights were still on in the main cabin, and heard the Rolling Stones erupting from Jack's stereo.

Perhaps it's only Charley, she thought frantically, or Jack and some of his friends. But her heart squeezed hard inside her chest and her limbs felt suddenly leaden. She told herself to go home, to forget the questions burning inside her. She told herself to walk away, to go back and pretend she hadn't come.

But something wouldn't let her. Every cell in her body warned her she would be sorry if she didn't leave, but instead she climbed the stairs and stepped onto the deck. Her legs were moving almost by themselves. She felt nearly as powerless as she had been in her dream.

She stood there in the darkness outside the cabin door, knowing she couldn't go in, knowing she had to. The sound of voices rose up — a woman's voice mingled with the husky tenor of a man's. She thought of Jack, of the time she had spent with him, the way he had made her feel. She thought of the way he had made love to her, of how much it had meant to her — and how little it must have meant to him.

She had known it would be like this — he had never lied to her about that — but somehow she had convinced herself it wasn't really that way.

Now she had to see for herself, had to confront the truth for what it was. She wished to God she had stayed away.

Jack's head pounded in rhythm to the beat of the Stones' latest song. Next to him, singing a little off key, Vivian crooned the words, repeating the lyrics to "Jumping Jack Flash," shaking her shoulders, jiggling her heavy pushed-up breasts.

Looking down at her, for the first time in a long time, he wished he had a cigarette.

Vivian smiled at him and batted her long, black-mascaraed lashes. She lifted his hand from her waist, kissed the palm, then settled it so he cupped a full breast. Beneath his fingers, he could feel the lacy cups of her push-up bra through the front of her thin black T-shirt.

Jack forced a smile and absently stroked her, trying to get in the mood, amazed at how his desire for her had waned instead of grown since the moment she had stepped aboard his boat. Somehow it didn't feel like she should be there.

Jack shrugged off the notion. Once he stripped her down, she would do just as well as any other woman. At least that's what he told himself, but his mind kept returning to Genny. He couldn't help thinking about her, worrying about whether she was sleeping, wishing he was there instead of here. For Chrissakes, he'd probably fantasize about Genny while he was pounding into Viv.

"Hey, Pete," Viv said when the song was finished, "how about something a little more romantic?" She ran a long-nailed finger along his jaw, making Jack clench his teeth.

"Good idea." Pete kissed one of the blondes on the mouth then knelt in front of the stereo.

Good idea, Jack thought. *Let's get laid and get these broads out of here.* Strange, he'd never thought of Genny that way. She wasn't a broad, she was a lady.

Maybe that was the problem.

A lady had no business with a guy like him.

Jack silently cursed. He'd thought about Genny so many times, he looked up and actually thought he saw her. She was standing in the open cabin door in that same bright yellow sweater she'd been wearing earlier in the evening.

Then Pete pushed the stop button on the stereo to change the disc, and silence descended — except the vision of Genny remained. She was staring at him standing there with Viv. And there were tears on her cheeks.

"Ah, Christ, Genny . . . what the hell are you doing here?"

She didn't answer of course, just turned and walked out, leaving Jack's mind in a fog he couldn't quite seem to clear.

"What's the matter, Jack?" Viv purred. "You didn't tell your new playmate she wasn't the only little girl in your sandbox?"

Jack came away from the wall, feeling sick to his stomach. All he could think of was the look on Genny's face.

"Jack?" Vivian grabbed his arm but he shook it off. "Wait a minute, Jack — where the hell do you think you're going?"

"Hey, Jack?" Pete called out, but he just kept on walking.

"See that Viv gets home," he said, jerking open the low cabin door, then ducking his head to step through.

"You asshole!" Vivian's glass shattered against the metal door frame, but Jack just kept on going. He slammed the door behind him as an ashtray crashed into the wall.

Crossing the deck in several long strides, he jumped down to the dock and headed for the gate at the end. He didn't see Genny till he reached the parking lot, then he spotted her slender figure running across the sand toward her condo in the distance.

Jesus, he felt like a bastard. He thought of how Genny must feel, and a knot balled hard in his stomach. He started walking faster, certain that every passing minute would only make things worse. Even more sure that with every tear she shed, the chance of mending the damage he had done dwindled to near nonexistence.

The knot in his stomach balled harder; a tightness squeezed inside his chest. God, he hated that she could make him feel this way. More than that, he hated the thought that she might never want to see him again.

Jack clenched his jaw, suddenly envisioning a

lifetime of women like Viv. A wave of nausea hit him and he stumbled in the damp, heavy sand. When Genny stepped inside her house and closed the door, beads of sweat broke out on his forehead. A few seconds later, Jack started to run.

Standing in the darkened interior of her living room, Genny leaned against the front door, hot wet tears running in rivulets down her cheeks.

She thought of Jack's big hand on Vivian Sandburg's breast and bent double. A keening sound came slipping from between her lips. God, it hurt. She had known it would, but she'd had to know for sure.

She hadn't suspected the pain would be so savage.

She straightened and turned her face toward the door, resting her head on a forearm, trying to stop crying. She jumped at the sudden harsh pounding that vibrated the thick wooden panels.

"Genny! It's Jack. Let me in."

She didn't answer. She couldn't believe he had come. Why would he, when he had the beautiful blonde?

"Genny, dammit, I know you're in there. You've got to let me in."

"G-Go away, Jack."

"Honey, please, just give me a chance to explain."

She swallowed past the lump still aching in her throat. "You don't have to explain, Jack. You promised me nothing. That's exactly what I got."

For a moment he didn't answer. "Please, baby . . . let me in."

"G-Go away."

Jack started pounding again, but Genny didn't care. There was nothing he could say to her, nothing he could do. He was just Jack Brennen. Just like he'd said.

Jack hammered away as Genny climbed the stairs. Turning the knob on her bedroom door, she woodenly crossed the room toward the bed. She stood there for a moment, looking down at the place where she and Jack had made love, remembering that she had invited him to share her bed again tonight. Jack had chosen the voluptuous blonde, as she should have known he would.

The pounding had stopped, but Genny scarcely noticed, caught up as she was in the misery that overwhelmed her. With trembling hands, she tugged the yellow sweater over her head, slipped out of her brown penny loafers, unsnapped and slid off her jeans. Opening a bureau drawer, she pulled out the long pale blue nightgown she had bought that day, hoping Jack would like it. She slowly drew it on.

She stared at herself in the mirror, assessing the way the nylon clung to her breasts, outlining the roundness, their uptilting shape, seeing the way the gown curved in at the waist then flared out over her hips. When she had tried it on in the lingerie shop, it made her feel sexy and feminine.

She'd wanted Jack to see her looking that way. Now Jack would never see her in it.

She listened for the pounding, but heard only silence. Jack had returned to the blonde.

Fresh tears gathered. Genny sat down on the edge of the bed, her heart aching fiercely, tears still washing down her cheeks. Then an odd sound drew her attention to the balcony outside the sliding glass doors. Her pulse speeded up as she realized that someone was climbing up the tall wooden trellis.

Hardly conscious that she moved, she walked toward the doors, listening to the rustle of the climbing rose vines against the plaster, hearing a soft muttered curse as a rose thorn bit into flesh.

In the sliver of moonlight, a long, hard-muscled leg swung over the railing, and Jack climbed up on the balcony. He was so tall and wide-shouldered, that he filled an entire pane of the sliding glass doors.

"Let me in, Genny. I've got to talk to you." He determinedly rapped on the door.

"Go away, Jack." She couldn't quite believe he would go to such lengths to get in.

"Open the door, Genny. If you don't I'll start pounding again. If that doesn't work, I swear

I'll break the damned thing in."

She knew he would do it. There was nothing he would not dare. And there was something about that tone of voice — whenever Jack used it, she always seemed to obey him. She found herself moving closer, turning the latch and sliding open the door.

Genny stepped back as Jack walked in. She waited for him to speak but he just stood there staring. A dark fathomless expression tightened the lines of his face.

"What . . . what do you want?"

Jack cleared his throat. He ran his palms down the front of the blue jeans hugging his muscular thighs. "I wanted to see you . . . I had to. I wanted to tell you . . . I'm sorry."

Genny tried to smile. "You don't have anything to be sorry for. You never lied to me. You warned me in the beginning. You told me this was the way it would be, I just wouldn't listen."

"Genny —" He took a step toward her, but Genny stepped away.

"Go back to your women, Jack. That's what you wanted, wasn't it? Go back to Vivian and leave me alone." She turned away from him, hugging herself, wishing she still had on her clothes instead of the clinging blue nightgown, which made her feel raw and tragic and exposed.

She felt Jack's hands on her shoulders, big powerful hands, strong yet somehow gentle, turning her to face him.

"That isn't what I want. I don't want Vivian," he said gruffly. "I want you. Unfortunately, until tonight, I didn't know how much."

Swallowing past the ache in her throat, Genny pulled away from him and walked over to the foot of the bed. She held onto the carved wooden bedpost to quiet her trembling hands and leaned her forehead against it. "Go away, Jack. Just g-go away and l-leave me alone."

He came up behind her so quietly she didn't hear him, his hands encircling her waist, resting gently on the curve of her hips. His warm breath fanned the hair beside her cheek. "I can't go, Genny. I wished to hell I could."

He pressed his lips to the nape of her neck, trailed soft kisses along her throat, and an ache welled up inside her. Through the thin nylon fabric, his fingers cupped her breasts, cradled them, molded them gently as he began to massage her nipples.

A shiver of desire rippled through her, coupled with a tremor of longing. "Don't, Jack, please."

"I didn't mean to hurt you, Genny. I swear it. I'm not used to feeling like this. I don't know how to handle it."

Genny said nothing.

"I'm sorry, baby. Please. Let me make it up to you. Let me take the hurt away in the only way I know how."

Genny shook her head.

"Tell me you don't want me. Say it and I'll leave."

"I . . . don't . . . want you."

"Liar," he breathed, pressing himself against her. She could feel the hard brass snap on his jeans and the heavy bulge beneath his zipper. Genny moaned as his hands slid inside her nightgown and he softly cupped a breast.

"You look beautiful in that. Did you buy it for me?"

She tried to say no, but his lips were burning across her shoulders. "Yes . . ." she whispered. When he leaned against her, she realized that he had stripped off his shirt. Coarse black chest hair brushed deliciously across her back while his mouth trailed kisses down along the ridges of her spine.

For a moment she swayed against him. Then an image of Vivian Sandburg rushed sharply into focus, and a soft sob slipped from her throat.

"You were with h-her tonight, Jack. I can still smell h-her perfume."

Jack swore softly, fluently. For a moment he just stood there. The muscles in his powerful body were so taut she could feel their vibration. Then he turned her around, slid an arm beneath her knees, and swept her up against his bare torso.

"What are you . . . ?" The words died off as he strode with her into the bathroom. Jack opened the frosted glass door, turned on and adjusted the shower, and before she could think to protest, simply stepped in. Both of them were drenched in an instant, she in her pale blue nightgown, Jack still wearing his jeans and boots.

"I wasn't with Vivian . . . not the way you mean. I haven't been with another woman since I met you."

Something sweet rolled over her. She clutched his neck and rested her head in the hollow of his shoulder. "Jack . . ."

She hadn't meant to say it with such sweet longing, but Jack must have noticed, for he let her go and she slid down the length of his hard body. Warm water rushed over them, splashing against her skin as he lowered his head to kiss her. The wet blue nylon teased her nipples, clung to the place between her legs. Water cascaded down her shoulders, moistened her trembling lips, and beaded like dew on her skin. When Jack groaned and pressed her against him, she tangled her fingers in his wet black hair.

"I know you won't believe me," he said, "but I thought of you a hundred times tonight." He ravaged her mouth, plundered it, took from it and forced her to give in return. In minutes he had peeled off her clinging wet nightgown and begun to run his hands over her naked breasts. "I'm crazy about you, Genny." He kissed her deeply again, teasing her bottom lip then plunging his tongue inside her mouth. "I know it's trouble for both of us, but I can't seem to help myself."

"Oh, Jack." Genny kissed him back. Her nipples grew hard and aching as he stroked them with his hands, bent his head and took one into his mouth. He ringed the stiff peak with his tongue, then closed his teeth around it and gently bit the end. Genny trembled at the sharp stab of pleasure. Water lapped at her feet, sprayed over her flesh, ran in erotic little rivulets down her breasts and furrowed into the cleft of her sex.

Her fingers bit into Jack's powerful shoulders; her mouth teased the ridges of muscle on his chest. Then he was unzipping his wet thigh-hugging Levi's, letting his hardened arousal spring free. Lifting her up, he wrapped her legs around his hips, spreading her wide for him.

His fingers found her, eased inside, discovered her wet and ready. He stroked her there until she trembled, felt the spiraling tightness begin to build.

"I've got to be inside you," he whispered. He brought her down hard, filling her completely, sliding into her damp wet heat. A deep groan rose from his throat. "This is what I wanted all along," he said, easing himself out, then plunging fiercely back in. "Only I was too damned blind to see it."

Shaking with the force that pounded through her blood, Genny wrapped her arms around his neck, and Jack gripped her bottom. Steadying her with an easy strength, he drove into her again and again, until the blood pumping through her veins felt hotter than the steam rising up from the shower.

She cried out as the first climax hit her, a long piercing wave of rippling pleasure. It slid over like a spray of hot water, shimmering deliciously, making her writhe and squirm. When she felt Jack's muscles grow tense, felt him stiffen with his own release, she came again, moaning and sobbing and pressing herself against his long hard length.

Trembling all over, she clutched his thick neck and Jack held her against him, kissing her mouth, her nose, her cheeks.

"Thank God," he whispered, though she wasn't quite sure what that meant, then he gave her another soft kiss. "I'm sorry, Genny. So sorry."

She almost said something she knew she'd regret. It was there on the tip of her tongue, there inside her heart. She swallowed the three little words and kissed him instead.

"You're so damned sweet." He leaned over and turned off the water, grabbed a fluffy white towel and began to dry her off. "And so incredibly sexy."

But no one was as sexy as Jack Brennen. No man could be so roughly gentle, so tender yet tough, so achingly compelling. Surely no man she had ever met had the audacity to make love in the shower — still wearing his jeans and boots.

Perhaps that was the reason she decided to forgive him. Or perhaps it was simply that she had no choice.

Fifteen

"She's a murderer, Jack."

Naked beneath the sheets, Jack eased forward and propped his back against the carved oak headboard. Earlier, they had made love.

"Who's a murderer? What the devil are you talking about?"

"The woman in my dreams."

His gaze grew more intense as he noticed the tension Genny tried to hide. "You saw it? You saw her kill someone?"

"Not exactly, but I know she did."

"Who'd she kill?"

"Her husband."

He sighed and rested his head against the smooth wood. "Doesn't it seem the least bit co-incidental that your husband was also mur-dered — just like the woman in the dream?"

"In a way it does, but —"

"But what, Genny?" He leaned toward her. "The doctors have said all along that your dreams are a result of your husband's death. I think this proves it."

Genny shook her head. "I know on the sur-face it looks that way, but I don't really think that's what this is about."

"Then what *is* it about?"

She glanced away, no longer able to meet his gaze. "I-I'm not sure. I need to talk to Charley, see what he has to say, but it still seems to me it's part of a story. Once I piece it together, maybe I'll have the answer."

Jack relaxed a little, shoved his hands behind his head. "I don't know, Genny, this whole thing is just so incredibly weird."

"I know." She snuggled down beside him, resting her cheek on his chest. He ran a hand through her hair, easing out the tangles, noticing how soft and silky it felt. Genny moved a little, trying to get more comfortable. He felt her bare nipple teasing his skin and desire pooled low in his belly. Damn, she always made him want her. No one else, just her. It was driving him crazy.

He forced his thoughts back to the subject. "Are you still searching for where the dreams might be taking place?"

"Yes. I've decided to research the South. If the natives were slaves, that might explain some of what's happened, although I can't figure out how those awful bloody ceremonies fit in."

"If I recall from my history class in college —"

"College?" Genny sat up in bed, holding the sheet up over her breasts. "You went to college?"

A smile of amusement curved his lips. "Is that really so hard to believe?"

295

"Yes . . . no . . . I-I'm not really sure. Where did you go?"

"UCLA. I was there on a football scholarship. That's where I met Ollie. We played together for a couple of years. He was one helluva tailback."

"Why didn't you tell me?"

He shrugged. "I didn't figure you cared that much about football."

She smacked him on the stomach with her fist and he grunted. "I'm not talking about football and you know it."

Jack grinned. "I didn't tell you because it isn't important. I went to college because my father was determined I should follow in his footsteps, which I knew I never would. Besides, I never graduated. I tore up my knee the third year, which ended my football career, then I got thrown out for balling the dean's youngest daughter."

Genny gave him a scornful glance and fell back against her pillow. "*That* I find very easy to believe." She rolled toward him. "What were you saying about your history class?"

"I was saying, that if I remember correctly, slaves were brought to the South mostly from West Africa. That's where you found the religious ceremonies most like the ones in your dreams, right?"

"That's right — yes. I see what you mean. They would have brought their religious customs with them. Eventually they would have been influenced by their new surroundings, but

296

in the beginning they would have been pretty much the same. But none were brought in after 1808."

"Yeah . . . that sounds about right. I remember a law was passed against the importation of slaves. Of course slavery didn't really end till after the Civil War."

Genny looked at him oddly, but Jack just smiled. "Actually, the connection to the Southern plantations crossed my mind earlier," she said, "but at the time it just didn't feel right. In my dreams, the jungle seemed taller, more overgrown than anyplace I could think of in the South. Now I'm beginning to believe that might be where it is."

"It might be. Assuming any of this makes any kind of sense — which I don't really believe it does. Especially not now that you're telling me the woman's husband has also been murdered."

"Yes, but this woman was the one who did it. I wasn't." In her exuberance, the sheet had slipped a little and one of Genny's small pink nipples peeked enticingly out from above it.

Jack groaned. "I think I've heard enough on this subject for the morning." He pulled her down in the bed and rolled her beneath him. "I've got a far more interesting topic to explore."

Genny laughed and dragged his head down for a kiss. They made love slowly, thoroughly, then she climbed out of bed and went into the bathroom to shower and dress. Jack might have joined her if the phone hadn't started to ring.

He debated answering, but Charley might be calling with some unscheduled work and they could certainly use the money. He decided if he didn't recognize the voice he could always hang up. Which is exactly what he should have done, but at the sound of Howard McCormick's irritating tone, something just wouldn't let him.

"Genny? Genny is that you? Genny, this is Howard."

An unwelcome twinge of jealousy rolled over him. "Good morning, McCormick. How's it hanging?" He didn't like the slimy bastard, but he had to admit the guy was good-looking. And he had money and power, and a substantial position in the community — all the things a woman like Genny ought to have.

"Brennen . . . what the hell are you . . . ? Where's Genny?"

"She's in the shower."

"Then why are . . . ? You son of a bitch."

Jack smiled tightly into the receiver. "Genny doesn't think so — at least not this morning."

Another long pause. "This time you've outdone yourself, Jack. You've taken advantage of a lovely young woman who is far too naive to deal with your kind. I ought to come over and throw your worthless carcass out in the street."

Jack bristled. "We both know you haven't got the balls for that, but you're welcome to give it a try."

Standing in the doorway buttoning up her white cotton blouse, Genny heard Jack's words and a gasp of horror slid from her lips. "My God, it's Howard!"

"Sorry, gotta run," Jack said to him. "I'll be sure to give Genny your regards." He hung the phone up in the cradle, suddenly feeling like a jerk and trying to ignore the pallor on Genny's pretty face.

"How could you?" She walked toward him, her expression angry and accusing. "How could you do that to me?"

Swinging his legs to the side of the bed, Jack sat up and raked a hand through his hair. "To tell you the truth, I didn't mean to. Something just sort of came over me."

Genny blinked furiously and he caught the sheen of tears before she turned away. Feeling like a heel, Jack hauled himself to his feet. Wrapping the sheet around his waist and tucking it in, he crossed the floor till he stood in front of her.

"Dammit, Genny, I'm sorry. There's just something about that guy that brings out the worst in me."

Genny turned away from him and used the back of a hand to wipe away the wetness. "He's Bill's partner, Jack. Can you imagine what he's thinking right now? Can you imagine what he thinks of me?"

A slight tension gripped him. "He thinks you spent the night in bed with me. Me — Jack

Brennen. If you're ashamed of that, Genny, you won't have to worry about it happening again." Leaning over, he grabbed his shirt up off the floor and started for the bathroom to gather his still-damp jeans.

Genny stared at him with amazement. She had hurt him, she saw. She could tell by the look in his eyes and the muscle that jumped in his cheek. She caught him before he reached the door.

"I'm sorry, Jack. I didn't mean it to sound that way. I'm not ashamed of you, or anything we've done. It's just that Howard's my friend and I don't want to hurt him. Sometimes he's overly protective. I thought it would be best if he didn't know about us . . . for a while."

"You mean in case there wasn't an 'us' later on."

Her chin came up. "Yes, I guess that's exactly what I meant."

"Maybe there won't be, Genny. There's no way to know that for sure. But for now there definitely is, and I don't give a damn if McCormick likes it or not."

Genny stared at him for several long moments. A slow smile tugged at her lips. "There definitely is?" she repeated.

Jack grinned, dimples appearing in his cheeks. "Yeah, there definitely is."

Genny smiled wider. She'd make it up to Howard, find some way to make him understand. "In that case, why don't I finish getting dressed and cook you some breakfast?"

"I've had a sneaking suspicion you could cook, ever since I saw those blue ribbons on the wall in your kitchen."

"I used to be a real gourmet chef before Bill died. We entertained a lot of his business contacts — Bill was really proud of my cooking."

"So how come I'm just now getting a sample?" He followed her into the bathroom, where she picked up his damp jeans, jockey shorts, and soggy black cowboy boots.

"We can put your clothes in the dryer while we're eating," she said. "Not the boots, of course."

"So how come?" he repeated, following her out the door and down the stairs, the sheet riding low on his hips. His dense black chest hair arrowed down his flat-ridged stomach and disappeared beneath the folds.

"To tell you the truth, after he died, I discovered Bill got more enjoyment out of my cooking talents than I did." She turned and grinned up at him. "Which doesn't mean I've forgotten how it's done."

Jack smiled. "My stepmom was a great cook," he said. "Probably the only reason my dad ever came home at all."

Genny stopped at the bottom of the stairs. "They were really that unhappy?"

"Worse. I think they both led the most miserable lives two people could."

"Why did they stay together?"

"I haven't the slightest idea. I told them that a couple of times, but they looked at me like I had six heads. I guess they believed in 'till death do us part.' That's probably the reason my dad killed himself."

Genny stopped midway through the kitchen door, turned and stared into Jack's face. "Your father killed himself?"

Jack looked suddenly uncomfortable. "Yeah. He just sat there at the desk in his office and calmly put a bullet through his head."

"Why did he do it?"

He shrugged in that off-handed manner of his. "Near as we could figure, exactly the reason I said. He hated his boring life. He didn't know what to do about it, so he took the easy way out."

"Oh, Jack, I'm sorry."

"Don't be. The life he led, he was dead long before he was actually gone."

It was beginning to make sense, Genny thought. The reason Jack had always been so reckless. He was determined to live a life that was full instead of empty, to pack as much in, see, feel, experience all of the things his parents never did.

"Come on." Genny tugged on his arm. "You can help me in the kitchen — make sure I don't burn your eggs."

Jack grinned mischievously. "Honey, you can burn my eggs any time you like."

Genny blushed and poked him in the ribs.

Howard McCormick stared down at the telephone sitting beside his bed and his fingers itched to fling it across the room.

"That bastard." He itched even more to put his fist in Jack Brennen's arrogant face. How could Genny have fallen for a jerk like that? How could she be screwing Jack Brennen when she could have been with him?

He thought about the way he had always been so careful of her feelings, gone to every length to treat her like a lady. He should have dragged her down on the sofa, shoved up her skirt, and screwed her till she couldn't walk. That was probably what she'd been wanting all along, and he'd been too stupid to see it.

Howard swore foully. Brennen would pay for this. He'd make damned sure of that. He had backed off the fee hikes and regulation changes he'd been pushing for down at the docks, not wanting to stir up too many problems when he had other, more important business to conduct. Now he'd make sure they went through.

The *Marauder* would be forced to dock someplace else — preferably Oxnard or Port Hueneme. He smiled viciously. No more Jack Brennen. Once the bastard was gone, he'd think about taking up where he'd left off with Genny. He still wanted to take her to bed. He just wasn't sure now about marriage.

Still, there were a lot of pluses to that situation, financial as well as political. Genny was naive when it came to men; he could almost understand how a stud like Brennen could have conned her into his bed.

Howard clamped hard on his jaw. He should have taken better care to protect his interests, should have kept a better eye on her. Long before now, he should have firmly settled her in his bed.

The phone jangled loudly, and he jumped at the unwelcome intrusion. Howard picked up the receiver and the caller identified himself as Marty James.

"I told you never to call here," Howard said coldly. "What do you want?"

"I tried to reach you Friday at the office, but you weren't in. I need an answer on that pick-up date by six o'clock tomorrow morning. Is the boat on schedule or not?"

Howard felt a surge of satisfaction. "She'll be right on time." Macklin had done exactly what he'd told him, as Howard had been certain he would.

"Good. Everything's set for the pick-up. The goods will be delivered the following day."

"I'll have your money ready." Howard didn't bother to say good-bye, just set the phone back in its cradle. At least his business dealings were going smoothly.

Glancing in the mirror over the fireplace as he walked by, he took the comb from the pocket of his sport shirt and ran it through his thick brown hair. Pleased with his appearance, he replaced the comb and casually walked out of the room.

Jack made love to Genny that Sunday night, but she didn't reap the deep refreshing sleep that usually came with it. Instead, at two in the morning, Jack took hold of her thrashing shoulders and roughly shook her awake.

"For Chrissakes, Genny, wake up!"

She was bathed in perspiration, she realized, looking down at her arms and chest as she groggily came awake, and one of her hands cupped a breast. Beneath her palm, her nipple was hard and distended.

"What the hell is going on?" Jack asked.

Genny wet her trembling bottom lip. It was slightly swollen from the way her teeth had sunk in, and tasted faintly of blood.

"I-I was dreaming, Jack." As the images returned, heat rushed into her cheeks and her eyes stung with unshed tears. "There was a man . . . he was . . . he was . . ."

"Making love to you," Jack finished, a subtle tension gripping the muscles in his body. "It goddamned well better not have been Howard McCormick."

She glanced into the distance, unable to meet his condemning gaze. "It wasn't me . . . and it wasn't Howard. It was the woman in my dreams."

Jack looked down at her still-taut nipples.

"But you could feel it, couldn't you?"

"Yes."

"Was it good?" he asked harshly.

A sharp pain knifed through her. She stared down at the sheet, her fingers knotted around it. "It shouldn't have been. The man was a b-big ugly brute. H-He didn't even take her clothes off, he just . . . bent her over an old wooden barrel out in the barn, pushed up her skirts, and drove himself inside her."

She looked up at Jack and a tear rolled down her cheek. "She told him to, Jack. She ordered him to do it. She likes it rough — that's what she said. She challenged him to hurt her." More tears welled, Genny blinked, then tried to brush them away with a trembling hand.

"Ah, Christ . . ." Jack pulled her into his arms, the harshness seeping from his features. "It's all right, baby. It isn't your fault. I shouldn't have gotten upset."

Genny clung to his bare shoulders. "I can't stand it, Jack. What am I going to do?"

He hugged her hard against him. "I don't know, honey. Tonight, after I get back to the dock, we'll talk to Charley. Maybe he'll know what to do."

Genny nodded. She burrowed her head against Jack's shoulder and slid her arms around his neck. When the trembling in her limbs began to ease, she closed her eyes. Jack held her that way until she finally drifted back to sleep.

Genny called Howard from work Monday morning. She felt guilty and embarrassed after his phone conversation with Jack, but Howard was still her friend and she owed him at least some explanation.

"Howard? It's Genny."

"Hello, Genny." Disappointment laced his voice.

"Howard, I'm sorry about . . . the phone call. I know what you must be thinking . . . the way you must be feeling about me, and I want you to know I never meant for any of it to happen. Somehow it just did."

Silence. "Are you in love with him?"

She started to lie. "I'm . . . yes. Yes, Howard, I'm in love with him."

"I should have guessed that, I suppose. A woman like you wouldn't go to bed with a man unless she felt something for him. I wish you could have felt that way about me."

"I care for you, Howard, you know I do. I've always felt a great deal of affection for you."

"I wanted to marry you, Genny. What does Brennen want?"

Genny didn't answer. She knew what Jack wanted from a woman, and she had already given him that. Her fingers tightened around the phone.

"Genny?"

"I'm sorry I disappointed you, Howard."

"I'm worried about you, Genny. The man is

nothing but a no-account hustler. He's out for only one thing."

"It doesn't matter," she said softly. An ache suddenly rose in her throat. "It doesn't change the way I feel."

"I'm still your friend, Genny. I hope you won't forget that. I'll be here if you need me."

"Thank you, Howard." Genny quietly hung up the phone. Howard had always been there for her. How much longer before Jack would be gone? She didn't want to think about it. It made her heart hurt too much.

After work on Monday night, Charley sat in the galley listening to Genny's story. He noticed the worry in her expression, though she worked to keep it carefully controlled. He watched as she flipped through the pages of her notebook, opened a file, and pulled out the research she had been doing.

This time she told him everything, leaving nothing out, not even the embarrassing erotic fantasies she had experienced. Desperation drove her. Charley could feel it in every halting word. She never looked at him once until she was finished and her cheeks were tinged pink when she did. Damn, he felt sorry for her.

Jack must have felt that way, too. The whole time she talked, he held onto her hand. Charley had never seen him act that way with a woman.

It gave him hope that maybe Jack could put the past behind him. Get more out of life than just the *Marauder* and a string of one-night stands.

"So what do you think, Charley?" Jack asked when she had finished. "You're into this kinda stuff. Maybe that doctor she went to was right. Maybe her husband's murder is really the cause. Maybe she should go back and continue her therapy."

"Maybe," Charley said, assessing Genny carefully.

"Bill's death might be part of it," she said, "but that still wouldn't explain that . . . other." Her cheeks grew pink once more, and Jack squeezed her hand.

"No, it wouldn't," he said. His worried look softened as he studied her troubled expression. "But the doctor might be right about that, too. Maybe something happened when you were a child. Something you don't recall. Maybe someone . . . hurt you."

Genny shook her head, but not with nearly the same conviction as she had done before. "I'd remember something like that. I know I would."

"Maybe you are remembering," Charley put in gently, and she turned more squarely in his direction.

"How can I be, Charley? These things happened more than a hundred fifty years ago. Unless I'd read it somewhere, I couldn't possibly —"

"There are people who believe you could," he said. "If you had lived before."

Genny just stared at him. "You're not talking about reincarnation?"

He nodded. "Past lives."

"That's crazy, Charley," Jack said. "I hope you haven't been talking to ol' Doc Bailey again."

"What if I have?" He turned to Genny. "Jack's never agreed with Richard's beliefs, but I'm a bit more open-minded. The two of us have been debating the notion for years."

"Bailey's Charley's best friend," Jack explained to Genny. "He's got a sailboat down at the yacht club. Spends most of his time down there. I always thought he was a little weird."

"He's retired now," Charley said to Genny, "but he used to be a child psychologist. We met when my boy Bobby first got into trouble. He loves boats almost as much as I do, and over the years we discovered we had other things in common. We've been good friends ever since."

"And Bailey believes in reincarnation," Genny said.

"He got interested when he was working with the children. You see when we're young, we aren't so set in our ways. We're more open-minded about things — we haven't been taught yet what's supposed to be real and what isn't."

"Now I remember . . ." Jack leaned forward in his chair. "You told me about a case he had of a little girl brought to him with an obsessive fear of water. She kept dreaming that she was ice-skating, that she fell through the ice and was swept away beneath it. She could see her parents' faces as they frantically tried to reach her, but the ice was too thick for them to break through."

"That's right," Charley said. "She kept saying that the people in her dream were her real parents, and she was crying about how much she missed them." He fixed his gaze on Genny. "Under hypnosis, the little girl recalled the year as 1891. It happened in Springfield, Ohio. Her name was Prudence O'Banyon."

Genny nervously ran her tongue across her lips. Perspiration glowed on her forehead and her face looked pale.

"Richard became so certain the child was telling the truth," Charley continued, "he went back to Ohio to find out for himself. He dug through old newspaper records for the year of 1891, and guess what he found?"

"What?" Genny asked softly.

"In December of that year, a little girl named Prudence O'Banyon had fallen through the ice and drowned. Her mother had nearly drowned trying to save her."

"Oh, my God."

"I think you oughta talk to him, Genny."

"Even if it's possible," Jack said, "it doesn't mean that's what's happening to Genny."

"No, it doesn't," Charley said, "but if she wants to find the answer to her problem, she's gonna have to look at all the possibilities."

"Are . . . Are you saying you think I might

have lived during the time of my dreams?" Genny asked. "That I was somehow involved in what's been happening?"

"I'm saying it's something to consider. You coulda been anyone who lived back then, someone who had dealings with the woman. Maybe you were one of the servants she mistreated."

"Or maybe even the woman herself." Genny's face was so pale it looked translucent.

"You couldn't have been the woman in the dreams," Jack argued. "You're nothing like that. You're sweet and gentle. You can't even kill an insect, let alone murder someone."

"Take it easy, Jack," Charley said. "We don't know what connection Genny might have had. I'm only sayin' she might want to try and find out."

"I'm sorry, Charley," she said. "I just don't believe in past lives. It has to be something else."

Charley reached for her hand. It felt as cold as ice and as brittle as a winter leaf. "I'm not sayin' it's that for sure. I'm only saying it's something to think about. Richard says once the patient discovers the truth, the residue in this life begins to fade. If it is a past life and you figure it out, most likely your dreams would go away."

Genny just shook her head. She gently touched Jack's shoulder. "I'm afraid I'm not very good company tonight, Jack. Do you think you could take me back home?"

"I'm sorry, Genny girl," Charley said. "I

didn't mean to upset you."

Genny smiled wanly. "It isn't your fault, Charley. Give me a little time to think about it, okay?" Charley just nodded. Genny left with Jack, and once they reached home, she felt a little bit better.

"I'm sorry Charley wasn't more help," Jack said as they curled up in bed, but Genny kept remembering the dreams, how real they felt, almost as if she had been there.

"It's all right. It's as good an explanation as anything else." But it worried her to think it might be true. She wished he had never brought it up.

And she wished she could stop thinking about what he had said.

Sixteen

Curled on her side in her big antique bed, Genny felt Jack's mouth brush the nape of her neck.

"That was so damned good."

She smiled contentedly. Letting the last warm remnants of their lovemaking drift over her, she sleepily closed her eyes and let him draw her against him. It felt good to have him there. His big male body made her feel small and feminine and oddly protected. But with the graying of dawn, over a steaming cup of coffee, she discovered that he would soon be gone.

"I've got to go away for a couple days, baby. I hate to leave when you're feeling so damned bad, but I'm making a last-ditch effort to get the money we need for the boat. I've got some people to see down at the harbor in Long Beach. If there's any chance at all of saving the *Marauder*, I've got to give it a try."

"Of course you do. I'll be fine while you're gone. Please don't worry about me."

But it was obvious he was worried, and the concern on his face gave her hope that it might work out between them.

She thought about the evening they had

spent with Charley, discussing her dreams, trying to decide what to do, and debating the possibility of having lived a life in the past. She appreciated Charley's attempt to help, but the concept of reincarnation was so foreign, so totally out of her realm of experience that she refused to give it any credence.

Of all the things she was willing to consider, a past life wasn't one of them. It was too far-fetched, too remote a possibility.

Just too darned scary.

Instead, she focused her attention on the problems she faced with Jack and finding a way to bridge the gap in their lifestyles that always came between them. After careful consideration, an idea occurred that offered at least some hope of a beginning. If she could make it work.

First thing Tuesday morning, she walked behind the reference desk to talk to Millicent Winslow.

"How was your weekend?" Millie asked. A slow smile softened the planes of her narrow face. Today she wore a simple blue suit, with her blond hair pulled back by gold clips at the sides of her face. "Scandalously delicious, I suppose."

"It definitely had its ups and downs."

Millie's eyes widened, and Genny laughed. "The truth is it started out bad, but ended up good. Now, what I really want to talk to you about is the favor I'd like to ask."

"Are you kidding? I owe you more favors than I can count. Who else but you would be willing to water my overgrown house plants and take care of my parakeet? Last time you even cleaned the bottom of Izzy's cage." Millie smiled. She had a very nice smile, Genny thought, wondering why some man couldn't see that. "So what's the favor?" Millie asked.

"I know this is going to sound crazy, but I want you to invite me over to your parents' house."

"That's no problem." Millie cocked a pale blond eyebrow. "What for?"

"If I remember correctly, your father has a billiard table. It seems to me, he's an expert pool player."

"Archibald Winslow III is an expert at nearly anything he sets his mind to. Pool just happens to be one of them." Millie gave her a searching glance. "Oh, I get it — you want Daddy to teach you to play, so you can shoot pool with Jack."

Genny smiled. "Exactly."

"I can do better than that."

"What do you mean?"

Millie's face lit up with a grin. "I'll teach you myself. Believe it or not, Daddy's little girl can make that old cue ball dance."

"You're kidding."

"Nope. Daddy needed someone to play with. I was the closest at hand. I'll make you a master of the green in no time at all."

Genny caught Millie's arm, excitement rushing through her. "Do you really think I can do it?"

"If I can do it, you can."

Genny reached over and hugged her. She could almost see the look on Jack's face when she showed him that she had learned to play. "I'll never forget you for this, Millie. Never."

"You better not say that yet. You don't know what a tough taskmaster I am."

But Genny just grinned and so did Millie. For the first time in days, she felt as if something positive was happening in her life. It was only a small step, but in the mundane world of Genny Austin, Assistant Branch Librarian, it was an important one. And with Jack out of town, there was no better time to start than the present.

With the Winslows visiting their Florida retreat in Boca Raton, Genny picked Millie up at her apartment right after work and they drove out to Montecito, to the family's eight-acre estate off San Ysidro Road. They were pulling through the high wrought-iron gates, driving up the circular gravel driveway toward the big stone house in the distance when Genny's hands began to tremble on the steering wheel.

Staring straight ahead, blinking furiously against what she had begun to see, she fought against the images flashing through her mind, but her vision continued to blur and retreat. Darkness tunneled in, sucking her back into the

317

past, until all she saw was a small square window of light in the distance.

Some remote part of her had the good sense to step on the brake, but she never heard Millie's frantic, worried voice, or the sound of the car door opening as her slender friend raced toward the house to get help.

She saw only the three barefoot black servants standing near the massive carved front doors of another huge stone house, listened as they spoke to one another in some odd-sounding language she caught bits and pieces of but couldn't understand. They were laughing among themselves, unaware that the woman with the long black hair also stood watching. Dressed in a burgundy riding habit, with a small matching hat angled perfectly atop her head, she stepped from behind a shrub, slapping her riding crop against the side of a petite black boot.

"I see you are all standing about instead of working, gossiping again as I have repeatedly warned you not to. Not enough to do, perhaps?"

"No, miztress," one of them answered nervously, hedging toward the door. "They's plenty for us to do. We all be gettin' back to it right now." They started to shuffle away.

"That is a very good idea," the woman called after them. "All of you get back to work — all but you, Flora." The woman grabbed the youngest girl's arm and roughly jerked her around.

When she did, a small round cameo fell from the girl's shaking hands. The other two women gasped at the tell-tale sight. Their faces seemed to pale beneath their shiny black skin.

"Well, look what we have here." The woman bent to retrieve the fallen object. "Isn't this interesting." She fingered the small carved, gold-encased gemstone she recognized as her own. "You're new here, Flora. Has no one told you the penalty for stealing?" A cruel smile curved her lips. "Do you know how we deal with thieves around here?"

"She just a young'un," one of the older women pleaded. "Don't got nobody to take her in hand. Let her go dis time and she won't neber do nothin' like dat again."

The woman's eyes grew hard. They were as black and shining as her hair. "Young or not, the rules are the same for everyone. After today, she'll remember to obey them." She jerked the girl forward, down the wide stone stairs, and around the side of the house. The overseer came running, the big ugly man who had been the woman's lover.

"The girl's a thief," she simply said. "You know what to do about that."

He twisted his woven straw hat in his massive, thick-fingered hands. "I dunno, she's awful young. Maybe just this once we ought to —"

"Are you contradicting my orders, Maubry?"

"No . . . no, of course not." He looked from

the woman to the girl, who squealed as he grabbed her arm and hauled her up on her toes. When she began to cry, he dragged her away. By the time he reached the barn, she was screaming and pleading, begging him to let her go.

Genny just stared straight ahead through the windshield. The last thing she remembered was the sound of the woman's biting laughter, and the smell of burning flesh as the hot iron brand pressed into the girl's bare skin above her breast.

"Genny! Genny — what is it? Genny — tell me what's wrong!"

A whimpering sound tore from her throat. Millicent leaned into the car, frantically shaking Genny's shoulder. She shuddered as her eyes finally came into focus, released a ragged breath, and let her head fall back against the seat. A hot stream of tears washed down her cheeks.

"I'm going crazy. Millie, I think I'm going out of my mind."

"Here — let me help you." With the aid of the housekeeper and an upstairs maid, Millie helped Genny out of the car, across the circular drive, and up on the porch.

"They're getting w-worse, Millie. I was seeing the people in my dreams — only this time I was awake."

"Oh, God."

They went into a downstairs parlor and the

housekeeper, a stout woman in a crisp black skirt and simple white blouse, hurried in with a pot of tea. Genny accepted the expensive Sèvres cup with a trembling hand and set it down on an antique marble-topped table. When she calmed a bit, she began to drink the tea. A sip or two and she felt a little more steady. Once she did, she was able to tell Millie what had happened.

"It's frightening," Millie said when Genny had finished. She uncrossed her long, thin legs. "I'm beginning to understand how terrible this must be for you."

"What am I going to do, Millie?"

"You could always go back to Dr. Halpern."

"If I thought it would help, I would, but I don't think that's the answer." She sat quietly for a while, sipping the strong hot tea, letting it seep into her bones, allowing its warmth to replace the despair she was feeling. Eventually her tension began to ease.

"Are you feeling any better?" Millie asked.

"Yes. I'm fine now. Thank you."

"Come on, I'll drive you home." Leaning forward, she set the delicate porcelain cup back in its saucer.

Genny looked up and slowly shook her head. "Going home right now is the last thing I want to do." She smiled but it came out a little forlorn. "Besides, I'm not letting you off that easy. We came here so you could teach me to play pool." Her lips curved up with a little more

321

ease. "That's exactly what we're going to do."

Millie smiled. "That's the spirit!"

The lesson went till late in the evening, and helped Genny keep her mind off what had happened in the car. Millie hadn't exaggerated — she was good at shooting pool. She was also a very good teacher, and Genny was a very determined pupil.

She returned home exhausted, but enthusiastic about the progress she had made. Still, as tired as she was, she wasn't the least bit sleepy. She was afraid to fall asleep, afraid of what she might see.

When she finally closed her eyes, the words the servants had spoken in front of the mansion rumbled around inside her head. Odd words that sounded like *d-weet, gwine, worra, irie, hoofa, cho, neber.* Tomorrow, she decided, she would try to decipher the language.

With the graying light of dawn, she finally drifted to sleep, only to awaken a few minutes later to the ringing of the alarm clock, telling her it was time to get ready for work. She dragged her weary body out of bed and forced herself to dress.

Oliver Madison Brown sat across from Charley Denton in the galley of the *Marauder*, playing a game of gin rummy. Bebe's mom was feeling poorly, so she had gone down to Orange County for a couple of days. He was taking care of the kids but tonight they'd asked to sleep over at their friends, Tabor and Debbie Swift's house. Since Vicki Swift was Bebe's best friend, Vicki had taken pity on him and agreed.

Which left him rattling around the house alone. He'd gone for a drive in the '64 T-bird he'd bought for a song and almost finished restoring. He wound up down at the dock, hoping Jack would be home. Instead he found Charley. What the hell, both of them were looking for something to do, so they sent out for pizza and sat down to a game of cards.

They were well into their sixth game of gin when someone knocked at the door. Charley went to open it, then motioned for Genny Austin to come in.

"Oh . . . I'm sorry, Charley, I didn't realize you had company."

"You remember Ollie, don't you?"

"Of course. Hello, Ollie."

"Hi, Genny. Nice to see you."

"I don't want to interrupt your game. I was just out for a walk and thought I'd stop in."

Charley eyed her shrewdly. Ollie spotted the fatigue even makeup couldn't hide, and remembered Jack mentioning her battle with insomnia and nightmares. Charley had mentioned them, too. Jesus, he felt sorry for her.

"What are you playing?" she asked, one hand twisting a button on her sweater.

"Gin," Charley said, "but Owl's beating the pants off me."

"I used to like to play hearts when I was a kid."

Ollie's interest picked up. "You play hearts?"

She smiled. "In my family, that was one game we took deadly serious."

Ollie grinned and rubbed his palms together. "Hot damn, Charley, a good game of hearts beats the hell out of gin. What do you say?"

"I say, pull up a chair, girl. We're about to deal you in."

She did just that, smiling with genuine excitement. There was a warmth about her, a gentleness that showed in her pretty brown eyes and sweetened the curve of her lips.

"I haven't played in years," she said. "I might be a little bit rusty." She sat down in the chair with such a hopeful expression it made Ollie want to let her win. Charley dealt the cards.

It didn't take her long to get into the game. She was damned good, too. He had to work hard to keep from losing. They were playing cut-throat, where the guy with the lowest number of hearts — the object of the game — got pounced on by his other two opponents.

When the pizza came, the three of them were just about even.

"So how's the research coming?" Charley asked, easing into the subject it was obvious he'd been dying to discuss since Genny walked in. She glanced in Ollie's direction, uncertain of how much he knew.

"Jack told me a little about your nightmares,"

Ollie said gently. "He says you're trying to find out more about them, figure out if it's something you might have seen or read."

"I wish it was that simple," Genny said softly.

Charley swallowed the bite of pizza he had just taken. "You been thinkin' about what I said?"

"Some." She took a slip of paper out of the pocket of her jeans, a black stone-washed pair that looked brand new. "Something came up the other day. I worked on it today at the library, but I wasn't able to track it down."

She handed Charley the slip of paper and he studied it thoughtfully. "What is it?"

"Words I heard the other day when I was . . . words from one of my dreams. I heard some of the servants talking. I was trying to figure out what language it is."

Ollie reached for the slip of paper. He read the words aloud. "*D-weet, gwine, worra, irie, hoofa, cho, neber.* They don't look like anything I've ever seen."

"I wrote them phonetically, just as they sounded." She looked at him oddly. "Say them again."

Ollie smiled and repeated the words.

"It sounds different when you say it. It sounds exactly like it did in the dream."

Ollie looked down at the paper and suddenly his smile turned into a grin. "I d-weet," he said in his big deep voice. "When you gwine do dat? Mebe neber. Ah worra did you say?"

"Oh, my God."

"It's Pidgin, Genny," he said.

"Pigeon. Very funny, Ollie."

He chuckled, the rumble coming from deep in his chest. "Not like a bird. Pidgin English. Sort of a combination of African slang and spoken English."

"Pidgin . . . yes, now I remember. I've seen it mentioned in articles I've read." She looked at Ollie. "I understood all but the last."

"Ah worra did you say?" he repeated. "That means, What did you say?"

"How did you —"

"My mother used to live on Barbados. We visited her folks there a couple of times when I was a kid. I remember they talked that way there."

"Barbados," Genny repeated.

"That's right."

"Not the South," she said, her eyes growing bigger, "the West Indies." She glanced to Charley, then back at Ollie. "And they have jungles there!"

"Some of the islands do."

"Barbados?" she asked hopefully.

"Not that I know of." Her pretty face fell. "Don't look so disappointed. There's a lot of islands in the Caribbean."

She studied the words on the paper. Her brows drew together in thought. "And back in the early eighteen hundreds, lots of plantations like the one in my dreams."

Just then footsteps sounded on the deck of the boat. Jack jerked open the cabin door. There was a murderous scowl on his face. He took in the sight of his two friends sitting with Genny, and relief swept over him. A pleased grin cracked across his face.

"I went by your house but you weren't home," he said, accounting, Ollie figured, for the black look he'd come in with. He glanced down at the empty carton of pizza, then at the rumpled deck of cards in front of Charley. "What the hell did you teach her to play?"

"We're playing hearts," Ollie answered. "And Genny's been teaching *us* a thing or two."

"You play hearts?" he asked, incredulous.

She only nodded. But her eyes were full of Jack, and it was obvious how glad she was to see him. Jack bent his head and kissed her full on the mouth. Apparently he was glad to see her, too.

Ollie chuckled. "I think it's time to go." Hefting his big bulk out of the chair, he clapped Jack on the shoulder. "Good to see you, my man."

"Don't let me run you off," Jack said, but already he was reaching for Genny, urging her to her feet and sliding an arm around her waist.

Ollie just grinned. Maybe his wife was right. Maybe Jack had found his match after all. He hoped so. Jack deserved to be happy. Then again the odds were against it. Jack Brennen had always been too restless to stay with one woman for very long. Ollie sighed as he headed for the door, hoping sweet little Genny wouldn't get hurt too badly.

If Charley was right, she had more than enough troubles already.

It was Charley's birthday. Today he was fifty-eight years old. As a special treat, Jack had asked Genny if she would mind cooking dinner — as long as he provided all the food.

"I'll round up a batch of fresh seafood," he promised. "Do you know how to cook lobster?"

"Are you kidding? You just bring me those tails and I'll make them melt in your mouth."

Jack grinned. "I was thinking a little bit fresher than that." One of his buddies had caught a mess of lobsters the day before. And he bought shrimp and oysters from a guy who sold them right off the deck of his boat.

Genny boiled the shrimp and served it cold, made oysters Rockefeller, steamed the lobster and vegetables, and made a big green leafy salad. She was fixing chocolate soufflés for dessert, which he figured would be the tricky part, considering the old propane stove in his galley, but Genny thought she could make it work.

He was watching her in the galley, thinking how cute she looked, up to her elbows in lettuce, dodging grease from a skillet full of bacon she meant to use with the oysters, when someone pounded on the cabin door. Wondering who it might be, Jack crossed the room and pulled it open to find three men in pin-striped suits standing on the deck.

"Hello, Captain Brennen," one of them said. "My name is Vernon Wilson and this is my associate, Ted MacArthur. We're with Santa Barbara National Bank. This gentleman is Allen Kline, one of our clients."

A shaft of tension speared through him. The hand propped on the doorjamb balled unconsciously into a fist. "What do you want?"

"We'd like to get a look at your boat, Captain Brennen. Mr. Kline may be interested in making a purchase, but time is of the essence. He'd like to be certain the *Marauder* will meet his needs."

Jack worked a muscle in his jaw, forcing himself under control. "Our note's not due for another three weeks. In the meantime, the *Marauder* isn't for sale." He looked at the blue-suited bankers. "Unless you're planning on extending our loan, I'd suggest you turn around and beat a hasty exit off my boat."

"We were hoping you'd be reasonable, Mr. Brennen."

"Yeah, well you hoped wrong. Now get the hell outta here." The men backed away, and Jack slammed the door in their faces. "Goddamned vultures," he muttered, anger still humming through him.

His trip to Long Beach had been no more fruitful than any of his other efforts. Now with the bankers pounding on his door, threatening foreclosure any minute, Charley's birthday party suddenly took a dismal turn.

Genny continued making dinner, but for Jack the joy had gone out of it. As good as the food turned out to be, as much as he wanted to make the day special for Charley, it was hard to get in the spirit. Both he and Charley remained quiet throughout the meal, and even Genny's efforts to lighten the atmosphere did little to help their plunging mood.

She pretended not to notice, of course, smiling with triumph as she served her beautiful soufflés, but when Jack walked her home, it was obvious his temper hadn't improved.

"I know you've got a lot on your mind tonight," she said, as they stood at her door. "You don't have to stay if you don't want to."

He'd be lousy company if he did. Hell, he wasn't even in the mood for sex. "If I don't, you won't get any sleep."

"Maybe I will. Besides, that isn't your problem."

He stared back toward the harbor, to the twinkling lights in the distance. He thought of the *Marauder*, of how close he was to losing her, and his insides felt leaden. "I've got some work I'd like to do, if you don't mind."

She cupped his cheek with her hand but even her gentle touch couldn't soothe him. "Of course I don't mind."

"Thanks for what you did for Charley. The dinner was really terrific."

She smiled. "My pleasure."

"You'll be all right, won't you?" He felt guilty in a way, but tonight he just couldn't help it.

"You don't have to baby-sit me, Jack."

He smiled at that. For such a willowy little thing, she sure had plenty of grit. Jack bent his head and kissed her, but his mind was on the boat and what his life would be like if he lost what he'd worked so hard for. "Good night, Genny."

Genny watched his tall frame fading in the distance. When he finally disappeared from view, she went into the living room and sat down on the sofa. At the opposite end, Skeeter awakened, stretched, and came over for a visit. Genny scooped him up and nuzzled him against her cheek, grateful for his tiny warm presence, and Jack's thoughtfulness in giving him to her.

She knew how bad he was feeling; she had seen it in his eyes all evening. She wished there was some way she could help him.

Jack called the next day, but he didn't have time to see her. He was working on the books, he said, digging for anything he might find that could help them save their boat. She tried to think of something she could do, but the money she had in her savings account wouldn't be nearly enough. As trustee of her shares, Howard would hardly agree to a request for a loan against her stock, and Jack probably wouldn't accept it anyway.

She wound up staying late at the library,

reading detailed histories of the Caribbean, but it soon became apparent that she would need more information. Her dreams could have taken place on any number of islands. Plantations were the norm, slavery the means used to work them. She left about seven-thirty, met Millie over at her parents' house, and spent the balance of the evening shooting pool.

Genny smiled to think of it. Millie really could make the cue ball dance. And to Genny's own surprise, she herself seemed to have a natural aptitude for finessing the ball and deciphering the geometric patterns that were the key to playing the game.

On Friday night, it grew cloudy. Genny paced the floor in her living room, waiting for Jack to arrive. He had called her at work to ask if he could come over. She had offered to fix him dinner, and he had agreed.

Genny stared out into the darkness. On the street below, gold and burnished leaves whirled in wind-twisted circles, and a stiff breeze whipped them against the window panes.

She spotted Jack's tall figure coming up the walkway and felt the usual fluttering in her stomach.

"Sorry I'm late," he said. "We had some trouble with the knuckle crane. Took us longer to finish than we guessed."

"That's all right." She smiled up at him. "Are you hungry?"

"Starved."

"How does lamb stew sound? I've got garlic French bread and a bottle of good red wine."

"Perfect. Let's start with the wine." He busied himself with the opener and Genny watched him from the corner of her eye. He seemed a million miles away. Genny set the steaming bowls of stew on the table, lit the candles she had set in the middle, and Jack poured the wine into glasses. He still seemed distracted. Genny worried about what he was thinking.

They ate for the most part in silence, with just an occasional attempt at conversation that seemed to go nowhere.

"Here, let me help you," Jack said when the meal was over, shoving back his chair as he came to his feet.

"Thanks." They cleared the table together, then stretched out on a blanket in front of the fire with a bowl of popcorn and two tall glasses of milk. Curling into a fuzzy ball at their feet, Skeeter dozed contentedly, while Genny studied Jack's somber expression.

"What will you do?" she finally asked as he absently rubbed her shoulder and broodingly stared into the flames. They both knew the question she was posing — what would happen if he lost the boat.

Using a long iron poker, Jack stoked the coals in the hearth, then watched a small red-gold shower drift up the chimney. "I'll have to look for work. There's at least two guys for every job around here, so I'll have to try someplace farther away."

"You mean like Oxnard or Port Hueneme?" Not that long a distance, only half an hour's drive. When Jack shook his head, Genny realized for the first time just what the situation meant to her. "You'd have to leave Santa Barbara completely? Where . . . where would you go?"

His shrugged his wide shoulders, bunching the muscles beneath his shirt. "San Pedro, maybe. I know some guys down there. Maybe San Diego, I'm not sure."

"San Diego . . ." Hours away, not minutes. It suddenly felt hard to breathe. "That's . . . that's so far away."

Jack shoved a hand through his curly black hair and sat up turning to face her. "Yeah, it is." Firelight flickered on his dark-tanned skin, the shade of burnished copper.

"What about Charley?"

"He's got a small monthly income from some property he sold a few years back. It doesn't take much for him to live, but I doubt he'll be able to afford Santa Barbara."

Both of them would be gone. A sweep of dread rolled over her, squeezing a tightness into her chest.

Jack saw the look on her face. "I know this isn't what you want to hear, Genny, but sometimes things like this happen for the best."

Her fingers curled into her palms. "You're

talking about us, now, aren't you?"

Jack's gaze swung away from her, then settled on crackling blue-tipped flames the color of his eyes. "I've been thinking things over lately. Trying to get my priorities straight."

Genny sat up, too, her insides turning to jelly. "And I'm . . . I'm not one of your priorities, right?"

"Don't put words in my mouth, Genny, that isn't what I meant. It's just that . . . right now . . . I'm not exactly sure how all of this is going to turn out."

Her heart tripped, twisted. "Are you saying . . . are you telling me you don't want to see me anymore?"

Jack closed his eyes. She felt his arm around her shoulders, drawing her closer. A big hand stroked through her hair. "No, baby, I'm not saying that. I'm only telling you that things may have to change. When they do, we can't be sure what will happen."

Genny's heart hammered. *Things may have to change.* No, please, she didn't want them to change. She didn't want to lose him. He had come to mean so much to her. Tears gathered in her eyes. Genny slid her arms around his neck. "Oh, Jack."

"Take it easy, honey. Nothing's happened yet. I'm only trying to warn you so you can be prepared."

Genny clutched him tighter. She would never be prepared to lose Jack. Never. "Make love to me, Jack," she whispered with quiet desperation. "I've missed you these last few days."

"I've missed you, too, baby." He turned her into his arms and kissed her. Dragging her down on the blanket, he began to strip off her clothes. He was as thorough as he always was, as passionate, as tender.

Yet it seemed like something was missing. Genny refused to consider what it was.

Seventeen

Standing in the navigation room, Jack stared out through the heavy rain toward the red and green lights signaling the mouth of the harbor. They'd been docked for about thirty minutes, running just ahead of a storm sweeping up from the south. He was damned glad to be home.

The day had been a bitch, fighting ten-foot seas that finally drove them back to the harbor and seemed to be getting worse as the hours slipped past. He was wet, cold, and exhausted. As soon as he finished his paperwork, he'd be ready for a change of clothes and a hot steaming shower.

Next to where he stood checking the fuel gauges, the radio crackled to life, and Jack's attention focused on the caller's barely audible words.

"Hey, Charley, listen to this." There was a mayday coming in. It was badly broken up — the operator's bearings muffled by static — but Jack was certain that's what he'd heard. Both of them listened hard in the silence.

"There it is again," he said when the familiar scratchy sounds reappeared.

Charley leaned toward the speaker. "Jesus,

Jack, that's the *Opus II*. She sounds like she's out in the channel."

"Wherever she is, she's in trouble. I wonder if the Coast Guard was able to lock onto her signal."

"Old Cap Macklin better hope so. There must be a twelve-foot swell out there tonight and the wind is howling like a banshee."

"Yeah, that's one hellion of a storm and it's only getting worse."

"The *Opus* is big enough to handle it. She must have had some kind of mechanical problem. Macklin never was much on keepin' things ship-shape."

"You got that right. He'd rather spend his money on booze and women than keeping his equipment in condition."

The radio crackled again and the mayday was repeated several times more, but each time the longitude and latitude of the ship's position was lost in the static. The coast guard responded, asking them to repeat their location, then Jack heard a loud eruption of noise that cracked like an explosion.

"Christ, Charley."

Both of them stood there frozen. They weren't fond of Bob Macklin, few people were, but they wouldn't wish disaster on him or anyone else.

"Doesn't sound good," Charley said into the quiet broken only by the Coast Guard's repeated attempts to get a fix on the ship's position. Silence was their only response.

"It sure as hell doesn't."

"Do you think he's goin' down?"

"God, I hope not."

They listened for several more hours, but no more broadcasts came across the channel. The Coast Guard kept up its efforts to pierce the ominous void, but nothing seemed to work. No sightings of Macklin's vessel were reported. No one had seen or heard anything that might be of help.

As the hour grew late, Jack called Genny on his cellular phone, told her what had happened, and that he was staying aboard. At first light, he planned to join the search for the ship. He wanted to be ready to leave.

That night he didn't sleep well. He was worried about the crew on board the *Opus*, and worried that again tonight he wouldn't be with Genny. Without him there, she wouldn't get a good night's sleep, or if she did, she might suffer one of her terrible dreams.

He woke up bleary-eyed and foul-tempered, angry that concern for Genny had put him so out of sorts. It bothered him that he was coming to care for her so much. He didn't want to feel that way about a woman. He couldn't risk getting that involved.

For thirty-three years, he had avoided commitment. He didn't want to settle down, to wind up spending the next fifty years on the couch in front of the TV. He had hoped to overcome his desire for her by taking her to bed. Now that he had, he kept telling himself that in a little more time, he would get over her. He'd be looking for a new piece of tail, someone else who turned him on.

But it still hadn't happened and he was getting himself in way too deep. Maybe leaving Santa Barbara wasn't such a bad idea. Maybe it would be the best thing for both of them.

At the crack of dawn, he rolled out of bed, dressed, and in minutes was standing in the wheelhouse, checking the weather and going over the charts. The seas were still white-capped and frothy, but the swell had receded enough they could make way without a problem. They checked in with the Coast Guard, who had plotted a grid-style search course, and with Raymond to help them crew, prepared to leave the harbor.

It was a grueling day of fighting high seas, rainy skies, and icy temperatures — and fruitlessly scanning the horizon. As late afternoon wore on, and the search boats continued to check in, it was becoming more and more obvious the *Opus II* had gone down. Apparently with a complete loss of cargo and crew.

"It makes me sick to think about it, Charley." Jack pressed his binoculars against his tired, gritty eyes for the hundredth time that day. The whop, whop, whop, of a rescue helicopter passing overhead grew louder then began to fade away.

"Wonder what he was haulin'," Charley said, and Jack's tired eyes swung toward him.

"Could be anything. His usual run was from Mexico to San Francisco. Or San Fran to Hawaii then south again. Last I heard, he was shipping mostly out of Manzanillo, copper wire from a smelter near Canyon Azul."

"Might be worth some pretty good money, if a guy could find it and bring it up."

Jack had started to think the same thing. If the ship had gone down, there was nothing they could do about it. But it just might be a means of saving their own boat instead.

"Yeah, it's the 'finding it' part that's the kicker."

"Not necessarily." Charley turned to him with a grin. "Not if one of the crew was to give us an idea where the *Opus* was when she exploded."

Jack saw then what Charley had already spotted, a small floating raft bobbing in the distance. Through the binoculars, he could just make out the letters *Opus II*.

"Crank her up, Charley." Any other time, he would have called the Coast Guard as soon as he saw the small craft. This time, he full-throttled the engines and prayed the chopper hadn't radioed in the raft's position.

"You didn't call 'er in?" Charley said as the big boat drove forward, battling the heavy seas.

"Not yet."

"What if one of those guys is injured?"

"Jesus, I hadn't thought of that. Think we dare to risk it?"

"We're damned near there. I say we hold."

Jack did so with mixed emotions. If one of the men had been hurt or badly burned, his conscience would have the devil to pay. He plowed ahead. Every wave seemed bigger than the last. When they finally reached the bobbing rubber raft, he called in their location, then left the wheel to Raymond while he and Charley made their way up on deck.

"Ahoy, *Marauder*!" someone in the raft called out.

Jack waved and called back a response as Raymond pulled the big boat in closer.

"Damn, you're a helluva sight for these old eyes," a craggy-faced man called out from the near end of the raft.

"Anyone hurt?" Jack asked as soon as they were close enough to hear him.

"None of us. We were working on the aft deck when the ship exploded. With all that copper, as soon as she heeled and the cargo shifted, she sank like she had lead weights tied to her tail. Far as I know, we're the only ones who got out alive."

Jack tied a line to the raft then helped the sodden men aboard. They were drenched and shaking with cold, suffering from exposure. He was glad he hadn't waited any longer to call for help.

There were four men in all, two of them in

their twenties, and two seasoned sailors in their forties. Except for the chilly night they had spent on the water, they seemed to have fared pretty well. Jack and Charley herded them into the galley, and Charley shoved a steaming mug of coffee into each man's shaking hands.

"Strip off those clothes," Charley ordered. "I'll round up something dry for you to wear."

They talked as they undressed, Jack picking up bits and pieces of information.

"What do you think caused the explosion?" he asked, easing into the subject of where the ship had gone down.

"Phosphate. We had several tons of the stuff on board."

"What happened?"

"The trouble started when the main electrical panel shorted out and caught fire," another man said. "Damn thing had been giving us fits since we left Manzanillo. Macklin knew it needed work. The bastard should have had it fixed before we left port."

"We thought we had it licked," the first man said. "We got the damned fire out and bypassed the panel to the sub-panel controlling the lights, but it overloaded and we got a fire in a junction box in the forehold. From then on, everything went to hell."

"You're sure Macklin didn't get out?" Jack asked.

"Sure as we can be. The blast cut clear through the wheelhouse, took it out and everybody in it before the ship even started to sink."

"Where was the *Opus* when it happened?" Jack asked.

"We were rounding Anacapa, trying to pick up the shipping lane. We were bearing 300 degrees, with Arch Rock directly astern when she went down."

"How far out?" he asked nonchalantly.

"About two miles when the trouble started. I heard Macklin say we'd be better off away from the islands, since there's a six-knot current close in. But after the controls went out, she started to drift. I'd say we were less than a mile off shore when she finally went under."

From the ladder leading down from above, Raymond called into the galley. "Coast Guard's on channel sixteen, Captain Brennen. They'll be here in just a few minutes."

"Thanks, Ray. Just hold her steady."

Charley reappeared with blankets for the men, and a few minutes later, the Coast Guard nosed alongside. The men were off-loaded with a grateful farewell and a variety of thanks, and the cabin of the *Marauder* returned to normal.

Almost.

"Well, Charley, what do you think?"

"We'd have to make arrangements, postpone some of our work or get somebody to take over for a couple of weeks while we searched. We'd be taking a helluva risk."

"Yeah," Jack said, "we'd need every last dime we've got to get the right supplies and equipment. By the time we hired someone to fill in for us on our regular jobs while we were gone we'd be risking everything we have."

"True, but if she sank close-in, we'd have a good chance of bringing up her cargo. And with the bank breathing down our necks, we're gonna lose everything anyway."

Jack grinned. "My thinking exactly."

Charley smiled. "I think that *somethin'* we been waitin' for has finally come up, boy."

"It'll take us a couple of days to get everything organized — but I think so, too, Charley." At least he hoped so. If they didn't find the *Opus II* and salvage what was in her hold, they wouldn't have a snowball's chance in hell of saving the *Marauder*.

Jack dragged in a lungful of salty ocean air, savoring the familiar taste and smell. It was more chance than they'd had that morning. And nothing felt better than having a longshot come in.

Howard McCormick leaned back against the sofa in his living room, watching the Channel 3 Evening News. The *Santa Barbara News Press* lay in a rumpled pile at his feet, the headlines glaring up at him in big bold black letters: OPUS II GOES DOWN. The smaller print read, Suspected Loss of All Hands.

Of course the newspaper had been wrong. Four of Macklin's crew had survived. Apparently their captain had not.

Serves the sonofabitch right, Howard thought, imagining Macklin in his watery grave. He never should have gotten involved with the bastard; it had just seemed the easiest solution to a very sticky problem. But Macklin ran a slouchy operation. Howard didn't normally do business with guys like him.

This kind of thing was exactly the reason why.

Howard pressed the volume button on the TV's remote control, and the newscaster's voice grew louder. He gave the details of the sinking as reported by the surviving members of the crew, mentioned the explosion and the speed with which the *Opus II* had gone down.

Howard swore foully. Nothing had been saved. Certainly none of his precious cargo. Worse than that, since no one knew of its existence, it wasn't even insured.

If that wasn't bad enough, now he couldn't meet the deadline on his contracts. There would be penalties to pay, to say nothing of the number of irate customers he'd have to soothe. Instead of the huge amount of profit he had envisioned, McCormick-Austin was about to suffer a terrible loss.

"What a mess," he muttered, dragging himself to his feet and heading for the bar. He rarely drank, but right now he needed a drink very badly. He poured a three-finger shot of Chivas into a Waterford crystal tumbler and took a healthy swig. He grimaced then relaxed as the smooth amber liquid burned a path into his stomach. Tomorrow he would assess the damage, try to plan his next move.

Tonight he'd curse Macklin to the icy depths and play hell trying to get to sleep.

Genny knocked hard on the door to the main cabin of the *Marauder.* Jack had called earlier to tell her he and Charley were going to be busy for the next few days with a salvage project that might save the boat. For the first time in over a week, she heard excitement in his voice.

"Jack?" she called out. "Charley? Is anyone there?"

"Come on in, Genny." Ollie Brown was in the galley unloading a case of supplies. His broad black torso gleamed with perspiration.

"Where's Jack?"

"He'll be back any minute. He and Charley are bringing in some equipment."

"Jack said they're getting ready for a salvage operation."

Ollie grinned, a giant flash of white. "A last-ditch effort to raise the money they need. If they can make enough off what they bring up, they can pay off the note."

Genny felt a shiver of excitement. Maybe Jack wouldn't have to leave. "I guess you're here to help."

"I used to dive some. I'm too damned out of shape to go down anymore, but I can help with the lines and gear."

"I wish there was something I could do."

"Jack says you get seasick," Ollie said, making Genny flush. "That's too bad. Jack's damned short-handed. A cook would give Charley more time to help."

Charley walked in just then, carrying two big boxes of groceries. Hearing Ollie's words, he frowned as he took in Genny's disappointment, then set the boxes down on the table. "We'll be workin' round the clock for four or five days at a time. Jack and Pete will be doing the diving. Jack'll be tired when we get in. You can take care of him then."

A long muscular leg kicked open the door. Jack walked in grinning. "You sure can." He set down a stack of heavy boxes, grabbed Genny around the waist and hauled her into his arms. "In fact, he'll need a little special care tonight." He bent his head and kissed her, a hot melting kiss that left her cheeks on fire and her body damp and aching.

"Jack —" she whispered, embarrassed. "Charley and Ollie are here."

He only laughed. It felt good to hear him laugh like that again. "I got everything on my list," he said to Charley. "Begged, borrowed or rented the stuff we're going to need. How about you?"

"I got through my list, too," Charley said.

"Me, three," Ollie put in.

"Good. We cast off at 5:00 A.M. Pete will be here and so will Raymond. With Charley and

Owl, we should have enough of a crew to get the job done . . . assuming we can find the damned thing."

"We'll find it," Charley said. "Then it'll be up to you and Pete to bring the darned stuff up."

"We'll get it up," Pete said from the doorway. He grinned. "That's never been a problem for Jack *or* me."

Genny's face grew warm at the men's bawdy jokes, but it felt good to be included, and the excitement they were feeling was definitely contagious. She only wished she could go with them.

She spent the night with Jack in his cabin, happy that he hadn't sent her home as she'd half expected. Instead he made passionate love to her, then slept with her curled in his arms. She stood on the dock early that morning as the big boat pulled out. She waved and prayed for his success; then she quietly made her way home.

That night, with Skeeter snuggled against her, she slept surprisingly well. Unfortunately, the next night wasn't so pleasant. Her insomnia kicked in, probably from her worry for Jack. She tried to keep her hopes up that he would succeed and not have to leave Santa Barbara, but her spirits were decidedly low. She slept for a couple of hours but mostly tossed and turned, and woke up feeling exhausted.

In her spare time, she worked on her re-search, narrowing down the islands in the Caribbean that might qualify as the settings in her dreams. Since the words she'd heard were Pidgin English, she singled out islands with a strong British influence. Antigua, Grenada, Barbados, Anguilla, Bermuda, the Bahamas, St. Kitts and Nevis, Jamaica, St. Vincent, the Virgin Islands — the list went on and on. There were separate islands in each of these groups, and many, like Trinidad and Tobago, or the Caymans, changed hands so often between the English, French, Spanish, and Dutch it was hard to tell who had the greater influence.

It was so frustrating that she wound up tossing her latest stack of books in an untidy pile on the living-room floor and phoning Millie. Genny picked her up and they spent the evening in Montecito shooting pool.

"I can hardly believe it," Millie said as Genny bent over the green felt table in the Winslows' walnut-paneled billiard room. "Jack is going to be amazed."

"If he's still here," Genny mumbled. She stroked the cue stick slowly, sending the white ball into the orange ball. She watched the orange roll into the corner pocket.

"Well, if he ever gets the chance to see you play, he's bound to be impressed. I know I am."

Genny set the cue stick down and walked around to Millie's side of the hand-carved table. "Thank you, Millie . . . for everything."

Impulsively, she hugged her. "You've really been terrific."

"It's been fun," Millie said. "Maybe you and Jack will invite me to go along sometime."

Genny arched a brow. "Are you kidding? Millicent Winslow — shooting pool at the Sea Breeze Bar?"

"Are you kidding — Genny Austin shooting pool at the Sea Breeze Bar?"

Genny laughed. "I see what you mean."

"You know, in a way, maybe Jack's been good for you. You look at things differently than you used to."

Genny pondered that. "I guess in a way, I do."

"Maybe going to bed with him wasn't such a bad idea after all."

Genny didn't answer. It wouldn't have been a bad idea, if she hadn't fallen in love with him. She wondered what Jack would say if he knew.

The fourth night he was gone, Genny spent the evening at Dottie's, catching up on the local gossip and Dottie's plans for the weekend. They talked about Dennis Mitchell, a policeman the buxom redhead had recently met, a relationship that seemed to have definite possibilities.

"I can't believe it," Dottie said, "I'm actually dating a cop. I know how fickle they are — their divorce rate is incredible. I swore I'd never get involved with one, but Dennis is different. He really cares about his job. He worries about people and making things better."

"Does he have any kids?" She wondered how Dennis would get along with Tammy.

"He's got two teenage boys he's raising from a previous marriage. Underneath that macho blue uniform, he's a real family man."

"I like him already," Genny said, meaning it. Dottie had never spoken in such glowing terms about a man. Genny hoped this would be the one who could finally break through her friend's barrier of male distrust.

They ate chili dogs and drank Diet Pepsi, since Dottie was always pressed for time before work and not exactly the world's greatest cook. As the evening wore on they talked about Genny's latest nightmares and about Charley's suggestion she speak to Richard Bailey, the doctor who believed in reincarnation.

"What do you think, Dottie? Do you believe something like that could actually happen?"

"I don't know, honey. It sounds pretty hokey to me."

"That's kind of what I thought, but Charley says Dr. Bailey has been able to document several cases."

When Dottie still looked skeptical, Genny told her about the nightmare she had experienced while she was actually awake — something she'd been afraid to tell either Jack or Charley. "It was even worse than the others, Dottie. It was almost as if I were there."

Dottie shook her head, wiggling the long red

ponytail hanging down her back. "I don't like this, Genny."

"To tell you the truth, it scares me to death. I wish I knew what to do."

"What about another psychiatrist? Maybe there's someone else you could talk to besides Dr. Halpern."

"I've thought about that, but it just doesn't feel like the right thing to do."

"You mentioned acupuncture once, or Chinese herbal medicine. But I can't imagine how that could help, either."

"Truthfully, neither can I, but I've got to do something." She sighed and accepted the bowl full of chocolate chip ice cream Dottie handed her. "In the meantime, I think I'll drown my troubles in all of these calories you're determined to feed me."

"Good idea." Both of them laughed and dug in.

Before Genny left, she worked up the courage to talk about Jack, in particular the conversation they'd had about his leaving Santa Barbara.

"I hate to say it, Genny, but it sounds to me like the guy's getting antsy, softening you up for the day he's ready to run."

"I was afraid you'd say that."

"I hate to be the bearer of grim tidings, but a guy like Jack isn't about to settle down." She picked up the empty ice cream bowls and started for the kitchen. "He's a real heartbreaker, honey. I just hope you don't get hurt."

Genny tried to remember Dottie's words, but it didn't do much good. Not when Jack called every night from the boat just before she went to bed.

"Hi, baby. Miss me?"

Her stomach fluttered at the sound of his deep sexy voice. "You know I do." Her hands fluffed through Skeeter's soft gray fur, and the tiny kitten began to purr. She smiled, hoping Jack could hear it in her voice. "I can't wait to see you."

"If we haven't found the *Opus* by tomorrow, we'll be coming back in for supplies."

"You've been gone four days. You must be exhausted."

"I'm a little tired, I guess. But nothing worth doing comes easy."

"I know you'll find it, Jack."

"You bet we will." He tried to sound positive, but she couldn't miss the strain in his voice. He asked if she'd been having nightmares and she told him that, surprisingly, she hadn't been. They talked for a little while longer, then he signed off with a weary, "Get some sleep, baby."

She wished his news had been better, but the hard truth was, after ninety-six hours of searching, they still hadn't found the *Opus II.*

Genny stood waiting on the dock the day the *Marauder* returned. Salt spray covered every inch of the teakwood deck, gray bird droppings spotted the rails, and the men looked even more battered and beaten than the boat.

Jack had a four-day growth of heavy black beard, and his face was so darkly tanned his eyes appeared an even brighter shade of blue. There were new sun crinkles across his forehead and the thick bands of muscle in his arms looked rock-hard.

Jack took her hand and helped her onto the deck. "You look even better than I remembered." He leaned over and kissed her. "Four days seemed like forever. God, I'm glad to see you."

Somehow those words surprised her. In the past few weeks, she had felt him pulling away from her, yet something always seemed to draw him back.

"I've missed you, Jack."

"Baby, I've missed you, too." They stood in the galley, while the men were busying themselves with end-of-the-day chores.

"Why don't you make yourself something to drink while I finish," Jack said. "As soon as I'm through, I'll grab a change of clothes and we can walk on over to your place." Tomorrow they would replenish the ship's stores, he said. The next day they'd be heading back out to sea.

Jack showered while she cooked his dinner, then she took him upstairs and put him to bed. He fell asleep while she was changing into her sexy blue nightgown — and he didn't wake up until morning.

Genny felt torn between disappointment that they hadn't made love, and pleasure that he would stay with her even without sex. She smiled into his dear, tired face. If there was anything — anything — she could do to help him, she would. She only wished she knew what it was.

Jack spent the day getting the *Marauder* and its crew ready to resume the search. Pete decided not to join them again until the sunken ship had been found. He had several other jobs pending and he needed the work. Ollie was in the same position. Charley, Raymond, and Jack would continue the search alone.

Genny slept aboard that night. Jack made slow, thorough love to her. Once during the night she started to dream, but he woke her before the nightmare had a chance to take hold. She smiled her thanks but Jack shook his head.

"I've got a different kind of thanks in mind." Cradling her buttocks against his groin, he eased her legs apart and sank himself inside her. Heat rolled over her as he held her hips and began to move. Afterward she drifted back into a restful sleep.

Each day the search continued. Genny used the time to continue her research, but nothing she read seemed the slightest bit familiar. Every night Jack called, but so far they'd had no luck. Jack's voice rang with fatigue and discouragement. Genny tried to bolster his spirits, but they both knew the money for the boat would soon be due and the bank wouldn't wait.

They also knew his chances for success were growing slimmer every day.

Eighteen

Jack called Genny that night from his boat. It felt good just to hear her voice. Too good. Damn, he wished he could stop thinking about her.

"When are you coming back in?" she asked.

"We've got supplies enough for a couple more days. We've got to keep going just as long as we can."

"I'll be praying for you, Jack."

For a moment he said nothing. Sometimes he wasn't even sure he believed in God. Obviously Genny did, and right now they needed all the help they could get.

"Thank you," he said softly. "Good night, baby." He was hoping she'd get some sleep. He smiled to think he'd been good for her in that department. As for himself, he was on a four-hour watch — four off, four on — alternating with Charley and Ray. Sleep right now was not a high priority. Finding the *Opus* was.

With time the limiting factor, they kept the *Marauder* in motion, working a grid pattern over the area where the *Opus* crew believed she had gone down. They were dragging a Ferros detector — a long, waterproof, tubular device that hung suspended from a cable beneath the hull. Monitored from a display screen in the navigation room, it outlined the shape of anything iron it found.

Jack had been watching that screen for the past four hours, watching it in alternating shifts every day since they'd started this project. His eyes burned and his eyelids felt gritty, but he didn't dare look away for more than a few short minutes.

They couldn't chance missing some object that might have been part of the *Opus II.*

"How's it going?" Charley sauntered into the wheelhouse, carrying a steaming mug of coffee. With his scraggly gray beard, he looked almost as disreputable as Jack. "Anything new?"

"Naw. We've been running right along the edge of the dropoff. I'm just praying she didn't go down farther out." All of the islands in the Santa Barbara Channel were surrounded by an underwater shelf. At the edge of the shelf the water deepened abruptly, from 40 to 50 fathoms to 100 fathoms and more. They had come equipped to go deep.

But not that deep.

"See any sign of the *West Wind?*" A hundred-and-twenty-foot salvage boat out of Port Hueneme which was looking for the *Opus* as well, to say nothing of the yachts and sailboats which were simply playing lookie-loo.

"They're searching farther north. I don't think they've been able to speak with any of the *Opus* crew, but sooner or later they'll be heading this way. I hope to hell we find her first."

Charley just nodded. "You ready for me to take over?"

"What time is it?"

"Twenty-three hundred."

Eleven o'clock. Charley had been in the Navy, too. "I sure could use a little shut-eye. How's Ray doing?"

"Tired, but hangin' in. He's a good man to work with."

Jack smiled tiredly. "I think he's got the fever."

"Salvage'll do that to a fella. Must be the thrill of the unknown."

"He's earned himself a share. Did you tell him?"

"No, but I will. If we find the damned thing, his take might be enough for him to quit work and go to college full time."

Jack just nodded. As long as they made enough to pay off the boat, that was all he cared about. He waved to Charley and headed down the ladder. By the time he reached his cabin, he felt so fatigued that he made a quick trip to the head, then crashed on his berth still wearing his jeans and T-shirt. His last thought was of Genny, how much better it had been when she was there with him, sleeping curled in his arms.

Four hours later, Raymond roused him from a drugging sleep. Charley would be taking over as engineer, checking the mechanical gauges and keeping the equipment running. Jack was back on duty steering the boat and watching the images on the detector screen.

They had supplies to last another day, maybe two if they were careful. At least the weather had been clear and the forecast looked good. Relieving Charley, Jack settled in. He meant to make each of those days count.

"Heard any news?"

Genny glanced up from the book review she had been reading. Millicent Winslow stood in front of her desk, a stack of heavy tomes clutched to her chest.

Genny shook her head. "It seems like he's been gone forever. Every time he calls, he sounds a little more discouraged. I feel so sorry for him, Millie."

"Well, Jack hasn't given up and neither should you."

"I'm not . . . it's just that I . . ."

"I know exactly what it is." Millie reached over and squeezed her hand, then left to return to her duties. Genny glanced down at the review she had been reading, trying to decide whether or not the library should purchase the book, but she couldn't seem to concentrate. She started to shove back her chair, find something else to do, but the phone jangled loudly, demanding that she pick it up.

"Genny, it's Jack." As tired as he was, his

voice sounded lighter, less strained. She could almost see him grinning into the receiver. "Guess what, baby — we found the *Opus II*."

For a moment Genny said nothing, just held on hard to the receiver, praying she'd heard him correctly. Then a film of tears clouded her eyes. "Oh, Jack, that's wonderful."

"We were going at it backward," he said. "We started at thirty fathoms and slowly worked our way into deeper and deeper water. We weren't having any luck, so yesterday we decided to take a chance and move in closer. We found the wreck in twenty-two fathoms of water — that's about a hundred and thirty feet."

"I knew you could do it, Jack. I'm so happy for you."

"Yeah, well, now's when the tough part begins." But he couldn't keep the excitement from his voice and Genny got caught up in it, too.

A few minutes later, she hung up the phone. Her heart was pounding, adrenaline pumping through her veins. She shoved back her chair and stood up.

"Millie!" Several heads popped up from the long oak table where a dozen people sat reading. They gave Genny a penetrating stare. "Sorry," she mouthed as she walked rapidly across the library toward the reference counter in the corner.

When she reached it, she leaned over and caught Millie's shoulder. "You won't believe it,

Millie — Jack just found the *Opus II*!"

The slender girl grinned up at her. "Oh, Genny, that's terrific! Maybe now he won't have to leave."

"That's what I'm hoping."

"When's he coming back in?"

"I'm not really sure, but I'll definitely be glad to see him."

"I don't imagine he'll stay long."

"I'm sure he won't." She sighed. "I wish I could go back out and help them."

Jack stayed gone an extra day, pushing his supplies to the limit, physically exhausted, she was sure, but infused with fresh hope. He wanted to establish the ship's exact location, he told her, and make at least a cursory examination of the wreck site.

To make the time pass more quickly, Genny continued searching for some clue to the past that might unlock the puzzle of her dreams. Plowing through the stacks of books she carried home each night, she read until her eyes burned and her head ached, but nothing helpful surfaced and she found herself wondering if it was just a waste of time.

She was sitting on the sofa in the living room, her nut brown hair clipped up in a topknot on her head and a pencil stuck behind her ear, when a picture on one of the pages of a history book caught her eye.

She was reading about St. Kitts, which along with Nevis, just two miles away, was ruled by the British, off and on, starting in 1623. On the opposite page was an etching done of a sugar plantation in the early 1800s. But it was the tall, sword-leafed cane fields stretching endlessly toward the ocean that made Genny's insides twist and her hand start to tremble.

The print on the page ran together, then grew fuzzy and blurred. The room started turning, seemed to shrink inward; the light grew dim and began to fade away.

"No," Genny whispered, fighting for control, trying to push back the images that began to whirl through her mind. Then she was spinning back in time, losing touch with her surroundings. Her mind became a hazy jumble of present and past. She was standing in the shadows down the lane from the great plantation house. If she looked in that direction, she saw a broad sweep of lawn and the rock-lined pond with the lily pads floating on it.

She faced the opposite way and scanned the horizon. In the distance, as far as the eye could see, cane fields waved like an emerald sea. They were taller than the tallest slave — a dense wall of green that seemed almost impenetrable.

A man on horseback rode near the edge of the field. He was a handsome man, well-dressed in a single-breasted chocolate brown frock coat and doeskin riding breeches tucked into a pair of knee-high Wellington boots. He dismounted beneath a flat-leafed tree and moved swiftly into the cover of the heavy foliage at the edge of the cane.

The black-haired woman stepped from the shadows, but her face was hidden by a short blue veil that extended from the brim of the riding hat angled atop her head. Dressed in a royal blue habit, the front trimmed with rows of starched white lace, she reached out to the man and he pulled her against him. In the shade of a tree behind them, the horses they had been riding nickered softly in the cool late afternoon breeze.

"I've missed you," the woman said softly, and the well-dressed man smiled. He was young, Genny saw, younger than the woman, somehow out of place in these surroundings. She slid her arms around his neck, and then they were kissing, her fingers slipping into his wavy brown hair. It was a soft kiss at first, a tender brush of lips and a welcoming sigh.

She felt his mouth over hers, tasted the warmth of his breath, and the sweetness of wine on his tongue. Her blood began to stir, to heat with the first hint of passion, her nipples began to ache and grow hard. She began to unbutton the white lawn shirt beneath his riding coat, to run her hands across the muscles on his chest. She could feel the hard ridges, the taut round circles of his flat male nipples, and a wave of desire washed over her. Heat rose up, stirred, hinted at the pleasure that would follow.

As quickly as it came, it was gone.

The man was no longer standing, but lying on the ground at the beautiful woman's feet. He was doubled over in pain, gripping his stomach, dragging in heavy labored breaths, and begging her to help him. His face looked stricken, his skin ashen, his cheeks sunken in. Beads of sweat trickled from his forehead along his throat to dampen the front of his snowy white shirt.

"Help me," he whispered. "Do something . . . please."

But the woman just stood watching, a slow smile curving her ruby lips. "You should have thought of the consequences before you slept with Pearl."

"It didn't mean . . . Please . . ." The anguished word ended in a strangled cry wrenched from somewhere deep inside him. He tried to sit up, screamed in pain, and once more slid into the dirt. He was staring with dull, glazed eyes that could no longer see. His labored breathing sounded like no more than a tortured hiss. He made an eerie gasp for air that ended in defeat, and his last breath whispered away on the wind.

The woman simply stared down at him. For a moment she thought of another handsome man, one she had loved with all her heart. She had been younger then, and foolish. In the end, he had betrayed her, just like all the rest.

She looked down at the man sprawled on the ground and hysterical laughter bubbled up from her throat, cutting into the silence of death that surrounded her. The man had been her lover . . . perhaps even more . . . but he had displeased her. She laughed until tears formed in her eyes, until the wetness trickled down her cheeks.

She laughed until the wicked, evil sound jolted Genny from her hellish vision.

She was breathing as hard as the man she had seen, gasping for air and sucking it in. She sat there for long, misery-filled moments, clutching the history book in her lap, tears rolling hotly down her cheeks. Sadness over-whelmed her. The dream left an aching grief that she could not comprehend. If only she could forget what she had seen, pretend it had never happened — but she knew that she could not.

With shaking hands, she reached for her tablet and picked up a pen, then began to scratch out the words describing the images she had seen. When she finished, she set the pen and paper away and rested her head against the back of the sofa. The woman had come again, not in a dream but in the same sort of vision she had suffered before.

She had come to continue her story — for Genny was now convinced that's what it was. She didn't know why, only that the woman meant for her to know, to make her live it — to actually *feel* it.

She was also convinced that the only way for

her nightmares to end was for the story to reach its conclusion. She shivered to think of it. Dear God, how much more could she stand?

Genny went to bed exhausted, but couldn't fall asleep. She wound up walking the beach, then returned upstairs, read for a while, and eventually slept off and on till morning. She awoke feeling tired and out of sorts. Only the knowledge that Jack would be returning saved her from complete depression.

Sitting behind her desk at work in a bright, cranberry suit she had chosen in an effort to buoy her spirits, Genny jumped at the sound of the phone. She heard Jack's voice and his unexpected call lifted her mood. She had just hung up when Millie walked over to her desk.

"That was Jack, I gather. Everything going all right with the salvage project?"

"He's on his way back in. They'll arrive this afternoon then spend tomorrow restocking supplies. I'll see him tonight after work."

Millicent's smile grew broader, making her thin face almost pretty.

"What?" Genny asked warily at her friend's smug expression.

"If I remember correctly, the last time we talked, you said you wanted to go out on the boat with Jack."

"That's right. They need someone to cook, and if there's one thing I'm good at, that's it."

"What would you do about your job?"

"I could take some time off. I haven't used up all of my vacation this year. Besides, Jack's only got a little over a week to bring up what's down there. After that it won't matter." She looked at Millie and frowned. "I don't know why we're even talking about this. I can't go out in the ocean, and you know it. I'd be deathly sick the whole darned time, and that would hardly do Jack any good."

Millie extended the hand she'd been holding behind her back.

"What's that?" Genny asked, staring at the small, rectangular box in Millie's palm.

"Ever heard of *scopalomine?*"

"Scope-what?"

She handed Genny the small dark blue package. "Scopalomine. Transderm Scop is the brand."

"Seasick medicine? You don't believe that stuff really works?"

"This is different. It's a patch you wear behind your ear. Jeff Mathison — he's a college professor I met a couple of days ago — told me about it. He also owns a sailboat. He said his ex-girlfriend used to get seasick every time they left the harbor. She tried the patch and after that she never had a problem. He says you can be out in ten-foot seas and never feel the least bit queasy."

"I've heard of it, but I never thought I'd be needing it and anyway I didn't have a whole lot of faith." Genny looked at the box. "This is prescription medicine. How did you get it?"

"Jeff had it. Since he and his girlfriend have broken up, he doesn't need it."

"Jeff?" Genny repeated, and Millie flushed. "You're dating this guy?"

"We've only been out a couple of times, but . . ." She glanced up and a bright smile softened her narrow face. "I really like him, Genny. And I think he really likes me."

"Oh, Millie, that's terrific." Genny looked back down at the box and read aloud the printed information. "Transderm Scop is a medicated patch that is slowly absorbed through the skin." She glanced up at Millie. "Do you actually think this stuff will work?"

"Jeff swears it does. He says each patch lasts three days. He says you can start with a whole one and if you discover you don't need that much, you can cut one in half. He says that's all his girlfriend ever needed."

Genny clutched the small box to her chest. "I'm going to try it, Millie. If it works, I can help Jack with his salvage project — and maybe even prove I can fit into his life."

"Just like learning to shoot pool."

"Exactly." Genny smiled brighter than she had in days.

"I hate to be a wet blanket, but what happens if . . . you know . . . you have one of those crazy awake-dreams like you had at my parents' house?"

Genny shivered to think of it. Still, she refused to be daunted. "I won't. There's nothing out there that could possibly set me off, and when Jack's around, I always seem to feel better." Genny smiled again. "I can't wait to tell him, Millie. He's going to be so excited!"

"You want to go with us? Are you out of your mind!" Standing next to the navigation charts in the wheelhouse, Jack felt Genny's light touch on his arm. Damn, he was glad to see her. At least he was until this.

"Wait, Jack, please. Won't you at least let me explain?"

"All right, I'm listening." He studied her eager upturned face. In the faint light of dusk, her big doe eyes looked like soft brown velvet and her skin had a warm pink glow. Every time he saw her she looked prettier than she had the time before. These last few grueling days, he had thought about her a thousand times. It wasn't like him, and the truth was, it worried the hell out of him.

"I know what happened the last time, but I've got this medicine — a patch I can wear to keep me from getting seasick."

"This is work, Genny, not a pleasure trip." He'd been waiting for her for the past half hour, more eager to see her than he could have imagined — and damned unhappy about it.

He was a dedicated bachelor, for Chrissakes. He didn't need — certainly didn't want — this growing attachment he felt for Genny. "Everything I've got is riding on salvaging the *Opus*. Even if you don't get sick, you'll just be in the way."

"Not if I do the cooking. That would free Charley up to work with the crew. Even with Pete and Ollie, you'll still be shorthanded. Ollie says you could really use someone to help."

He raked his fingers through his hair, which still felt damp with sea spray. His jeans and shirt clung wetly to his skin, his muscles ached, and he was tired clear to his bones. "Ollie said that?"

"Yes, he did. I can help you, Jack, if you'll just let me."

"What about your job?"

"I've already made arrangements. All I have to do is make one quick phone call to set things in motion — and Millie will take care of Skeeter."

Jack sighed wearily. He'd never had a woman aboard when he was working. He didn't like the idea of it now, especially not one who made him hard every time he looked in her direction. "I don't know, Genny . . . a woman out there with the crew. It's not a good idea."

"They aren't just any crew, they're your friends. They aren't going to mind my coming with you, as long as it helps you finish your salvage work."

Jack turned a searching look on Charley. "You think this medicine she's got will work?" He held up the small blue box.

"Now that you mention it, I heard something about this stuff before. I should have thought of it myself."

"Let me come along, Jack, please."

Jack fidgeted under her close regard. He had forgotten the way her big brown eyes lit up whenever she was excited, the blush he could bring to her cheeks with only a few soft words. He'd been wanting her for days. Now he worked to ignore the blood pooling low in his groin.

"I don't think —"

"You need a cook, Jack. I'm a great cook and you know it. Besides, I really want to help."

Jack scowled, but looking at Charley, he knew when he was beaten. "All right, you can come. But that damned patch had better work — and you had better resign yourself to taking orders — just like everyone else."

Genny gave him a jaunty salute. "Aye, aye, Captain."

"And don't be surprised if the cook has a few extra duties . . . down in the captain's cabin."

She grinned. "Whatever you say, Captain Brennen."

Jack eyed her tight blue jeans and sexy tank top. Maybe having her along wasn't such a bad idea. At least she could lessen the strain he was under in one way. Besides, if she was with him, she'd probably be able to sleep, another unwanted worry off his mind.

"We'll be resupplying tomorrow, then leave at

first light the following day."

"I can start in the morning," Genny said. "I'm sure there's plenty for me to do."

Jack gave her a slow perusal that made her cheeks turn as rosy as her lips. "All right, tomorrow it is. I'll walk you over to collect your things." He'd be collecting something else while he was at it. Something he'd been dreaming about for the last five days.

"I guess I'll see you two in the morning," Charley said.

"Why don't I make dinner for the three of us?" Genny suggested. "I might as well start my duties tonight."

Charley smiled indulgently. "I think Jack's appetite is running in a different direction. I can fend for myself this time. You'll have a whole crew to cook for, soon as we leave port."

Jack grinned. "Thanks, Charley." He caught Genny's hand and tugged her toward the door. "We'll see you bright and early." Charley just smiled as they took the ladder down to the deck.

"Are you hungry?" Genny asked Jack when they stepped inside her condo.

"Starved." Jack leaned over and nuzzled her ear. "But not for food." He carried her upstairs, hurriedly stripped off her clothes and his own, then both of them fell onto the bed in a tangle of arms and legs. They made love with hasty abandon, with hot hands and eager mouths, with

374

hearts pumping and perspiration-slick bodies.

Afterward they lay quietly contented, legs entwined. Genny's hair was trapped beneath Jack's thick-muscled shoulder. As she worked herself free, she noticed his gaze was focused on the stack of history texts piled on the bedside table.

His eyes swung to her face. Coming up on an elbow, he cupped her cheek with a big suntanned hand. "We haven't talked about this since I left. I guess I didn't want to deal with it while I was out there on the water. It was selfish, I know. I want you to tell me now. What about your nightmares, Genny? What's happened while I've been gone?"

She shifted uncomfortably. She didn't want to tell him about the cruelty and death she had seen, about the dreams she'd had that weren't dreams at all but more like a window into the past. She didn't want to spoil the days ahead.

"I've learned a few more things," she evaded. "I'm narrowing down my research area. I'm almost sure it's someplace in the Caribbean. It's coming along fairly well."

"That's it?"

"Please, Jack, let's not talk about it now. I haven't seen you in days. I don't want anything to ruin the time we have together."

"Are you seeing Dr. Halpern?" he pressed.

"No."

"Dammit, Genny. How the hell are you ever going to get over this?"

"I think the dreams will end when the story is finished . . . when I know all there is to know about what must have happened."

"You think the woman in the dream wants you to know?"

"Yes. I think that must be it."

"Who do you think she is? A ghost who's talking to you from beyond the grave?"

"I don't know. Charley thinks she's someone I knew in another life."

"I know what Charley thinks. I think it's a bunch of bull."

Genny stared down at her hands. "Let's not talk about it, Jack. I'd rather you just held me."

"Dammit, Genny." But already he was reaching for her, pulling her into his arms. She rested her head against his chest and listened to the slow, steady rhythm of his heart.

"Thank you for taking me with you," she said.

Jack combed his fingers through her hair. "Are you kidding? I plan to run you ragged. Besides, that's the only way I can be sure you'll get to sleep."

Genny smiled. "Hungry?" Lifting her head, she searched his face.

"Starved," he said, as he had before. But instead of getting up, he slid a hand behind her neck and pulled her mouth down to his for a kiss. Feeling the hard male ridge rising up against her leg, Genny guessed supper was still a ways away.

Sitting behind the wide mahogany desk in his office, Howard McCormick slammed down the phone. "Goddamn it!" His fist pounded hard on the leather-trimmed green felt blotter. "Of all the rotten luck!"

Across the room, his secretary Winifred Daniels swung open the heavy paneled door. "Mr. McCormick — are you all right? I thought I heard someone shouting."

Howard scowled. Sometimes Win's over-protectiveness grated on his nerves. "I'm fine, Win. I just got some more bad news, that's all." Worse even than the loss of the *Opus II* with all his precious cargo.

"Anything I can do?" Win asked, her pretty face lined with worry.

"Yes. Get out and leave me alone." Win stiffened, hurt by his cold tone of voice, but he didn't care. She wouldn't quit; she was too damned loyal. She was used to his occasional bad moods, and besides, he paid her too well. She walked back into her office, pulling the heavy door closed behind her.

Howard stared hard at the phone, thinking of the call he'd just received from Marty James. It galled him, what he was about to do, but the way he saw it, he didn't have much choice. Shoving back his chair, he rounded his desk, jerked open the door, and strode out of his office.

Reaching his private parking space at the rear

of the building, he climbed into his Lincoln Continental and drove a little too fast toward the beach. The sooner he dealt with this, the sooner he could put it behind him.

The traffic was light on the freeway. He pulled off on Castillo, turned right at the stop sign and right again onto Cabrillo. The parking lot down at the harbor wasn't crowded. He found a space, turned off the engine, then sat there working up his nerve.

Or should he say working to set aside his pride.

He took a last long breath to steel himself and fortify his resolve, stepped out of the car and crossed the parking lot toward the boats tied up in the distance. Using his slip key, he opened the gate to Dock H, and walked down the wooden pier toward the *Marauder*.

He'd have to proceed with caution — and a good deal of restraint — if he expected to succeed. He squared his shoulders and tried to wipe the grim look off his face.

Nineteen

Jack could hardly believe his eyes when he returned to the boat with Genny in tow, stepped into the galley with a load of supplies, and spotted Howard McCormick.

Walking beside him, Genny made an odd sound in her throat. She stopped dead in her tracks. "H-Howard. What on earth are you doing here?"

"Good question, McCormick." He set the heavy box of groceries on the table. "What brings you to our humble corner of the world?" He took the bag Genny carried and also set it down.

"I'd like a word with you, Jack, if you don't mind. Strictly business."

"Go ahead."

Howard looked at Genny. "It might be better in private."

Jack glanced between the two. "I don't think that's necessary. We're all . . . friends . . . here, aren't we?"

A muscle ticked in Howard's cheek. "All right, if that's the way you want it." He carefully smoothed his features. "Word on the street is you've been searching for the *Opus II*."

"So?"

"Today, word has it you've found her."

"What's that got to do with you?"

"Actually, it has a great deal to do with me — or should I say it has a great deal to do with Genny and I." Her head snapped up. She studied Howard's face, but his expression remained inscrutable. "McCormick-Austin had a load of computer parts coming in from its plant in Mexico. It was being carried aboard the *Opus II*. The items were extremely important to some contracts we have pending."

"They were bound to be insured," Jack said. "Why don't you simply replace them?"

"Because the parts would have to be rebuilt and there isn't that much time. It would be far more advantageous to make use of the ones aboard the ship."

Jack eyed him coolly. McCormick's expression remained controlled, but there was a wild, slightly frantic look in his eyes. The skin along his jaw appeared taut and a muscle jumped in his cheek. "So what's the deal?" Jack said.

"I'll pay you for the parts. Fair market value, the same as the insurance company will be paying me."

"How much is that?"

"They were second-grade items, less expensive than those made here. They're worth about fifty thousand dollars."

"What's the catch?"

"There is no catch."

"I wouldn't think they'd still be good. Won't

the saltwater make them useless?"

"They're packed in air-tight aluminum containers. Assuming the explosion didn't destroy them, they should be as good as they were when they were shipped."

"Then, assuming we find them, I don't see any problem in selling them back to you."

"Fine." Howard looked oddly relieved. "I'll have my attorney draw up the agreement." Without further words, he started for the door.

"Wait a minute," Jack called after him. "I didn't say anything about signing an agreement."

Howard turned around very slowly. The knuckles on his hands looked white. "I thought we had a deal."

"We do. Assuming the parts are worth what you say. If they are, then you can have them for the fifty thousand. If they're worth more, then you can go fuck yourself."

"Jack!" Genny gasped.

"I've made you a reasonable offer," McCormick said. "In return I need something in writing. I can't rely on whatever whim you might take once you've brought them up. I'll be happy to show you the sales invoices, showing the quantity shipped and the cost."

Jack shook his head. "Sorry, that won't cut it. I want an independent opinion of value. Once I've got it, you can buy them for whatever they're worth. I'll be happy to sign an agreement to that. A right of first refusal. If you aren't willing to come up to whatever price is fair, then somebody else gets a chance to bid."

Howard's face turned red. An angry scowl marred his forehead. "You're a real bastard, Brennen."

"And you're a crook, McCormick. Everyone here knows that except Genny."

"Stop it, Jack," she warned. "Howard came here with a business proposition. He doesn't deserve to be treated this way."

Jack clamped hard on his temper. McCormick had always been a bone of contention between them. It was obvious Genny cared a great deal for him. Jack suddenly wondered how deep her feelings for the bastard really went. "You heard the deal, McCormick. Take it or leave it."

For a moment he said nothing. Then his mouth curved into a frigid smile. "I told you, Brennen, I don't have time for your games. I'll find another solution to my problem and it won't include you. You just cost yourself fifty thousand dollars." Turning away, he stomped toward the door.

"Howard, wait!" Genny started after him, but Jack caught her arm.

"Let him go, Genny."

She whirled to face him, planting her hands on her hips, her cheeks pink-tinged with anger. "Dammit, Jack — you need that money. How could you let him walk away?"

"Fifty thousand won't solve my problem. And if I know McCormick — which I do — that's stuff's worth a lot more than what he's offered."

"Did it ever occur to you that I own half that business? Howard's problems are my problems, too."

Jack winced at the hurt in her pretty brown eyes. He hadn't thought of it quite that way. "Listen, baby. We haven't got any idea what's down there with the *Opus*. Those parts may have been blown to kingdom come. Why don't we wait and see? If we find them and McCormick's telling the truth, I'll be happy to cut a deal with him — one that's more than fair to McCormick-Austin. Good enough?"

Genny gave him a reluctant smile. "I suppose so. But I hate for him to worry."

A thread of irritation snaked through him. "If you want to stay here and comfort your good friend Howard, that's fine by me. Is that what you want, Genny?"

"You know it isn't."

"Then let me get to work, so first thing in the morning we can be ready to leave."

"Fine," Genny snapped with a fierce little lift of her chin.

"Fine," Jack said, but already his anger at Genny was fading. It was McCormick who occupied his thoughts. He wondered what the bastard really had in those cases aboard the *Opus II*.

They left at dawn. Ollie and Pete had arrived well before first light. Jack and Genny had slept aboard that night, so Jack could take care of some last-minute details, and they would be all set to go.

It didn't take long to reach the wreck site a half mile north of the south end of Anacapa Island. As Jack had finally discovered with his limited information, the *Opus* hadn't gone down on the edge of the island shelf, but drifted inland even farther than he had first believed.

The three-hundred-foot ship was sitting on the ocean floor angled onto the left side of her hull in twenty-two fathoms of water.

During the two-and-a-half-hour trip to the island, Genny stood at the rail, mesmerized by sun and sea. The patch she wore was working perfectly. She hadn't suffered even a moment of queasiness. Which meant that for the first time, she had been able to enjoy her surroundings: a cloudless blue sky, graceful sea birds, and a beautiful azure ocean, its foamy salt spray breaking over the bow of the *Marauder*.

In the distance, she could just see the outline of the Northern Channel Islands: San Miguel, Santa Rosa, Santa Cruz, and Anacapa, their rugged peaks rising through the early morning haze like a far-off range of mountains. The weather was early November, California perfect — crisp cool air, a warm yellow sun, and a hint of mist in the breeze.

The men in the crew paid little attention. They were too immersed in their duties, too hopeful of what they might find once they reached their destination. All of them but Jack. Unlike the others, Jack seemed to soak up his surroundings, to mesh with the salt mist and waves as if he had been born to it.

Until today, Genny had never realized how much a part of him the ocean really was. She glanced up from her musings and saw him, one foot propped on a deck box, breathing in the salty sea air as he stared off toward the islands. His T-shirt clung to his thick-muscled shoulders. His faded jeans hugged his narrow hips and the sinews in his long-boned thighs. Sunlight glinted on his curly black hair and made his dark skin glow like burnished copper.

He turned when he felt her eyes on him. He smiled, and started walking in her direction. The sight of him so tall and magnificently built never failed to make her heart beat faster.

"You look fit enough," he teased, eyeing the color in her cheeks and warm, welcoming smile. "How are you feeling?"

Genny's smile grew broader. "Fine — no, better than fine — I feel terrific." She glanced past him toward the ocean swells, watching the way the sunlight formed patterns on the surface of the water. "It's so beautiful, Jack. Not like anything I could have imagined."

A glow of pleasure softened the planes of his

face. "I'm glad you like it. To me it's the most beautiful place in the world."

"I love it. And I think I'm beginning to understand why all of this means so much to you. I don't think you could ever be happy anywhere else."

Jack's relaxed smile faded. "I couldn't be, Genny. This is the life for me. The *only* life for me. It always has been."

"And you don't think a woman could fit in?"

Jack gazed out across the water. A group of dolphins cut the surface, diving in unison, reflecting silver and blue in the sunlight. "I don't see how." He turned to face her. "Do you?"

"We've been doing all right, so far."

"We're attracted to each other, yes. I've never denied that and neither have you. But a woman like you needs more from a man than that. More than a semipermanent relationship. With us, that's all it ever can be."

Genny said nothing, but her heart wrenched painfully.

"So far we've been lucky," he said. "My work has been here in the channel. There were times in the past when I was out at sea for weeks. What would you do then?"

Genny looked him straight in the eye. "I'd wait for you, Jack — that's what I'd do. If I thought you . . . cared enough . . . I'd wait for you to come home."

Jack said nothing but something flickered in his eyes. "Now isn't the time for this kind of talk." He smiled but it came out forced. "I want you to enjoy your time out here." He gave her a brief absent kiss. "I've got to help Ollie set things up for our first dive. I'll see you a little bit later."

Genny just nodded and watched him walk away. She shouldn't have said what she did. She shouldn't have made her feelings so obvious. At least she hadn't told him she loved him. She could imagine what Jack would have said to that.

"I gather your seasick patch is still working." Pete sauntered toward her. His red hair was partially covered by a short-billed cap with a blue and gold Oceanographic's Ltd. emblem on the front. He had a lanky build, mostly sinew and bone, but Jack said he was a tremendous diver, and he looked incredibly fit for the job they needed to do.

"I can hardly believe it, but the crazy thing really works." She wasn't sure yet how she felt about Pete. She gathered he had the same mixed emotions about her.

"To tell you the truth, I'm surprised Jack brought you along. He's never had a woman in the crew before."

"Desperate times require desperate measures."

"That's true, I suppose." He looked past her out at the lightly rolling water. "It's obvious he likes you. Unfortunately, if you're expecting more than that . . . if you're falling in love with him, I'd advise against it."

Genny stiffened, her defenses going up. "Oh? Why is that?"

"Because he won't be able to love you back."

Genny tried to ignore the sharp sting that came with his words. "How is it you know so much about him?"

"We've been friends since the Navy. We were both divers, assigned to underwater demolition." Pete's expression remained friendly, but there was something in his eyes that warned her to beware.

"And that makes you an expert on his emotions?"

Pete shrugged, but he looked far from nonchalant. "Jack was never one to get entangled in a relationship — not that the women he knew didn't want to. From Singapore to the Middle East, he could just about pick and choose. The hard truth is, Jack left a girl in every port. Which is not to say he led them on. He warned them from the start. They always thought they could change him, but instead he broke their hearts."

A tightness contracted in Genny's chest. She thought about what little she knew of Pete Williams, of the night he'd been with Jack at the Sea Breeze Bar, and the time he had been on the boat with the blondes.

"What about you, Pete?" she asked coldly. "Did you leave a trail of broken hearts, too? Or did you just ride on Jack's coattails, hoping he could stir up enough women for the both of you?"

Pete's hazel eyes darkened almost imperceptibly. "Maybe back then that was true. I didn't have much experience with women. Jack always had more than he could handle. Since we were friends, it was only logical I wound up with some of them."

"And now?"

He stiffened, his shoulders going tense. "Now I do just fine by myself."

"Are you sure about that?"

"Damned sure. I don't have to settle for Jack Brennen's leftovers anymore. I can get all the women I want."

Genny smiled tightly. "I would appreciate it, Pete, if in the future you would try to remember that."

Pete arched a bright red eyebrow, sizing her up, then looking at her in a way he hadn't before. "Pretty shrewd, aren't you? Maybe you *aren't* like the others. Maybe that's what Jack sees in you. That still doesn't mean he'll stay with you."

"Maybe not. Then again, maybe he'll discover that it's nice to have someone who cares for him. Maybe he'll find out there's more to life than drunken parties and one-night stands."

Pete said nothing, but an odd look crept into his face. "Maybe he will. Maybe he won't. I guess we'll just have to wait and see."

Genny watched his long-boned, leggy frame walk away. Perhaps it wasn't just self-interest that motivated Pete's concern, but worry for his friend. Then she remembered his words about Jack, and a sweep of dread washed over her. She was risking so much, betting on something with almost no chance of success. Genny's insides clenched to think she might be nothing more than another in Jack's string of broken hearts.

As the island drew near, the engines slowed then finally came to a shuddering halt. They were towing a twenty-by-sixty-foot equipment barge Jack had rented to haul back the heavy reels of copper wire they intended to bring up. Using the *Marauder* to position the barge over the wreck, he spent the next half hour setting the anchors, then they tied the boat up alongside, using the barge as a floating dock.

From the corner of his eye, Jack spotted Genny walking toward the stern to watch them getting ready for their first descent. He couldn't help thinking about what she had said. *I'd wait for you, Jack. If I'd thought you cared enough, I'd wait for you to come home.*

He hadn't expected that. Another woman might have said, "You could sell the boat and get a real job, Jack." Or, "You could always take me with you," or, "You don't have to take jobs that keep you away from home."

Anything but, *I'd wait for you, Jack.* Those

words did funny things to his insides. Made him think about things he'd never had, never thought he wanted. A real home, one full of warmth and caring. Someone who was there for him, not a house occupied by strangers — a father who was never around, a stepmother who cried too much, and a son who could never live up to his dead older brother.

It filled him with a kind of desperation — and it scared him to death.

He watched Genny walking toward Charley, smiling sweetly, enjoying the sun and the wind, alive in a way he had never seen her. Genny, with her terrible dreams and sleepless nights, who had lost a husband and wound up with a bastard like him. Yet she rarely mentioned her troubles. She was far more worried about him and the chance that he might lose his boat.

She had worked since early that morning, cooking breakfast for the five of them: hotcakes, sausage, bacon and eggs — enough food for a man the size of Ollie, and damned near that much for him and Pete, since they had a mountain of work to do and were running on nervous energy that burned up calories big time. Then there were dishes to do and pots to scrub and keeping things ship-shape, not an easy task with the crew they had on board.

She kept the coffee hot and plenty of it, kept everything running smoothly and the men in good spirits. Just looking at the way she smiled at Charley made something soften inside him.

"Say, Genny girl." Charley waved her over. "How ya holdin' up?" Now that the engines were stopped, the boat had begun to roll in the motion that had made her so deathly sick before.

This time Genny just grinned. "I'm doing great, Charley. My stomach never felt better — in fact, I'm getting hungry. It's time I started thinking about making you guys some lunch. How long will the first dive take?"

"Jack'll be down almost an hour, then Pete'll go down."

"They aren't going down there together?"

"Under normal circumstances they would, but we have to make every minute count."

"I would think if they can stay down for an hour —"

"Thirty minutes at depth, a little over twenty-three minutes comin' back up, then they've got to spend time on the surface."

"I don't understand."

Jack left them talking and walked over to Ollie, who was making a last-minute inspection of their wet suits and diving gear. Behind him, Charley grabbed a chart, flipped through the pages, and began to explain.

"When a diver goes down that deep for any length of time, his bloodstream fills with nitrogen."

"Yes, I think I've read that."

"That's why he has to decompress. He's got to come up slowly, let the nitrogen escape from his blood so he won't get the bends — you know what that is, don't you?"

"Yes," Genny said weakly, her mind suddenly clouding with images she had seen in an old John Wayne movie, of men doubled over in agony being rushed into a decompression chamber. "That's what happens when little bubbles of gas get trapped in the diver's bloodstream. It causes excruciating pain."

"It can kill you, if you aren't careful." He studied the chart in his hands. "Half an hour at a hundred and thirty feet requires a three-minute stop at twenty feet then an eighteen-minute stop at ten, plus the time it takes to make the ascent. Jack'll stay on the surface for a little over three hours, which will clear his blood a bit more, then go back down."

Genny's heart had begun to thud dully. "I didn't realize this would be so dangerous."

"It won't be — not for these two. They're both ex-Navy divers, and we'll be in constant contact."

"How does that work?"

"Pete's borrowed an Aquacom. It's a radio that transmits through the water. Jack and Pete will be wearing full face masks with mikes and earphones so we'll all be able to talk back and forth."

"I see."

"Jack's already been down once on our last trip. He's charted the ship's position, gauged her depth, made an inspection of the damage from the explosion, and figured approximately where the load she was carryin' ought to be."

She glanced over at Jack, who stood next to Ollie and Pete. Dressed now in his shiny black wet suit, he looked even more formidable than he usually did, yet she couldn't help being afraid for him. Genny started walking in his direction.

"All set?" she asked, trying her best to sound cheerful.

"Almost."

He picked up the dive light at his feet and turned it on to be certain it worked. "It'll be dark down there, even in the daytime. And I want to see exactly how much wire we're actually dealing with. Plenty, I hope."

"How do you plan to get it up?" she asked, and Jack flashed her a devastating grin. "Don't you dare say what you're thinking."

Jack laughed and so did Pete, and some of the tension eased.

"We'll be using a flotation device called a Carter Bag. They're lift bags made of urethane-coated nylon in different shapes and sizes. We'll attach them with cables to the reels of copper wire and fill them with air. Once they're buoyant, they can lift up to twelve thousand pounds."

Genny smiled, impressed by Jack's knowledge. "Sounds like a good idea to me."

"You ready to make some money?" Ollie said to Jack, handing over his face mask. "Or you just gonna stand here and chit-chat all day?" He was acting as tender, Charley said, helping the divers with their tanks and equipment, generally seeing to their comfort and safety.

"Ready as I'll ever be."

"Be careful down there," Charley said. He was the timekeeper, monitoring depth and calculating decompression times, which was done before the dive began, but had to be altered if any critical factors changed. As an added protection, Jack wore an air-integrated computer on his belt that kept track of those same things. He was wearing dual tanks filled with Trimix gas to solve the problem of narcosis — underwater delusions divers called the martini effect — not the normal oxygen surface divers usually breathed.

"It's a mixture of nitrogen, helium, and oxygen," Charley had told her. "The bad news is it ain't been approved yet, not by OSHA or the Coast Guard. They'd have a fit if they found out what we were using."

"Then how did you get it?"

Charley shrugged as Jack might have done. "We got our ways."

Jack looked over at Ray. "You got those cables all lowered?" Ray would be handling the winch, the air lines they called umbilicals that filled the flotation bladders, and all of the cables they would be using.

"They're all in the water. Soon as you get the lift bag in position, I'll start the air flow from the compressor." They had two air lines going down, so two bags could be filled without Jack having to wait and move the hose, which would take too much time.

"I don't know how many reels I'll be able to rig up on this first trip. I'll know more once I get inside the hold."

Though he wouldn't go down for nearly an hour, Pete was already suited up, just in case something went wrong. They tried out their communications system, which seemed to be working properly. Jack sheathed his diving knife, checked his wrist compass and watch, then climbed onto the diving platform they had rigged at the back of the boat.

"See you in an hour," Genny called out to him, trying to hide her nervousness.

"You just have plenty of chow on the table when I come up," Jack said with a grin. He pulled his face mask into position, gave her a thumbs-up sign, and lowered himself into the water. She heard his voice coming over the radio sitting on a table they had set up on deck, and as long as she could hear him, her worry stayed under control.

There was a hole through the middle of the ship, Jack reported, though he had seen it on his preliminary dive. Now he could see the spools of drawn copper wire. They remained intact — about two hundred one-ton reels of them. The hole in the ship made access to them easy, he said.

Over the next twenty minutes, he was able to attach a line to the first ten, five-foot wooden spools, but his time at the bottom ran out. Genny waited till he started back up the cable they were using as a descent line and Ray began inflating the two giant air bags. Then she could relax enough to resume her work in the galley.

Fortunately, she had done some of the preparation in advance. Twenty-five minutes later, she was waiting on the deck, searching the water for the first sign of Jack. Ham and cheese sandwiches on crusty wheat bread, crunchy dill pickles, homemade potato salad, and a big bowl of cole slaw sat on the table, along with a pot of hot coffee.

Near the stern of the boat, Jack's dark head broke the surface of the water. Handing his dive light to Ollie, he jerked off his mask, flashed a broad, white-toothed grin, and with Ollie's help, levered himself up onto the swim step. A few minutes later, the water started to churn, a dense mass of bubbles seeped upward, then the first of the two big nylon air bags popped up.

Suspended from a cable beneath them, ten reels of one-eighth-inch pure copper wire waited to be lifted aboard the equipment barge.

Ollie grinned and so did Pete.

"Ten tons of copper wire," Jack said, dripping water like a big black seal as he reached down to pull off his fins. "Salvage value roughly a dollar a pound — looks like we just made twenty thousand dollars." A cheer went up all around.

"How you feelin'?" Ollie asked.

"Never better," Jack said. Pete slapped him on the back, grinned, and stepped into the water.

Twenty

Jack leaned back against the sofa in the main salon. His head was pounding, he felt drained and exhausted, yet he couldn't suppress a feeling of elation. Before nightfall, they had recovered forty reels of copper worth somewhere near eighty thousand dollars. Not enough to pay off the boat, but it was a damned good start.

"Are you feeling all right?"

He opened his eyes to see Genny leaning over him, her fine brown eyebrows knit in a worried expression. He smiled. "A little tired is all. Nothing a good night's sleep won't cure." Taking her hand, he dragged her down on the cushion beside him. "You were great today. You worked your pretty little tail off and believe me, the guys were really glad to have you along."

Genny flushed with pleasure. "I enjoyed every minute. I haven't felt that useful in years."

"We've got another tough day tomorrow. We'll bring up as many spools as we can, then tow the barge back to the harbor in Port Hueneme." The wire would be off-loaded into a warehouse area, where potential buyers he had contacted before they left could get an early look at the product. "We'll get a few fresh supplies, refill our tanks, and head back out."

"You haven't mentioned McCormick-Austin's computer parts. Did you find them?"

"Not yet. But that load of wire was scattered all over the hold. They may well be buried beneath some of those spools. We'll be keeping an eye out for them."

Genny cupped his face with her hand. Her palm felt cool and smooth against the roughness of his day's growth of beard. "You look done in, Jack. I think you ought to get some sleep."

He turned his head and kissed her fingers, then flashed her a wicked grin. "I was hoping you'd say that."

The rest of the crew was sitting around the table in the galley, talking, or quietly reading. Pete was on watch in the wheelhouse for the next four hours, then Ray, then Charley. Jack and Ollie would take the night watch tomorrow. Other captains might not take the precaution, but Jack had always been cautious by nature, and with so much at stake, he didn't want any unexpected problems.

It seemed to pay off, since things continued to go smoothly the following day. They made the trip into Port Hueneme late in the afternoon, off-loaded eighty-two spools of copper, resupplied, and returned to the wreck site, arriving at nine o'clock that night. With time of the essence, he wanted to be ready to make his first dive as soon as the sun came up.

Working in the galley, Genny put away the supper dishes while Jack and the others relaxed in the main salon. When she finished, she came up behind where he was sitting in a sofa chair, and peered over his shoulder. He was reading a crisp new paperback book, she saw, scanning the pages with what seemed undivided interest. Surprised, to say the least, she was almost afraid to interrupt him, but her curiosity nudged her till she finally gave in.

"What's that you're reading?"

Jack dragged his gaze away from the print with obvious reluctance, then looked up at her with a slightly sheepish grin. "I decided to take your advice. I picked this up off the bestseller rack at the supermarket in Santa Barbara while we were buying supplies." He turned it around so she could read the title. "Tom Clancy. *Clear and Present Danger.*"

A feeling of warmth spread through her at the effort he was making. "I read *The Hunt for Red October*, but not this one."

"It's great. I guess reading isn't so bad if you find the right book. I'll loan it to you when I get done."

"Thank you. I'd really like to read it." Something passed between them. She could see it in his eyes. Then he marked the page, closed the book, and stood up, stretching a little to work the kinks from the muscles across his back. "I'd better go relieve Pete. I've got the watch until two, and a lot of copper wire still left to bring up tomorrow." He took her hand and kissed the palm. "Why don't you go down and get some sleep?"

It was probably a good idea. She would be up before dawn, cooking breakfast. She was windburned and tired, and even the sunscreen she'd been using wasn't enough to keep her totally protected from the sun. She loved the rosy glow her skin had taken on, but not the freckles. She'd have to be more careful in the morning.

"I am kind of tired." She smiled. "If you're feeling reckless, you can always wake me up when you come in."

Jack grinned. "Reckless is my middle name." He brushed her mouth with a kiss and then he was gone, carrying his paperback with him.

They got off to the early start Jack had planned and the first reels of cable came up without a hitch. Pete's load got hung up in some of the bulbous green seaweed that had broken loose from the dense kelp forests surrounding the island, but eventually the heavy reels rose to the surface. When they did, Jack let out a loud bark of joy.

"We're almost there, baby. One more load and we'll have enough to pay off the note."

"Oh, Jack, I'm so happy for you."

Jack lifted her off her feet, spun her around, then gave her a resounding kiss. "We haven't got it yet, and with the cost of the supplies and equipment; Ray's share, as well as Pete and Ollie's, we're still not out of the woods. But there's plenty more down there, and with our next load we should have a little over two hundred thousand dollars."

Jack grinned and so did Genny. He pulled her against him and gave her a hug. Ray was working the crane. Jack and Pete were both in the water to guide the load aboard the barge. Genny went into the galley to make herself a quick cup of tea. She searched the cupboards, found a box of Earl Grey tea bags — her favorite — then filled a kettle with water and set it on the stove.

When the kettle started to sing, Genny went over to turn it off. In the process, she knocked Charley's calendar off its magnetic hook on the wall. She'd paid no attention to it before. Now she saw it was the travel kind with color photographs of romantic faraway places. Charley had forgotten to change the month, so Genny flipped the page — and froze.

The picture at the top was an island scene: gorgeous blue-green water, rows of beckoning palm trees, and lovely white sand beaches. Against a golden sunset, steep mountains rose in a jagged line. Their slopes bore a canopy of towering trees and lush green foliage blooming with tropical orchids.

She stared at the page, unable to look away, and the hand that held it started to tremble. Genny's vision began to spin. The picture was fading, becoming fuzzy and blurred.

"No," she whispered, frantic to stop what she knew was coming, struggling desperately to blot the images she had already begun to see. "Not here . . . please . . ."

But the room continued to dim and her legs went weak. Genny leaned against the wall then slid bonelessly to the floor. Her body was trembling all over. Little by little the galley of the boat slid away and she was standing in the jungle, surrounded by palm fronds and a forest of giant ferns. Cool green moss cushioned the soles of her bare feet.

She recognized the clearing she had seen before. There was a palm-thatched roof above it, supported by a stout pole down the center and others around the edge. In front of a primitive altar, signs had been drawn in the dirt, the five-pointed star and an odd assortment of symbols: crisscrossed circles, geometric figures, and a number of wiggly lines that looked familiar from before. Whale fat candles burned at the crude wooden altar, and drumbeats thrummed in her ears. A goat was tied to a stake near the center of the clearing. Its high-pitched bleating sounded mournful.

Dancers appeared in the dream, nearly naked, writhing and squirming and fondling themselves. A huge wooden phallus appeared. Two of the women lay on the ground, arching their backs, their bare knees bent and drawn upward, their callused feet flat on the dirt. A thin man thrust the wooden phallus between their legs while they rubbed themselves against it, caressing it with their bodies. Their eyes rolled back until only the whites shone in the flickering light of the fire.

A tall dark-skinned man in a loincloth moved stiff-legged toward them, his spine and limbs rigid as he bounced up and down, babbling incoherent words. A knife appeared, glinting, wicked. She couldn't see who held it, only heard the goat's soulful bleat of pain, saw the blood spurt upward from the gash across its throat.

Her own throat seemed to swell. She tried to swallow, but couldn't. She fought to wake up, to drag herself back to the present, but she had lost her way. The blood of the goat flowed toward her, covering the ground in a scarlet wave, building until nothing but red appeared and the jungle began to recede.

Around her the images changed. The three hideous corpses stood before her. She recognized one face. The man on the bed, the man who had been the woman's husband. Another corpse joined them, the handsome younger man who had died at the woman's feet. They started walking toward her, stiff-limbed like the man who had killed the goat. Their mouths were stuffed with cotton, their jaws tied shut. Though their eyes were closed, they seemed to be watching, accusing.

She wanted to run. She tried to force her

frozen legs to move, but she was as helpless as the sacrificial goat. The corpses leaned forward, leered down at her. One of them wrapped his hands around her throat and began to squeeze. She fought to pry his fingers away, tried to suck air into her burning lungs —

"Genny!" Jack's shout of alarm carried over the shrill hum of the tea kettle as he raced across the room and knelt beside her. Frantically, he shook her shoulders. His heart was pounding till he thought it might tear through his chest. "Genny! For godsakes — what's wrong?" She seemed to be unconscious, but her eyes were open. She sagged against the wall, trembling all over, staring at the pages of the calendar she gripped in a white-knuckled hand.

"Good God, what's going on?" Charley hurried across the galley and knelt at Genny's side. She was gasping for air, her neck muscles straining, struggling desperately to breathe, yet it was obvious she wasn't really choking.

Jack pried her stiff fingers loose from the calendar and slid her icy hand between his warm ones. His own throat closed up and his chest heaved with fear. "Christ, Charley — what's wrong with her?"

Charley didn't answer. "Genny — it's Charley — can you hear me?" A soft little whimper escaped. Her head fell back. Her eyelids fluttered as she continued to gasp for air, but none seemed to reach her.

"She can't breathe, Charley. We've got to do something!" Her face was so pale her skin looked translucent. Her lips were tinged an odd shade of blue. Jack's heart constricted. He had never felt so powerless, so utterly useless. Fear for her squeezed his insides into a hard tight ball.

"Get me some water," Charley said to Pete, who stood frozen in the doorway. Ollie stood behind him, peering worriedly over his shoulder. With unsteady hands, Pete hurried to fill a glass then handed it to Charley, who tossed half the contents into Genny's face. She came up sputtering, dragging in lungfuls of air, coughing and gasping, but she had begun to breathe.

A shudder of relief rippled through Jack's big body. "It's all right, baby." He eased her into his arms. "Everything's going to be all right."

"Jack . . ." Genny started crying. Her arms slid up around his neck as she clung to him. "Hold me, Jack. Please don't let me go."

He buried his face in her hair. "I've got you, baby. I won't let you go."

They sat like that for painfully long moments. Genny was crying softly, curled in Jack's arms on the galley floor. Jack was trembling almost as much as Genny. Eventually she calmed, and he smoothed back her tear-dampened hair. "What happened, honey? Can you tell me?"

She glanced across at Charley, but seemed

afraid to look at Jack. "The dreams," she whispered. "They've started to come when I'm awake."

"Jesus." Jack tightened his hold, pressing her cheek against his chest, cradling the back of her head in his hand.

Genny still looked at Charley. "I-I'm ready to see your Dr. Bailey — as soon as we get back to port. Will you fix it for me, Charley?"

"You bet I will, honey."

Jack helped her up, then carried her over to the couch and sat down with her in his lap. "Don't think about it anymore. It's all over now." He stroked her back and held her against his chest, but Genny eased away.

"I-I'm fine, now, really I am." It was obvious she was embarrassed. "I'm sorry, Jack. I didn't mean to cause you any trouble. I just never thought it would happen out here."

"How many times have you done this?" A knot of tension still balled tightly inside him.

"It happened twice before. Both times something triggered it. This time it was the c-calendar."

"You should have told me," Jack said darkly.

Genny flushed and glanced away. "Where is it?" Her dark eyes searched for the calendar. Charley handed it over, but Genny shook her head. "No, you'd better read it. Just tell me the name of the island in the picture."

Charley scanned the print beneath the photo. "Jamaica," he said softly.

Genny's eyes slid closed and Jack felt a shiver run through her. "That's where it happened, Charley. I know it. I'm not sure how, but I do."

"Nothing happened," Jack argued. "Not on Jamaica or any place else. This isn't real, Genny. None of this is real."

"Leave her alone, Jack." Charley put a hand on his shoulder. "Let her rest for a while. We can talk about it later."

"I think we should take her back in, let the doctor have a look at her."

"No!" Genny came up from the sofa. "There's nothing wrong with me . . . at least nothing physical. We're staying out here till you've finished. I won't be a liability to you, Jack — I won't!"

"Dammit, Genny —"

"Dammit, Jack!"

He felt the pull of a smile, then sighed with resignation. "What do you think, Charley?"

"I think Dr. Bailey's her best bet. I'll arrange things as soon as we get back to the harbor. In the meantime, we'll keep an eye on her, make sure nothing triggers another attack."

"I don't like this, Charley." That was putting it mildly. He had never been so frightened in his life, which showed how much he had come to care for her. Damn — how could he have let that happen? How could he have gotten so involved?

"If Genny's okay," Pete said, "we had better get back to work, if you're planning to bring up another load today."

"We had indeed," Charley put in. "The weather report shows a storm comin' in."

"Once it gets here the current will be a bitch," Jack said. "We won't be able to dive until it's over." In the meantime, if they kept at it, they'd have enough copper wire to make the big balloon payment on the note due the end of the week.

Another barge load — the rest of today and tomorrow — would make a profit for everyone. "Are you sure about this, Genny?"

"I'm fine, Jack, really. Besides, if it happens again, I'd rather be here with you and Charley."

The thought of it happening again made the sweat break out on his forehead. He could still see her gasping for breath, fighting to suck air into her lungs. What would have happened if he hadn't found her when he did? Sweet Jesus — surely she wouldn't have died!

The thought so unnerved him, Jack swayed a little on his feet. "I'm going back outside," he said thickly. "I need a little fresh air." But even that didn't help. Nothing could erase the memory of the sheer stark terror he had felt when he'd thought he might be losing Genny.

Charley stood at the rail, watching Jack get ready for his last dive of the day. Jack had been quiet and remote since the incident with Genny, pensive in a way Charley had never

410

seen him. By unspoken agreement, they were all keeping tabs on her. No one wanted a repeat of what had happened, and none of them wanted to think about what might have occurred if Jack hadn't found her when he did.

Especially not Jack. Charley noticed his brooding expression, the tension that still gripped him every time he looked in her direction. Jack had never been protective of a woman. He had never been that involved with one. He hadn't been close to his father before he died, and his stepmother had merely been the woman who saw to their home. Charley wondered if Jack had ever felt the soul-deep kind of caring he appeared to feel for Genny.

Charley watched him check the pressure on his air tanks, the numbers on his dive calculator, and his dive knife in the belt at his waist. Adjusting his face mask into position, he spoke into the microphone, testing their communications, and Charley responded through the mike that sat on the table. Wearing twenty-six pounds of weight, Jack's six-foot-four, two-hundred-ten-pound frame slid into the water with an easy grace, then silently slipped below the surface, leaving only a few air bubbles to mark the spot.

They talked back and forth during the dive, discussing the placement of the next set of cables and saying he intended to bring up as many reels as the air bags would lift. Standing next to Charley, Genny listened quietly. She tried to smile, but he caught her biting her lip and knew she was anxious, as always, for Jack to return to the surface.

The radio crackled to life. "Good news, Charley. I just found McCormick-Austin's computer parts. They're wedged behind three of the reels we'll be lifting in this next load. Unfortunately, my air's getting low. Pete will have to bring them up on his next dive. Tell Genny she can play the heroine and save good old Howard's ass when she gets home."

"Will do."

Jack didn't speak for a few minutes more. Then, "Just about through here. I've got two six-ton loads rigged up and ready to go. Tell Ray to start the air."

"You got it."

There was a long uneasy pause. "And tell him not to waste any time. It looks like I've got company."

"Son of a bitch," Ollie's voice boomed out behind them. Concerned for Jack, he hurried to his place next to Pete on the diving platform.

Standing just inside the hold, Jack aimed his light toward the lift bags beginning to fill with air. Through the tear in the hull he'd swum in through, the hum of an underwater sled pierced the murky silence, followed by a single beam of light moving forward through the tall leafy growth of underwater plants. Jack listened to the sled's approach but the humming stopped some distance away, and the light went out.

"Don't make contact again until you hear my voice," he whispered into the mike. Turning his own light off, he blended into the surrounding darkness inside the hull.

For a moment he saw nothing, then a pair of divers fanned bright yellow beams in his direction. Cones of light turned plant life a brilliant green and the hull of the ship turned a startling shade of blue. A huge eel slid past but the big-boned diver didn't seem to notice.

They must have come in off the island, or off a boat anchored somewhere out of sight around the point. Whoever they were they knew what they were doing. They were carrying spear guns, loaded and ready, but he doubted they were there to fish.

"Christ," he muttered, and in reply heard Charley's voice urging him to the surface. Jack glanced down at his dive computer. A repetitive dive like this one had to be shorter. He had a total of seventeen minutes at depth, and only six of that remained. He waited in the darkness as the men approached. One of them towed a big net bag fixed with a number of CO_2 cartridges, to act as self-inflating floats, and they were headed into the hold.

He watched them move toward the lift bags filling with air and realized what they had come for. Even now the bags had begun to drag one of the reels away from the aluminum containers filled with McCormick-Austin computer parts.

Good old Howard had said he'd find a way.

Bastard, Jack swore inwardly, condemning the man to an early grave, but he made no move from the shadows. Apparently the divers believed he'd already gone up as he usually did, once the bags began to be filled with air. As he would have to do now, since his time at depth was almost up.

Shrouded in darkness, he started to slip through the crack in the hull and make his way toward the descent line leading to the surface. Then he thought of Howard McCormick, could almost see his smug expression once he got his hands on those parts, and turned back instead.

Moving in as close as he dared, he aimed his light toward the men and flipped it on, holding the beam like a spotlight, illuminating their efforts to dislodge the aluminum cases. Catching them dead to rights stealing his salvage, he hoped would be enough to make them panic, cut and run. If they simply swam up through the gap in the hold just as the bags did, they could make their way back to their sled and escape.

It was a slim chance, but thinking of McCormick, a risk he was willing to take.

He held the light steady, pinning them within the bright yellow arc, and oddly enough, it worked on one of them. The smaller diver jerked toward the light, pointed frantically toward Jack, then to the hole and escape. The other man motioned that he should stay but instead he kicked his fins, stirring up the sand that had seeped into the broken hull, took his light, and started swimming away.

The other diver spun toward Jack, aimed and fired his spear gun without the slightest hesitation. There was no time to move from its path. Jack felt a searing pain in his shoulder, saw the projectile angled through a tear in his wet suit, and a wash of his own blood. The momentum carried him backward against a bulkhead. Shaking his head to clear the swirling black circles, ignoring the sharp throb of pain, he saw that the spear had gone in at a shallow angle. He clenched his teeth and jerked it free. Pulling the dive knife from the belt at his waist, he shoved off the wall, and swam forward.

There was nothing for it now — the man meant to kill him. He'd damned well succeed if Jack didn't stop him.

The diver cast his spear gun aside and yanked a long-bladed, serrated knife from its sheath. Avoiding a quick slashing move, Jack grabbed his wrist, and the man grabbed his, then they started spinning in the water. Bubbles of air rushed upwards; sand swirled past their face masks.

"Jack? Dammit, Jack where are you?" Pete's voice came to him through the earphones. From the sound of it he was already in the water.

"Hull," Jack said, trying to conserve his strength. "Got trouble."

"The cavalry's on its way." That was the last Jack heard till he saw Pete's light. The distraction drew his opponent's attention and in that moment, Jack freed his knife hand. He slashed upward, cutting into the man's thick arm and releasing a cloud of blood. It looked blue in the light of the lamp. His own shoulder seeped that same bluish hue, and his strength was quickly ebbing.

He didn't try to stop the diver when he turned and headed upward, working his fins to sweep him out through the hole left by the explosion. Jack felt a wave of relief, along with the fleeting knowledge he had stayed too long below.

"We'll have to let him go," Pete said, reading Jack's thoughts correctly. "You're hurt pretty bad, and you've been down here too long. Your decompression time's going to be a whole lot longer."

Jack just nodded. He felt light-headed and his shoulder ached like hell. Jerking off one of his rubber gloves, he shoved it into the wound to help stanch the flow of blood. Then he let Pete guide him out of the hold, through the murky water to the descent line. Pete's light fanned toward it through the emerald green sea plants waving in the current, illuminating a school of bonito that flashed silver in the yellow beam. Neither of them mentioned the sharks Jack's blood might attract as they made their way up to the surface.

"What's going on down there?" Charley's voice cracked with worry over the line.

"Jack's been hit in the shoulder. Spear gun. He's bleeding, but not too badly."

Only a moment's pause. "I'll get things ready up here. Ollie's set to go in. Just sing out if you need help."

"I'll make it," Jack said, his voice a little shaky as they reached their first decompression stop, the time recalculated now that he'd been down an extra eight minutes. At each of the stops, a mixed gas tank complete with regulator and mouthpiece had been tied to the cable, just in case the diver ran low on air. Right now, Jack was damned glad it was there.

"What happened?" Pete asked as they held onto the cable to steady their position at the twenty-foot depth.

"They were after the computer parts."

"McCormick again. That bastard."

Jack rested his head on the cable. His dizziness was increasing along with the pain in his shoulder. "One of them got away clean. He may come back."

While Pete pondered that, Genny's voice came over the line. "Jack, it's Genny. Charley and I have everything ready." Her voice broke. "You just get back up here, you hear me?"

Jack frowned at the fear he heard in her voice. He'd felt that same fear earlier for her. He didn't like the feeling either way. "I hear you."

Pete gripped his wrist to catch his attention. "You'll be okay if I leave you here a minute?"

Fifty feet behind them, Jack watched the air bags carrying the reels of copper wire to the surface, and tightened his hold on the line. "Sure, but —"

Pete was gone before he could finish the sentence. He didn't stay long and kept talking to Jack all the while, making sure he was all right and explaining what he had in mind. He returned with a thumbs-up sign and a wide grin shining through his face mask. Pete had gone back to the hold to move the aluminum cases. Even if McCormick's men returned, they wouldn't be able to find them. They'd be sure the *Marauder* had already brought them up.

Jack chuckled to think he might have bested McCormick after all. Then a wave of dizziness hit him, followed by a rolling bout of nausea, and it was all he could do to stay conscious.

As the minutes ticked by, he concentrated on holding the line and making it back to the top. He refused to think of Genny. That was a subject his mind had carefully begun to blank out.

By the time Pete helped Ollie pull Jack out of the water and onto the diving platform, Genny's nerves were stretched to the breaking point. Her blood pounded inside her head and perspiration ran in hot damp rivulets into the space between her breasts.

Then she saw the ugly weeping wound in

Jack's shoulder. "Oh, my God . . ."

"Easy, Genny girl." Charley patted her hand and moved off toward the men. Using extra care, Ollie draped one of Jack's thick-muscled arms across his beefy shoulders. With Charley's help, Pete hurriedly removed Jack's diving gear and went around to lend a hand on the opposite side.

They crossed the platform with no little effort and climbed up the ladder, into the stern of the boat.

"Jack? Jack, it's Genny." When he didn't look up, and made no effort to lift his chin up off his chest, Genny's stomach muscles tightened. "Is — is he going to be all right?" Her worry increased again at the imprint of pain etched on his face.

"He needs a doctor," Charley said. "We've got to get him back just as soon as we can."

Jack roused himself, stumbled, then wearily shook his head. "We're not going anywhere — not until we get that copper aboard."

"Forget the copper." Pete tightened his grip on Jack's waist. "You've got to get that shoulder taken care of."

"Jack, darling, listen to Pete. You have to . . ."

Jack stopped walking, forcing the men at his side to do the same. "I said we're not going back until that copper is loaded. I'm still the captain of this vessel." He swayed a little. Pete and Ollie steadied him. "Those are my orders. I expect the men in my crew to carry them out."

"Jack, please —" Genny reached for him, but he jerked away.

"Not now, Genny."

"You sure about this, Jack?" Pete asked, but Jack just glared at Charley.

"Stubborn S.O.B.," the older man grumbled. "Hop to it, Ray. The faster you get that stuff on board, the faster we can get him back to port. For now let's get him inside," he said to Pete, "then you and Ollie can help Ray finish his work."

"What — what are you all talking about?" Genny pressed forward, feeling suddenly sick. "Jack's badly injured. We've got to take him in. He's got to have medical attention."

Stumbling through the doorway into the main salon, Jack tossed a hard look over his shoulder. "Stay out of this, Genny. We've got to collect this load or we lose the boat."

Genny moved through the door and planted herself in front of him. Her legs were ridiculously unsteady. "I won't stay out of it. This boat isn't worth risking your life."

"It is to me." With Pete and Charley's help, Ollie got him into a chair in the galley. "Besides, it's only a shoulder wound. I'll be just fine."

"Jack, please listen —"

"I told you I'm fine. Get her out of here, Ollie."

"Come on, Genny." Ollie gripped her shoulders, but Genny broke away.

"No, Ollie, I want to stay with Jack." A few feet away, Charley peeled open the front of Jack's rubber wet suit. Blood and water pooled, as the bright pink liquid made trails down his massive chest. Fresh blood seeped from the hole where the shaft of the spear had gone in, weaving a crimson path through his curly black chest hair.

"Oh, Jack . . ." Genny pressed her fingers against her trembling lips. She felt tears welling, stinging the backs of her eyes. She knew she was making things worse, but she couldn't seem to stop herself.

Charley tenderly probed the wound and Jack gave in to a low groan of pain. Genny bit hard on the inside of her cheek. Her hands closed over the back of Jack's chair. "I can't stand this, Charley. I can't stand to see him hurting." Fear for him nearly overwhelmed her.

"He's tougher than he looks," Charley said, trying to lighten the moment, but another moan from Jack made Genny's insides churn.

She reached over and clasped his hand, which was damp with perspiration. "I wish there was something I could do." Her eyes swung up to his face. "I love you, Jack. I love you so much."

Around her, the room fell silent. Bright blue eyes swiveled down at her, then fixed on her face with a look as cold as the bottom of the sea. "I don't want you to love me, Genny. I've never asked for that. I just can't deal with it."

His gaze swung up to Ollie. "I thought I told you to get her out of here."

Genny stared at Jack, trying to see past his black expression and the taut lines of pain that must surely have colored his words. She didn't let go of his hand until she felt Ollie's grip on her arm, gently drawing her away.

"Come on, Genny. Let's let things settle down a little in here." Genny let him guide her through the cabin door and out onto the deck.

"You mustn't worry," he said, "Jack knows what he's doing. There's been more than once, he's been hurt worse than this." He lifted her chin with a thick pink-palmed hand. "This boat means a lot to him, Genny. Everything. He's not about to lose it — not when he's this close to keepin' it."

Genny swallowed hard. She felt miserable for causing Jack trouble again. "You're right, Ollie. I-I was just so frightened. I couldn't stand to see him hurting that way."

"Charley'll do what needs to be done till we get back to port." The big hand cupped her cheek. "And he'll be hurtin' a whole lot more if he winds up losing his boat."

Genny stared down at her feet. One of her white deck shoes was speckled with pink dots of blood. Her stomach rolled and she fought to control it. "I'm sorry, Ollie. I didn't mean to make things worse."

"It's all right. When somebody loves somebody, they ain't always thinkin' too clearly."

"I-I shouldn't have told him — I shouldn't have said that I loved him."

Ollie sighed. "Prob'ly not. God knows the man's gun-shy when it comes to love. Says he's got to have his freedom."

"So what do I do now?"

"Give him time to get used to the idea, I guess. 'Bout all you can do. Man like Jack, settlin' down's the last thing he wants to do. Leastways, that's what he thinks. I know that's what I used to think."

"You did?"

He nodded, his broad face softening into a smile. "Now I got a wife and two kids I wouldn't trade for all the so-called freedom in the world. You ask me, I think the single life is damn-well overrated. If you're the right woman, maybe Jack'll see it that way, too."

Genny smiled at Ollie, and held on tightly to his words. Once they got back to the dock, they'd get Jack to a hospital and he would be all right. He'd have time to think over what she'd said. Maybe he would accept it. If he did, maybe he would allow his feelings for her to grow.

Maybe it would all work out.

Maybe . . . maybe . . . maybe. So many maybes.

Genny shuddered to think of an equal number of *what-would-happen-ifs*.

Twenty-one

"You sure you won't come with us?" Charley asked.

Standing in front of the mirror over the built-in dresser in his cabin, Jack absently rubbed his bandaged shoulder, ignoring a dull throb of pain, then he started on the buttons down the front of his blue wool Pendleton shirt.

"No thanks, Charley. You know I don't believe in any of that mumbo jumbo." A gust of wind slammed against the side of the boat and howled through a crack in the porthole. They couldn't dive in this weather. But neither could anyone else. "Genny doesn't need me — she's got you to look after her — and I've got plans of my own."

Charley frowned. "You haven't seen her since we got in."

They had patched him up in the emergency room of a Port Hueneme hospital. Afterward, they'd dropped their load of copper and returned to port. All the while, he'd been thinking about McCormick trying to steal those cases, wanting to knock the bastard on his high and mighty ass. But as Charley had said, without any proof, all he'd get for his ef-

424

forts was a whole lot more trouble.

Charley moved closer. "Genny's bound to be worried about you. Don't you think you ought to call her? At least let her know you're okay?"

Jack ran a comb through his curly black hair, checked his image in the mirror. "You can tell her, Charley. Tell her I'm doing just great." Surprisingly, he was. He figured he'd be sucking wind, once he decided not to see her, but it hadn't been so hard. He'd known what he had to do the moment he'd heard her say she loved him. Maybe even before.

A woman in love. Christ, that was the last thing he needed.

"Going out again tonight?" Charley asked. Jack ignored the hint of censure. "You sure you're up to it?"

No, his shoulder hurt like hell, but he was going anyway. He had a date with the redhead he'd picked up in the bar last night. She was a great piece of ass. At least he thought she was. He'd been so drunk, he really couldn't remember. Jack smiled into the mirror. Just like the old days. Wine, women, and song. God, it felt good to be back in the saddle.

"I'm fine, Charley. I'll see ya later." He left the older man standing in the doorway and climbed the ladder into the main cabin. Grabbing his rain slicker off the peg beside the door, he yanked it on and headed out into the storm.

For the first time in days, he felt calm inside, not like he was riding on some damned roller coaster. He wasn't worried about Genny, afraid that she might not be sleeping, concerned about her terrible dreams. He didn't torture himself when she wasn't with him, didn't think about her every damned minute of the day. He didn't give a damn what she did — hell, he could hardly remember her face.

The fact was, he wasn't worried about Genny, or anybody else. He had the money coming in to pay off his boat and not a care in the world. He had made the right decision. Genny was gone from his life and he was a free man again.

His conscience should have nagged that he had hurt her, but it didn't. He had warned her from the start, and it was better this way for both of them. Someday Genny would thank him.

Besides, to suffer any guilt you had to have feelings.

Jack had succeeded in locking his away.

Beneath Charley's big black umbrella, the rain ran off in a steady stream. He knocked on Genny's front door and a few seconds later she swung it open.

" 'Evenin', Genny." Unconsciously she glanced behind him searching for Jack, but both of them knew he wouldn't be coming. "I'm sorry, honey." Jack hadn't called her. Genny wasn't a fool. She knew it was over between them. Damn, he felt like hell about it, but there was nothing he could do.

"It isn't your fault, Charley. It isn't his fault either. He never lied about what he wanted."

"I don't think the fool knows what he wants," Charley grumbled, thinking of the Jack who had been standing in front of the mirror. A Jack he hardly recognized as the man he had come to know these past few months. "My car's still runnin'. You ready?"

They were meeting Richard Bailey aboard his sailboat down at the harbor. Not far away, but it was raining too hard to walk.

Genny grabbed her purse, stepped outside, and closed the door. "All set." The cheery smile didn't fool him. There were circles beneath her eyes and her skin looked waxy and pale. It hurt to love someone. He wasn't too old to remember just how much.

They shared the umbrella. Clasping her hand in his, he ran with her to his car — an old blue Ford pickup he'd been driving for years — and drove the short distance down to the harbor.

Though Richard owned a sprawling hillside ranch house up in the exclusive Riviera, he stayed aboard his fifty-five foot Hatteras as much as he could. It was a comfortable, beamy boat, but reliable in blue water, and Richard was one helluva sailor. He was a man who loved the sea, the smell, the sound, even the taste and feel. Charley understood that kind of love, too.

Once they reached the harbor, he shoved the pickup into park, turned off the ignition, and reached for the door.

"How is he, Charley?" He knew who she meant. They hadn't talked about Jack. He wished they didn't have to.

Charley inwardly sighed. *How's Jack Brennen? Stubborn and headstrong. Hell-bent on destruction.* "Shoulder's healin' just fine. Doc says he'll be able to dive again in a couple of weeks."

"Surely you won't wait that long to go back to the wreck site." There was a hollow ring in Genny's voice, a haunted look in the eyes that clung to his.

"Pete'll be diving. Now we got money, we'll hire a couple of fellas to help him. Safer that way, anyhow."

"I hope you still don't think Howard was the man responsible for Jack's injury."

He wasn't about to answer that one.

"I spoke to him yesterday, Charley. He was stunned when I told him Jack had been attacked. He didn't know anything about it."

"Might be best if you left off tellin' your friend what Jack's been doin'. I don't think he'd like it much."

"No, I don't suppose he would, but Howard is my business partner . . . and my friend. I owe him a certain amount of loyalty. I don't think I owe Jack anything."

"I'm your friend, too, Genny. Maybe you could do it for me."

Color rushed into Genny's cheeks. "I'm sorry, Charley. I didn't think of it that way. I only wanted to be sure that Howard wasn't . . . At any rate, I'll be careful what I say."

He reached over and patted her hand. "Good girl. Now let's get goin' before you lose your nerve." Fighting their way through the slashing rain, they hurried along the wooden dock to Richard's boat. He was waiting for them beneath a canvas awning he had strung up over the stern.

"Welcome aboard." He was a tall man, younger than Charley by at least five years, with a mane of salt and pepper hair, a slightly Roman nose, and a wide, smiling mouth. He had dark, intelligent eyes that seemed to have a way of seeing through you. Intuition. That's what Richard had. It was a quality Charley had, too, and maybe that was the reason they had become such good friends.

The three of them dashed down the ladder into the cabin, which was roomy for a sailboat, with lots of portholes to let in light and air.

"This is Genny, Rich. You already know a good bit about her." With Genny's consent, he had filled Richard in as best he could on her husband's unsolved murder, her nightmares, and the treatment she had been receiving.

"Hello, Genny." Richard reached out and shook her hand, clasping it warmly in both of his.

"I'm happy to meet you, Dr. Bailey. Charley has told me a great deal about you, too." The cabin was neatly arranged. Everything was in place, with very few frills. Comfortable, just a brown tweed built-in sofa, a couple of matching chairs, and a low teakwood coffee table. Richard was a widower, just like Charley.

"Are you nervous, Genny?" the doctor asked.

She smiled. "If you want the truth, I'm terrified. The idea of letting someone control my mind . . . I don't know . . . it stirs up all sorts of negative connotations."

"There's nothing to be afraid of. The fact is, I won't be able to hypnotize you if you won't let me. Even then, I can't make you do anything you don't want to do."

"I want to do this, Dr. Bailey. I've got to find out what's going on."

Richard studied her a moment, taking in the simple brown wool slacks and soft beige sweater that emphasized the highlights in her hair and the rich chocolate color of her eyes. "Would you like something to drink before we get started? Some hot tea, perhaps, or maybe a soda?"

Genny lowered her purse strap off her shoulder and set the leather bag on a nearby chair. "No, thank you, I'm fine."

"Charley?"

"Not right now."

"Since this is your first time here, do you have any questions before we begin?"

"Charley's explained the way you work. I believe I'd rather go forward and ask questions later, after we see how it goes." Genny seemed to like him, Charley thought. Richard had a way of doing that.

"Why don't we get on with it, then?" He motioned for Charley to take a seat on the sofa. Then he had Genny sit in one of the over-stuffed chairs. "Are you comfortable, Genny?"

"Yes."

"Good. Now just lean back. I want you to take a few deep breaths and try to relax." She sat back farther in the chair, set her feet flat on the floor and let her hands rest loosely in her lap. Taking a long deep breath, she released it slowly then repeated the action again. She had resigned herself to this, he saw. She was far less tense than he had expected.

"I know this is hard for you, Genny," the doctor said, "but perhaps the results will be worth it."

Anything that helped would be worth it, Charley thought, recalling her pale face and blue-tinged lips as she had struggled for air on the galley floor. Anything.

"I want you to look at the candle, Genny." Richard lit the long white taper that sat in a small brass holder on the coffee table. A notebook and pen sat beside it, next to a compact, battery-operated tape recorder. "I want you to concentrate on the light as you listen to my words."

Speaking in a soft monotone voice, he encouraged her to relax, to let go of her cares and concentrate only on the flame.

"I'm going to count backward." He sat down in the chair he had placed beside the candle. "As I do, you will begin to feel sleepy." He started counting softly, almost indistinctly. "Your eyelids are heavy. They will start to drift closed." The counting continued, down from twenty to ten, nine, eight, seven, six . . . she didn't seem to hear the last.

"Are you relaxed and comfortable, Genny?"

"Yes."

Richard leaned over and pressed the start button on the tape recorder. "We're going to play a game, now, Genny. In it, you're going to look backwards in time, to see your life as if it were a movie. You'll be able to watch each portion on a different screen, but you will remain detached, just as you are at the movies. Do you understand, Genny?"

"Yes."

"All right, now we're going to move backwards in time till we reach the first screen. You're fifteen years old. What do you see?"

She smiled — an impish warm smile that parted her pretty pink lips. "My birthday party. Mama made a big chocolate cake with my name on the top in scrolly red letters."

"Where are you?"

"At the beach. We had a picnic. I always ask to go to the beach."

"Who's there with you?"

"Mama and Daddy, my little sister Mary Ellen. They're building sand castles, but I'm looking out at the water."

"What are you looking for, Genny?"

"Him."

Richard's gray-streaked black brows hitched a little closer together. "Who, Genny? Can you tell us his name?"

"I-I don't know."

Richard glanced over at Charley, who continued watching Genny closely. He'd told the doctor about the choking incident in the galley. They had to go carefully. Neither of them wanted a repeat performance.

"All right, Genny, let's go backwards to the next movie screen. You are seven years old. Where are you?"

She doubled up her fists as if she were a child, and her soft lips pulled into a pout. "In Mary Ellen's bedroom. She stole my seashell. I came to get it back."

"And did you?"

She nodded, an exaggerated motion like the little girl she thought she was. "Mama made her give it to me, but she says I have to share it, and I don't want to. It's just like the one *he* gave me."

"Someone gave you a seashell? Who was it, Genny? Who gave you the shell?"

She frowned, her eyebrows drawing together. "I don't know. I can't remember."

Charley laid a hand on Richard's arm. "Maybe we should pursue this," he whispered. "Her therapist believes someone may have molested her as a child. Maybe this is the guy."

Richard studied the look on Genny's face. "Something tells me this isn't an unpleasant memory. Whoever this guy is, she doesn't seem afraid of him. I think we should go on as we planned. We can always come back to her early years if we need to."

Charley nodded and the tall graying doctor returned his attention to the woman still seeing images of herself at seven years old. "All right, Genny, you're doing very well. We're going to go back even farther. Way back, now, to a time before you were born. Tonight it will be easy to remember." He shifted, easing his chair a little closer. "Can you do that for me, Genny?"

"Yes."

"This time, I'm going to let you pick the year. You choose the movie screen and tell me where you are."

The muscles in her arms went tense. She started shaking her head. "No. I don't want to choose." For the first time, she looked uneasy.

"All right, I'll help you choose the screen." He glanced at Charley, who reached for the notepad on the table, penning the numbers 1800 to 1835.

"It's a long time ago, Genny. More than a hundred and fifty years. Somewhere between 1800 and 1835. What do you see on the screen?"

She said nothing for the longest time, just chewed her bottom lip and stared off into space. Maybe there was nothing there to see. "A girl," she finally said, her voice an octave lower that it had been before. "She's twelve years old."

"Where does she live?" Richard asked.

"We live in Haiti. I live with Mama and Papa." Charley felt the blood begin to pound in his head. It wasn't Jamaica but it was damned close.

"And the year?"

"The year of our Lord, 1812."

"Can you tell us your name?"

"I'm Annie Patterson."

Charley relaxed a little. That didn't sound too ominous.

"What else can you tell us?"

She smiled, squared her slender shoulders. There was an air of strength about her, yet the hint of a young girl's shyness seemed to be reflected there, too. "People say I'm smart. Papa says so, Mama, too. My teacher says I can do anything, be anything I choose."

"Your teacher, Annie? Tell me about her."

"Tahara is Mambo, high priestess. She is a friend to Christophe, the king. My father is one of his advisors."

Richard turned to Charley. "There's a set of encyclopedias over there against the wall. Look up Haiti; see if it says anything about Christophe." He turned back to Genny while Charley dug through the volumes. "Patterson. That is English?"

435

"Mama is English. Papa is Irish. He's a very successful merchant."

"It's right here," Charley said softly. "Henry Christophe crowned king of Haiti in 1811. 'Course she coulda read that somewhere."

"Let's talk a little more about your teacher," Richard said, and a soft smile crept into Genny's face.

"Tahara gives me presents, beautiful wooden dolls and stones that glitter in the sunlight. Papa says she helps him with the king because she likes me so much. Sometimes I go with her into the jungle. At night when I hear the drums, I climb out the window and she's waiting to take me with her. They say the drums call the gods. That the rhythms must please them."

Richard eyed her carefully. "Where is it that Tahara takes you?"

She shook her head. "I'm not supposed to tell." She flashed a secret smile. "But I have seen things . . . I have seen magic."

Richard picked up his notebook, flipped to a clean page, and made several notations on his pad. He glanced back at Genny. "You've seen magic, Annie? What kind of magic?"

"I've seen the gods. Tamara teaches me about them — Damballah, the serpent; Papa Legba, the guardian. I've learned about Agoue, god of the sea; and Ofun Badagris, god of war. Tamara can control the *loa*. She shows me the ancient ways."

Charley felt a shiver run through him. "What the hell is she talking about?" He sat back down on the sofa, the encyclopedia still clutched in his hand.

"I'm not sure. But if she's in Haiti . . . perhaps the woman taught her something of voodoo."

"Black magic?" A memory of the rituals Genny had once described rushed into Charley's head. "Jesus, surely it can't be something like that." But he had seen films of modern-day voodoo, and now that he thought of it, the descriptions somehow fit.

Richard leaned forward. "All right, Annie, let's go forward in time to another screen. You're a woman, now. The year is" — he calculated quickly — "1830. You're thirty years old. Where are you?"

Genny didn't speak, but her eyelids began to twitch and she shifted in her chair. She started shaking her head. "Don't . . . don't want to go there." Charley watched her swallow and noticed the difficulty she seemed to have. A ripple of tension rolled over him.

"Where are you, Genny?" Richard pressed. "What is it you see?"

Her head moved back and forth. "N-No. Nooo!" Genny gripped the arms of her chair. "Can't . . . see her. Won't . . . see her." She started breathing faster, her skin growing flushed and beginning to gleam with perspiration. Moisture beaded on her upper lip. "Can't

. . . see her." Her hands crept up to the base of her throat.

"You're all right, Genny." Richard sat forward, his shoulders going tense. "It's only a movie screen. You're detached from what you're watching." But the words did no good. Genny's eyes snapped open. Enormous brown circles stared into the flame of the candle. Her face looked as pale as the white blouse she wore beneath her sweater.

"Can't . . . see her. Won't . . . see her."

Charley came up from the sofa. "Bring her out of it, Richard. Do it. Now — before something terrible happens."

He hesitated only a moment. Each case was different. He couldn't afford to take the chance. "The screen is growing dark, Genny. You're moving away from it, forward in time." She had started to shake all over. "Do you hear me, Genny? You're back in the present. You're Genny Austin. You're a librarian and you live in Santa Barbara. Can you hear me, Genny?"

"Y-Yes."

"The images you saw on the screen have faded. They're once more nothing but memories. There is nothing to be afraid of. Do you understand me, Genny?"

"Yes." Her eyelids slid closed, and Charley felt a wave of relief. The muscles at the back of Richard's neck began to ease.

"When I count to three, you're going to wake up. You're going to feel relaxed and comfortable and totally unafraid. Are you ready, Genny?"

She nodded.

"One. Two. Three."

Her eyes came slowly open. She sagged against the chair. Her body was limp from exertion. She smiled weakly. "I guess it didn't work." She stared at the men for confirmation.

Charley looked at Richard, who looked back with a face set in stone. Charley thought of what she would hear on the tape and almost wished they hadn't succeeded.

Genny walked beside Charley up to the door of her condo. Before she had left the doctor's boat, he had explained what had occurred under hypnosis, then played the recording he had made. The whole time, Genny sat there shivering, listening to every word, feeling oddly disconnected from the voice on the tape that sounded so different from her own.

And she felt more than a little bit frightened.

Was she really the little girl named Annie Patterson who had once lived in Haiti? Had she really lived another life? The young girl's experiences with her teacher's primitive religion would explain the pagan rituals in her dreams, but the puzzle of the black-haired woman remained unsolved. How did the girl fit in? How was Annie Patterson connected to the wicked, evil woman in her dreams?

From the sound of the tape, Annie was just

as frightened of the woman as Genny was.

And she still wasn't convinced that what she had experienced was a previous existence.

"There may be another explanation," Dr. Bailey had said. "You may be inventing the story for some reason. You may have read it. There is even a chance you might be receiving the story paranormally, the way psychics tune in to vibrations given off at the scene of a crime. Some of them seem able to actually experience the tragedy that occurred."

Genny just shook her head.

"Or you may simply be playing out a fantasy. The story may be nothing more than a powerful metaphor of the subconscious, intended to help you deal with your husband's murder. I *will* tell you that even in past-life cases that appear to have no basis in fact, the patient is often cured of the malady that drove them to seek out regression in the first place. People with phobias, for example, or some sort of obsession. In your case, the end of your nightmares."

"How does it happen?"

"Let me give you an example. A woman came to me with a dangerous allergy to coconut. Whenever she accidentally ate some, she had a massive reaction — heart palpitations, choking, coughing. Once she nearly died. Since the doctors could find no medical reason for the phenomena, she came to me. Under hypnosis, she recalled a life as a tribal chieftain on an island in the South Pacific. She remembered that another tribe attacked them and during the fray, she was mortally wounded by a lance through the throat. She also recalled that the tip of the lance was carved from the shell of a coconut.

"What happened then?"

"Jane's story could not be verified, of course, but two months after her last session, she bit into a cookie that turned out to be a coconut macaroon. She had finished it before it occurred to her she should be having a reaction. She didn't, and she has never had once since."

"That's incredible."

"On another occasion, a woman came to me who was plagued by chronic asthma. Under hypnosis, she recalled a past life as a slave in the Middle East. At some point during her hopeless existence, she saw herself riding in the back of a wagon filled with wet straw. The wagon overturned, trapping her. The slave girl died of suffocation beneath the straw. Soon after reliving that experience, her chronic asthma disappeared. Do you understand what I'm telling you?"

"I think so."

"What I'm trying to explain is that, verified as fact or not, whatever you discover may help you. Once you've dealt with it, your nightmares, your visions, will very likely end."

She had left the office exhausted but, with the lure of freedom from her dreams, more determined than ever to find out the truth.

"You sure you'll be all right?" Charley asked, breaking into her thoughts as they walked along the sidewalk to the door of her condo.

"I'll be okay."

"You don't want to change your mind about returning?" Another session was scheduled for the day after tomorrow.

"I have to go, Charley. I have to know the rest of it."

"You fought it, Genny. It scared hell out of me, I'll tell you. If you do it again, there's no tellin' what might happen."

"It could happen anyway, Charley. Just like it did on the boat."

He didn't try to argue with that one. "All right, I'll pick you up at eight, same as tonight."

Genny just nodded. She waved to Charley, went inside, and closed the door. Her head hurt and her muscles ached from the tension that had gripped her during the session. She wondered if she would be able to sleep, then sadly wished that Jack was there to help her.

Jack. She allowed herself to think of him as she'd tried so hard not to these past few days. She could see his tall figure almost as if he stood there. His shoulders were so wide he nearly filled the door frame. If Jack were there, he would make slow, sensual love to her. He would look at her with those beautiful bright blue eyes and make her forget the turbulence roiling inside her. She would feel nothing but love and a hot, spiraling desire for him.

But Jack wasn't there. He was gone for good — Genny didn't doubt that for a moment. Just as he had warned her from the start.

Forewarned should have been forearmed, she thought bitterly, but it hadn't helped one bit. Instead she'd lost her heart to him, fallen head over heels in love as she had never been before.

Her hand curled over the banister to steady herself as she climbed the stairs. She didn't realize she was crying till she felt the wetness on her cheeks. Dear God, she loved him. They were so different, yet somehow they seemed to fit together. Like cogs on a wheel, meshing notch for notch. What one didn't have, the other did.

He had made her life more fun, changed her from the drab, mundane person she was, to something brighter, more sparkling, more aware of the beauty around her.

She had changed him, too. She had made him see inside himself, made him understand that sharing simple pleasures like sitting before a fire with someone you cared about, or popping corn together, or discussing a good book could bring joy to life, too.

Genny brushed the tears from her cheeks as she wearily climbed up to her room. Her heart felt crushed, her spirit bruised and aching. She had to quit thinking of Jack. He was gone from her life and she had to go on without him. In the morning she would go through her history books, learn as much as she could about Haiti and its ghastly religion.

No — not a good idea. Since Jack had been gone, she couldn't seem to think clearly, seemed to function mostly by rote. She shook her head, forcing his tall dark image from her mind, forcing herself to concentrate. She couldn't do more research, at least not for a while. The more she read, the more she would be able to repeat. Under hypnosis, the more she might invent.

So far, her studies had never included Haiti, since the island hadn't fit her fleeting impressions; nor had she read up on Jamaica, the place in the calendar that triggered the incident aboard Jack's boat. Until then, she'd been convinced the island was Nevis or perhaps St. Kitts.

Now she knew differently, but considering the course she had chosen, the less she knew of these places the better. If she waited till the sessions were over, drew what knowledge there was from her mind, then listened to the recordings, perhaps she could discover if what she said on the tapes held any truth — if in fact she had actually lived another life.

Genny refused to dwell on that possibility. Instead, she forced one tired foot in front of the other until she reached her room. Once inside, she began to strip off her rain-soaked clothes. Sleep was what she needed. She hoped she wouldn't dream, not of the black-haired woman — nor of the handsome blue-eyed man

444

who haunted her nights even more.

"Jack, honey, you know the way I like it." Kristin Hamilton cupped his face in her hands, ran a long red nail down his cheek. "I want you that way now." They were standing in the entry to Kristin's lavish marble-floored apartment. Jack had been kissing her, leaving tiny dark love bites down her long graceful throat.

"I know what you like," he said. "You'll get it when I say so."

She drew her pouty lips into a moue and he kissed her again, harder than he should have, grinding her teeth against her mouth. The faint taste of blood just turned her on.

"I love it when you talk tough like that," she whispered against his lips. She pressed her mound against his groin, and he filled his hands with her breasts. Her short red leather skirt crept up till it barely covered her ass, and her low-cut silk blouse gapped open whenever she moved.

She had full pink-tipped breasts and a pretty face framed by a mass of unruly dark blond hair. He had known her for years. She was twenty-seven, as spoiled as they came, a promiscuous little piece living off Daddy's old Santa Barbara money. She had goaded him tonight into taking her home, reminding him of the last time they had been together.

Nearly two years ago, three nights after his father had shot himself, he had picked her up in a jazz bar in Montecito. Unfortunately, he'd been so drunk he'd passed out on the sofa before he'd been able to give her a proper servicing — or at least that's what she claimed. He owed her one, she told him, and tonight she meant to collect.

"Give it to me, lover. You know you want to. Give it to me good."

Jack reached inside her blouse, unhooked her bra, and rubbed her tits till the ends grew hard. He'd give it to her all right. He'd screw her till she couldn't walk, then he'd get the hell outta there.

He dragged her over to the sofa and shoved her skirt up to her waist. "This is the way you like it — right, Kristin? Hard and fast. Rough and tumble."

Wearing thigh-high stockings and a pair of sheer black panties, she shivered in delicious anticipation. Massaging her breasts, pressing his hardness against her, he bit her nipples, then jerked down her panties and squeezed her ass.

"Jack . . . oh, God, that feels so good."

"You'll get yours, darlin', I promise. I'll give you the ride of your life." Reaching into his pocket, he pulled out a condom, unzipped his Levi's, and rolled it on.

She was hot and wet. He gripped her hips, slid himself in, and started pumping. She climaxed almost instantly. He made her come again before he allowed himself to finish, then he eased himself away.

There wasn't much to it. Just a fast fuck, a quick come, and he was ready to leave. Find 'em, feel 'em, fuck 'em, and forget 'em.

He stripped off the condom and zipped up his jeans.

"You're not leaving yet?"

"You got yours, didn't you?"

"Yes, but —"

"Fine, then I'm outta here. See you next time, baby." The minute he said the word, his chest went tight. He wished he hadn't said it. She wasn't his baby. She meant nothing to him. Less than nothing. And he meant nothing to her.

His hands were shaking when he opened the door. His chest felt heavy and his mouth was dry. His shoulder throbbed but he hardly noticed, for his heart seemed to ache even more.

"I need a drink," he muttered, convincing himself it would help. It would, he knew. By the time he got home, he'd feel better. He wouldn't remember the flashes he'd had of Genny when he'd been making love to the blonde. He wouldn't recall how much he hurt for her. He'd be able to block it, forget her, pretend he was happy without her.

He wouldn't remember what it had been like to hold her, how good it felt to be inside her. He wouldn't think of how much he still wanted her. How much he missed her.

His whole life lay ahead of him. He had to make the most of it, seize each moment and hold on. He would do what he had to do. And then he would go on.

Twenty-two

Seated at an intimate table in the dining room of the El Encanto Hotel on a hill overlooking the city, Howard McCormick reached across the sparkling white linen to cover Genny's hand.

"I'm glad you decided to come." He gave her his most understanding smile. The dining room was opulent: molded ceilings, green-striped silk chairs, silver, crystal, and china, and a small porcelain vase of delicate fresh flowers. The kind of room he felt comfortable in, the kind that made him glad he had been so successful.

"I needed a friend tonight, Howard. I'm glad you called."

Howard brought her fingers to his lips. "You look tired, Genny. I know you've been under a strain. What about your nightmares, are you getting any sleep at all?"

She smiled wanly. "Funny thing is, I haven't been dreaming, not for the past few days. Having . . . someone . . . there for a while seemed to have helped in some way."

"Brennen, you mean." It galled him to say the man's name but Jack was gone from Genny's life now. Besides, he had come tonight hoping for a little information.

449

"I fell in love with him, Howard. God, help me, I didn't mean to, but I did."

"I tried to warn you, Genny. I didn't want to see you get hurt."

"I know. I should have listened. I guess I just got in way over my head."

"You went out on the boat with him. I take it that's the last you've seen of him."

She nodded, looking wan and pale, yet the softness was there, the gentleness that had drawn him from the start. "It was a wonderful trip. I had a marvelous time . . . up until Jack got hurt."

"You know I had nothing to do with his unfortunate mishap. I'm sure he tried to convince you I did, but it isn't the truth."

"I know, Howard. I never believed you'd be responsible for something like that."

"Of course not. I wanted those cases, yes. McCormick-Austin still needs them, but I believed then as I do now that, sooner or later, Jack would come to his senses."

"He will, Howard. Jack's got a terrible temper, but he isn't a fool. He'll sell you those parts at a reasonable price, just as soon as he brings them up."

Howard's stomach muscles tightened. "Then he hasn't found them yet?"

Genny hesitated, thinking of Charley and what he had said. But Howard was her partner. She trusted him, and she owed him the truth. "Jack's found them, but he was injured before he got the chance to bring them in." She squeezed his hand. "But you mustn't worry about it. As soon as the weather clears, they'll be going back out to the wreck site again. They'll bring up those cases, and when they do, I'm sure Jack will let you buy them for whatever price is fair." Genny moistened her full lower lip, and a curl of heat slid through him. He wanted her. Even after she'd been with Brennen, he wanted her. Perhaps even more than before.

"He promised me, Howard, and whatever he is, Jack isn't a man to break his word."

"I'm sure he isn't." His eyes ran over her. She looked more fragile than she usually did, more delicate somehow, like a flower that had just survived a windstorm. It made him want to destroy Jack Brennen. It made his desire for her grow until he went hard beneath the table.

And yet she had betrayed him. Slept with Brennen without the slightest care for his feelings. He had wanted to marry her, make her his wife. He had placed her on a pedestal. Brennen had treated her like the dirt beneath his shoes.

"Howard?" Behind her, the lights of Santa Barbara sparkled like amber gemstones the color of Genny's knit dress.

"Yes, my dear?"

"Can you ever forgive me?"

He wished he could. He wished he could carry out the plans he'd had for a life together with Genny. "Of course, my dear. There is nothing to forgive." But it wasn't the truth. He would never forgive her for choosing a man like Jack Brennen over him.

He would take her to bed, of course, it was something he needed to do. But he would never offer marriage. He would use her just as Brennen had, cast her aside when he grew tired of her. It wouldn't take long to woo her. He would prey on the guilt she felt for treating him so badly and sooner or later she would willingly come to his bed.

Howard smiled to think of the things he would allow himself to do to her. Things he wouldn't have considered if she had been his wife. Perhaps, in the long run, it would all work out for the best.

Assuming he could get his hands on those cases.

That thought was a grim one. He wouldn't allow it to ruin what looked to be an extremely pleasant evening.

Lifting his wineglass, he held it up in a toast. "To us," he said.

Genny's hand shook as she lifted her own glass and clinked it against the side of his. "May our friendship last forever," she said.

Howard just smiled. They would be friends all right. Close friends. Closer than his fragile little flower could ever have imagined.

Jack filled his glass to the brim with Wild Turkey, took a sip, grimaced at the burning sensation, then shot the remainder back.

"That isn't going to help, you know." Charley eyed him from across the room, taking in the lines of fatigue beside his eyes and the haggard look on his face. Jack shifted beneath his close regard as if he were still a schoolboy.

"How do you know what will help?" he growled. He was standing in front of the liquor cabinet. Charley sat over at the table in the galley.

"I know because I'm older and wiser. Whiskey doesn't help much of anything, except maybe a bout of the flu." The rain was still coming down, a gale predicted to last the rest of the week.

"Yeah, well, this is different." The storm and Charley be damned. He was heading for the Sea Breeze Bar. "Don't you think I deserve a little celebration?" The check had come in from the copper they'd sold. They had paid off the bank note today. He should have been ecstatic, instead he felt mildly relieved. "It wouldn't hurt you to get out a little yourself. Why don't you join me when you get finished?"

Maybe he'd do Vivian tonight. She'd been coming on to him again all week, playing her sexy little mind games. She could keep him entertained till the weather broke and they could all get back to work.

Charley eyed him sadly. "You're in love with her, you know."

His hand stilled on the barrel of the whiskey

bottle. His pulse picked up as his gaze collided with Charley's. "You're crazy."

"Am I?" Gray eyes remained locked with blue.

"I haven't thought of Genny in days."

"You haven't allowed yourself to think of her. You're afraid to. That's how I know you're in love with her."

Jack's hold grew tighter on the bottle as he poured himself another drink. An image of Genny rose up in his mind. Genny laughing softly that day down by the river. Genny wearing her seasick patch, her warm brown eyes shining with excitement as the boat plowed through the waves. Genny lying next to him, her pale skin flushed with passion, her lips softly bruised from his kisses.

Something clenched inside him. He took a deep breath and forced the tightness away. "You're wrong, Charley."

"There's nothing wrong with loving someone, Jack." Charley came up silently behind him, rested a hand on his shoulder. "Not everyone who gets married winds up like your mother and father."

There it was. In all its blazing glory. "You're full of it, Charley." He finished pouring the shot, tossed it back, then slammed the whiskey glass down on the table. "You don't know what you're talking about — and I'm outta here." His long legs carried him across the room. He grabbed his slicker, yanked it on over his jeans and Levi jacket, then pulled open the door.

"Think about it, Jack."

He slammed the door a little too hard behind him. It didn't matter what Charley thought. He wasn't in love with Genny. He wasn't in love with anyone. He had his freedom back, his life back the way it was, and that was exactly what he wanted.

His Mustang sat in the parking lot, looking forlorn in the gray, sleeting rain. He opened the door, slid behind the wheel, cranked the ignition, and the engine blazed to life. Throwing the car into gear, he roared out of the parking lot.

At the Sea Breeze Bar, he stopped on the sidewalk just outside the door and looked in through the window below the red neon beer sign. Viv was there, tight pants, hot box, and all. Tonight he'd finally get a piece of her. Or maybe he'd pick up the redhead he'd screwed when he'd first come back to port. Whoever he was with, it wouldn't be Genny.

He refused to think why the truth of that should make him feel so sad.

Richard Bailey helped Genny Austin down the ladder into his boat. He didn't have an office anymore. He saw very few patients, but when he did, he liked doing it aboard his sailboat.

He'd owned the *Lady El* for the past ten years, had been retired since the year his wife, Ellen, passed away.

That was the same year he began to get interested in the theory of reincarnation, just after he discovered his first documentable case.

Perhaps he was more open to it at the time, subconsciously hoping that someday in the future he might have another chance with Ellen. Whatever the reason, he didn't attribute the young girl's recurring memories to an overactive imagination or childhood trauma as he might have a few years before.

He wouldn't overlook the distinct possibility that Genny Austin's troubles sprang from memories of a previous existence. Certainly, as he had told her, there might be some other explanation. But he had seen many cases, and he believed that past lives did indeed exist.

He wondered what it would take to make Genny Austin believe.

"Good evening, Dr. Bailey."

"Good evening, Genny. You're looking very pretty tonight." In her long, gray wool skirt and jacket, a burgundy blouse, and a pair of gray leather boots, she also looked very determined.

"Thank you." She wore a trace of makeup as she hadn't before, perhaps to disguise the paleness of her cheeks. A matching shade of lipstick brightened her lips.

He smiled at her with warmth. "You don't look so nervous tonight. I think you're ready for this." He glanced at the man who had accompanied her. "What do you think, Charley?"

"Looks like it to me." He could always count

on Charley to be cheerful and optimistic — and to keep an open mind. Someday he would like to regress him, see if they shared some connection from another time.

"What do you say, Genny? Are you ready for this evening's endeavor?" She was a pretty little thing, slender and delicate yet somehow resilient. He was glad of the underlying strength he perceived. She might well need it tonight.

"I'm surprised to say I'm almost looking forward to it. This has gone on so long, the thought of it coming to some kind of resolution makes anything seem bearable."

"Well, then, why don't we get started?" He went through the same sort of motions he always did, relaxing the patient, focusing her attention then pulling her down into Alpha and beyond. He moved her back through her childhood, pausing to listen to a story of her family at the zoo, and one about the neighbor's kitten playing with a ball of string in the kitchen, then he moved her back farther, to the screen beyond this existence. The one where she had lived as Annie Patterson.

"Do you see yourself, Annie?"

She nodded.

"How old are you?"

"Ten."

He looked over at Charley, who seemed to know what he was thinking. She was safe here. As a child she faced no problems. "Let's go forward, Annie, to a later time in your life. You're all grown up now, a woman in her thirties. Where are you?"

Genny said nothing. Not a muscle moved. Then her head shifted from side to side in a negative manner. Her bottom lip began to tremble and her fingers dug into the arms of the overstuffed chair. She still made no effort to speak.

"Think hard, Annie. You're a woman, now. A woman in her thirties. You can see yourself clearly. Where are you?"

She moistened her lips. Her throat moved as she swallowed. "J-Jamaica." Her voice had changed, deepened.

"How long have you lived there?"

"I moved here from Haiti when I was sixteen."

"What do you look like?"

Genny shifted in the chair, deeper in the trance now, remembering the life she had lived. She straightened. Her posture became erect. She gave an arrogant tilt to her chin. "They say I'm very beautiful. It may seem vain, but in truth I cannot disagree."

"I want you to describe yourself."

Her smile looked a little bit smug. Her voice went deeper, more throaty. "I have long, thick black hair, wavy but not unruly, and pale, very smooth skin. My figure is lush, ripe, the men say. I have used it often to my advantage."

Richard wet his lips, which had suddenly gone dry. He was silently praying Genny wasn't the woman in her dreams, but remembered past lives were often the most unpleasant. "Is there a mirror in the room?"

"No. I'm standing out on the veranda."

"The veranda of your home?"

"Of course. I've just walked through the French doors, on my way to the stables for my morning ride." Her brows drew together in a frown.

"What's the matter?" Richard asked.

"One of the slaves has apparently misbehaved. Canto. I can see them in the compound below. The man has always been a troublemaker. My overseer, Maubry, disciplines him now." A hard smile curved her lips. "Unfortunately, he is often too lenient in his judgment. I believe I shall see to the matter myself."

Richard waited in silence as the scene progressed in Genny's mind. "What's happening now?"

"I have reprimanded Maubry. The punishment should be ten lashes, not five. I administered the other five myself." She turned her head a little, as if she watched the man across the way. "Cut him down, Maubry, and have someone see to his back. I expect him in the fields again by tomorrow . . . unless he wishes another dose of the same."

Silence fell. Charley sat stiff and unmoving. Genny said nothing more.

"What are you thinking?" Richard asked her, noting the subtle changes taking place in her face.

She shook her head, as if she couldn't quite grasp it. "There is . . . something inside me. It is always there, eating away at me. Trying to swallow me up. I feel such . . . sadness. So much grief. I try to control it. Control is my only weapon against it, yet such a force is elusive. Sometimes even that is not enough."

"Can you tell me what makes you feel this way?"

She only shook her head. There was a bleakness in her expression that hadn't been there before, a despondency that seemed rooted in the very core of her. It pulled at him, made him want to know more.

"I think that perhaps we should move forward," he said softly. The end of a lifetime was often the most traumatic. Perhaps it would give them the answers for which they searched. He took a steadying breath. "I want you to look ahead now, Annie, to the last several screens of your life. Where are you now?"

Her chin came up. "In my bedchamber at Rose Hall."

"That is the name of your home?"

"Yes."

"Walk over and look in the mirror. Can you see yourself?"

"Yes. I'm preparing for bed. I'm dressed in a wrapper of ice blue silk I ordered from Paris. It displays my breasts in a most erotic manner." She reached up and touched herself there, cupped herself with her hand.

A cold shudder slipped through him. "What year is it?"

"1831."

"Then you are thirty-one years old."

"That is correct."

"Is it late in the evening, or early?"

"The hour is late, but I prefer this time of night." Genny frowned. "I hear footfalls. Some-one is coming up the stairs." She leaned forward. The muscles in her shoulders grew tense. He noticed the pulse picking up at her temple. "Too many footsteps. It cannot be one of the servants. I locked the door as I always do but —" She turned, cocking an ear as if she could hear them. "They're pounding, trying to get in." Her fingers curled into the palms of her hands.

"Who, Annie? Who is pounding on your door?"

"*Houngan. Obeahman.* Batu and his followers. Most of them are slaves, some are free men of color. He and I are well acquainted." In her mind she saw him clearly, this man she had conspired with. Batu knew the art of poison as no other headman on the island. He had helped her on more than one occasion, but only be-cause he feared her. Apparently his hatred now overruled his fear.

She jumped as the door slammed back against the wall and a dozen bare-chested, black-skinned men rushed into the room. "How dare you! How dare you come in here like this!"

461

Batu stepped forward from the others. He wore only a loincloth, which left his long, thin legs bare. His black skin glistened in the light of the whale oil lamps.

"You, evil one, have killed Mara, my brother's daughter." A ruff of feathers wrapped around his lean black throat, around his ankles and wrists. "You set the *Loup-garou* against her, then you poisoned her. She is dead because of you." An amulet filled with charms and potions hung from a leather thong and bobbed against the bony protrusions on his chest. His fist shook as he lifted it into the air. "You will die for what you have done."

"Mara was a disobedient fool. I ordered her punished, but I did not kill her. You, Batu, are an even bigger fool if you believe you are strong enough to see me dead."

He took a threatening step forward and Annie raised her hand. She needed time to gather her energy, time to call forth the *loa* to do her dark work. She'd had nothing to do with the slave girl's death, but to Batu it did not matter. He had other grievances against her.

"Do you wish to see the three-legged horse?" she threatened, trying to concentrate, to summon the strength she needed, but the nearness of the men distracted her. "You know I have the power to bring it forth." She laughed, high-pitched and long, and the men recoiled several paces. "Do you all wish to die here this eve?"

"It is you who will die," Batu said. "Your cruelty must no longer go unpunished."

"Stay back, I warn you." She made several signs with her hands as they started easing toward her again, then separated and began to circle around her. She recognized a number of the faces — Simon, Mingo, and three of the others were her own Rose Hall slaves. "You'll pay for this — all of you." They would suffer as they never had before. "I warn you, Batu, do not come nearer. I promise you I will —" Her leg collided with the edge of the stool in front of her mirror and she stumbled. The moment she did, they were on her.

Batu's hands went around her throat, thin, veiny hands but strong. Stronger than she would have believed. She gripped his fingers and tried to pry them loose, but his thumbs pressed into her windpipe, cutting off her air.

Genny's eyes popped open, bulging from their sockets as she fought to drag oxygen into her lungs. Her body slammed hard against the chair and her head tilted backward. Her hands came up to the base of her throat. "Get . . . away . . . from . . . me."

"Bring her out of it." Charley lurched forward, his hands shaking where they gripped Richard's shoulders.

"Not yet, Charley. She has to see that this is really the end."

"The end? What do you mean?"

"She has to experience her own death. She has to feel it. She needs to know that Annie is dead, that this existence is over."

"Good God, man, what if Genny dies, too? Bring her out of it, dammit!"

"I know what I'm doing!" Richard said, beginning to get angry. "If we want to succeed, we have to take the risk. We owe that much to Genny." Richard swallowed nervously as he watched her writhing in her seat, fighting her unseen attackers. She was choking violently, coughing and fighting for breath. In that moment, Richard knew, as Genny would, this was a lifetime that had reached its ghastly end.

"All right, Genny," he said, leaning forward, urgency in his voice, "listen to me carefully. The screen is growing dark now. You are no longer in the past." Her face had turned purple. Odd bruise marks began appearing at the base of her throat. "Can you hear me, Genny? This is Dr. Bailey. You're back in the present. Do you hear me, Genny? You're back in the present."

When she didn't respond, his hands grew slick with perspiration. Inside his chest, his heart set up an unsteady rhythm. Nothing quite this severe had ever happened before.

"I want you to listen very carefully," he said, working to keep his voice under control. "Your name is Genny Austin. Genny Austin. You are back in Santa Barbara. Back in the present." Her face was completely blue. She twitched several times, and for a moment he feared that she had actually stopped breathing. Then she jerked her head in his direction and finally seemed to hear him. "You are a librarian, Genny. You live in Santa Barbara." Her hands, still clutched around her throat, relaxed, and so did Richard. Genny's struggles subsided. Her eyes slid closed, and she sagged down in her chair.

Richard's breath sighed slowly outward. "When I count to three, you will awaken. The past will be only a memory you no longer recall. You will feel relaxed and comfortable and totally unafraid. One. Two. Three."

She opened her eyes. Genny blinked several times then looked over at Charley. His face was as pale as her own. "What happened?" she whispered, frightened by the look on the two men's faces.

"It's over, Genny," the doctor said gently. "When you listen to the tape, I think you'll have enough of the pieces to put your puzzle together. The woman in your dreams is dead."

Genny slumped back in her chair, exhausted but wildly relieved. "Who was she?"

Charley glanced away.

"You've had a very trying evening, Genny. Perhaps it might be better if you returned another time to hear the tape."

Her relieved smile faded. "Why do I have to return? I want to hear it now."

"Genny, Dr. Bailey knows best about these things," Charley said gently. "We can always come back tomorrow."

She frantically shook her head. "I want to know now. I have to." Her hands clenched nervously into fists. "Please. You have to play the tape for me."

Richard came out of his chair. He looked at her then slowly reached over and pressed the rewind button that began to backup the tape. "All right, Genny, I'll play the recording. But you must understand that the life you've been recalling is separate from the life you're living now."

"If that is the case, then why have I been remembering?"

"You told me yourself, your husband's murder triggered your nightmares. The connection to the dead men in the dreams is obvious. You remembered nothing before that. Most likely you never would have."

"Play the tape," she said. "I want to hear it."

"Perhaps we should talk about it first," Richard said, as the tape began whirring softly behind him, "so that you might be better prepared."

Genny stared at him, suddenly wishing she hadn't come. "What is it, Dr. Bailey? God in heaven, what did I tell you?" Then, in a moment of insight, she knew. "The woman," she whispered. Her heart started picking up, thudding dully inside her chest. "That horrible creature. That vile, despicable person who tortured young girls, and used her body, and murdered young men, that woman — it was me, wasn't it? That woman was me." Through her tears, the candle flickered, became an indistinct blur of yellow tipped with blue.

"It was another lifetime, Genny. You're living this life now."

"Listen to him, Genny." Charley's face appeared distorted, then she blinked, dislodging the wetness, and his features came back into focus. Tears cascaded down her cheeks. Ignoring both men, she reached over and turned on the tape.

"You're a different person now, Genny," the doctor repeated as the tape began to play. "You must remember that."

She heard noises in the background, the doctor's hypnotic words, then a woman started speaking. She didn't recognize the voice at first; the woman's sounded deeper, almost a throaty purr. The more she listened, the more she recalled it from before. She had heard it in her dreams.

Genny's stomach twisted. Her breath seemed frozen inside her ribs. She listened as the arrogant woman described herself. She knew the woman well, and now she could see her clearly. When the laughter started, she recoiled from the sound, just as she always did. Bile rose in her throat.

Dear God, don't let it be true. She couldn't have been that wicked inhuman creature. A woman involved in torture, in murder and black magic. Dear God, she couldn't have done such terrible things. But way down deep inside her, in a place she had refused to see before, she feared that it was the truth.

Her eyes slid closed when she heard the woman choking, gasping for breath as someone squeezed the life from her treacherous body, as she suffocated beneath the strangling hands of her attackers, just as Genny had imagined more than once.

By the time the tape ended, she was sobbing. Charley put his arms around her shoulders and she cried against his chest.

"It's over, honey. Now you know the story. Whether it's true or not, don't make a damn. The important thing is — now you can put it behind you."

She lifted her head. "Do you really believe I can do that, Charley? Just turn around and walk away? I have to know if this really happened. I have to know if a woman that vile existed . . . if she did those terrible things. God in heaven, I pray it isn't the truth, but I have to know."

"It might not be that easy," the doctor said. "A number of my clients have tried to track their former lives down. The past is elusive. Most of them have met with little success."

"The woman is a murderer," Genny argued, wiping at the tears still clinging to her cheeks. "She had power and wealth. I know where she lived and when, even the year she was killed. If this is real, I'll be able to prove it."

"What will you do then?" the doctor asked gently.

"I don't know. If it's true, I don't know how I'll be able to live with myself."

The doctor rested a hand on her arm. "I told you before, it doesn't really matter whether or not it's the truth. What matters is that you've faced it. Once that's happened, the past will begin to recede. The pain will, too, Genny. Please believe that."

"I wish I could, Dr. Bailey. I only wish I could."

Sitting at a small round table in the corner of the Sea Breeze Bar, Jack leaned back in his chair. His gaze was fixed on the half-empty beer bottle in front of him. Vivian Sandburg sat across from him, sipping a gin and tonic. Both of them were surprisingly pensive.

"Jack?"

He roused himself, looked up from the bottle, allowed some of the noise in the place to seep in. "Yeah, what is it, Viv? You want another drink?" He wasn't drunk. God, he wished he was. He didn't have the heart for this, tonight. Not like he thought he would. But after the way he'd treated her last time, he couldn't walk out on her again. Even he wasn't that big a bastard.

"No, I'm fine." He saw her reach across the table, felt her fingers curling over his hand. "I've been watching you all week, Jack. You've been acting kind of strange ever since you got back into port."

"I've had a lot on my mind."

"The boat, you mean?"

"Yeah," he lied. He hadn't even told her his good news.

"Maybe, but I don't think that's it. I've been flirting with you all week and you've been flirting back. Tonight I figured the time for us had finally come, but something seems to be missing."

"What are you talking about?"

"Something's wrong, Jack, and I think I know what it is."

He straightened, sat up taller in his chair. "Yeah, what's that?"

"It's Genny, isn't it?"

His stomach clenched. His mouth went dry as he stared across at Viv. "What's she got to do with this?"

"I've known you quite a while, Jack. In an odd sort of way, you might even say we're friends."

He smiled faintly. Perhaps in a way they were. "I guess you could say that."

"I remember the first time I saw her. I was jealous of the way you looked at her. I've never seen you look at a woman that way."

Jack shrugged, but he felt far from nonchalant. "Genny's different. She's not like other women I've known. I suppose that's the reason."

"Maybe it is . . . or maybe it's something else.

Are you in love with her, Jack?"

His head came up. He started to give her a smart-ass reply but the words stuck in his throat. "It doesn't matter one way or the other."

"I think it does, Jack. Does Genny love you?"

"Look, Viv — talk about acting out of character — since when have you been concerned with the welfare of another woman?"

She smiled at that, a bright white smile in a pretty face framed with long blond hair. "Maybe just this once I'd like to see a guy like you find the real thing. Love — you know what I mean? We're a lot alike, Jack. We always have been. If there's hope for a guy like you . . . then maybe there's hope for me."

Jack looked at her, studied her in a way he hadn't before. It occurred to him that she wasn't just a shapely body, someone to screw when a guy got horny. She was a woman, trying to make her way in the world, a woman with her own wants and needs. Before he'd met Genny, he wouldn't have been able to see that.

"It isn't me you want tonight, it's Genny. Why don't you just admit it?"

"Like I told you. It doesn't really matter. It's too late for me and Genny. It's over between us."

"Maybe it isn't too late. Maybe that's just an excuse you're using because you're afraid. If it's any consolation, I'd be frightened, too." Vivian slid back her chair and slowly came to her feet.

"Think it over, Jack."

He watched her walk away and didn't try to stop her. He felt like he'd just been granted a reprieve.

Propping his elbows on the table, he rested his forehead in his hands and released a slow breath of air. First Charley now Viv. *"You're in love with her,"* Charley had said. It was becoming painfully clear those words were true. Achingly, bitterly, sorrowfully clear. Even Vivian Sandburg could see it. Why the hell couldn't he?

Shoving back his chair, the grating sound lost in the boisterous crowd around him, Jack stood up behind the table. His head hurt and his stomach felt tied in knots. He dropped a five and some ones beside the Budweiser bottle, to cover his drinks, then crossed the smoky room toward the door. Outside, the air smelled cleaner, yet his chest still ached with every heartbeat.

He walked straight to his car and drove back to the boat, determined to seek out Charley. He needed to talk to him, say the things he'd been afraid to say before, things he had refused to even consider.

He needed his best friend's advice, though in his heart he figured it was probably coming too late. Genny was lost to him. He had severed the connection as cleanly as if he had cut her out of his heart with a knife.

Downing a cup of black coffee, while the

storm was still raging outside, Jack paced the floor of the galley. His mind filled with images of Genny. It hurt just to think of her, yet the pain felt better than the numbness, which was all he'd allowed himself to feel since they had parted.

"Damn it, Charley, where are you?" Jack muttered aloud as he made another turn and started pacing back the other way.

"Right here, son. What the devil's going on?" As Charley stepped inside and removed his heavy wool coat and the scarf around his neck, Jack sank down on the sofa, trying to think what he should say.

"How is she?" he finally asked, his heart throbbing painfully, knowing where Charley had been.

Charley's bushy gray brows rose a fraction. "Is that concern I hear? I thought you could hardly remember her name."

Jack said nothing, but guilt slithered through him like a serpent.

Charley sighed. He rubbed his face with his hand. "She's not so good, I'm afraid."

"Why not?" His guilt spiraled upward. He'd hurt her, he knew. He wasn't sure how bad.

"Besides being trod upon by you, she's finally remembered the woman in her dreams. It was her, Jack. Genny was the black-haired woman in Jamaica."

"That's crazy. Richard Bailey told her that? What the hell kind of quack is he?"

"It had nothing to do with Richard. Under hypnosis, Genny remembered the life she led back then. At the end, she was murdered by some of the people she mistreated. She was strangled, Jack. She choked to death. Does that ring any bells?"

A wave of nausea rolled over him as he thought of Genny gasping for air on the floor of the galley. "I don't believe any of it, especially not that. From what Genny says, the woman was sadistic. A ruthless, vicious killer. Genny is nothing like that. She would never hurt anyone."

"It doesn't really matter whether it's true or not. What matters is that Genny believes it. This isn't an easy time for her, Jack."

He bent his head, raked a hand through his curly black hair. "You were right, Charley. It's just like you said. I'm in love with her." The words hung in the air. Charley made no comment; he had known the truth all along. "I tried to fight it. I tried to ignore it. I've done everything in my power to pretend it isn't true, but it is. It's killing me, Charley. I'm in love with Genny. The problem is, it doesn't make a damn bit of difference."

His friend walked over and sat down in the chair across from him. "Why not?"

"You know the answer to that as well as I do. Genny and I — we're two different people. For God's sake, Charley, the woman's a damned librarian. Even if I am in love with her, what

474

kind of life could we have?"

Charley chuckled softly. "A 'damned librarian.' I think I've heard those words before. Funny thing is, it seems to me the two of you aren't so different after all. Think about it, Jack. Genny's changed since she met you. She's one of the most fun-loving, adaptable females who ever came down the pike. She's adventurous, and she certainly isn't boring. And come to think of it, you've changed a good bit, too. You want to know what kind of a life you'd have? A damned good one, I'd say. The least you can do is give the two of you a chance."

The knot in Jack's stomach clenched tighter. Charley was right. Genny had changed and so had he. They weren't so very far apart. Fear was what had made him go so crazy. Fear of losing her that day in the galley that had made him realize how much he loved her. Terror at the thought that she might love him. Panic that together they would suffer the same awful existence as his parents.

It was the same fear that had driven him to avoid any sort of attachments, that had led him to be wild and reckless all his life. "I don't think she'll have me, Charley. I treated her badly. I don't think she'll forgive me this time."

"You won't know that until you ask her." He smiled gently. "I remember those bankers when they came to see the boat. There wasn't a snowball's chance in hell you were gonna let them have it. I can't imagine you'd let a guy like Howard McCormick steal your lady away from you."

"McCormick? What the hell does he have to do with this?"

"She's seein' him again. He wants her, Jack. Real bad. This time he might just get her."

Jack's fist unconsciously clenched. His wound still ached from the spear McCormick's hit men had fired into his shoulder.

"I may not be perfect, but I'm a damn sight better man than Howard McCormick. If there's any way in hell to make Genny see that, I've got to try." If he hadn't been so worried, he might have smiled. It felt good to admit his feelings. For the first time in days, he felt like himself again. It surprised him to realize the hard-drinking, conscienceless man he had portrayed since his return was no longer the man he was inside.

"You know, Charley, it might not be so bad being married. And having a couple of kids around wouldn't be too bad, either. You know how much kids like boats."

Charley felt a sharp, sweet blossoming inside him. A sheen of moisture glazed his eyes. He had wanted this for Jack, wanted him to have the happiness he would have wished for his own son. He tried to smile, hoping Jack wouldn't see. "Maybe you're not so dumb as I thought, boy," he said gruffly. "All you got to do now is find a way to convince Genny."

Jack looked at his friend and knew exactly

what he was feeling. His own emotions ran much the same. They wavered from elation to hope to bitter despair. After the way he'd behaved, he didn't deserve a second chance with Genny. How could he possibly convince her to believe in him again?

"Thanks, Charley," he said, as he strode to the door. It was late, but he didn't care.

"Good luck, son."

Jack nodded grimly. It was going to take a whole lot more than luck to win Genny this time. He had never been so sure of anything in his life.

Twenty-three

Genny sat curled on the sofa in her living room. It was nearly midnight, but she couldn't sleep. She was more afraid of her nightmares than ever. Now she would see them as a terrible reflection of herself.

She had tried to convince herself that there might be some mistake, or some other explanation, as Dr. Bailey had said. But she didn't really believe it. Deep down in the core of her, down in the very marrow of her bones, she believed that what she'd seen in her mind was the truth.

Still, she couldn't know for certain, and until she did, she would cling to the chance that it was all a fabrication — some psychotic fantasy she had spun in response to Bill's murder. An hour ago, she'd decided she would travel to Jamaica. Research books had their limits. She wanted to go to the source. She wanted to see the place. To *feel* it.

She wanted to know about Annie Patterson, and to do that she needed to go where Annie had lived. And the research would be far easier. She could sort through old newspaper accounts, study history books on the area. Such materials would take weeks to locate through inner branch library loans.

She was going to Jamaica. When she returned, one way or the other, she would finally know the truth.

Genny leaned back against the sofa and closed her eyes. When she wasn't thinking about what had happened at Dr. Bailey's, she was aching for Jack. She had tried to forget him, to put him out of her mind, but she couldn't. Part of her hated him for hurting her so badly, but the other part said it was her fault, not his.

Jack was the same man he was on the day she had met him. The man he had always claimed to be. He didn't want to be tied down. He didn't want that kind of involvement — or responsibility.

He had warned her.

Pete had warned her.

She was the one who had fallen in love.

Genny squeezed her eyes closed to block his handsome face, to try and block the pain. It felt like a dull wound throbbing inside her chest, like a heavy stone crushing her heart. It felt as if time would go on, but her life had ended the minute she had left him on the boat.

She could still see him lying there, his shoulder swathed in bandages, refusing to take the pain medication the doctor had prescribed, until the copper had been safely off-loaded on the dock.

He had hardly spoken to her, just a brusque word or two, a polite but distant glance. She had known it was over by the look on his face, known that the moment she had told him she loved him, Jack had pulled away.

Genny brushed the tears from her cheeks with a shaky hand. Crying wouldn't help. Hurting wouldn't help. Nothing would. Jack was Jack. Whatever they had shared was over and done. Jack had made certain of that.

Though she hadn't seen him, she knew what he had been doing. She remembered the last time he had run, the night she had found him with Vivian Sandburg aboard his boat. She would never forget the crushing emotion she had felt, as if she were dying, as if the life were being ripped from her heart. She couldn't go through that kind of pain again, and the sooner she faced the fact, the better off she would be.

Genny rested her head against the sofa, wishing she could fall asleep, praying that if she did, she wouldn't dream. Instead she heard a soft, insistent pounding on the door.

Pulling her terry-cloth robe more tightly around her, she went into the entry and looked out through the tiny glass peep hole. *Jack.* Her stomach twisted, clenched.

"Genny, it's Jack. I've got to talk to you. Please let me in."

She bit down hard to keep her lip from trembling. "I-I'm sorry, Jack. I can't do that."

"I know you have every reason to hate me, but —"

"You didn't want me, Jack. You made that perfectly clear. Please don't hurt me anymore."

"Genny, you've got to listen."

"I know what you've been doing." Her throat constricted, ached with unshed tears. "I know about the drinking. I know you've been seeing other women. That's what you wanted, now please just go away."

"Genny, you have to let me talk to you, try to explain."

Tears brimmed in her eyes. She tried to blink them away, but they spilled onto her cheeks. "I know about the redhead. Dottie Marshall saw you with her. You went to bed with her, didn't you?" She had no right to ask him . . . or perhaps she had every right. She was fighting for her life.

For a long while Jack didn't answer. "I won't lie to you, Genny. Not now. All I can do is tell you that it won't happen again. Let me in, Genny, please. All I'm asking is that you listen to what I have to say."

Genny pressed her forehead against the door. She was shaking all over. Hot tears were streaming down her cheeks. If she let him in, she might forgive him. She loved him. When it came to Jack Brennen she was weak. "I can't do that, Jack. It's over between us. It never should have gotten started."

"Genny —"

"It isn't your fault, Jack. You tried to tell me and so did Pete. Please . . . please go away and leave me alone."

"Dammit, Genny —"

She straightened, sucked in a breath of courage. "If you pound on the door or try to come in through the balcony, I'll call the police. I mean it, Jack."

It was quiet for the longest time. "I'll go away, if that's what you want. But I'm not giving up. Not until you talk to me."

"Good bye, Jack." Pressing a hand to her mouth to stifle a sob, Genny turned and ran from the entry. In the living room she paused. Her knees were wobbly, her heart aching fiercely. Skeeter rubbed against her legs. Genny reached down and picked him up with a shaky hand, and buried her face in his soft gray fur.

She had to be strong. No matter what happened, she couldn't let Jack Brennen come back into her life. The pain was just too great.

Climbing the stairs, she went into the bathroom. In the medicine cabinet, she found a bottle of sleeping pills Dr. Halpern had prescribed over a year ago. She took double the prescribed amount, went into the bedroom and crawled beneath the covers. Almost immediately, the drug kicked in and buried her in a deep, sluggish sleep.

In the morning, the doorbell rang and she roused herself, fearing for a moment it was Jack. Instead it was the florist, carrying a beautiful gold foil box. Through the cellophane window she could see a branch of white orchids. Their throats were a deep, shimmering purple. Surely they were from Howard. He knew white orchids were her favorite. Genny removed the card with a trembling hand.

What I have to say, I have to say in person. I know I don't deserve it, but please give me the chance. Jack.

Genny pressed the card against her lips. What could Jack possibly have to say that she hadn't heard before? Worst of all, how would she react when he said it? Genny couldn't bear to think of falling back into the trap of loving Jack and worrying day and night about the next time he would leave.

Instead she phoned the travel agency, made arrangements to leave in the morning for Jamaica, then packed her bags and spent the night with Millie so Jack wouldn't be able to find her.

Carrying a passport she had gotten for a trip to Mexico with Bill but never had had the chance to use, she left Millie's the following morning. By 8:00 A.M., she was on a flight to Los Angeles that connected with a nonstop to Miami. From there she'd fly directly to the airport at Montego Bay. Nothing was going to dissuade her. Not Jack Brennen, or Charley, or even her own heart.

"I can't find her, Charley. She isn't at work,

she isn't at home. Her car was gone when I got there last night, and she never came back." Jack knew because he'd looked in the window of her garage, then sat in his Mustang parked at the curb, watching for her return till the early hours of the morning. "God, Charley, what if she's with McCormick?"

Charley speared him with a glare. "Then you'll just have to forgive her that mistake, just like you're asking her to forgive yours."

Charley was right, of course, but the thought of Genny — *his* Genny — spending the night with that slimeball McCormick made his insides curl.

Charley laid a hand on his shoulder. "Listen, son. I don't think she's done anything foolish. She's just trying to stay away from you. Believe it or not, it may be a very good sign."

"Sure, Charley. She hates me so much, she won't come near me. That's always a damn good sign."

"Did you ever think she might be avoiding you because she's afraid you'll convince her to see you again? She thinks you want things back the way they were, and she's afraid you'll hurt her again."

Guilt crawled through him. "So how can that possibly be good?"

"She loves you. She's afraid she'll do it, even if she knows she shouldn't."

Jack just shook his head, feeling like a worse piece of scum than Howard. "I don't think you're right, Charley. I think she's with Mc-

Cormick. She likes him a lot more than you think."

"Why don't you find out?"

"How?"

"Talk to her friend, Millie, down at the library. Chances are, she'll know where Genny is."

"What makes you think she'll tell me?"

"Not many women say no to Jack Brennen."

A corner of his mouth curved up. "I hadn't thought of it quite that way. All right, if Millicent Winslow knows where Genny is, I'll figure a way to get her to tell me." Jack grabbed his jacket, winced at the pain that shot into his shoulder, and headed out the door. He drove too fast to the library, then tried to calm his racing heart as he walked in.

From Genny's description, and the knowledge that Millie was a reference librarian, he spotted her tall slim figure almost instantly and made his way over to her desk.

"Miss Winslow?"

She turned, a thin, reedy young woman who looked at him through big round eyes a lighter shade of blue than his own. "Yes?"

"I'm Jack Brennen. I hate to bother you, but —"

"Jack! Of course. It's nice to meet you. Genny's told me a lot about you." She was smiling. Was that a good sign or bad?

"I need to talk to her. I thought maybe you could help me."

"Yes, well, I'm afraid she doesn't wish to see you."

"Where is she?"

"I-I'm really not at liberty to say."

McCormick. He knew it. He thought he might be sick. "I know I've treated her badly. I want to make it up to her. I have to talk to her, Millie, I have to tell her . . . I love her. I want her to marry me."

Millicent Winslow's deep-set eyes went as round as silver dollars. "You love her?"

"Yes." It wasn't so hard to say. Not after the first few times.

Millicent grinned broadly. "Well, that's different. Of course I'll tell you where she is. Genny's gone to Jamaica."

"Jamaica!" He faltered. He hadn't expected that. "Surely she didn't go by herself." Please, God, don't let her be with McCormick.

Millie nodded. "All by her lonesome. She stayed with me last night then took off early this morning. She wants to find out about the woman in her dreams."

"When's she coming back?" Instead of feeling relieved, he grew dark with worry. With the problems she'd had, Jamaica was the last place Genny should be going by herself.

"I'm afraid she didn't say."

Before he left the library, Jack got the details of Genny's trip, including the hotel in Montego Bay where she would be staying. Then he went back to talk to Charley. Ollie was there when he walked in.

"Genny's gone," he said without preamble, sliding into the booth in the galley across from his two friends. "Flown off to Jamaica. She's gone to find out about the woman in her dreams."

Charley's face went pale.

Even Ollie looked shaken. "You got to stop her, man. You saw what happened to her on the boat. All she did was look at a picture of the place. What if somethin' like that happens again?"

"The same thing occurred at Richard Bailey's," Charley said. "He had a helluva time bringing her out of it. She left the doctor's office with bruises on her throat."

"Bruises?" Jack sat up straighter in his seat. "How the hell did that happen?"

"Richard figures marks like that must have been made on Annie Patterson's throat the night she was strangled. When Genny remembered, they reappeared. Richard says it's psychosomatic, a physical manifestation of a psychological trauma."

"Jesus." Jack raked a hand through his hair.

"Charley says this Annie was mambo," Ollie said. "A high priestess of voodoo. That stuff's bad shit, man. You don't want Genny messin' with that kinda thing."

"I can't just up and leave," Jack argued. "We've got to finish the salvage project. We've got to replenish our capital if we intend to stay in business."

"There's another storm front movin' in behind this one," Charley said. "If you're lucky, you'll be back here with Genny before the weather clears enough to dive. Besides, your shoulder's still not healed. You shouldn't be divin' yet anyway. And we've got enough money left from that first batch of copper, we can hire the men we need."

"I can help you out," Ollie said. "Pete prob'ly can, too."

Jack smiled. "Thanks guys. Thanks a lot." He started across the room to the ladder leading down to his quarters.

"When will you be leaving?" Charley asked.

Jack's smile turned into a grin. "I've got a seat on a plane heading south in an hour and a half."

Charley laughed and so did Ollie. "Maybe he really has changed," Ollie said, "— at least in some ways."

"Yeah, no doubt about it. And definitely for the better. You'd best get a move on, son."

But Jack didn't need to be prodded. He was already halfway down the ladder, grabbing his duffel bag, stuffing in shirts and shorts and jeans. A few minutes later, he was heading for the airport in nearby Goleta, scheduled on a flight to Los Angeles. He'd lucked out and found a direct flight from LAX to Jamaica, which would save him a couple of hours flying time. Six hours after takeoff, he'd be landing in Jamaica.

He just prayed Genny would be all right until he got there. And that once he did, he'd be able to convince her to come home.

Genny stepped off the plane at Sangster International Airport in Montego Bay. The standard package from the Half Moon Golf, Tennis, and Beach Club where she would be staying included a transfer, so she climbed aboard a van with the hotel name stenciled in small gold letters on the door. At the curb, a smiling Jamaican loaded her luggage into the rear. With the time change, it was early evening.

She was tired, since she hadn't slept well at Millie's. She planned to have supper in her room then go to bed and hopefully get some sleep. She would begin her search in the morning.

Genny leaned back against the seat of the van. Her eyes strayed outside to the sights and sounds of the city.

"Dis you first time in Jamaica?" the driver asked, speaking to the only passenger on board.

Was it? A chill swept over her. Perhaps tomorrow she would know for sure. "Yes . . . yes, it's my first time here."

He grinned, exposing big white teeth. He wore a short-sleeved blue flowered shirt, and his hair had been plaited into dozens of three-inch braids. Typically Jamaican. But then that was probably the way the hotel wanted him to look.

"Since dis you first trip, I give you quick look-see at MoBay."

"MoBay?"

"Montego Bay. Dat what we call it."

"I see. Thank you, that would be nice." It would be, if she wasn't so nervous. She kept worrying that something she saw might trigger another choking attack. Though the bruises on her throat had faded as magically as they had appeared, she hadn't forgotten the episode she had suffered. Dr. Bailey believed that since she knew what had caused it, it would not happen again. She was praying he was right.

They wove their way through the busy streets, past brightly dressed Jamaicans selling everything from woven baskets and straw hats, wood carvings, pottery, shell goods, and flowers, to fresh fish, and vegetables.

"Be sure you try Jamaican fruit," the driver said. "Star apples, sweet sop, sour sop, jack fruit, guinep, naseberries, paw paw — You will like, I promise."

She smiled faintly. Such wonderful, rhythmical names. "I'm sure I will." The whole place seemed to have a rhythm all its own.

The van stopped at a red light and a tall willowy cocoa-skinned woman walked past, balancing a basket filled with bananas and coconuts on her head. Her hips swayed in a graceful motion as old as the first inhabitants of the island. Genny closed her eyes, trying to imagine what it might have been like to live here a hundred and fifty years ago. In the days when there were no cars, no planes, no buses. When the crowded square might have been filled with slaves, instead of vendors hawking their wares, or artists painting at their easels.

"Better we go to de hotel now. You can see more in de morning."

"Yes, it is getting late."

She checked in at the resort and was taken to a deluxe room on the second story with a balcony overlooking the blue-green Caribbean sea. An ancient palm tree shaded the windows, giving the place added privacy, and beyond a grassy expanse, the ocean lapped softly at a mile-long stretch of white sand beach.

The room itself was tastefully decorated in muted tropical tones and polished dark rattan furniture. A mini-bar with a small refrigerator hummed softly, across from the big king-size bed.

Genny spent an hour or so unpacking, ordered a meal of cream of banana soup, baked chicken and sweet potatoes. She meant to eat but only picked at the food as she sat on the veranda. Then she went in. Stripping off her clothes, she climbed into bed, but she couldn't fall asleep.

Two hours passed and she still wasn't sleepy. All she had done was worry about what she might discover tomorrow; or think about Jack, which alternately made her angry then filled her with bitter despair. She sighed with resignation, tossed back the crisp white sheet, and came to her feet.

Dragging on a pair of khaki shorts and a dark green scoopnecked blouse, she left the room and went down to walk on the beach. Halfway there, she made a quick detour to ask the desk clerk to have the latch fixed on her small in-room refrigerator. She'd noticed earlier that it wasn't working. From there she made her way out into the darkness. Her senses honed in on the lure of the ocean.

Jack stood at the counter of the Half Moon Resort behind a fat, balding man in a pair of god-awful pink flowered shorts and a T-shirt that didn't quite cover his belly. Anxious to see Genny, fidgeting from one foot to the other, he wished the man would decide which kind of room he wanted, stop complaining about the price, and get the hell out of there. When the bald man finally left, grumbling as he walked away, Jack took his place at the counter.

"Name's Jack Brennen. I made a reservation earlier today."

The desk clerk pushed a button on his computer. "Of course. We have you right here, Mr. Brennen." He pulled a registration card from the file and pushed it across the counter. Jack filled it out and shoved it back, and the clerk gave him a key. "Room 144. Ground floor with a very nice lanai."

Jack just nodded. "A friend of mine is staying here as well. Her name is Genny Austin. Could you tell me if she's checked in?"

Again the computer hummed. "Yes, sir. She arrived several hours ago."

"Which room is she in?"

"I'm sorry, sir. It's against our policy to reveal that information."

He'd known it would be, but it was worth a try.

"Do you have a house phone I can use?" He had hoped to confront her in person, though it didn't really matter. He had come this far to see her. He intended to do just that.

"Yes, sir. The phone is right over there. But now that I think of it, if you're planning to speak to Ms. Austin, I'm afraid she isn't in. There was a maintenance problem in her room. She went for a walk on the beach while our service people were repairing it."

Jack set his duffel bag up on the counter, along with a handful of Jamaican currency he had just purchased at the exchange. "Have the bellman put this in my room, will you?"

"Of course."

Jack turned and headed out the door. He checked his watch. It was ten o'clock in the States, but after one in the morning here. He made his way past the pool area, where the tinkle of steel band music drifted toward him on the wind. He crossed the grass, and stepped out onto the sand. He scanned the distance but at first he didn't see her, she had walked so far away. A full moon rose above the water, forming a silver path that arrowed toward the beach. The long stretch of soft white sand was nearly empty.

He waited a moment for his eyes to grow accustomed to the darkness. Then he spotted a small figure ankle-deep in the surf way down the beach.

Jack started walking in that direction, his nerves strung taut as a bow line. What would he say to her? What *could* he say that would make her understand why he had done what he did? And even if she forgave him, would she also believe he wouldn't hurt her that way again?

He had walked more than half a mile down the beach and Genny was still some ways ahead. It was a beautiful, secluded stretch, framed by rustling palms amid lush tropical foliage scented with night-blooming jasmine. Fireflies mated a few feet away, flashing their neon love songs.

Moonlight and warm Caribbean breezes. Perfect for the words he wanted to say. If only he could persuade Genny to listen.

Genny shoved her hands into the pockets of her khaki shorts and tilted her head back to look up at the huge full moon that seemed to hang in the night-dark sky. A light breeze sifted through her hair, which hung loose around her shoulders. Longer now, it curled softly in the humid Caribbean air. The ocean felt warm where it gently lapped at her ankles, and the fragrance of flowers scented the light wind blowing out to sea.

Surrounded by such beauty, she should have found it hard to feel sad, yet the tropical night only made the ache she felt for Jack grow more poignant.

She had come here hoping that once she immersed herself in the search for Annie Patterson, the loss she felt would ease. Instead, her feelings only seemed to grow stronger, as if the island itself held memories of Jack and the love she felt for him, no matter how hard she tried to force it away.

Genny bent down, picked up a small speckled seashell, and skipped it across the dark glossy surface of the water. When she turned, she paused, spotting a tall man outlined by the moonlight walking toward her on the beach. For one brief, heart-stopping moment, she thought it was Jack. It was silly, insane to think that he would come thousands of miles in search of her.

Yet as she watched the man draw near, her pulse started pounding, throbbing inside her chest. Her palms went damp, and her heart swelled up with a fierce, unbearable longing.

He had almost reached her when the moon

came out from behind a passing cloud, illuminating his features in its softly shimmering rays.

"Jack . . ." she whispered, but in that instant something happened. Time began to spiral, to tunnel her backwards, to pull her into another age and place. The man walking toward her was Jack and then again he wasn't. The eyes were the same compelling shade of blue, but the hair was not so dark. It was a deep reddish brown, and his skin was not as swarthy. He was as tall as Jack, but his body was leaner, his muscles longer, more bone and sinew. Strength of character shone in the hard lines of his face.

Jason. She began to tremble all over, knowing that face, remembering it with a brilliant rush of warmth and a burning need to touch him. He was here. He had returned. It was *him*.

"Genny?"

She barely heard the word. She could see him now as he was then, in his navy blue uniform, with its rows of shiny gold buttons up the front, epaulettes riding his wide shoulders. She saw him as she had that last day on the dock, waving back to her as he headed for his ship. The *Voyager* would be leaving, but Jason had promised to return. He loved her, he said. Madly. Fiercely. He would come back to her as soon as he could make the arrangements.

He called her name once more, reached out to her, and she went into his arms, feeling his solid strength, remembering it as he tightened his hold around her.

"I love you," he said. "I love you so damned much." He held her face between his hands, brought his mouth down to hers and kissed her so tenderly, her heart expanded inside her chest. His tongue slid gently between her teeth and sweet sensations rippled over her. He took her mouth, claimed it, took it again and again.

All she could think of was how much she loved him. How she had missed him through the eons of time, and that he was finally here. She ran her fingers over the line of his jaw, felt the firm, determined set, saw the beautiful blue eyes that had drawn her to him all those years ago. She wanted to hold him, to touch his bare skin, she wanted to feel him inside her.

She would do anything to have him. Anything to once more be his.

"Genny," he said softly, her name coming out on a hushed breath of air.

"Make love to me," she whispered, "please . . ." He paused, his eyes turning a deeper shade of blue yet suddenly uncertain. "Please." Then he was lifting her up, carrying her to the edge of the sand, laying her down on the soft damp grasses that hid them from view. He was opening the front of her blouse, filling his hands with her breasts, bending his dark head to kiss them, suckling them into small tight buds.

He had always loved her breasts, she recalled. Revered them, practically worshipped them. Just as she worshipped him.

"Jack," she whispered, then frowned. It was Jason she remembered, Jason who had loved her, who had taken her innocence that day beneath the ferns at the edge of the pool, a pool lined with lovely white orchids. It was Jason who loved her now, who kissed her breasts, ran his hands over her hips. It was Jason who stripped off her clothes and his own, who knelt between her legs to kiss her belly and thighs, who whispered soft words and settled his mouth over the hot damp core of her.

Genny arched upward, feeling his tongue, accepting it, craving it. She burned for him, loved him, needed him as she never would another human being. Waves of heat slid through her, ripples of desire so intense she began to shake with the force of them. His mouth took her body with intimate care, suckling gently. His tongue went sliding in, knowing how to please her. Aching to, it seemed. He gripped her hips and lifted her, delved his tongue more deeply inside her. He held her there, determined to give her pleasure, knowing exactly the way. He stroked her lovingly, tenderly as she thrashed and moaned and the fires built inside her. She would die of the pleasure, she thought, shaking with heat and shivers of delight, then the sweetness of release washed over her.

Pressing her down in the soft green grasses, he came up above her. His curly black chest hair was rubbing sensuously against her breasts. She could taste herself in his kiss, in the brush of his tongue first against the walls of her mouth, then sweeping lightly across her lips as he whispered how much he loved her. Her desire returned, swelling with each of his words, each touch of his hands on her breasts. He stroked her nipples, caressed them, eased his hands between her legs and parted the folds of her sex. She was damp with the moisture of desire, ready to accept him, craving the feel of him inside her.

"I love you, Genny," he whispered, filling her with his hot heavy length. And she knew she would always love him.

"Jack . . ." He was thick and solid, touching the top of her womb, at the same time touching her soul. How long had she waited? Why hadn't he returned?

His muscles tightened as he began to move, kissing her thoroughly, thrusting deep inside her. She clutched his massive shoulders. Her head was falling back into the soft green grasses, her nails biting into his sweat-slick flesh. Her eyes were closed but still she could see him, so beautiful, this man that she loved, this man she had always loved.

She clung to him and felt the tight spirals coiling inside her, the release that only he could bring. Her body gripped him, tightened around him, and she heard him groan. Then she was spinning upward, whirling, soaring, breaking through the clouds, drinking in the sweet, sweet pleasure. Shivers of delight spread through her, and a feeling so intense she could taste it on her lips.

She felt his muscles go taut, felt his hot wet seed spilling inside her, and tears stung the backs of her eyes.

"You didn't come back," she whispered. "I waited and waited. I watched the horizon for hours on end. I never gave up, but you didn't come back."

She felt him move off her, gather her close. He leaned his head against her forehead. "I'm here now," he said. "And I'll never leave you again."

Genny slid her arms around his neck. Her heart felt swollen and bruised, yet unfettered from the shackles that had bound it. She felt the light brush of his lips on her eyes, her nose, her mouth, saw the infinite love in his beautiful blue eyes. Jack and Jason, they were one and the same, the man she had loved for all time.

Genny touched his face with a trembling hand, brushed his mouth with a last soft kiss, and started to weep.

Twenty-four

The night sounds intruded. The lap of the ocean against the shore, the chirp of an insect, the rustle of long-bladed leaves in the tropical wind. Jack was glad for the intrusion. He didn't want to think about what had happened. He didn't want to recall the intensity of their lovemaking or the odd words he and Genny had spoken. He didn't want to remember the sound of her soft weeping.

"Did you mean it, Jack?"

He felt her hand on his chest, the faint tremors still running through her body. Fighting the ache in his shoulder he'd been able to ignore until now, he leaned over and kissed her forehead. "Did I mean it when I said I loved you? I meant it, Genny. I've never meant anything more." His hands were shaking as they framed her face. Something had happened between them, something so intense, so profound that even their passionate lovemaking hadn't drained the tension from his body. It frightened him, yet it felt so right he knew he would never run again.

Genny's hand whispered over the stitches in his shoulder. "You took off the bandage," she said softly. "You shouldn't have. You could have hurt yourself when we . . . when we . . ."

He smiled faintly. "My shoulder's getting better. Besides, it'll heal faster this way."

Genny sat up next to him. Her big brown eyes searched his face. "I can't believe you came here. I can't believe we made love. Considering the things that have happened, I never intended to see you again."

She meant the women. His insides churned. He thought of the way he had felt when he had imagined Genny with Howard McCormick and understood the anguish he had caused. He wished he had understood sooner, that he could undo what he had done.

"I would have come after you, no matter where you had gone. I would have gone to any length for a chance to explain."

"You don't have to do that. I know the way you are." There was sadness in her eyes and a wisdom far beyond her years.

"I'm sorry, Genny, for everything that's happened. If I could change things I would. We both know I can't do that. But I can tell you that from now on things will be different. That if you'll give me another chance I'll make it up to you."

Tears misted her eyes. Genny looked away. "It wouldn't work out, Jack. You'd get tired of me and then you would leave."

"You're wrong, Genny. I ran because I was frightened. I've never felt like this before — I've never been in love. I didn't know how to deal with it. I was afraid to even try. But I'm not afraid anymore."

She looked up at him with surprise. "What would a man like Jack Brennen have to be afraid of?"

He sighed and stared off toward the water. Along the shore fireflies flashed their tiny neon lights. "Life, I suppose. Or more accurately, not living life. Growing old without knowing what it's all about . . . the way my parents did. Now I realize that living without you would be the same thing — going through life without knowing what it's about. I love you. I want us to get married."

Genny's throat went tight at the unexpected words. She had never thought to hear them. She hadn't believed he would make that kind of commitment. "I-I don't know, Jack. An awful lot has happened." More than she cared to think about. More than she thought she could handle. So much still remained unsettled, her own problems as well as those between them.

Jack ran a finger along her cheek. "A lot has happened because I was too stupid to admit the way I felt. Once I did, everything suddenly seemed clear. Since then I've had time to think things through." His features brightened, matching the hope that had risen in his voice. "My boat is finally paid off. With the money I'll get from the rest of the copper, we'll have a good stake for the future. There's plenty of work in the channel. I won't have to be gone that much from home. You can keep your condo. We can live there, if you want, or we can move someplace else. We can make things work, Genny, I know we can."

"We've never talked about marriage. I never thought it was something you wanted." It was something *she* wanted, she began to realize. More than anything else in the world. But besides the problems with Jack, what about her own? What if she had really lived another life? What if she was really the evil, vicious woman in her dreams? If she had actually done those terrible things — how could she live with herself?

Yet after what she remembered tonight, hope blossomed fresh in her heart.

The beautiful young girl who had made love to Jason Sommers wasn't wicked or evil. She was a woman filled with love, with a heart overflowing with dreams, and a shining hope for the future. Perhaps Annie Patterson wasn't the awful woman of her nightmares. Maybe it was a mistake. Maybe they were actually two separate people. Perhaps Annie Patterson was merely related, a cousin or even a sister.

She wanted to believe that. Desperately. And she wanted to marry Jack Brennen.

As if she had spoken, he reached for her, turned her face with his hand. "Once you said I never promised you anything. At the time, it was the truth. I'm making you a promise now.

504

I'm promising to love you. Not just for this moment, but for the rest of our lives. I'll do everything in my power to make you a good husband. Do my best to be a good father to our kids. That's my promise. I may be a lot of things, Genny, but I don't break my word."

Tears touched her eyes, began to spill down her cheeks. Once she had said that same thing about him. Now she wasn't so sure. Lieutenant Jason Sommers had made just such a promise, and he had certainly broken his word.

She remembered that young girl now, intelligent, courageous, fiercely loyal to the man she loved. They had met when she had first come to Jamaica, after her parents had died. She was only sixteen, but her father had been a well-respected merchant, and white women were scarce. The wealthy planter society was only too eager to embrace another of its kind.

The night she met Lieutenant Sommers, she was attending a party at one of the nearby plantations. Jason was an officer of His Majesty's Navy, aboard the sailing ship, *Voyager*, which had stopped in Jamaica to make repairs. He was the handsomest man on the island.

"They're playing a waltz," he had said as the orchestra in the ballroom began another tune. "Have you ever waltzed, Miss Patterson?"

She smiled. "Once or twice, perhaps. And I shall have you know I don't think it's one bit sinful."

"Neither do I." He smiled. The most beautiful smile she had ever seen. "I don't suppose this dance is open."

She looked down at her dance card, knowing not a single space was empty. "As a matter of fact, it is."

He grinned, certain it wasn't the truth. "Then may I have the pleasure?"

Over her shoulder, she saw the stout little man who should have been her partner, but all she could think of was what it might feel like to dance with Jason Sommers. "I'd be delighted, Lieutenant."

They waltzed together as if they had done it a thousand times and afterward he escorted her in to the midnight supper. The next day Jason paid a visit to the very proper boardinghouse where she was living and from that time on they saw each other nearly every day. She was innocent and trusting, Jason said he loved her, and she certainly loved him.

That day in the mountains beside the secluded pool, she gifted him with her innocence, and he took it with infinite care. Afterward he asked her to marry him, promising to return as soon as the *Voyager* reached England and he could make plans.

And then he had sailed away.

Week after week, she awaited his return, staring out at sea, watching the horizon, hoping and praying, certain that he would come. But no word reached her.

And Jason never came.

"Genny?" Jack's deep voice dragged her from the past. "I know you weren't prepared for this, but I'm asking you to marry me. Please say yes."

Her heart twisted, throbbed. There was a time she had prayed he would say those words. Now she was not so naive. Jack had left her before, just as Jason had.

Still, this time things might be different.

Perhaps, after all, he had come for her at last.

"Are you certain, Jack?" Genny looked into his darkly handsome face. "Are you sure this is what you want?"

"I love you, Genny. If you love me, this is exactly what I want."

She leaned forward and kissed him. "I love you, Jack. I always have and I always will."

"Then you'll marry me?"

She smiled, forcing away the memories, convincing herself that whatever she discovered wouldn't change the way she felt. "I'll marry you, Jack."

Still beautifully naked, Jack stood up and hauled her to her feet. He was aroused again, and the fierceness of his desire made her own desire swell. His springy black chest hair rasped against her nipples, sending a warm delicious shiver along her spine. She felt his muscles bunch, and heat tugged low in her belly.

Taking her hand, he raced toward the water. His laughter sounded deep and warm. Genny found herself laughing, too, daring to hope again. Daring to dream.

The ocean lapped against their skin as they sank into the sea. Jack was kissing her with tenderness and an intimacy different from any they had shared before. He wasn't holding back, she realized. He was giving himself, wholly and completely. The hope inside her expanded, convincing her that a marriage between them might actually work.

Neck-deep in the water, Jack lifted her up and wrapped her legs around his waist. Genny sighed with pleasure as he lowered her onto his hardened arousal. They made love slowly, like the timeless lovers they were, then returned to the foliage wet and dripping to pull on their clothes.

"I suppose it's time we went in," Genny said with some reluctance. "I've got lots to do in the morning."

Jack stopped her as she buttoned up her blouse. "I was hoping . . . now that things are settled between us . . . you'd forget about Annie Patterson, that we could spend a few days together and then go home."

She wished she could. Dear God, how she wished she could. "I have to find out, Jack. I have to know if these feelings, these things I remember are real." In her heart she believed they were, but she had to know what had happened to Annie Patterson, and if Annie was the awful woman in her dreams.

Beneath the silver disk of moon, Jack's blue

eyes searched her face. "All right, if that's what you want, I'll help you. We'll stay here until you find out the truth. But there's something I want in return."

"What's that?"

"A day for us. A single day in paradise. For just one day, I want you to forget the past and think about the future. Think about you and me. I want to swim in the ocean, climb waterfalls, take a boat ride down the river. I want to drink rum punch and make love beside a pool lined with orchids. Will you do that, Genny? Will you give me that one day?"

Make love beside a pool lined with orchids. Did Jack remember, too? For a moment when they were lying together, she had wondered if his memories might be the same as hers.

"All right," she said softly. "Tomorrow will be ours. Whatever happens, we'll always have tomorrow to remember." A shiver of unease slid through her. Memories. So many memories.

They could free her. Or they could destroy her.

She wondered which one it would be.

A single day in paradise. It started with breakfast in bed, drinking thick black Blue Mountain coffee, feeding each other coconut and mango and juicy fresh pineapple, licking the sweet stickiness off of each other's fingers. That led to a round of passionate lovemaking. Genny remembered the night before with only a moment of embarrassment, which slid away completely as Jack brought her to a mind-spinning climax.

Afterward he tugged off the sheet she had pulled up to cover herself, and he playfully dragged her from the bed. "Come on, sweetcakes, it's time for a nice hot shower. I've got plans for you today and they don't include sleeping."

"Sweetcakes?"

He grinned wickedly. "Why not? I can't think of anything sweeter than the taste of —" The pillow hit him full in the face. Genny raced by him and climbed into the shower, but a few minutes later Jack joined her there.

While she dressed and dried her hair, he arranged for a rental car, which was delivered to the hotel. They were on the road by ten and heading into the city, making a stop at the Harbour Street Market, where a woman braided pretty glass beads into Genny's hair. Then they decided to explore some of the surrounding countryside.

A little nervous to be driving on the wrong side of the road, they drove west instead of east out of the city, taking the less-traveled road to Negril. A few miles later, they spotted a sign for a turn off to the Rocklands Bird Feeding Station.

"Let's go there, Jack. It'll only be a few miles out of the way."

"Why not?" Jack flashed her a lazy smile, happy and carefree as she had never seen him.

Two hundred and fifty species of birds made their homes in Jamaica, Genny learned, once they reached the sanctuary. There were four varieties of hummingbirds, including the tiny bee, one of the smallest birds in the world; as well as interesting specimens like the tody, which made its nest on the ground instead of in a tree. Most spectacular was the incredible array of parrots in their flashing bright colors.

Genny and Jack watched them feeding, then headed on down the road to a spot on the Great River.

"How did you find this place?" Genny asked.

"Read about it in a travel brochure. We're going to go rafting."

"Oh, Jack . . . I don't know . . . I'm not that good a swimmer."

He reached across the console in their rented little Ford Escort and squeezed her hand. "It's not that kind of raft. Besides, you trusted me on the Harley. You went out with me on the boat. You wound up enjoying yourself, and this won't be one bit different."

"What about your shoulder?"

"I'm not paddling and neither are you."

Genny grinned, suddenly filled with excitement. "All right, rafting, it is. How much worse can it be than the ride you gave me in your Mustang?"

Jack laughed as they pulled into the parking

lot. Half an hour later they were headed up the Great River on a small wooden raft. A lean black guide poled the boat toward a secluded spot deep in the tropical forest. The guide would leave them there to explore, then come back three hours later and return them to their point of departure.

On a seat festooned with flowers, they trailed their fingers in the slow-moving current. Once ashore, they walked the tranquil rain-forest paths, climbed steep waterfalls, took off their clothes and swam naked in secluded pools the color of perfect emeralds.

They made love, of course, just as Jack had promised, beside a quiet pool beneath huge lacy ferns. Lying in his arms, Genny couldn't help recalling another time they had made love like this. A time in the long distant past.

She trailed a finger down Jack's chest, drew a circle around his flat male nipple. "I was wondering . . . does the name Jason Sommers mean anything to you?"

Staring at the thick green canopy above his head, Jack plucked a long stem of grass and rolled it between his fingers. "No. Should it?"

"I-I just thought maybe you might remember him."

"Where's he from?"

"England . . . over a hundred and sixty years ago."

Jack's lazy expression faded. He propped himself up on an elbow. "Don't, Genny. Not today. You promised me a day all to ourselves. I don't want some man from the past to intrude."

"He isn't just some man. He was . . . you."

"Me!" Jack's face closed up even more. "I don't want to talk about this — especially not now." To prove it, he leaned over and kissed her. Not such a gentle kiss this time, but one of fierce possession. She was his, his body said, he wasn't going to let her forget it. His hands came up to her breasts, cupped them, plucked her nipples into hard tight peaks. He deepened the kiss and Genny moaned into his mouth, beginning to tremble beneath him. Soft damp moss cushioned her back. Jack's hard-muscled thighs pressed against her. Her body was still moist from the time before. She accepted him easily as he gripped her hips and thrust himself inside her.

He took her wildly, passionately, forcing the same response from her. Pounding into her, he rode her hard and fast, taking her to heights of incredible sensation. She felt the tension coil and the hot sweet moment of climax. Jack followed her to release.

"This is our day," he whispered as he curled her beside him. "I won't let tomorrow intrude."

She couldn't argue with that. Tomorrow was still too uncertain.

It was late afternoon when they returned to their car then drove on to Long Bay in Negril. They explored the lighthouse on West End

Road, then stopped at Rick's Cafe — on the cliffs above the shore — to watch the sunset. The place was renowned in the area for its beautiful view.

At Rick's they ate baked crab and pepperpot soup, sucked fresh oysters from their shells, "to restore their strength," Jack claimed, then stuffed themselves with West Indian lobster.

"At this rate, I won't fit into my swimsuit," Genny complained as she shoved back her chair when they were through.

"So far you haven't needed one." Jack's heated glance made the color rush into Genny's cheeks. The hot look didn't diminish on the hour-long drive back to their hotel.

All in all, it was everything Jack promised. A day in paradise. It made her want to forget what she had come to Jamaica to do.

It made her want another day to be with him.

Clifford Turner-Smythe, the desk clerk at the Half Moon Beach Club, also served as concierge. He was working in that position, sitting behind his glass-topped dark rattan desk in the lobby when he caught sight of the handsome pair walking hand in hand in his direction.

Magnificent, he thought, studying the tall dark man he remembered from the night he had checked in. The girl was lovely, too, of course, but in a softer, simpler, less striking manner.

"Good morning," he said pleasantly at their approach. "I see you two found each other." He almost wished they hadn't. Perhaps the beautiful blue-eyed man . . . ah, but that was merely wishful thinking. He had known the moment they met, the man had an appetite different from his own. "How may I help you today?"

The woman spoke up. "I was wondering if you might know a bookstore nearby, someplace I might find a list of the old plantations." She looked soft and feminine in her ankle-length white cotton skirt and simple lace-trimmed peasant blouse. She wore her light brown hair clipped up on one side, enhancing the dark brown color of her eyes. She was taller than average, with a willowy build, yet her breasts were full and high.

He smiled. "Then you're interested in the history of our island."

"More or less," said the big man beside her. "As Genny told you, we're particularly interested in the early plantations."

His smile grew broader. "As they say in Jamaica, 'No problem.' The ones still standing are very big tourist attractions." He brought out a printed sheet of paper the size of a place mat, which sported a drawing of the island. The major tourist attractions were marked in red. Placing the map on the counter, he used his pen to point out the small red stars which located the plantations.

"There are quite a number, as you can see."

"The one I'm particularly interested in may no longer exist," the woman said, "but this will certainly give us a place to begin."

He started circling the names, forcing his eyes not to drift to the tall handsome man. "Let me see . . . Greenwood Great House in Falmouth isn't that far away. It was built by a cousin of Elizabeth Barrett Browning. Harmony Hall is an old Victorian, part of a pimento estate. There's Prospect Plantation near Ocho Rios, and Brimmer Hall in Port Maria. Colbeck Castle is on the opposite side of the island. Oh, and I nearly forgot. The most infamous plantation of all is just seven miles from here. That's Rose Hall Great House."

The woman's hand tightened around the tall man's powerful bicep. "Rose Hall?" she whispered, her cheeks going suddenly pale.

"Why, yes. That's where Annie Palmer lived. The mansion is supposed to be haunted." Tourists were always enthralled with this sort of nonsense. Actually, he found it rather fascinating himself. "Supposedly Annie was involved in black magic. She used her powers to murder three husbands, as well as a couple of lovers. She tortured her slaves until they strangled her to death in 1831. They called her the White Witch of Rose Hall."

Genny swayed on her feet.

"Easy, baby." Jack gripped her arm and steadied her against him.

"Annie P-Palmer," Genny repeated, feeling numb all over. "Not Annie Patterson?"

The desk clerk frowned. "That name does

sound familiar." Rummaging through his files, he took out several flyers with pictures of Rose Hall Plantation on the front. Genny recognized it immediately as the place in her dreams. Her legs began to tremble. Opening the brochures one after another, he skimmed through each of them and quickly tossed them away.

"Ah, here it is. This one tells a bit about Annie. It says she was Irish and English. That she married John Palmer in 1820. This says her maiden name was Patterson. I thought there was some connection."

Annie Palmer. Annie Patterson. The bile rose up in Genny's throat. She could hear the names ringing in her head. Dear God, just as she feared, the women were one and the same! Her stomach roiled violently.

"Genny?" Jack called out. She reached for him, but dark circles moved in front of her vision and the room began to spin. Blackness dropped like a curtain. Her legs gave way as she tumbled into unconsciousness.

"Genny!" Jack barely caught her before she hit the floor. A jolt of pain shot into his shoulder as he lifted her up in his arms.

"Ohmygod." The desk clerk clapped his hands against his chubby cheeks.

"Call a doctor," Jack said, lowering Genny onto a nearby sofa. He shoved a cushion beneath her ankles, then knelt beside her and began to rub her limp, icy hands. She moaned softly as she started to come around. When she tried to sit up, he gently pushed her back down on the sofa.

"Give it a minute, baby. There's a doctor on the way."

"Doctor? I-I don't need a doctor." She came up from the couch. "I-It was just a shock, is all."

Jack eased her back down. "It can't hurt to have him take a look."

But Genny stubbornly shook her head. "I'm all right now. Really I am." Swinging her legs to the floor, she carefully sat up, but didn't try to stand. "I'll be back to normal in a minute."

The desk clerk returned with a flurry. "Dr. Milo is on his way. He should be here in just a few minutes."

"I guess we won't be needing him after all," Jack said with some reluctance. "Sorry for the trouble."

"Are you certain?" The little man turned solicitous eyes to Genny. "She still looks awfully pale. I hope it wasn't those dreadful stories I told her. I should feel quite distressed to think I had caused her to faint."

"It wasn't your fault," Genny assured him. "And I'm feeling much better already. I can't imagine what could have happened." A glance at Jack and she saw that he was frowning at her lie. He helped her unsteadily to her feet. "I'm sorry for the inconvenience. Perhaps it's a change in the weather."

"You're absolutely certain you're all right?

The hotel has a certain liability, you know."

"I'm fine." She looked again at Jack, then back to the clerk. "If you wouldn't mind, I'd like some of those brochures. I presume they give directions to Rose Hall Great House."

"As I said, it's merely a few miles away."

"Genny —" Jack's glare of warning didn't deter her.

"I'm going, Jack. That's what I came here for. I've got to see it. I've got to try to understand." But the truth was she would never understand how a beautiful young girl like Annie Patterson could wind up the vicious, evil woman who was Annie Palmer.

Perhaps, if she had the courage, the answers awaited her at Rose Hall.

Twenty-five

"Genny, are you sure this is a good idea?"

"How can you ask me that, Jack? You know what I've been through. I've dreamed about this woman for the past two years. I don't have any other choice." They were just past the Half Moon golf course, driving on the left hand side of Route A-1 on the road to Rose Hall Great House.

"I still say this is bull. I don't believe your dreams have anything to do with reincarnation. It could just be something you've read. The guy said this place was a tourist attraction. Maybe you saw a pamphlet somewhere, read about the Palmer woman in the library. That has to be the explanation."

"I wish it were. There is nothing on this earth I would rather believe, but in my heart I know it isn't the truth." She knew it even more clearly when they drove up in front of the house. It was just as she remembered, a huge three-story Georgian mansion with tall paned windows and massive carved front doors. Seeing it, her mind came alive with images, bits and pieces of a past that should have been long forgotten.

Still, it was different now, as Dr. Bailey had told her it would be. Now that she knew what had brought the images on, she could handle them. It was still like looking through a window to the past but without being immersed in that past as she had been before.

It also helped that though the house was much the same, it was also very different. The original Palmer mansion had been destroyed, she learned as the short, stocky cocoa-skinned guide led them on a tour of the mansion. All but the exterior walls of the house had burned up in a fire long ago. The present structure had been carefully restored from the burned-out shell, using as much detail as the owners could glean from their intensive research.

Still, the differences formed a sort of protective barrier, allowing her to look, to experience the terrible memories, fit the pieces together, without the threat of being consumed by them.

The pain came only from the knowledge of what she had done. And with each new secret revealed, her face went a little bit paler. Her stomach felt queasy while her head throbbed with a dull ache that set her nerves on edge. Mostly what she felt was overwhelming grief. The same grief that had come after each of her dreams.

"You don't look good, baby," Jack said. "I think we ought to leave this place before something bad happens."

"No." She shook her head. "As long as you're

with me, I'll be all right."

Jack's features remained grim but he squeezed her hand. "I'll be with you every minute."

They walked through the entry with its sweeping mahogany staircase, toured the morning room, and then the magnificent ballroom. The elegant furnishings looked much as she remembered: beautiful Queen Anne tables, William and Mary side chairs, crystal chandeliers and Oriental carpets. There was a Hepplewhite table in the dining room nearly identical to the one she remembered.

They continued upstairs. Genny was clinging to Jack, grateful for his solid support. Outside a bedroom Annie had always kept sealed — one once occupied by one of her murdered husbands — Genny was swamped by a violent wave of emotion. As she was leaning against the wall outside the door, her heart was beating oddly. She closed her eyes and dragged in deep breaths of air.

Jack swore softly. "Dammit, Genny —"

"Just give me a minute and I'll be all right." Forcing down ugly memories of death and despair, she made her way on down the hall. They caught up with the group of tourists as they entered Annie Palmer's bedchamber. The place where she had spent the last night of her life.

Standing at the rear of the tour group, with Jack's arm protectively around her waist, she leaned against him and listened as the guide relayed the gory details of the slave revolt that had led to Annie's death by strangulation.

"The room was . . . different," Genny whispered, her mouth so dry she could barely form the words, her limbs wildly unsteady. "She always kept fresh flowers in a vase on the dresser, but it was here" — she pointed toward the opposite wall with a trembling hand — "not over there. It sat next to a beautiful hand-painted porcelain pitcher her mother had brought from England. And there was a thick, dark red Oriental carpet beside the four-poster canopied bed. She hated to step on the cold hardwood floor."

A muscle jumped in Jack's cheek. He didn't argue, but it was obvious he didn't like what he was hearing. Genny didn't like it either. It was beginning to seep in, exactly who she was and the terrible things she had done.

The group went out to the back of the house, and both of them followed. A wide lawn sloped down to the rock-lined pond, just as she recalled. Off to the left was the place near the edge of the cane fields where Annie's young lover had been poisoned. As Genny stared off in that direction, an agony of pain tore into her chest. The grief she felt expanded until she thought it would consume her. Hot salty tears began to roll down her cheeks.

"All those people — dead because of me."

"That's it — we're outta here." Gripping her hand with a strength that said he meant business, Jack started walking back up the grassy slope, leading her around the mansion toward the car. If he thought she meant to argue, he was wrong.

"Th-there's just one more thing."

He stopped and turned to look at her, his jaw set determinedly. "What is it?"

Her lips felt bloodless and numb. She knew her face was as white as the flowers in Jack's short-sleeved navy blue shirt. "The gift shop. I need to buy some books. I have to find out as much as I can about Annie."

"I don't think that's a good idea."

"I have to, Jack." On legs that shook with every step, Genny started walking toward the souvenir shop with its small bookstore section. Jack caught up and captured her hand, gripping it tightly and easing her fears a little.

A number of volumes had been written on Annie Palmer and the legend of Rose Hall Great House. By the time they left the mansion, Genny had purchased an armload, some on Rose Hall and Palmyra, also owned by the Palmers; others on Annie herself, the legendary White Witch of Rose Hall.

As Jack drove the car out of the parking lot, Genny sat curled up in the passenger seat, hugging the books to her chest, hot tears streaming down her cheeks. Pain still throbbed at her temples and her heart ached unbearably.

Jack turned her face with his hand. "It's over, Genny. This house and everything you supposedly remember, happened more than a hundred and sixty years ago. It's all in the past — over and done with. You've got to forget it."

But she only leaned her head against the window and cried all the harder. Now that the pieces fitted together, she knew what she had suspected all along. The beautiful young girl who had loved Jason Sommers, the woman filled with passion and hope, had gone completely insane. Jason's betrayal, coupled with the knowledge that their one forbidden moment had left her pregnant with his child, had reduced her to a bitter shell that finally crumbled altogether.

She had been so alone, so desperate. She had waited for word, certain that Jason would come. When no word came and the weeks rolled past, her fear and desperation grew. With no one to turn to, she sought the help of a woman in the village. She wanted Jason's child so badly, yet survival demanded she destroy it.

But Annie had waited too long.

Genny could still see the blood. So much the dirt floor ran crimson. And the pain — dear God it nearly tore her in two. She awoke several days later, racked with fever, hovering near death. In the end, she survived, but there would never be another baby. She had wept until her throat ached and her lungs felt as if they were bursting. She wept for the child she had lost. Wept for Jason. Wept for herself.

For the men who followed, men who took

advantage of her loneliness, her battered heart, and vanquished spirit, she felt nothing but a violent disgust. The terrible grief she was forced to bury along with her child led her down the path of self-destruction.

Annie's bitter resentment of men had begun.

"She spelled it A-N-N-E-E," Genny said softly, staring straight ahead as they drove back toward the resort. "Haiti was French, you know. Her parents thought it was such a pretty name."

Jack gripped her hand. "Don't do this, baby. Please." His skin felt warm in contrast to the iciness of her own. "Let it go, Genny. It has nothing to do with us."

But it had everything to do with them. Jason Sommers's betrayal had driven poor Annee insane. It had led to her return to black magic, to the deaths of at least four men and the torture of dozens of others.

Now Jason Sommers was back. Already Jack Brennen had betrayed her. What would happen if he did it again? She could only begin to imagine what the horrible consequences might be. She didn't doubt they would occur. The pieces of the puzzle had at last come together. The circle was complete.

But this time she meant to change things. Whatever monstrous outcome fate had in store, she would not allow it to happen.

"I think we should go back in the morning," Jack said. "I don't think it's good for you to be here."

"All right." Her voice sounded thick and sluggish, yet it was an easy concession. She wanted to be away from the past as badly as Jack did.

What he didn't understand was that she would also be parting from him.

Twenty-six

Genny sat next to Jack on the big United DC-10 to Los Angeles. They had hardly said a word since they'd left Jamaica that morning, not since the argument they'd had the night before when she had told him that she couldn't marry him. And there was still an hour's flying time before they arrived in L.A. The plane was less than half full, so the service was good; yet neither of them had anything to eat or drink.

It was cloudy most of the way. The gray cast outside the window was seeping into the atmosphere inside. The interior was chilly and dim, reflecting Genny's mood. From the corner of her eye, she watched Jack sitting beside her, though it hurt just to look at his dear, handsome face. He must have seen her for his gaze swung to hers, and he searched her eyes for some sign of what she was thinking.

"This is crazy, Genny." His softly spoken words cut into the misery she felt.

"Maybe it is. Maybe I'm as crazy as Annee. Or perhaps I'll simply go mad just knowing the things I've done." She had told him last night that it was over. She'd told him about Jason Sommers and Annee Patterson, and why she could not marry him. Jack had railed as she knew he would; he had argued and raged and sworn. He had begged and he had pleaded.

None of it did any good.

He turned in his seat, cramped as he was by his long muscular legs and wide shoulders. "Listen to me, Genny. I know the things you believe, but they can't be true. If they were, I wouldn't be in love with you. You're nothing like that woman — surely you can see that. You're sweet and kind and good. You believe in people. You care what happens to them. I could never love the kind of woman you believe you were. Doesn't that prove something?"

Perhaps it did, but she couldn't be sure. She only knew the risk of loving Jack was too great. The consequences were too grave to even consider.

"It's no use," she whispered, her throat clogging up with tears. It seemed she had been crying forever. "We've been through this, time and again. Nothing you can say is going to change my mind." Her bottom lip trembled. "I think in your heart you know that."

She had never been so implacable, so set on a course without the slightest chance of alteration. Jack must have felt it. He must have seen it in her expression for his own reflected despair.

She had never seen him look that way, his features so empty, so resigned. He was always so robust, so full of life. It exuded from his pores like a fine sheen of exertion. But today the vibrance was gone, replaced by the hollow-ness in his eyes, the grim set of his jaw, the bleakness around his mouth.

She reached out and touched him, cradled his cheek with her hand. Already she could feel the faint dark roughness of his beard. Jack leaned into her palm and closed his eyes, shielding her from the brilliant blue gaze tinged with defeat.

"My darling, Jack," she whispered. "I love you so much."

His thick black lashes swept up as his eyes fixed on her face. "Genny . . ." The harsh pain in his voice twisted her insides, cut through her heart like a blade.

"I wish it could be different," she said. "I should have known it was too much to ask."

Jack leaned back in his seat. His face seemed a little pale beneath his tan. His features once more were masking his emotions. "Funny thing, the way it's turned out. It took me a life-time to find you, to discover what I really wanted in this world. Now that I have, it isn't going to happen."

Genny felt a searing jolt of pain.

"I deserve this," he said softly. "For the things I've done to you. For the women who loved me I couldn't love back. Now I know how they felt. Until I met you, I never understood how much it hurt to love."

Genny's throat ached harder. "Jack, please don't say any more."

He didn't. Just stared out the window without really seeing. He reached for her hand, laced his fingers through hers, held it in his lap. She could see the muscles in his throat constricting. She knew his pain was the same as her own.

"I never believed you would care this much," she said. "I love you. I never meant for any of this to happen."

He pressed her fingers to his lips. "I'm the one to blame, Genny. I just don't have what it takes to make you believe in me. If you did, you'd trust me enough to know I'd never let anything hurt you. To believe I could protect you from whatever it is you fear."

"Don't say that . . . please." But in a way it was the truth. As much as she loved him, she was certain in the end he would betray her. Just as Jason Sommers had.

It didn't make the hurting any less painful. It didn't make her love for Jack go away.

She watched him as he stared out the window. The lines of his face seemed set in stone. Tension seeped from every pore of his body. And yet he tenderly clutched her hand.

Dearest Jack. In a way, he was as vulnerable as he was beautiful. In the beginning, she hadn't believed he was the kind of man she would ever want to marry. She hadn't recognized his intelligence, or his determination. She hadn't seen his courage or his loyalty to his friends. She hadn't understood his passion for life, or his secret need to be loved.

Now that she saw it, it was too late.

Genny swallowed against the harsh ache in her throat. She was going to lose him. There was no other choice. She wondered if it was retribution. If instead of cheating fate, she was accepting what fate had planned all along.

They departed the plane in silence, crossed the tarmac at LAX, and boarded a smaller flight to the airport outside Santa Barbara. It was raining when the wheels touched the runway. A heavy sleeting downpour formed great puddles on the asphalt, dampened her clothes, and weighed down her spirits even more.

Jack said nothing as he walked beside her into the terminal to retrieve their luggage. Then they continued through the doors leading out to the parking lot. He loaded her suitcases into the back of her Toyota. His face seemed an emotionless void.

"I'll follow you home," he said gruffly, "make sure you get there safely."

Genny shook her head. Her lungs ached with the effort not to cry. "No, Jack, please. I can't handle another good-bye."

Jack's face contorted. His careful control snapped like a dry branch in the wind. He gripped her arms and hauled her in front of him. "Do you really believe I'm going to leave you like this? Say good-bye forever in this god-damned parking lot? Christ, Genny. I love you.

You told me you loved me."

"I told you why this has to happen. I'm not asking you to believe it. I can't make that happen and I won't even try. I'm just asking you to try to understand."

"I don't understand. I'll never understand. I love you. I don't want to lose you again."

She couldn't swallow. Her throat ached too much. Tears welled in her eyes and slipped in great silent tracks down her cheeks. Sliding her arms around his neck, she pressed herself against him, felt his hand stroke gently through her hair.

"We have to do this, Jack. We can't take the risk. Please don't make it any harder than it is already." Jack said nothing, but his hold grew tighter around her. "Promise me you won't call. That you won't come by to see me. If you love me, you'll promise me that, and you won't break your word."

"God, Genny . . ."

"Please, Jack, I'm begging you. If you love me —" He stopped the words with a hungry, anguished kiss. It burned into her heart and scorched all the way to her soul. She could taste the salt of her tears and feel Jack's big body trembling. He crushed her against him, buried his face in her hair.

"I love you, Genny — I don't want to leave you. But I've hurt you enough already. I'll do whatever you say."

"Jack . . ." They stood like that for long,

heartbreaking moments, then finally he pulled away.

"If you ever change your mind —"

She pressed her trembling fingers against his lips to stop the words. "Good-bye, my darling Jack. I hope you try to love again."

He only shook his head, his dark locks glossy with a mist of rain. "There's only one woman for me. I know that now. I know it in here." He pressed her hand over his heart and she could feel the uneven beat that matched her own. "And I'm not brave enough to try again."

Genny bit hard on her lip. She thought of the past, of the fate that had brought them together, and she believed it was the truth. The knowledge was her undoing. Bitter sobs tore from her lips and Jack swept her into his arms.

"I love you," he whispered, crushing her against him, shattering her self-control. He kissed her one last time, kissed her with ravaging tenderness. And then he was gone.

Genny watched him walk away, biting hard on her bottom lip but unable to stop the tears. *It wasn't meant to be,* she told herself. *If it had been, you wouldn't have remembered.* But if she hadn't remembered, she wouldn't have walked the beach that night and she never would have met him. Or maybe they were fated to meet. Perhaps they would have met somewhere else. Dear God, it was all so confusing.

She looked across the parking lot and spotted Jack's car. He was standing just inside the open door, his head hanging forward, his black hair spilling across his forehead. He propped an elbow on the top of the rolled up window and hid his face in the crook of one thick arm.

Jack Brennen was crying.

Genny felt as if someone had just ripped out her heart.

Twenty-seven

Howard McCormick picked up the telephone receiver in his den on the second ring. He was late for a City Council meeting, but he was expecting this call and he wanted to be there when it came in.

"All right, Marty, let's have it."

"Everything's set, boss. I got the men lined up, just like you said. Reynolds is out of the picture. That knife wound in his arm got infected. He's pretty screwed up, but Collins is still in." The divers who had clashed with Brennen at the wreck site. "And I hired a guy named Peterson. He's real good with explosives."

"Good. As soon as the weather breaks, Brennen will be back on the salvage operation. This time, we'll let him do the work. When he brings up those cases, we'll simply go in and take them. When we leave, we'll dispose of our good friend Jack, and that will be the end of it."

Marty chuckled into the receiver. "An old-fashioned boating accident — Brennen will never know what hit him."

"Exactly." Howard glanced at the clock ticking softly above his mantel. "Oh, and

Marty, one more thing."

"Yeah, boss?"

"When you make that final trip. I want to go with you."

Marty paused only briefly. "You got it, boss."

Howard felt a surge of anticipation. Jack Brennen had humiliated him, made him look like a fool. He'd been a thorn in his side for the past three years. Worst of all, he had stolen what should have belonged to him. He smiled grimly. Getting rid of Brennen would be an even better high than making another tax-free million dollars.

Howard hung up the phone and stared at the rain beating hard against the window. The damnable stuff had been coming down all week. He wished to God it would end. He wanted this business over and done with.

And he was eager to taste the triumph he would feel in putting an end to Jack Brennen.

The nightmares were gone, but Genny still couldn't sleep. She couldn't eat; she couldn't think. Her heart felt torn in two. She had gone back to work as soon as she'd returned to Santa Barbara, but her energy was depleted. It took all her will just to get out of bed in the morning and drive herself down to the library.

She'd told Millie what had happened, and her friend had been supportive. They'd grown closer in the last few weeks since Millie had been teaching her to play pool. Dottie called several times, but neither of them had been able to cheer her.

Instead the hours seemed endless. She felt dull and listless, and she worried for Jack. She wondered what he was doing.

Surely he was drinking again, carousing with other women, drowning his sorrows in the only way he knew how. Or perhaps his love for her had only been a whim, a momentary lapse from the bachelor existence Jack had always seemed to love. A life that by now had probably returned to normal.

Sitting curled up on the sofa, with Skeeter purring softly in her lap, Genny turned the page of the novel she had been reading. It was a depressing tale of three married sisters whose relationships had all gone sour.

She had already finished the pile of books she'd brought home from Jamaica. Afterward she had been better able to understand her dreams. She also saw how things from the past had spilled over into this life.

Her love of the sea, for example, the strange pull she had felt since she was a child. How many hours had she stood at the window watching the distant horizon? Waiting. Searching. Until this had happened, she hadn't understood what she was waiting for.

And there was the matter of children. She hadn't wanted a child, not until she met Jack. She had never confessed her secret fear that somehow she might hurt her own baby. Annee

Patterson had aborted her child. Perhaps the guilt still lingered. Annee Palmer had been terribly cruel to children. Perhaps somewhere in the woman's twisted mind, she resented them for being alive while her own child lay dead, another victim of Jason's betrayal.

It occurred to her that even her spelling might have been a remnant of the past. All her life, she had misspelled the oddest words: *moulding, parlour, theatre, armour* — even the simple word *grey.* Years later she realized these were the English spellings. But she had never even been to England.

And her nightmares — she understood them, too, now. She had learned, for instance, that the huge ugly spiders in her dreams actually lived on Jamaica. The symbols in her dreams were voodoo gods, called *loa.* The wiggly lines represented two twisted serpents, the sign for Damballah the snake. Odd dots and circles meant Papa Legba, guardian of the gate. Triangular shapes like sails were Agoue, god of the sea.

It was an odd religion, she learned, a combination of ancient West African animistic beliefs distorted by layer upon layer of Catholicism imposed on the early slave inhabitants of the island. When voodoo was outlawed in the late 1700s, slaves used Catholic saints as the names for their deities: Ogoun, god of war, became St. Jacques; while Erzulie, the goddess of love, the most important of the female *loa,* became the

Virgin Mary. The bizarre twist gave Genny an uneasy shiver.

The books she brought home also explained her grisly nightmares about the walking corpses. In voodoo, believers feared above all else that at death their souls would be stolen, leaving their bodies enslaved, to work for eternity as mindless *zombies.* To prevent it, the mouths of corpses were sealed, their noses plugged with cotton, and their jaws sewn shut.

A thirst for power drove the religion. The sorcerer set out to conquer the universe, to put things the way he believed they should be. That meant mastering evil as well as good, cruelty as well as mercy, pain as well as pleasure.

Perhaps Annee sought power to right the wrongs she had suffered, the loneliness she must have felt during her early years. She struggled for mastery, but there was fear there, too.

Genny had felt Annee's fear. And always her terrible grief.

She could sense the hopelessness in Annee, the bleakness in her soul that had finally destroyed her. By the time she arrived at Rose Hall, she suffered bouts of depression, sporadic fits of temper, and periods she couldn't recall. Her cruelty was legend. She murdered and terrorized the people she ruled, yet singlehandedly, a young woman in her twenties, Annee Palmer oversaw a vast plantation. She was as brilliant as she was ruthless, as beautiful as she was wicked. In the end, she was killed by the people she abused, and in that there seemed some small measure of justice.

As far as Genny was concerned, the search for her past was complete. She knew more than she ever wanted to know, and, as Dr. Bailey had predicted, the memories of that life continued to fade.

She lived in the present now. Reading more about those days would only make it that much harder. Nor could she risk the connection to Jack. In Annee's life, Jason had been her undoing. In this life, Jack was her weakness. She couldn't let it happen again.

Genny set the novel aside, unable to remember what had happened on the last three pages. The doorbell rang, saving her from a second attempt. Gently lifting Skeeter off her lap, she got up from the sofa and crossed to the entry. When she opened the door, Pete Williams stood on the porch.

"Hello, Genny."

"Pete! What on earth are you doing here?"

He seemed nervous, fidgeting from one long leg to the other. "I came to talk to you about Jack."

Her heart wrenched painfully. "Wh-what about him? He's all right, isn't he? His shoulder isn't worse? I was worried that he might have injured it in Jamaica. I was afraid —"

"It isn't his shoulder," Pete interrupted. "May I come in?"

"Of course." Feeling foolish for leaving him

standing in the cold, she motioned him into the entry.

"I was afraid I might not be welcome."

"Don't be silly. Of course you're welcome."

Pete sat down on the living room sofa while Genny went into the kitchen, to fix them each a mug of coffee. "I'm afraid it's only instant," she said.

"It's hot, isn't it? That's good enough for me." He took a sip from the steaming mug she handed him, then looked at her over the rim. "So how have you been?"

"Okay, I guess. What about you?"

A thick red eyebrow went up. "I'm fine. It's Jack I'm worried about."

"But you just said —"

"I said his shoulder was fine. It's you, Genny. You're what's wrong with Jack."

She swallowed past the lump in her throat. "Did he send you here?"

"Are you kidding? He promised me a punch in the nose if I did anything to bother you. I figured it was worth the risk."

Genny glanced away. The mug of coffee held in one hand was somehow forgotten on its way to her lips. "In a way I'm surprised he's still upset. I thought maybe . . . once we got home . . . he'd be glad things didn't work out. He's always valued his freedom."

"You know what they say . . . freedom's just another word for nothing left to lose." His thin smile faded altogether. "I was wrong, Genny. I

542

didn't realize how much Jack cared for you. He won't eat. He can't sleep. Charley's worried about him. Ollie says he holes up in his cabin like a hermit. I've never seen him this way."

"I never meant to hurt him."

"I thought you were in love with him. You said so that day on the boat."

"I love him," she said softly. "I'll always love him."

"Then forgive him, Genny. He won't let you down. Jack isn't like that. Not when he cares about someone. You can trust him with your life."

Genny sighed. "It isn't a matter of forgiveness, Pete. It has nothing to do with that."

"That's what Charley said. He says you think you knew Jack before . . . maybe in some other lifetime."

"I know it sounds crazy, but —"

"Even if you did, that was then and this is now. Give the two of you a chance, Genny. I don't think you'll regret it."

Genny smiled sadly. "You're a good friend, Pete. Jack is lucky to have you."

"I'd like to be your friend, too. That is, if you'll let me."

Her mouth curved up. "I'd like that."

"Will you think about what I've said?"

She nodded, but she wouldn't change her mind. Not when she considered what had happened the last time the two of them were together. "How's the salvage operation coming?"

she asked, steering away from a subject that was just too painful to discuss.

"We're ready to go back out, but the weather's been so unstable we can't risk it. Down that deep, the current's just too strong." Pete set his half-empty mug on a coaster on the clawfoot oak coffee table. "I guess I'd better be going." He stood up and offered her his hand. The freckles across the back matched those on his face. His hair looked even redder in the glow of the lamp than it had out on the boat. "I just wanted you to know about Jack."

Ignoring his hand, she leaned over and hugged him. "Thank you, Pete. It was kind of you to come." She walked him to the door and he stepped out into the wind.

"Take care of yourself, Genny."

"I will, Pete. Do me a favor?"

"Sure."

"Take care of Jack."

Pete smiled sadly and nodded. Shutting the door behind him, Genny leaned against it, closing her eyes against a moment of pain. When a tear seeped out from beneath her lashes, she brushed it aside with the back of her hand.

The phone rang just as she returned to the sofa. She picked it up and pressed the receiver against her ear.

"Genny?" Her mother's familiar voice washed over her, easing some of the ache in her heart. "We've been worried about you, honey. You haven't called in ages."

"I'm sorry, Mom. I've had a lot on my mind." That was the understatement of the year. "How's Daddy?"

"He's fine, honey. We were hoping you might come down for the weekend. We'd certainly love to see you."

"I-I don't think so, Mom. I've got some catch-up work at the library." And she wasn't ready to face them, knowing one look at her pale distraught features would tell them the strain she'd been under. "Thanksgiving's coming up. You know I'll be coming for that."

"You aren't having man trouble, are you? Your father thinks that's what it is. He thinks you're dating someone, that you're afraid we'll disapprove of whoever this man is. Is that it, dear?"

"Mother, I'd rather not —"

"If it is, you can put your mind to rest. We've gotten over that phase quite some time ago. If you like him, that's good enough for us."

Her chest went tight. She should have known they would welcome Jack into the family, if that was what she wanted. "It isn't man trouble. Not anymore. I was seeing someone, but it's over now."

"Oh, dear. Maybe your father and I ought to come up there. You don't sound quite yourself, dear."

"I'm fine, Mom, really. I'm a little tired tonight, but I'm not having those nightmares anymore."

"But I thought those were over some time ago."

Genny bit her lip. She had forgotten the small white lie she had told them, more an error of omission. She hadn't wanted them to worry. "I'm glad you called, Mom. Give Daddy a hug and tell him I'll see him Thanksgiving weekend."

She hung up the phone, thinking how lucky she was to have parents like her mother and father, instead of the distant, remote kind of family Jack had been born into. She thought of him and pain washed through her. She thought of Pete's worry and resolved not to let his arguments dissuade her.

They didn't. It wasn't until the following night when Charley arrived at her door that the first spark of hope began to flicker in her burned-out, deadened heart.

He came about nine and brought someone with him. "It's good to see you, Genny girl."

"It's good to see you, Charley. You, too, Dr. Bailey." Stepping into the foyer, Charley leaned over and hugged her. His weathered face was comfortingly familiar. Inhaling the smell of rain and sea on his Navy issue pea jacket, she found herself clinging to his reassuring warmth. It wasn't raining anymore, but even in the fire-warmed living room, the November chill seeped in. "Why don't you both come into the living room?"

She was happy they had come, yet she was

afraid she knew why, and she wasn't up to another assault on her defenses. As they made their way toward the peach chintz sofa, Charley's eyes ran over her, noting the weight she had lost, the hollows beneath the ridges in her cheeks.

"Look at you — why you're nothin' but skin and bones." When she glanced down, he caught her chin and lifted it, forcing her to look at him. "Now you listen here, Genny girl. I know what's goin' on in that female brain o' yours and the whole damned thing is gonna stop right here and now."

An ache rose in her throat. "I wish it were that simple, Charley."

"Tell her, Doc. Talk some sense into this girl. My boy's over there heartsick for his woman. She's over here, pinin' away for her man. That ain't the way it's supposed to be."

Taking a seat beside her on the sofa, Dr. Bailey shifted toward her and looked down his slightly Roman nose. "He's right, Genny. If I'd known where this would lead, I wouldn't have regressed you in the first place."

"I'm glad you did. My nightmares have ended, just as you said. Even my awful memories are beginning to fade."

"Good. That's the point of past life regression. So the person can put it behind, and get on with life in the present."

"I wish I could do that." She turned away unable to meet his gaze. "The truth is, I don't know if I'll ever be able to forget it, at least not completely. In the past, I did unspeakable things, hurt a lot of innocent people. Now, I've met the same man I loved then. What happened between us was the cause of what occurred. God only knows what could happen this time."

Charley made a sound of disgust. "I know what you're thinkin'. You're afraid you'll turn into the same kind of woman Annee Palmer was. Well, I don't believe it. Not for one damned minute. You're too darned sweet, Genny girl. Too damned good. If you still owed some kind of debt, you wouldn't be the way you are now."

"I-I don't understand what you mean."

"Charley's talking about Karmic Debt," the doctor said.

"What on earth is that?"

"Put simply, it means that if, in the past, you committed the heinous crimes you believe, you would have to do penance for them in another existence. The Hindus believe people come back in the lowest possible form for the sins they've committed in a previous lifetime. If that is so, the person you are in this life would reflect the person you were back then. Perhaps you would be bitter and resentful, violent or abusive. By their beliefs, you would hardly be pretty. More likely you would be maimed or deformed. You are none of those things, Genny."

"What are you saying?"

"I'm telling you that you have solved the puzzle of the life you lived as Annee Palmer, but between that life and this one, you must have lived other lives as well, lives in which you rectified your mistakes. That is the only explanation for the generous, decent person you are in this life."

"I-I don't know. I've never studied Eastern religions, except for a course or two in college. What you're saying seems so unbelievable." She shifted her gaze, staring thoughtfully into the flames of the fire that still burned in the hearth. "And there are other considerations."

"Such as?" A log snapped in the grate, sending up a shower of sparks.

Genny watched them disappear, then returned her eyes to his face. "What about heaven and hell, Dr. Bailey? Don't you believe in those things?"

"Yes, I do," he said softly. He reached over and took her hand. "But I also believe in the benevolence of God, and in His wisdom to understand human frailties. There may well be a heaven and hell — but who is to say Purgatory's not right here on earth?"

Genny fell silent. She had never thought of it that way. And who was she to argue? For all she knew, none of this was real. And yet she believed that it was. "What about Jack? If what you're saying is the truth, why have we been brought back together?"

"I don't know. Sometimes acquaintances

from one life return together again and again, until the lesson they are meant to learn is finally understood. Or some past wrong is righted. I can't tell you what the reason is. You'll have to discover that yourself."

"I can't afford to take the risk."

"Are you certain you can afford not to?"

Genny pondered that, more than a little uneasy. "Do you really believe my debt might already be repaid? I can't imagine there is anything I could have done to make amends."

"Perhaps it wasn't done all at once. Perhaps it took several different lifetimes."

She looked at him, wanting to believe his words, searching for hope where there had been none before. "You could help me find out."

He eyed her thoughtfully. "You're talking about another regression."

"If there's a chance I can uncover something that might make things different, that's exactly what I'm talking about."

"That isn't why I came here. I came to help you put things in perspective."

"Please, Doctor. If I could find even one life where I somehow made things right, perhaps I could learn to forgive myself."

"It might be dangerous — we had problems before. I don't really think your other lives had such a negative influence, but we can't be sure."

"I'm willing to take the risk."

He studied her intensely, trying to reach a decision. "All right, Genny. If you've the courage, we'll see where it leads. I'm free Wednesday night, if that would be convenient."

"Well, of course, but —"

"What about doin' it now?" Charley said. "Every day she waits, only makes things harder."

"Yes!" Genny said excitedly, coming to her feet. "Why can't we do it here? Right now? Tonight?"

He looked at her long and hard, his dark eyes piercing. Then he sighed. "All right, we'll try it tonight."

"Thank you." The hope she was feeling expanded, settled around her heart. "Thank you so much, Dr. Bailey."

"It should be easier for you to go back this time, since you've done it twice before, and you seem to be a very good subject. Hopefully it will also be less painful, since whatever you may recall has heretofore left you untroubled."

"If there were other lives in between, why has my life in the present been so influenced by my life as Annee?"

"Probably because it was such a painful incarnation. Even if your karma is clear, the residue of that lifetime could have remained."

"I see."

"If you've no more questions, I think we ought to get started. We don't know where to begin, so this may take some time."

She nodded, nervous but hopeful of what she might find out. They got up from their chairs and bustled around the room arranging things, adding several logs to the low-burning fire. Settling herself more comfortably on the sofa, Genny anxiously rubbed her damp palms on her dark green plaid wool trousers.

"Are you ready?" The doctor sat down across from her, pulled the comfortable peach chintz overstuffed chair a little closer.

"I'm ready. And I pray with all of my heart that you are right." Staring straight ahead, he used the flames of the fire to focus Genny's attention. When her eyes slid closed and her breathing went deeper, the doctor began to take her backwards, back through time to the years before she was born.

"All right, Genny. You're relaxed and comfortable. Your mind is clear and you are ready to begin your search. In front of you, you see a number of screens from which you may choose. You know what we're looking for. I want you to pick a screen and tell me where you are."

She struggled for a moment, groping through the shadows of time, trying to force her mind to see. Then a picture appeared, fuzzy at first, but soon growing stronger. She clutched at it, dragged it to the forefront of her mind. It was a young girl in her teens, crippled at birth. She lived somewhere in England in the late 1800's, but the memory was weak and the details were sketchy. With Doctor Bailey's help, they discovered that the girl was an orphan, that for a while she had lived in the streets, that she had gone hungry much of the time. From the age of ten, she had worked in a textile factory sixteen hours a day, under the most abominable conditions.

One day the factory caught on fire. The fabric went up in a blazing inferno. The girl was caught in the flames and grotesquely burned. She died three days later, consumed by the agonizing pain that she suffered. Her death and those of the others who were killed resulted in better working conditions in the factory over the years to come.

Richard must have known that the memory of that lifetime wouldn't be enough to convince her, because he continued to search. "You're moving ahead now, Genny, to another screen. Can you see it? You know what we're looking for. Do you see it yet, Genny?"

"Yes . . . I can see it now."

"Tell me where you are."

"I-I'm out in the ocean. I seem to be on board some kind of ship."

"What year is it? Can you tell me?"

The trance drew her deeper, sucking her in until she had completely lost track of the present. "It's the end of October 1944. I'm aboard the Navy cruiser, *Atlantis*." Her voice sounded different now, the cadence of her speech becoming higher, more refined. Perhaps the East Coast, she thought. Then she remembered she had been born in Boston, in August of 1923.

"What is your name?"

"Regina. My name is Regina Lynn Wilcox. I'm an Army nurse assigned to the base on Midway Island. The ship is transporting about thirty female nurses."

"What do you look like?"

She grimaced a little. "I'm rather plain, I'm afraid, and quite a tall woman. Long-boned, people would say. I'm ridiculously thin, and I'm too high-waisted. My hair is straight, rather a mousy brown, and particularly hard to manage. I've always had very bad teeth."

"How would you describe your personality? Tell us what kind of person you are."

She sighed. "I've rather a nasty temper, I suppose, if one must be truthful. I'm a bit condescending, and not particularly well-liked. Perhaps that's because I keep a great deal to myself. I'm a very good nurse, though, and not one to shirk my duty. That much no one disputes."

"Let's go forward a bit," the doctor suggested. "You know what we're searching for, don't you, Regina? The time in your life we'd like you to tell us about?"

"Yes, but I would rather . . ."

"You would rather not see it. I'm sure it's painful for you. Still, I think you must. Tell us what is happening now."

Her muscles tightened. Her fingers were

clamping into the arm of the sofa. Her pulse speeded up, began to thud uncomfortably. "The call for All Hands just sounded. The sirens are blaring. Every time we've had this drill, I've hated that miserable sound."

"Is that what this is, Regina? Just another drill?"

"No." Her palms felt sweaty. She wiped them against her starched khaki uniform skirt. "Not this time. There are Japanese planes in the air — at least several squadrons. Good God — they're coming straight at us." She could see them now as she looked out the porthole in the sick bay. They were strafing the ship with heavy bursts of machine-gun fire, raining bullets into men and equipment.

Soon the hospital ward would be filled to overflowing with the wounded and dying. Moving with urgency and no little fear, Regina helped a medic roll in several empty beds, then she staggered backward as a huge explosion rocked the ship. "Good heavens."

"What is it?" the doctor asked. "What's happened?"

"Jap kamikaze. Rode his damnable plane right into the deck. One of the ammunition bays has exploded." She braced against a second massive blast. The blare of sirens continued to fill the air. She was shaking now, with adrenaline pumping through her veins. She worked hard to control it. "I think we may have to abandon ship."

"Come on, Regina!" one of the nurses called out. "We've got to get these patients out of here!" Outside the door, fire roared down the passage, flames licking up through the ladder from the decks below. The screams of dying men echoed from every corridor and doorway.

With the help of some of the nurses and a few of the men, they carried the sailors already in sick bay up several ladders and out into the open. She shivered at the sight of the blood-slick deck, at the burned and charred bodies of the men. Good Lord — she had never seen such carnage.

A sailor named Greg Perkins cried out to her for help. She remembered seeing him in the mess hall that morning. Shoving her fear away, she hurried to his side and helped him stagger to his feet. Shrapnel had torn into his stomach, leaving a gaping hole slick with blood. She ripped the shirt off a dead man lying a few feet away and tied the sleeves around Greg's torso to hold his insides in place.

"Let's go." Draping his arm over her shoulder, she helped him cross the deck, each of his slow, shaky steps bringing him an agony of pain. Almost half the lifeboats had been destroyed in the blast, she saw, or burned up in the fire consuming the ship. Regina found an empty space in one and helped the wounded sailor aboard.

For the next thirty minutes, she loaded injured men into the last remaining lifeboats. The burning decks were still littered with suffering men. As the ship listed onto its side, she helped them adjust their life jackets and jump into the water, working to avoid the slicks of burning oil.

"She's going down," one of the officers told her, hurrying up beside her on the deck. "You'd better get overboard, Lieutenant Wilcox."

She nodded vaguely, numb with the agonized shrieks of the dying men, wishing there was more she could do to help them. A wounded sailor came up from below and staggered piti-fully toward her. She linked her arms around his waist and together they jumped into the water. She bobbed to the surface, but lost her hold on the sailor. For a moment, she thought she had lost him.

Then his head popped up. He sputtered and groaned.

"Hang on, sailor." She helped him up on a floating piece of wood then climbed halfway up herself, hoping to conserve her strength. She wondered how long the hundreds of injured men could survive, fighting the white-capped seas.

"Did you watch the ship go down?" the doctor asked Genny, intruding on her thoughts.

"Yes."

"What happened to Regina?"

For a moment she didn't answer. The images were there, but they were too awful to speak. "One . . . One of the men floated past where she was clinging to the flotsam. His head kept going under. Regina turned him onto his back and hauled him up on the makeshift raft, giving her place to him. Hours passed but no one came to help them. The men who hadn't already drowned were beginning to go under, so she found them something to cling to, hoping they could stay afloat till someone finally came."

"And Regina?" he pressed.

She swallowed the bile in her throat. "Sh-sharks. They were drawn to the wounded, attracted to the blood in the water. Regina and dozens of others, they —" Pain slammed into her midsection, ripping her apart, just as the shark had done. "God have mercy —"

A note of urgency infused the doctor's voice. "The screen is going dark now, Genny. Do you hear me? The past is fading and you are returning to the present. Do you hear me, Genny? You're name is Genny Austin. You're back in the present. Back in Santa Barbara."

She swallowed hard, felt the pain receding. "I hear you. I-I'm back in Santa Barbara. My name is Genny Austin." She heard his sigh of relief.

"When I count to three, you will awaken. You'll feel relaxed and comfortable and totally unafraid. This time you will remember the story you've just told, but feel none of the emotions you suffered when it occurred. Do you understand?"

"Yes."

"One. Two. Three."

Genny opened her eyes to find the fire had once more burned low. She felt exhausted, barely able to hold up her head. Charley sat hunched forward in his chair, his face a little pale. Dr. Bailey's salt-and-pepper hair looked rumpled, as if he had driven his fingers through it.

"How are you feeling?" he asked.

"I'm all right . . . now that it's over."

"For a moment I was concerned. Do you remember what you told us?"

She nodded.

"Do you understand now, what I've been trying to explain?"

Genny slumped against the sofa, rested her head against the back, and smoothed the wrinkles from the legs of her trousers. She thought about the memory she'd had of Regina Wilcox. "Perhaps I do."

Charley bent forward and gently touched her shoulder. "You see, Genny girl, every lifetime has its problems, as well as its solutions. You can't run away from them. We don't know how many lives you've led, how many people you may have helped in some way, how many times your debt might have been repaid. But it appears to me, you've got nothing to fear in this life, at least no more than anyone else. I want you to remember that when you think about you and Jack."

She reached over and clasped his hand. "Do you really believe in all this, Charley?"

"I can't say for certain. None of us can. But

it makes an odd sort of sense. I came to that conclusion when my Sassy died. I haven't changed my mind in the years since then."

"I'll give it some thought, Charley, I promise. But please don't tell Jack about tonight. I need time to think things over." She wasn't ready to see Jack yet. She wasn't sure she ever would be. But for the first time in a long time, a tiny ray of hope brightened her heart.

She came to her feet and turned to the tall imposing doctor, who had also risen from his chair. "Thank you, Dr. Bailey. I won't forget what you've done."

"Think about what Charley said. Think about what happened to Regina, what may have happened in other of your lives as well, and think about the woman you are today. Karmic Debt is a powerful force. I believe, as Charley does, that yours has been repaid."

Genny nodded, feeling a tight knot in her chest. Her mind was whirling with questions, with fears and uncertainties, and once more with hopes and dreams. Was it possible she had redeemed herself from the terrible things she had done? She wanted to believe that.

She wasn't sure she could, but she desperately wanted it to be the truth.

Twenty-eight

Standing on the diving platform, dripping water like a big black seal, Jack pulled his face mask off and tossed it to Ollie. "The load looks good. It's well secured and on its way up."

"Any sign of McCormick's aluminum cases?" Ollie asked.

"I took a quick look around, but didn't see them. Pete tried to explain where he'd hidden them, but either somebody's already found them or he did a damned good job of stashing them away. As short as our air time is down there, I figured we'd be better off waiting for him to go after them. He'll be diving with us the day after tomorrow. Another couple of days won't make any difference."

Charley grinned. "Good old Howard might not agree. He seemed damned anxious to get his hands on those cases."

"Yeah, well too bad for him."

"Unless he's already got 'em," Ollie said.

Jack just shrugged. He was all business these days, which he usually was on board, but lately his rigid demeanor didn't lessen once he got back to shore. Charley wished he could mention his evening with Genny, give Jack some hope that things might work out between them. But he had given Genny his word and he still wasn't sure what her plans were.

In a way, he couldn't blame her. She'd been through a lot in the past two years. She'd uncovered things people weren't meant to know, been taunted with the past and driven damned near crazy.

He didn't know why it had happened. He believed Genny and Jack were fated to meet, but he wasn't so sure about her dreams. Something seemed to have gone awry there, bent things way out of kilter. Maybe he and Richard had helped set things right. Charley certainly hoped so.

"What time we headin' back to port?" Ollie asked Jack, peeling him out of his wet suit with special concern for his friend's still-tender shoulder.

"Soon as Marvin and Kelsey bring up that next load of copper." They were the divers they had hired to help with the salvage operation, now that they could afford it. Jack's shoulder was healing well, and he was diving some, too, but there was no sense in pushing it.

Ollie picked up Jack's tank and the three of them crossed the diving platform toward the ladder leading up to the stern. "You got plans for tonight?" Ollie asked. "Bebe's cookin' homemade barbecue. How 'bout you guys comin' over to eat?"

"Come on, son," Charley urged Jack. "You know Bebe makes the best damned barbecue in seven counties. Do you good to get out some, forget your troubles for a while."

"No thanks, Charley. I've got a good book going — the new John Grisham. Think I'll stay home and read."

Charley scoffed. " 'Think I'll stay home and read.' Can you believe that, Owl?"

Ollie looked at Jack and knew he was thinking of Genny. "Yeah, man, I can believe it. Don't worry, Jack. I'll send some barbecue home with Charley. You can have it for a midnight snack."

"Thanks," Jack said distractedly. With a brief glance at the water, he turned and started striding toward the aft steering station where Raymond worked the winch, hoisting the heavy reels of copper up on the barge.

If Genny never came back, Charley wondered, how long would it take Jack to get over her? Then his mind flashed on his pretty wife, Sassy, on how much he still missed her, and he wondered if he ever really would.

It was a crazy idea. Still, the library was Millie's forte. After all, she was a reference librarian. If anyone could locate the facts, she could.

She wouldn't tell Genny, not unless there was something to tell. But she was getting pretty good on the modem and it wouldn't take much to lock onto the Naval Historical Records in Annapolis, records of ships that had been sunk in World War II. Was there really an *Atlantis*? Had it actually gone down under Japanese fire somewhere in the waters off Midway Island?

So far everything else Genny had remembered appeared to be true. Millie had listened to the story, told haltingly at first, since Genny worried what her friend would say. Even if all of it were true — and there was no way to be one hundred percent sure — how could Millie possibly condemn her? It had happened more than a century in the past, and besides, if there were such a thing as reincarnation, who knew the kind of lives *she* might have led?

Settling back into her chair, Millie watched the screen and waited for the proper files to come up. It took a series of tricky machinations, but she finally found the data bank she wanted.

"WW II," she muttered aloud, skimming the contents for old Navy records, then hunting through year after year of files until she came to 1944. She slowed her efforts there, searching with painstaking care through the weeks and months, through the arrivals and departures of hundreds of American ships.

The library got busy, so she had to quit for a while, but eventually things settled down and she returned to her perusal. During her break, she went out for a Snickers, polished it off, and returned to her desk with a big icy Coke. It was a wonder she didn't gain weight.

She broke off at five o'clock, still finding no

mention of a ship named *Atlantis*, and hurried home to get ready for her date with Jeff Mathison. Things were going great between them. She was crazy about Jeff and he seemed equally enthralled with her.

She was busy the following morning, and sleepy from her late night out. She hadn't gone to bed with Jeff yet, but they were getting pretty close. Just thinking about making love to him made her pulse go crazy. She forced her mind back to her work.

In the afternoon, she found a couple of hours to dedicate to her search. She didn't see Genny until she walked up right in front of her desk.

"You're certainly hard at it today."

"I guess so," she replied evasively. It must have been her slightly guilty expression that made Genny round the desk to see what it was she was working on.

"My God — you're searching old Navy files! You're looking for the *Atlantis*!"

"I-I wasn't going to tell you. Not unless I found something interesting."

Genny eyed her with a mixture of chagrin and unmistakable interest. "Have you?"

"Not yet."

Releasing a slow breath of air, Genny leaned toward the computer screen. "Actually, I thought about doing this myself. But I wasn't exactly sure where to start and I . . . wasn't exactly sure I wanted to know."

"Maybe I won't find anything."

Genny straightened, smoothed a wrinkle from the front of her plum wool suit. "Let me know if you do. I might as well find out if there's any truth to what I supposedly remember."

Millie just nodded. She wished Genny hadn't found out what she was doing, but maybe it was for the best. She rubbed a kink in her shoulder, sat up straighter in her chair, and started forwarding pages. At 3:15 P.M., Millie's fingers stilled on the keyboard.

The *Atlantis* appeared, a newly commissioned Navy cruiser on its maiden voyage. The ship left San Francisco harbor on October 15, 1944. Destination: Midway Island.

Millie's palms began to sweat. God, it was uncanny. Pulling up another file, she started scanning the list of those onboard. It showed four hundred and ninety-six crewmen.

"And thirty Army nurses," Genny read, staring at the screen from over Millie's shoulder, her voice sounding reedy and strained. "There really was a ship, just like I said."

Millie nodded. "It's real, all right."

"Is . . . is Regina listed among the nurses?"

"I don't know yet." Millie forwarded to the next page. "I read somewhere that the Army didn't assign female nurses to duty in a battle zone until sometime into the war."

"I think that's right. But they should have started before 1944."

Millie skimmed down the column of nurses.

The entry for Regina Wilcox jumped out at her and her heart ricocheted inside her chest. "Holy moly!"

Genny wet her lips. "Holy moly is right. God, I can hardly believe it!"

"Believe it." So far Genny's memory appeared correct. But had the *Atlantis* actually gone down? The following page confirmed it. A direct hit by a kamikaze pilot had exploded an ammunition bay. Two hundred and twenty-three men were lost. A list of casualties as well as survivors was included. There was a notation of those who had received Purple Hearts, and those who had been awarded medals for valor.

Regina Wilcox posthumously received a Distinguished Service Cross, for bravery above and beyond the call of duty.

Both of them stared at the entry in silence.

"It doesn't say how she died," Millie said softly, "but she must have done something very brave."

Genny's face looked pale. "Yes."

"Are you okay?"

She nodded. Millie reached over and dragged up a chair. "Sit down. If you don't, you might just fall down."

"I wonder if Dr. Bailey could be right — perhaps Annee Palmer's debt really has been repaid. If that's true, then maybe Jack isn't here as some kind of retribution." She frowned. "But if he isn't, why have we been brought together after all these years?"

Millie sighed. "I wouldn't have the slightest idea. This is all too heavy for me." She glanced back at the computer screen. "What was the name of that ship you said Jason Sommers was on?"

"The *Voyager*. Why?"

"No reason. I just figured since we're into the maritime files, we might as well go back to the days of the *Voyager*. See if we can find out anything about your handsome lieutenant."

"Do you really think we could?"

"I don't know. Maybe." She started digging backward through time, changing from one file to another, opening one, closing one, opening something else. In the end, she had to redial the modem and start all over with a different source of information.

Genny left several times to answer the phone or handle some problem but returned to the chair next to the computer just as the entry they'd been searching for popped up.

"There! There it is!" The *Voyager* appeared in a batch of old British Naval records from the early 1800s. Millie followed the records forward, then went to a file that dealt with information specific to the *Voyager*.

"There's his name!" Genny cried, coming to her feet. She'd been sitting on the edge of her chair, on tenterhooks since they'd spotted the sailing ship's records.

"Lieutenant Jason Sommers," Millie read, "His Majesty's Navy. According to the record, his ship was never scheduled to stop in Jamaica."

"There was a problem with the rudder. The *Voyager* was forced into port for repairs."

Millie scrolled through the pages. "Look at this."

Genny read the entry. "It says the *Voyager* encountered a storm off the Azores. It says the ship went down. My God, Millie. The *Voyager* was lost with all hands." She sank back down in her chair, her fingers curling over the arm rests. "The *Voyager* never reached England. Jason never arrived back home." Tears began to slide down her cheeks. "He never returned to Jamaica because he couldn't. Jason died when the ship went down."

Millie reached over and gripped her hand. It was trembling so hard, she had to hold on tightly. "He loved you," she whispered, her throat closing up, her own eyes filling with tears. "Jason loved you, just like he said."

"He didn't betray me."

"No, he didn't."

Genny hugged herself, rocking forward in her chair, her arms wrapped tightly around her. "Jack loves me, Millie. He loved me then and he loves me now. Just like I love him."

Millie wiped tears from her cheeks. "He's come back for you, Genny. He's come back after all these years. It's crazy . . . and it's so romantic."

But all Genny could think of was Jack. How wrong she had been. How she had hurt him.

How desperately she wanted to see him. To touch him. To tell him how much she loved him. Inside her chest, her heart beat with a painful throbbing, ached as if it needed to be freed. Only Jack could do that. Only Jack.

"How come Annee never knew what happened?" Millie asked, breaking into her thoughts.

"I-I don't know. No one in Jamaica was directly involved with the ship — it wasn't even supposed to be there. News from England was rare and it took months to get there. By the time word arrived, Annee had probably lost the baby. She was sick for a long time afterward." And buried in her grief. "I guess she just never found out."

Millie smiled softly. "I think you should marry him."

Genny swallowed past the lump in her throat. "Yes." She gave Millie a lightning-bright smile. "That's *exactly* what I should do." Leaping up from her chair, she leaned over and hugged her. "Thanks, Millie. You're the best."

Rounding the desk, Genny called back over her shoulder. "Cover for me, will you? Charley called earlier. Jack's due in with his last load of copper today. It's getting dark early so he'll probably be back some time soon. I want to be there when he gets in."

"It might be hours yet," Millie said, causing her to pause. "You're just going down there and wait?"

"I want to surprise him. Besides, I've waited all my life for Jack. A couple hours more won't bother me a bit."

Millie smiled. "Give him a big hug for me, will you?"

"I don't know," Genny teased, walking once more toward her office. "Jeff Mathison might not like it." Millie laughed as Genny went inside, grabbed her purse, and headed for the door.

As she walked to the car, her thoughts returned to Jason and how he had died so young. Was that the reason Jack always tried to cram so much into his life? Why he lived every moment to the fullest? She would never really know, but it made a kind of sense. And it really didn't matter. She intended to enrich the life they would share, give everything she could and more. She meant to make him happy — wildly, insanely glad that he had come back to her after all these years.

Howard McCormick pulled into the harbor parking lot at four o'clock in the afternoon. Marty James would be waiting on the boat. He had called an hour ago to tell him Jack was bringing up the last few loads. The cases were bound to be among them. Marty knew because the men he had hired had been watching the *Marauder* from aboard a small commercial fishing boat that prowled the waters near the wreck site. They reported the *Marauder*'s progress but with all the activity in the channel, so far the boat hadn't drawn particular interest.

The boat would be waiting at a rendezvous point several miles away. Collins and Peterson would come aboard the *Sea Siren* and then they would go after the cases.

Eager for the coming confrontation, Howard got out of his spotless white Lincoln and locked the door. He started across the parking lot, took two paces and stopped. In a space several cars away sat Genny's brown Toyota. He read the license plate to be sure, but he knew it was hers by the little stuffed mouse that dangled from the mirror.

Howard glanced around but didn't see her. Still, he knew the reason she was there — the only possible reason — and anger formed a hard knot in his chest.

Damn her. Damn her lying, treacherous little soul. He had spoken to her only that morning. She hadn't mentioned Brennen and neither had he. He had thought she was through with him, that their brief affair was ended. Damn her deceiving heart to hell!

With his thick hands balled into fists, Howard walked past the Ship's Chandlery and the Sailor's Emporium toward his forty foot Bertram tied up at Dock J, just one dock over from where the *Marauder* tied up, which after today, wouldn't be happening again. The thought gave him a surge of satisfaction.

When he reached Dock H, he turned, determined to discover if Genny was waiting for Jack. Inserting his card in the lock, he pushed open the tall metal gate and walked down the ramp of the floating dock. Genny wasn't standing in front of the *Marauder*'s slip as he had expected. Then he saw her at the far end of the dock, staring off toward the mouth of the harbor.

The bitch was waiting for Brennen, just like he'd thought.

Fury swept over him, making it hard to breathe. He kept on walking, forcing himself under control, forcing his temper to calm. Genny whirled at his approach.

"Howard! Wh-what are you doing here?" A guilty flush crept into her cheeks, but it couldn't dim the excitement on her face as she stood there waiting for her lover.

"Hello, Genny. I might ask the same question of you, but it's obvious what you are doing. You're waiting for Jack. I thought you said you were through with him."

She looked at him with a measure of pity. It only made him madder. "I'm sorry, Howard, I really am. I hope I haven't hurt you. I never intended that."

Howard said nothing. He was afraid he couldn't control his voice.

"The truth is Jack and I are in love. For a while, things got mixed up, but everything's straightened out now. I love Jack. I'm going to marry him."

Heat surged into the back of his neck. "Marry him? You're going to marry Jack Brennen?"

"He's a good man, Howard. I love him and I know he loves me."

He stared at her for long, blood-pumping moments, working to control his blinding rage. She had chosen Brennen over him. Not once, but again and again. She had played him for a fool, made him look like an idiot. He clamped down hard on his temper, on the desire to slap that look of pity off her face.

"If that is the way you feel, then you had better come with me." He gripped her arm a little too hard, eased his hold, and started leading her back along the dock.

"Wait a minute, Howard. Where are we going?"

"I'm taking you to Brennen. That's what you want, isn't it?"

"Yes, but . . . I don't understand, Howard. He's probably on his way in. Why can't we just wait for him here?"

"He isn't on his way in. He's had problems with his engine. He's still at the wreck site." He hauled her through the gate.

"But —"

"I'll explain everything, once we get underway." She started to argue, to ask him more questions, but she believed he was her friend. She trusted him. More fool she.

She walked beside him down the gangway to

Dock J, where his cabin cruiser bobbed at the end of its line. "Give the lady a hand, Marty," he called out to the man who stood on deck.

"You got it, boss." He was auburn-haired, wiry, a man in his mid-thirties. Marty had worked for him off and on for years. He was a jack of all trades, a master of getting things done — no matter how sticky they happened to be.

He helped Genny climb on deck, then Howard came aboard. Taking her hand, he led her into the main salon while Marty climbed up on the flying bridge to get the boat underway. A few minutes later, the engines fired up, and the boat eased away from the dock. The movement alerted her. She began to rummage through her purse.

"I-I have to put on my patch. I brought it with me in case Jack had to go back out. I'll get seasick if I don't wear it."

"Then by all means, put it on. There's a mirror over the sink in the head. It's just down those stairs."

"I hope it works," she muttered, more to herself than to him. "You're supposed to put it on sooner."

Howard said nothing. Since this was her last voyage as well as Jack's, it wouldn't make a damned bit of difference. He wondered if anyone had seen them together. If they had, he would have to think of something to tell the authorities about why he had taken her out to the

Marauder. She was in love with Jack. It shouldn't be difficult for people to believe she had simply wanted to be with him.

Besides, the explosion would simply be an accident, nothing that might arouse suspicion.

Genny went down to the head in the master cabin, then returned to stand in front of him. "All right, Howard, now tell me what's going on. Tell me why we're here, how you know about the problem with Jack's engine, and why we're going out to see him."

He smiled at her grimly. "You want to know what's going on? I'll tell you. I'm going after those computer parts that went down on the *Opus II.* That, my dear, is what's going on."

"What!"

"That's right. For days now, my men have been watching Brennen's salvage operation. This afternoon, he brought up those aluminum cases. I want them and I'm going to get them."

"For heaven's sake, Howard, Jack will sell them to you. I already told you that."

His expression turned harder. "I'm afraid it's too late for that. Brennen's had his chance. Now it's my turn."

She looked incredulous, her light eyebrows arching upward in dismay. "I can't believe this, Howard. Have you gone completely insane? You can't just steal those cases. Good Lord, Jack could have you thrown in jail."

"Let me worry about Jack. In the meantime, I'd suggest you make yourself comfortable."

Genny didn't move. "You said Jack's had engine trouble. Did your men have something to do with that, too?"

His eyes skewered her. "A clogged intake. It causes the engine to overheat. It'll take him a while to figure it out. By then we'll have arrived for our little 'discussion.' "

"I can't believe this. What on earth's gotten into you, Howard?"

"Nothing having those cases won't cure."

"I won't condone your stealing them. I'm your business partner. I have at least some say in the matter and I won't let you do it."

Howard just smiled. "Yes, well, we'll talk about all of that later." In a way, it was going to work out for the best. As executor of Bill Austin's estate, he'd been managing Genny's shares of McCormick-Austin stock for the past two years. In August, she would take control herself.

He had planned to be married to her by then. Now, well . . . he was also executor of Genny's estate. With her out of the way, he would control her shares again. They would have to be sold, of course, the proceeds going to her heirs. But he would make sure that he was the only interested buyer — at a price that was more than fair.

In fact the amount would be ludicrously cheap, if the true worth of the company were known.

And lately another problem had crept up.

The matter of Genny's hypnosis. She had mentioned it only briefly, but it was enough to alert him. He'd discovered her sessions with Richard Bailey and he didn't like it. Not one little bit.

Who knew what she might remember?

Yes, as much as all of this pained him, in a way it would work out for the best. He glanced once more at Genny, seeing her troubled expression.

"As I said, we'll talk about all of this later. In the meantime, there are things I must see to before we reach our destination. If you'll excuse me . . ."

Genny watched him go with a feeling of dread in her bones. What in the world was Howard thinking? He couldn't just steal those computer parts from Jack. She sat down on the gray wool sofa in the luxurious salon, elegantly appointed in mauve and gray. Smoked glass mirrors lined the walls and a sculpted acrylic coffee table sat in front of the couch. A built-in bar sat open on one wall, displaying crystal decanters and cut glass snifters, in carefully crafted holders to insure against breakage.

She sighed as she leaned back on the sofa. Surely Howard would come to his senses. If not, somehow she would have to convince Jack not to press charges. No matter how ridiculous this feud was between them, Howard was her partner and he had always been her friend. Besides, everyone made mistakes. That was a lesson she now knew only too well. Things would work out, she resolved. She would make sure of it. And once it did, she would be with Jack.

That thought buoyed her spirits. Genny watched the frothy sea spraying up against the windows, glad she had run into Howard at the dock, glad he had brought her along. As long as she was there, she could keep things from getting out of hand.

At least that's what she told herself as she worriedly chewed her lip.

Twenty-nine

Jack bent over the engine, a monkey wrench in his hand, his shirt stripped off, his chest bare, a smudge of black grease along his jaw. "It has to be the intake," he said to Charley. "We've tried about everything else."

"We tried that, too. Pete said he didn't see anything."

"I know, but maybe it's been sucked farther in."

Charley peered over his shoulder. "Might be worth another look."

"I'll go down this time. Maybe I can find it." He turned away from the powerful twin diesels and headed up the ladder from the engine room, with Charley right behind him. He made it as far as the deck when the hum of an approaching boat drew his attention.

"Looks like we may have visitors," Charley said.

"I wonder who it is."

Charley went up to the wheelhouse and returned with a pair of binoculars. He scanned the horizon till he picked up the big white cabin cruiser through the lenses. "Good lookin' Bertram. 'Bout a forty footer. Got those fancy blue canopies and all."

"Canopies? Here, let me see that." Jack took the binoculars from Charley's hand, brought them to his tired eyes, and focused. "McCormick's got a Bertram. Got those blue canvas canopies, too. You don't suppose that bastard would come clear out here?"

"The man ain't shy," Ollie said, walking up to join them. "And you got his cases, don't you?" He and Pete, Jack, Charley and Ray were working alone this last day, enjoying the feeling of triumph, of completing the job they had set out together to do.

Charley chuckled. "I hope he's got his checkbook handy."

"Not a chance," Jack said. "For him, it's cash on the barrelhead." He turned to look at Pete, who stood a few feet away, staring over the railing.

"It probably is McCormick," Pete said. "He's gone after those cases before."

"Where did Ray put them? I want to see what's so damned important about them."

"They're sitting over there on the deck." Pete pointed in that direction. "They came up with that last batch of copper, but I had Ray haul them aboard instead of loading them onto the barge. I thought you might want a look inside on the way back to port."

"I would have opened them up already if we hadn't gotten sidetracked with that overheated engine." His gaze swung sharply to the boat, which was drawing closer. "You don't suppose

581

McCormick had anything to do with that?"

"I don't know," Pete said, "but I think I'll go down and take another look at that intake before he gets here." He was still wearing the bottom half of his dive suit. As Jack crossed the deck toward Howard's aluminum cases, Pete went over the side.

"You remember that fishin' boat that's been workin' nearby?" Charley asked. "They been fishin' these waters pretty hard the past couple days." They had spotted it on radar, of course, but there were dozens of boats in the area. It was gone now, though neither of them had noticed it leaving. "You think McCormick's smart enough to think of somethin' like that?"

"He's a low-life," Jack said, "but he's not dumb." He pulled one of the shiny aluminum cases out from the wall and knelt beside it. Each case was about four feet wide and three feet high, tightly sealed and secured by a heavy stainless steel padlock. Reading his intentions, Ollie left for a moment and returned with a heavy pair of bolt cutters. He centered the tool on the first lock, and with one powerful squeeze, bit through it.

Jack knelt again and tried to lift the lid. A watertight seal still held it firmly in place. Pulling a pocket knife from his faded blue jeans, he opened the blade and used it to break the seal. Beneath a layer of plastic, row upon row of computer chips lay in machine-pressed, Styrofoam sheets, each chip carefully protected. Jack dug down through the rows, checking the contents thoroughly, but there seemed nothing unusual about the chips.

"Looks like computer parts to me."

"Yeah, well, who can figure McCormick?" Ollie said. Just then Pete hopped up on the swim step, holding a long narrow piece of driftwood in one hand. "I found it shoved way up into the intake hose. Should have seen it the first time." He triumphantly waved the wood that had been used to block the water coming in to cool the engine. "I cut out the section where it was jammed and pieced the hose back to the through-hull." Whatever he said next was muffled by the roar of Howard McCormick's engines.

He finally turned them off and the boat bobbed in the water twenty feet away. "Ahoy, *Marauder*!" came the call through the bullhorn blaring across the distance between them.

"Ahoy, *Sea Siren*!" Jack called back. "What the hell do you want, McCormick?"

"You know what I want. And now I've got something that you want."

"What's he talking about?" Jack said to Charley, but the bullhorn remained silent as Howard made his way up on deck. He was shoving someone in front of him, a slender figure at least six inches shorter than Howard. It was a woman, Jack saw, noting the shapely legs showing beneath the knee-length plum-colored suit.

He knew those legs. "Genny," he whispered, his heart slamming into his ribs. What was Genny doing with McCormick? Then he saw that Howard had her arm wrenched up behind her back, that he gripped her across her chest, his forearm pressed tightly beneath her throat. He saw the flash of the gun Howard held, and his breath froze somewhere inside him.

"Christ, Charley, that's Genny. What the hell does McCormick think he's doing?"

The boat had drifted closer. Howard's voice carried clearly without the bullhorn. "I've brought you a present, Jack. All I want in return is what is mine already. If you want Genny to remain unharmed, I suggest you hand over those cases."

"Genny — are you all right?" Jack motioned for Pete and Ollie to go get the computer chips.

"I-I'm fine." There was fear in her voice. It made his own worry heighten. "I'm sorry, Jack. I was wrong. I didn't know Howard was —" McCormick cut off her next words by tightening his grip on her throat.

"Just give me what's mine, and I'll send Genny over."

Jack surveyed the boat, trying to determine the best course of action. Giving up the cases wasn't a problem. He wouldn't put Genny at risk for any amount of money. Besides, he'd made plenty already. Along with the valuable copper they'd already brought up, yesterday they'd found a load of silver ingots.

No, the cases weren't a problem. But Mc-Cormick was. Jack didn't like the smell of this. Not one bit.

"Ray's ready with the knuckle crane," Ollie said, hurrying toward him. "We can winch them over anytime you say."

Jack nodded. "Listen, McCormick, you can have the cases, okay? We're getting things rigged up right now to send them over. It'll only take a few more minutes. In the meantime, just take it easy. Don't do anything that might hurt Genny."

He studied the deck of the *Sea Siren* and the two men standing next to Howard. They were hard-edged men, the kind who didn't play games. He didn't know why Howard would want to harm Genny, but assessing the other two men, he didn't doubt for a moment the threat they posed was real.

As the men set to work, lowering McCor-mick's Boston whaler into the water to make the exchange, Jack turned and walked back toward the boxes sitting on deck.

"Open those other two cases."

Ollie set to work and in minutes they were open. Jack dug through them, seeing exactly what he had seen before — rows of neatly pack-aged computer chips. "I don't get it. No drugs, no smuggled Mexican antiquities — I figured it had to be something like that."

Ollie knelt beside him, his massive black body throwing the cases into shadow. He lifted out one of the chips and studied it closely. "Take a look at this, my friend." He handed Jack one of the chips. "You know what that says?"

"I.N.T.E.L.," Jack read. "It says, Intel. What about it?"

"It says Intel, all right, one of the most widely used, in demand computer chips in the world. They're expensive — and they sure as hell aren't made in Mexico."

"Forgeries?"

"You got it."

"He wants the boxes back so no one will find out what he's doing."

"To say nothing of the value of those chips. The difference in profit between a load of Intel chips and the cheaper ones made across the border ain't exactly small change."

Jack frowned. "Why do you suppose he's involving Genny in this?"

Ollie scratched his head through his wiry black hair. "I don't know. Unless maybe she found him out."

"Close the box." Ollie lowered the lid, and Jack strode back to the rail, thinking about the .45 caliber automatic he kept in the drawer of his night stand. But bringing another weapon into the already dangerous equation might just get Genny killed.

He looked across at her, and even from a distance, he could see her bloodless face and frightened eyes. He forced himself to ignore the anger surging through him.

"Everything's ready, McCormick! Send Genny over and you can have the cases."

"Sorry, Jack, I'm not that stupid. My men will be coming aboard. We're taking out the radio and your cellular phone. In the meantime, you can have your men load the cases. When I've got them safely aboard, then Genny can come over."

Jack swore foully. He didn't trust McCormick. There was no way the man could afford to just let them go. But before he could take any action, he had to get Genny onboard the *Marauder.*

"Bring Genny with you when you come," he said. "We'll make the exchange at the same time. Otherwise, I open those cases and dump them into the ocean."

Howard didn't hesitate, which only made Jack more suspicious. "All right, that's fair enough. We'll do it your way."

A few minutes later, McCormick's two henchmen climbed into the dinghy, and Howard helped Genny aboard. Her gaze found his, locked and didn't waver. Something clenched inside him. He was afraid for her, afraid of what McCormick meant to do. He'd give up his own life before he'd let anyone hurt her.

His hands gripped the rail as the small outboard engine came to life and the dinghy nosed into the waves. Genny seemed frozen to the seat, her face as pale as the tiny whitecaps the boat created. When the small craft pulled alongside, the guy at the tiller, a wiry, auburn-haired man in his thirties, stared hard in his direction. He held a gun to Genny's head.

"You can winch over the cases while my friend here takes out your communications." He gestured toward a black-haired man with a scar running down along his neck. "When we're finished, you can have the girl."

Jack nodded. Motioning toward the dog house, where Ray sat at the controls, he waited tensely for the chips to be loaded aboard the dinghy. The man with the scar returned, carrying the mike from Jack's radio and four feet of dangling wire, along with his nearly new cellular phone. He tossed all of the objects into the water, where they landed with a nerve-jarring splash and disappeared. Climbing into the boat, he lifted the lid on one of the cases, then nodded to the man at the tiller.

"All right," he said to Genny, "you can go."

The small boat rocked as she tried to climb out, her unsteady legs threatening to give way beneath her. Jack gripped one of her trembling hands, Ollie grabbed the other, and they lifted her easily aboard. As the dinghy's engine revved up and it started its return to Howard's boat, Jack pulled her into his arms.

He could feel her shaking against his bare chest, and his anger and worry heightened. "Genny . . ."

"I'm s-so sorry Jack. About everything."

His throat constricted. She pressed her face into his shoulder, and he rested his cheek against the top of her head. For a moment, he said nothing. Then, "Baby, are you all right?"

She nodded and looked up at him. "Jack, I can't believe it. Howard he — he —"

"He didn't hurt you did he?" He held her away to look at her, to study the tears that had dried on her cheeks. "If he did, I swear I'll —"

"He didn't hurt me." She clung to him again, this time even tighter. Jack glanced from Genny to the forty foot yacht now departing.

"I thought you said McCormick wasn't dumb." Charley stood beside them, staring out at Howard's boat, it's powerful wake cutting across the water.

"He's a lot of things, Charley, but dumb isn't one of them. That's why none of this makes sense." He felt Genny shudder, and tightened his hold protectively around her, but his eyes were fixed on Howard's boat. McCormick still stood at the rail, a shrinking figure as the boat moved away. Jack frowned, seeing something different about the scene, something he hadn't noticed before. "Where'd that diver come from?"

"What diver?" said Pete.

Jack's pulse began to race. "The one that wasn't there a few minutes earlier." His gaze swung to Charley. "McCormick can't afford for us to know his secret. He can't afford to let us live. Somehow he has to stop us."

Pete's ruddy face turned ashen. Jack knew exactly the reason why. "Explosives!" Pete said. "My God, he's planted a bomb beneath the hull!"

"Get everyone into the lifeboat!" Jack ran in that direction. "We've got to get off this boat as fast as we can."

Men raced about the deck, Pete, Ollie, Charley, and Ray all working seamlessly together in a desperate race for survival. Jack loaded Genny aboard the lifeboat, instructed her to put on her vest, cupped her face between his palms and kissed her quick and hard. "Get her out of here," he said gruffly.

"What about you?" Genny frantically gripped his arm, but he eased her hand away.

"I'll join you in a minute. There's something I have to do."

They lowered the boat, Genny pleading for Jack to come with them, Charley grumbling about his being a fool, Ray silent, as always. Ollie just looked worried, while Pete's gaze followed Jack, trying to figure out what he meant to do. They powered the dinghy a safe distance from the boat, in case the explosion they all feared occurred, but close enough to go back in after Jack.

"Where is he?" Genny cried, fear for him making her shiver with dread. "What on earth is he doing?"

Charley frowned. Ollie scanned the deck but saw no sign of him. "Son of a bitch," Pete said, suddenly standing up and ripping off his life vest. "He's gone under the hull to search for that bomb." Without another word, he dove over the side of the boat and into the sea.

"Shit," Ollie stripped off his vest, too, and went in, his bulk hitting the water like a giant bowling ball. He came up, caught a breath of air, and began to swim toward the *Marauder.*

"Crazy fools," Charley growled, grabbing Ray's thin shoulder as he tried to rise. "Just because they're determined to get themselves killed, don't mean you have to do it, too. Besides, those three are all divers. They know what they're doin'."

"I hope so," Ray said, but Genny saw how worried both of them looked.

"God, Charley — what are we going to do?"

His bushy gray brows drew together. "Pray, Genny girl. Sit here in this damnable boat and pray. There's not a damn thing else we can do."

Genny stared at Jack's beloved *Marauder* and fought not to cry. She thought how much he was risking to save it. She thought of Howard and what he meant to do, and the tears in her eyes began to wash down her cheeks. "I came to tell him I'd marry him, Charley. I learned the truth about Jason and I finally understood. But now . . . now it might be too late."

Charley gripped her head. "It ain't over till it's over, honey. That's a truth I've learned. You just keep prayin' and holdin' good thoughts for Jack."

She tried to. Dear God, she tried to. But with

every second that ticked past, every time she saw Ollie's head break the surface, or Pete come up for another breath of air, she thought of what would happen if the bomb went off while they were under water. If the blast didn't blow them to pieces, if parts of the ship didn't tear them in two, the concussion alone would be enough to kill them.

She didn't doubt the threat was real. Not after the way Howard had treated her aboard his boat. Not after she had seen the ruthless men he had hired to do his dirty work.

Not after what she had finally remembered.

Long minutes passed. Jack never surfaced. She guessed he was wearing an oxygen tank, and prayed it was the truth. Pete and Ollie looked exhausted. Even from a distance, she could see their chests heaving in and out each time they came up and dragged in a great gulp of air.

Finally Jack's head broke through the water, his black hair wet and glistening, the muscles in his shoulders flexing as he moved. Ollie and Pete popped up, too, treading water next to Jack, who held something in his hand. He raised his arm and threw it as far as he could in the opposite direction. Then with smooth powerful strokes, he began to cut through the water beside his two best friends.

Charley revved the motor on the dinghy and aimed the boat toward the men. He had just about reached them when the blast went off.

White water seethed, erupted, showered the men, sprayed over Genny and Charley, and filled the bottom of the boat. The waves it made nearly swamped the engine, but none of the men were hurt.

"Jack!" Genny hurled herself toward him as he thrust himself over the gunwales and collapsed into the bottom of the boat, his air tank still clinging to his broad back. Pete and Ollie climbed in, panting and heaving with the effort. Ollie wore a big white grin.

"You did it," he said to Jack, helping him out of his air tank. "You found the damn thing. I can't believe you were crazy enough to try, but I'm damn glad you did."

Jack said nothing. Instead he searched the horizon. "Get us back to the boat. McCormick may be watching. We've got to get out of here before he comes back." As the small outboard motor revved up, he reached for Genny and dragged her into his arms. Capturing her face between his hands, he gave her a ravaging kiss.

"Don't tell me you won't see me — this time, I won't listen. I'll camp on your doorstep every night until you let me in. I'll send you flowers, I'll write you poems. I'll seduce you into making love to me. I'll enslave your beautiful body until you can't live without me — until you agree to marry me."

Genny smiled at him through a flood of tears and slid her arms around his neck. "You've already seduced me. I *can't* live without you. And

I can't wait to marry you."

He kissed her again, crushing her against his water-soaked chest and ignoring Ollie's deep-throated chuckle. "You mean it?"

"That's what I came to the dock to tell you. Unfortunately, I ran into Howard instead."

Jack frowned and glanced back at the horizon. No sign of a boat, but they couldn't be sure Howard wasn't lurking just out of sight. He kissed Genny again, then held her close until they reached the *Marauder* and everyone hurriedly boarded.

While Charley got the big boat underway, Jack went down to his cabin and grabbed his .45. He shoved it into the waistband at the back of his wet Levi's, then returned to the wheelhouse, where Genny and the others were waiting.

"Any sign of him?" he asked Charley.

"If McCormick was watching, he had to do it from far enough away that we wouldn't get suspicious. Too far away to stop us, once we got underway. If he saw what happened, he must have taken off."

"What will you do?" Genny asked.

A grim smile curved Jack's lips. "Make sure he doesn't get away with this."

"That shouldn't be too tough," Pete said. "He hasn't had time to reach the harbor."

"All we've got to do is find another boat," Jack said. "We can use their radio to call the Coast Guard. They'll catch the bastard red-handed."

Determined to do just that, using the radar to guide their search, Charley steered the *Marauder* toward a dot on the screen that appeared to be a boat. Meanwhile Genny sat in silence, thinking about all that had happened.

And about what she now knew.

Jack broke into her thoughts. "I can understand why he wanted me out of the way. Even without those cases, he's been itchin' to get rid of me for years. What I still can't figure is why he wanted you dead, too."

Genny swallowed hard. It was all so clear now. Why hadn't she been able to see? "Partly because he's executor of my will. If I'm dead, he can control the disposition of my shares of McCormick-Austin. He can finally get his greedy hands on the other half of the company."

"And?" Jack urged, squeezing her hand.

"And partly because he was afraid I would remember what he did to my husband." She looked up at him, feeling a tightness in her chest. "And I did, Jack. After all this time, I finally remember what I saw."

Jack frowned. "I don't think I understand."

"Howard murdered Bill. That night on the sidewalk beside our house."

"Jesus."

"That's what all of this has been about. The dreams I was having weren't triggered simply by Bill's death — but by seeing my husband's murder."

"You saw it? You were there?" Jack hugged her hard, his cheek pressed to the top of her head. "Christ, baby."

Genny dragged in a steadying breath and pulled herself together. "When I got home that night, I saw Bill's car in the garage. I walked in calling his name, but he didn't answer. When I looked out the window, I saw his body lying on the sidewalk and I fainted — at least that's what I thought. But the truth is Bill wasn't dead when I got home."

She fought to blink back tears. "I saw him from the window, standing on the sidewalk out in front, partly hidden among the shrubs. I s-saw someone with him, but I couldn't make out who it was. They were arguing. Then I-I heard a gunshot and . . . and pieces of Bill's head . . . p-pieces of Bill's head j-just exploded away. It-It was all gray and wet, a-and his face . . . his face was covered in blood. I just stared at him out through the window. I knew he was dead."

She brushed at the wetness on her cheek. "Just before I fainted, I saw Howard walking away."

She felt Jack's tension as he smoothed back her hair. "He won't get away with it. Not this time. I promise you that, baby." Lifting her cold hand to his lips, he gently kissed the palm. "And I don't break my word."

Genny shook her head. "It was so terrible, I must have blocked the whole thing. When I finally came to, I thought I'd just walked in, that all I had seen was Bill's body. That he was already dead."

Charley scowled and scratched his graying head. "It all fits together. Like a giant jigsaw puzzle that's finally been solved."

"Yes," Genny said. "The killing triggered my dreams, just like the doctors said. Only my dreams weren't about my husband's murder. They were about Annee Palmer's husbands, murdered all those years ago. I didn't remember anything about Howard . . . not until today. Not until he held that gun to my head and I thought he might kill me. I must have felt something like that the night he killed Bill because that's when it all came back. And that's the reason he wanted me dead."

Jack held onto her hard. "Your husband must have found out about the forged computer chips. Maybe he tried to stop McCormick from bringing any more of them into the country."

Genny looked up at him. "Howard was forging computer chips?"

Jack nodded, his arm held tightly around her waist. "He was having them made in Mexico."

"Bob Macklin was smuggling them into the States aboard the *Opus II*," Ollie said.

"I thought I knew him." Genny leaned back against Jack's hard frame. "I thought he was my friend."

"He's a killer," Pete said. "And we've got to stop him." Everyone's eyes swung toward the horizon as if they could will a boat to appear.

Then a sailboat came into view, a long, sleek Transpac 49. Jack hailed the Oxnard-based *Dolphin* through the bullhorn. He identified himself and told them what had happened, then he carefully relayed the message he needed to send.

The *Dolphin* hailed the Coast Guard by using their cellular phone, so McCormick couldn't intercept the call. The captain told them what the men aboard the *Sea Siren* had done, and where McCormick might be headed. He told them what they could expect to find aboard.

Assuming McCormick didn't panic and dump the stuff overboard first.

But the Coast Guard was prepared for such an occurrence. They located the *Sea Siren* not on its way to Santa Barbara, but headed south for Mexico. Howard must have realized his scheme had failed and tried to make good his escape. They tracked the boat, but didn't try to board, hoping McCormick would put into port somewhere. In shallow water, even if Howard dumped the load, they'd have a chance to recover the cargo.

It happened just north of San Diego, when the boat was forced to stop for fuel. The Coast Guard was waiting. They found the cases still aboard, and McCormick and his henchmen were arrested.

Genny's nightmare was finally over.

And she was once more with Jack.

Epilogue

In a pair of hip-hugging jeans and a white cotton tank top, Genny stood next to Jack, her inlaid pearl-handled pool cue clutched in a slender hand, her body outlined by the single overhead lamp suspended above the green felt table.

Other than that, the Sea Breeze Bar was empty. It was Monday night, and the place was closed. Jack had convinced Pixie Murphy to give him the key.

He smiled at Genny and her lips softly parted. Tonight was a special occasion, their first year anniversary. Tomorrow night he'd promised her French champagne and dinner at the Biltmore Hotel, and he'd bought her a pretty diamond pendant, but tonight . . . tonight he had something very different in mind.

Genny bent over the pool table, giving him a seductive view of her tight little round derrière. Her light brown hair was long now, falling softly to well past her shoulders. She gently stroked the cue and the striped nine ball rolled into the pocket.

"Nice shot," Jack said, his voice a little rough as he watched her. She moved around the table and when she bent over, he was looking right between the mounds of her high full breasts. He was already hard, but his body tightened even more. She shot the ball firmly this time, bounced it off the edge of the felt, sent the seven ball in, and set herself up for a good shot at the three.

A smile tugged at his lips. "Keep that up and you just might beat me."

She grinned, looking so damned pretty he wanted to kiss her. "That's exactly what I intend to do."

A surge of pride rolled through him that she had learned to play so well. She had tried wind surfing, which wasn't her best sport, but she loved white-water rafting. She was learning to snow ski, and she seemed to have a natural knack for that. Pool was still her favorite. She was a damned good player, too. Any other time, he would have had to concentrate to win, but tonight he didn't care. There was something he would far rather do.

She rounded the table, returning to his side, and bent over the green felt again. What an ass, he thought as he moved forward, pressing his hardness against her, cupping her breasts from behind. She sucked in a breath, but kept her aim steady on the ball. She didn't shoot, not until he'd unsnapped her jeans and slid them down. Not until she'd stepped out of them and stood there in a pair of tiny white thong panties.

A corner of his mouth curved up at the sight

of them. Pretty brazen for Genny — and incredibly seductive. She was learning. His groin throbbed. And damned did she learn fast.

He gently squeezed a breast, making her squirm. She stroked the cue a little more roughly than she meant to and the ball went askew. All he could think of was how much he wanted to be stroking her. When she straightened, he kissed the back of her neck and rubbed her nipples through her T-shirt. He plucked them into tight little buds, and Genny softly moaned.

Jack unsnapped the button on his jeans and unzipped his fly. He was rock hard and aching. Alone in the back room of the bar, no one could see them. He meant to have her there, bent over the pool table, just as he'd imagined the first night they had come here. Christ, he had envisioned this scene a thousand times, but he couldn't have guessed how much the real thing would turn him on.

Genny felt Jack's hands on her bottom, smoothing the roundness, sliding softly between her thighs. Her heart was pounding; she was damp and aching, already wanting him inside her. It was always this way between them. And in other ways, it was good, too. They were far more compatible than either of them had guessed — Jack easily fitting in with her friends, her parents increasingly charmed by him.

They had gone to see Jack's stepmother and

though it seemed there was little affection between them, Genny was certain Jack felt better
for having gone.

His powerful body moved closer behind her.
His tongue found her ear and he traced a line
around it. One hand squeezed her bottom. He
moved lower, eased her panties aside. She was
wet and ready, trembling with need for him.

"Can you feel how much I want you?" he
whispered in her ear, sending shafts of heat
through her body. She moaned a soft reply, letting him slide down the panties, letting him
spread her legs with his jean-covered knee. She
felt his hardened arousal, then he was easing
himself inside her. He turned her a little and
gave her a long wet kiss, taking her mouth with
the same fierce possession as he claimed her
body. Then he firmly gripped her hips and
began to thrust hard and deep.

It took only minutes for her to reach her
peak. The moment was just too erotic. Besides,
Jack had been at sea for the past two days and
she had missed him. As he drove her to a
second frenzied climax, her body clenched
around him, eliciting a groan. His muscles went
rigid and he spilled his seed, but there wouldn't
be a baby, at least not this time.

These first few years were for Jack. And for
herself. When they were ready, she would have
Jack's baby. She wanted it. Desperately. And so
did he. But they were still young and they deserved this time together.

After all, they had waited through time and beyond.

Of course Jack didn't believe any of it. Not one word. She had never tried to convince him, and in reality there was no way to know if it was the truth.

To Genny it no longer mattered. She slept peacefully at night beside the man she loved. Her nightmares were gone and her days filled with pleasure. The dreams they shared now were dreams of the future.

"I love you," Jack whispered, turning her to face him then holding her in the circle of his arms. "This has been the happiest time of my life."

She gazed into his brilliant blue eyes, eyes that had haunted her through time and beyond. "I love you, my darling, Jack." She smiled and cradled a hand against his cheek. "I always have, and I always will."

Author's Note

As wicked as she was, Annee May Palmer was a
true life character from history. Though the facts
of her life differ from source to source, most of
what I've written about her appears to be true.
As a young girl, her parents died, leaving her or-
phaned on Haiti. She moved to Jamaica shortly
thereafter and eventually married a wealthy
planter named John Palmer.

She began to dabble in voodoo, to continue
what she had started to learn as a child. Annee
became a master of sorcery, a high-priestess of
voodoo who was feared by the slaves on the
island. It was said she could project the demons
of hell — the three-legged horse, the rolling calf
— any number of apparitions of doom — into
the midst of those who crossed her. The terrifying spectacle was witnessed by dozens of
people, including a number of wealthy white
planters.

It is believed she killed all three of her husbands, and perhaps even several of her lovers.
And her brutality to the slaves she owned was
legend. They were often flogged, Annee on occasion wielding the whip herself. She was beautiful and unpredictable. It is said she rode the

plantation at night dressed in men's clothes —
a scandalous occurrence at the time.

For the next eleven years until her death in
1831, through three dead husbands and untold
lovers, Annee commanded her world. In the
end she was strangled by the people on her own
plantation during a slave rebellion.

I took liberties with the story of Annee's early
years and her love affair with Jason Sommers. I
felt that whatever forces caused a brilliant, sophisticated woman like Annee Palmer to de-
scend to such horrifying depths must have been
powerful indeed.

Perhaps, as I wrote in the story, through the
decades of time that have passed, Annee was
somehow able to redeem the terrible debt she
owed. Like most of our fantasies, it is something we will never know. It would be nice to
think she paid for her sins and wound up as
someone like Genny, that the ending of her
story might be happy instead of sad.